BOURBON PROMISES

A Bourbon Canyon Novel

WALKER ROSE

LE Publishing

Copyright © 2024 by Walker Rose

Editing by Razor Sharp Editing

Proofreading by Fairy Proofmother Proofreading, Deaton Author Services, and Judy's Proofreading

Cover art by Okay Creations

All rights reserved.

No part of this book may be reproduced in any form or by any electronic or mechanical means, including information storage and retrieval systems, without written permission from the author, except for the use of brief quotations in a book review.

The characters, places, and events in this story are fictional. Any similarities to real people, places, or events are coincidental and unintentional.

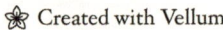 Created with Vellum

I left for a weekend in Las Vegas and came back with a husband.

Gideon James isn't just any husband. He's the wealthy CEO of a Vegas hotel casino, he's devastating in a suit—and he's Bourbon Canyon's very own prodigal son. Now he's returning to claim the land my brothers are in the middle of purchasing from his father. With me at his side, Gideon will finally be able to stop the sale.

Why else would someone like him marry me? I may just be a small-town schoolteacher one step away from cat-lady status, but I'm not clueless. I know exactly why Gideon chased me into that all-night chapel. If he wants my help to sell this union and get his land, he's going to have to give me something in return.

A baby.

Then we'll go our separate ways.

Only the longer we're under the same roof, the harder it is to remember our relationship is fake. The easier it is to forget there's an end date on this contract. The plainer it is to see this marriage could be more than bourbon promises.

CHAPTER ONE

Autumn

Brightly lit slots surrounded me, and the smell of old cigarette smoke was suffocating at times. The Silver Hotel and Casino was a sophisticated hot spot in Las Vegas, but a casino was a casino. My eyes watered, and I wanted to curl up in my hotel room and catch some Hallmark movies before *The Golden Girls* came on.

Being a single lady in my golden years was looking more and more like a reality. I used to reassure myself that I'd have my sisters with me, but two were enjoying wedded bliss and the third was reported with a new beau every six months.

I could always take my boss up on his offer. We'd been out a few times, and he'd given me a sweet kiss. The sex would be perfectly adequate. I could live with adequate. Sex wasn't the glue of a relationship.

Right?

My coworkers and I were parked at the nickel slots.

We all worked at the elementary school and they were friends too, but I usually didn't hang out with them after work. Yet when my coworkers had asked me if I wanted to go on a trip to Las Vegas, I'd jumped at the chance. It didn't matter that they joked I was the mom of the group or that I was yawning by nine and that was when they were ready to begin. I needed to get out. Nothing like a weekend with younger women to help me figure out the Mark situation.

Brittany, a kindergarten teacher, leaned toward me. "Autumn, do you think he's here?"

Awareness tingled over my skin every time the *he* in question was mentioned.

Brittany was not talking about Mark.

Gideon James. The local boy who'd grown up into a dark-haired god in a suit. He was the CEO of the hotel casino we were staying in. There was absolutely no reason for us to cross paths, but that didn't stop any of us from peering around corners to catch a glimpse.

After the sale of his family's land had been announced, Gideon had come to town to face off with my brothers, who were buying it. Now, he was the talk of the town, and the ladies had insisted on making his casino the destination for our trip.

I hadn't fought them. I was the only one of the group to have glimpsed him in real life. I'd heard how deep his voice was. I'd seen him storm out of my family's distillery. Looking him up wasn't necessary. His image was emblazoned in my memory.

"Maybe we'll see him," I answered. "If he's working late. Do CEOs work on the premises? Live here?"

"Could you imagine?" she gushed. "Like one of those

places you see on TV where the elevator opens into the apartment."

"Isn't that a penthouse?"

She wrinkled her nose. "I exist on a teacher's wage. I don't know a thing about penthouses."

"We could ask him if we see him."

She giggled. "I can't believe you don't remember him."

Oh, I remembered him and those wide shoulders. "He's a little older than Tate, and Tate's seven years older than me."

"I do love an older man." She punched a button on her slot. I'd quit playing several minutes ago when I'd started daydreaming about my hotel room. "Does he really look like his pictures? *Gideon James*." She purred his name.

No headshot could do that man justice.

A shiver ran down my spine when I thought of how he'd stalked across the parking lot to his car. His black suit had to have been stitched onto his body, and his dark hair hadn't dared to move in the wind. And when he'd turned his head? I'd caught a glimpse of stormy eyes.

I hadn't seen the color from across the distillery. Blue? Green? What was the color for Melt My Underwear?

I, apparently, liked a brooding man.

That brooding man would not like me, a Bailey. He'd argued with my brothers about buying his family's land, and while my last name was Kerrigan because my sisters and I had been adopted, I was still a Bailey.

"Jackpot!" Kaitlyn, the school's admin, yelled from the other side of Brittany.

Destiny laughed, the phys ed teacher, leaning in from farther down the row of slots. "Don't spend it all in one place."

Kaitlyn grinned. "Fifty bucks is fifty bucks. Next round is on me."

Brittany scooted off the plush stool attached to the slot machine. "Should we go to the club?"

"Absolutely." Kaitlyn removed her casino card from the machine and waved it around. "If we don't get in, I can bribe 'em."

Laughing, we all followed her. She teetered on her four-inch heels, but her lack of balance was likely from our day of drinking and not the actual shoes. The girls were all a little tipsy from the steady stream of cocktails. I was the soberest of them, but not because I was the elder of the group.

I'd learned how to taste bourbon when I was fifteen. That was the first time Daddy had *known* I'd had a drink. With three older brothers, an older sister, and numerous foster kids who Mama and Daddy had taken into the fold for what time they had with us, I had been exposed way before my first "official" taste.

Destiny tugged down her short skirt. I owned volleyball shorts with a longer hem than hers, but if I had her legs, I would buy ten of those skirts. The others were dressed like her—short skirts, high shirts, and fuck-me makeup. The opposite of how they dressed at work.

I wore ankle boots with a chunky heel and rust-colored leggings. My cream wrap dress was the opposite of what I'd wear teaching too, but only because I wouldn't want to get watercolor on it. I could blame my style on being a teacher approaching my midthirties, but the truth was that my style had been the same when I was their age.

Brittany squealed. "The line isn't that long. This is our night!"

They'd been so excited to go to Glitter & Gold, an ultraposh club that a normal person could still get inside.

I eyed the outside dubiously. Black with sleek silver lines, it fit into the theme of Silver while standing out. The posts for the waiting lines were gold and so were the bouncers' vests.

We got in line.

"At least we're indoors," I muttered.

Destiny nudged me. When she leaned in, I almost got a face full of cleavage. Definitely not her work clothes. "You're such a cat lady."

"I only have one cat."

She winked. "I'm sure Mark will let you get more."

I gawked at her. Mark Knutson. My boss. "It was only three dates." The first of which shouldn't count. We'd both happened to be at Mountain Perks on a Saturday to get our caffeine fix. For the second date, he'd asked me out by saying, *If you were to go out with me, Fatima would have to do your evaluations*. Fatima was the school's assistant principal.

I'd said yes. A biological clock could only be ignored so long, but I was courting speculation in and out of the workplace by dating my boss. It was also flattering that he'd been willing to risk tarnishing his brand-new position by dating me. But then, it was Bourbon Canyon. Small dating pool and all, which I knew too well.

Brittany spun around. "I heard he wants you to meet his parents."

He had asked me to meet his parents. In Spokane.

Which would make the visit an overnight trip. "He's moving a little fast."

I liked sex as much as the next girl, but an overnight trip was serious for someone I didn't think I'd been seriously dating.

Still, a girl had needs.

Could Mark fulfill them?

Small dating pool.

I was the sister who'd never left Bourbon Canyon except for college. It was looking like I'd be the last to settle down. Junie might have a round-robin of boyfriends, but based on sheer numbers, her odds were better than mine. Something that loomed over me in Vegas.

"As long as he moves slow when it counts," Brittany whispered.

We crept forward. The others chattered about how excited they were, lobbing questions back and forth. *What's the dancing like? The drinks? The men? The women?*

When we reached the front, the bouncer in his black sport coat, gold vest, and black slacks nodded at Brittany while raking his gaze down her mile-long legs. "Welcome to Glitter & Gold, ladies."

Brittany did a happy shimmy and rushed in. Kaitlyn and Destiny followed her, getting ogled by the bouncer.

He held his hand up to me.

"Wait here, ma'am," he said, then turned to the side with his hand to an earpiece.

Ma'am?

Wasn't I one of the *ladies*?

He muttered a few things. Was his earpiece real or for show? I wasn't well traveled, but I also wasn't an idiot. This place wanted to seem exclusive. The girls who got in wanted to feel special. Superior. Like gold.

I was dressed like fool's gold.

How was I going to get in? I wasn't the sexy Kerrigan sister. I might as well have worn my *Sorry, I have plans with my cat tonight* sweater.

"Excuse me." The bouncer ushered me back, creating more distance between us, like my plainness was a contagion. A second bouncer politely gestured for my friends to move to the side. A tall blond with heels I swore were twice the height of Kaitlyn's strode through us like we were the sea and the bouncer had parted us for her. She disappeared down the dark entry.

Well then. I didn't catch her face, but her long, glossy blond hair hung down her bare back. Her gauzy red dress was shorter than Destiny's. She was a polished ruby compared to us river rocks.

When she passed, my friends started down the entry after her. I glanced from them to the guys who'd moved to block me again.

"We're full at the moment," the first bouncer said, his gaze skipping over me.

"Oh. Okay." Embarrassment flooded my cheeks. The whole not-well-traveled-but-not-naive thing could be a curse. I knew why I wasn't being allowed in.

I wasn't fuckable.

My throat grew thick, and the cozy haze of the two cocktails I'd had in the last three hours burned off.

Brittany stopped past the entry threshold and so close to the official opening of the club. Her eyes were wide. "Autumn?"

The rest of my friends spun to stare at me, the excitement draining from their faces.

"Why can't she come with us?" Brittany asked, her voice sharp.

One of her students might've started crying, but the bouncer didn't flinch. "We're full. You want in?"

She tried to extinguish the longing in her eyes, but I caught it.

"You can go," I said hastily, hating the attention on me.

"No," they all said and started in my direction.

I backed up, holding my hands up. "It's fine. They're full. I'll wait."

They hesitated. They wanted to be ride or die, but they also wanted to go into the trendy casino nightclub run by a hot CEO. It was all they'd talked about on the flight down.

Kaitlyn frowned, wringing her hands together. "We can't."

"Go." I shooed them away. "Really. I'll be fine. I might even go back up to my room. I'm really tired." That was the truth, but humiliation was better experienced in private.

Destiny shook her head, the light dancing off her glossy black hair. "Autumn—"

"Last chance," the first bouncer barked at my friends.

"Go on," I stressed. "Really, it's *fine*. I'll be in in a few minutes."

"Only if you're sure," Kaitlyn said, her glossy lower lip pouty.

The second bouncer ushered them into the silver-tinged shadows. I waved and forced a big smile. "Have fun."

I watched them rush away, tears poking the backs of

my eyes. I turned a direct gaze toward the first bouncer. "I'm not getting in, am I?"

To his credit, his expression contained mild regret, and he shrugged. The bouncer next to him waved three more girls inside. Each of them wore a handkerchief and little else.

Right. I pushed a lock of hair behind my ear. I'd left it down for once. I might have a matronly style, but my red hair screamed young and vivacious. It was the only part of me that was wild. Most of the time, I was okay with that.

I might've wished to be lying in bed and watching a movie a few minutes ago, but the reality of doing so because I hadn't been sexy enough for a club in Vegas stung.

I stepped out of the line, but I didn't want to go back to my room. There was a bench by the wall. Maybe I'd wait for a few minutes. The club might be so boring my friends would pour out and we'd go do something fun, something we could all enjoy.

I'd just wait for a few minutes.

Gideon

For fuck's sake, she was still there.

I glared at the screen on my desk. I could scroll through any part of Silver any minute I wanted. I could go back three months, or I could watch live like it was my very own streaming show. Rarely did I need to. But when the reservation system had sent a flag to my office weeks ago, I'd made sure I was ready.

That fucking family.

I had put the goddamn Baileys into the system. If they used a credit card or tried to reserve a room, I'd put a stop to it. On a whim, I had added the Kerrigan sisters too. Were the Baileys trying to get dirt on me?

There were no secrets. I'd worked fucking hard to get this corner office and an entire casino of staff under me.

Like my grandfather had said, *What a man owns defines him.*

I didn't own the place, but I ran it. I controlled it. I grew rich from it. Rich enough to buy anything I wanted —only to have my father ensure I didn't have a say about the one property that mattered to me.

Goddamn him.

You need to make this yours. A man is nothing without his legacy. My grandfather's words had been running nonstop through my head since Dad had called to tell me he was selling.

I squeezed a fist as I watched the woman on the edge of my screen. The image was slightly grainy. She had one leg crossed over the other and was scrolling through her phone.

She hadn't been allowed into Glitter.

What had she been thinking? Couldn't she tell she was way out of her league? The girl wasn't showing more than an inch of skin at her collar line. Her bare neck wasn't enough to gain entrance into the club.

Glitter's manager was relentless about his "standards," and I'd had more than one argument with the board about that jackass, but Glitter's bottom line spoke louder than me.

I studied my screen. I didn't know Autumn Kerrigan personally. I knew she taught third grade at the lone elementary school in Bourbon Canyon. I knew she and her sisters had been adopted after their parents had died in a nasty wreck. And I knew that she was staying in room 1405, ten floors below my own suite.

She must've known that she wasn't getting inside.

Her friends had ditched her?

A tingle of dismay crossed through me. I didn't like her, but getting ditched hit a sore spot with me. Who needed enemies when you had friends like that?

Autumn was buried in her phone, hunched over the device like she was trying to disappear in a casino full of cameras that caught every angle.

I'd seen all those angles.

Ever since she'd checked in. I'd seen the way she'd tapped her foot while waiting for her card to run. How she'd laughed with her head back and that wavy hair falling down her back. How she'd held the door for all her friends to enter the public restrooms first, like a damn gentleman. She'd shown them more consideration taking a piss than they had for her a half hour ago.

My phone buzzed. I didn't bother to check it.

Taya was at the club and wanted me to join her. We'd have our own private booth. As the brains behind the casino's financials, she'd want to talk shop. Then she'd want more. I hadn't succumbed in a while.

A part of me was . . . restless. Taya and I worked together, and occasionally, we fucked. She looked good on my arm, and she liked how my name opened doors for her.

I glanced at the screen. **I'm waiting.**

She didn't like to wait.

I had told her we could talk over the plans to restructure the parking garage and renovate several rooms into luxury suites. Rich people didn't want to park with the masses.

I clicked out of the surveillance system and left my office. In the elevator, I snapped my suit coat straight and buttoned one button.

When I got to the second floor, I exited. The nightclub was street level, but I hated walking through the casino. The barrage of sounds would only make me cranky before a financial discussion with Taya that was sure to be irritating. There was another bank of elevators closer to the nightclub.

Half the time, we fucked because we had to release the tension from arguing over finances. I got told what the investors wanted and it was up to me and her to carry out their wishes.

I rolled my shoulders. I should schedule a massage and get these kinks worked out.

I ignored the gawking of tourists. They were used to the tuxes of the casino staff, but I stood out. How, I didn't know, but it was a reaction I'd accepted over the years.

An older couple loaded into the elevator in front of me.

She grinned, eyeing my suit. "Don't you look fancy? Plans for tonight?"

"Yes."

Her brows rose like she was waiting for me to continue. Her shirt matched her husband's. A picture of dice with snake eyes on the front. Very Vegas. Very touristy.

She finally nodded and exchanged a *get a load of this guy* glance with her husband.

I suppressed a sigh. If only I could get a private elevator to the club, then I wouldn't have to deal with the public. I ran the casino. I wasn't the PR team.

When the elevator dinged, I hung back to let them out first. I was about to follow when a short bundle of cotton-candy-smelling woman crashed into me. I caught her by the shoulders before she staggered backward and fell.

"Oh, crap. I'm sorry." Her rich voice rolled over me like a warm wave.

I hated the slots in the casino—anywhere a ton of people congregated, talking, talking, talking—but my ears liked when she spoke.

She blinked up at me. My brain shut off, and I drowned in her emerald gaze.

No, emerald was too plain. Occasionally, people felt comfortable enough to comment on my eyes. *They're such a light green. You don't see that often.* I never commented back.

But this woman's eyes were a deep jade and each iris had a small chunk of brown close to the pupil. Technically, her eyes were hazel, but someone would have to get very close to notice.

I could have done without that knowledge. Just like I wished I could erase her sweet scent from my memory. I didn't want to know details about this woman.

Autumn Kerrigan.

Her eyes flared wide and her lips parted, drawing my attention.

Goddamn. Couldn't her lips be a boring pink? Instead, they were a soft red and the tongue that licked out to wet those red lips reminded me of the cotton candy she smelled like.

Would she taste as sweet?

"I—I'm sorry." She tried to step back just as the elevator doors attempted to close. She was in the opening.

I had two seconds to make a decision. Let her take the elevator while I met Taya, or . . .

I drew her farther in. Her eyes widened like I was a wolf dragging her into my den.

"It's fine," I said smoothly, my mind kicking into gear after being stunned senseless by Autumn Kerrigan, of all people.

Why hadn't she been let into the nightclub? Hadn't the bouncer seen her fall of thick, coppery hair? The dusting of freckles over her creamy skin? Those damn eyes should've been an instant entry.

Her gaze slid to her shoulders, where I still gripped her.

I peeled my hands off her. "Apologies." I never thought I'd apologize to a damn Bailey.

The elevator started moving. She spun toward the controls. She was about to hit a button, but I couldn't have her going to her room and hiding from my spying.

"Are you enjoying your stay?" Look at me, doing PR.

She clenched her fists and pivoted back to me. Her shoes, while sensible, made her legs look long and curvy. And while she'd been turned, I'd gotten teased by a glimpse of her lush ass.

"I was, but I didn't make the fuckable cut at the nightclub."

I recoiled at the acid in her voice. Not what I'd expected from the soft, curvy woman. "Oh?"

Instead of a tirade, all I got was a shrug. "Whatever. It's tasteless."

I bristled. Nothing about Silver was tasteless. I'd made sure nothing about this building resembled the dusty and dirty place I'd come from. Glitter & Gold was the crowning glory of the structure.

I also agreed with her. Fuck.

She punched the *14* on the elevator panel.

A sense of panic took over. She was getting off. She'd insulted my place of work and was leaving. I should let her go, but—

The elevator jerked into motion. She leaned against the back wall. Unaffected by both me and Glitter's rejection.

I could take a different route to get to Little Miss Bailey. That whole damn family thought they were untouchable. There was a reason she was here, a purpose to her presence. There had to be. My world wasn't tilting sideways for nothing. "You're right. It is tasteless."

We stopped on the fifth floor, and I moved to her side of the elevator car. She tracked me, shrinking against the rear wall. Her gaze dropped down my suit and skated away.

Was it possible she was affected by me?

Did she know who I was?

Two giggling women got on. They were comparing shiny gold bands on their ring fingers. The Silver Linings Chapel was on the fifth floor. Autumn might also think Vegas weddings were tasteless, but we made sure even impulsive vows were sophisticated.

"I'm surprised you agree," she murmured.

I took advantage of her continued conversation to lean against the wall adjacent to her. She drew back like I was going to steal the small cream purse hooked over her bandolier-style.

I stuffed a hand into my pocket, knowing I looked exactly like an ad for Zegna. "It's business. Pure and simple."

"Yeah, but I didn't come to Vegas to get insulted."

The elevator eased to a stop on the twelfth floor. Dammit. We were almost at her stop.

The couple got off, and we were alone again. She scooted an additional foot away from me. I almost slid closer. We continued our ride.

"On behalf of the Silver Casino and Hotel, I apologize." My sincerity startled me. I knew the exclusiveness of the club hurt feelings, but I'd never witnessed it. I should've fought the board harder. Otherwise, what was the perk of being in charge?

It shouldn't bother me. She was a Bailey.

She lifted her chin. "Thank you," she said stiffly.

I narrowed my eyes on her. Were her cheeks naturally that flushed, or was she angry? Embarrassed? Overheated?

We came to a stop on the fourteenth floor. The doors opened and the panic was back. She'd step out. I'd never know why her group had chosen Silver or if she knew who I was.

What did it matter?

But it did. It had to. Her family was closing on the sale in a month, and she was in my casino.

So when she took a step toward the exit, I let spill the words I was sure would give her pause. "You're welcome, *Miss Kerrigan*."

CHAPTER TWO

Autumn

He knew who I was?

My heart jackhammered against my ribs. Gideon James knew who I was?

I stared at him so long the elevator doors closed, and once again, this space seemed too small to hold someone as tall and powerful as him. I should've gotten off, but my astonishment kept me immobile.

"You, uh, know—"

"I make it my business to know what the family who's trying to destroy my legacy is doing."

My brothers didn't share a lot of nitty-gritty details about the distillery and ranch with me, but I'd heard about the land purchase. All of us had had to approve it, but it was little more than a formality. Teller told us our brothers' plans, and if we didn't argue, it happened. If we did have an issue, most likely, my brothers would get their way regardless.

Tate wanted to hire someone to farm the James land. Its official name was Percival Farms. Some of it was only fit for ranching, but a couple of sections made for good farming. The family distillery, Copper Summit, would be able to source some of its own grains instead of being subject to the whims of the market and Montana farmers. We'd be the farmers and we'd be the market.

Well, my brothers would. They ran both businesses and rarely asked for my input.

Gideon tilted his head. His hand was still in his pocket and he continued to lean against the wall. The man was mouthwatering.

The way his mouth tipped up, a little taunting, a little sardonic, should've grated on me. But before Daddy had died, he'd given each of his kids a portion of the Bailey land. I'd gotten the section closest to the distillery. There was a creek that ran through the property, multiple wildlife trails, and my favorite—huckleberry bushes. Lots of them. How would I have felt if Daddy had tried selling before he'd died?

I'd have been heartbroken. "I don't think anyone anticipated how hard it would be for you."

We came to a stop. I didn't pay attention to the floor number. Three guys crowded on and a wave of booze washed over me. I inched closer to the wall of cedar citrus surrounding Gideon.

The corners of his jaw flexed. "It's not as if they care."

"It's business. Pure and simple."

He ground his teeth together and pinned me in place with his dark gaze. His pale-green eyes darkened. "Touché."

The small beat of triumph was fleeting. "For what it's

worth, I understand how upset you are. If I was in your place, I'd be angry at my brothers too."

We stopped and the guys got out. Again, when the doors closed, we were alone.

We didn't move apart.

"Isn't Copper Summit a family company?"

I knew what he was asking. Didn't I have a say? Weren't all of us the brains behind the operation? Um, no. But I wouldn't let on how little say I had. "It is, but Bailey Beef is doing the purchasing. I'm only one Bailey."

"I thought you might argue you're a Kerrigan."

"I assume you know my first name, *Gideon*. You can use it. You're not one of my students."

His eyes lightened. "Autumn."

The elevator stopped. When the doors opened, the chatter from the main floor filled the small space. The dull bass of the club traveled through the floor, reminding me of my earlier humiliation, the one I'd confessed to the most handsome man I'd ever seen.

That guy and I would part ways. I'd go to my room, and he'd . . . I didn't know. Go to his mansion in the hills? Walk into Glitter ahead of the line because he was the boss and the finest man to enter the place? Meet his equally beautiful girlfriend?

None of it was my business, but when I was about to tell him goodbye, I found him studying me.

"Tell me, Autumn." His voice was smooth, filling me with a warmth only Copper Summit's best bourbon could produce. "Would you like to see the parts of the casino that are more tasteful?"

Gideon

I hung on her answer much longer than I normally would've if I'd asked a girl out. And I hadn't for years. Decades, even.

Since college, probably.

For the most part, women made me feel like I was a teen again, hoping for attention and approval from those around me and not getting it. For the last few years, dating hadn't been worth the trouble. Hence why I had sex with Taya when it was convenient for both of us.

Shit. Taya. She was waiting for me.

Autumn narrowed her eyes but walked out of the elevator. I followed, like a moth to the flame of her hair.

She stepped to the side and faced me. "There's nothing you can show me that'll redeem how utterly worthless your club made me feel. But thank you for the offer. I might just wander for a bit."

How utterly worthless. There was a matching emotion inside me that rose up, hearing those words. That knew how she felt.

I stuffed that feeling away. The land sale was unearthing all sorts of thoughts I hadn't had in a while. Anger was nicer. Resentment was more useful.

But thank you for the offer.

No, her flippant attitude would not do. I couldn't have her returning to Bourbon Canyon and sharing what a poor experience she'd had.

"One moment, please." I withdrew my phone and shot off a quick message to Taya.

Can't meet. I have a VIP to show around. We're starting at the club.

That was her cue to leave me the fuck alone. She didn't like catering to VIPs. It's why she worked with numbers and left the schmoozing to me. I disliked the task; I wasn't good at it, but talking business was what I was paid for.

I tucked my phone back into my jacket pocket and held an arm out. "Allow me."

Autumn gauged me warily. Finally, she wrapped her small hand through my arm. Her warmth seeped through the fabric and the sweetness of her scent increased.

Was that perfume, or was she naturally sweet?

I led her toward the entrance to the club. The line was longer than earlier.

Her grip on me stiffened a moment before it loosened. I put my hand over hers.

"It's all right, Autumn."

I kept my hand on hers as I walked past the bouncer. I didn't know which guy had turned Autumn away, but I gave each one a stern glare.

The first bouncer blanched, and the second mouthed "fuck" when he thought I couldn't see him.

My phone buzzed in my pocket. It was likely Taya, but I was with my VIP.

Autumn remained stiff as we strode by the mass waiting to gain entrance.

Someone muttered, "Why the hell does she get in?"

A group of women snickered. The guys with them wore smug expressions. All of them looked like they were ready for a professional photo shoot.

They were exactly the crowd Glitter & Gold wanted to attract.

Fuck.

My heartbeat hammered between my ears. Autumn was correct. This was tasteless. I'd have to figure out a way to deal with that. Exclusivity and luxury did not need to be insulting.

I maneuvered Autumn toward the dark wall. "Give me a moment."

She glanced around. A caged little bunny. If someone said boo, she'd take off. This wasn't the woman who'd spoken her mind in the elevator.

I approached the bouncer. "That group that insulted my guest?" I said softly enough for only him to hear.

He inclined his head. "Yes, sir." He barely moved his mouth.

"They're gone."

"Absolutely, sir." He cleared his throat. He must be nervous. The guy was as stiff as Autumn.

"If my guest gets insulted one more time, it's your job on the line." I tipped my head so the other bouncer knew I was talking to him. "And yours."

He dropped his chin.

"We run a classy nightclub. I don't care what your boss says; class does not correlate with the amount of skin showing." Glitter's manager would clamber over me to get to the board once he heard what I'd done. I didn't care. I'd be ready. "If someone's not respectful, they're gone. Got it?"

Both men nodded.

I half turned to check the message on my phone.

Taya: **Ugh. I'm already gone. Catch you in the morning?**

Gideon: **Sure**

Relief that I wouldn't have to juggle Taya's questions about why Autumn was a VIP cooled some of the anger from the bouncers' behavior and the crowd. She'd use the employee exit, so I didn't have to worry about explaining my guest to her.

I couldn't explain why I was so defensive of the new arrival. Her family's company, a business she had a part in, was trying to take Percival Farms. But I couldn't escape the thought that she might be useful. I just needed more time around her to know how.

Autumn was hugging her arms around herself like she was trying to shrink into the wall. The red waterfall of her hair would never allow it. Neither would those curves.

How had she gotten passed over?

I stuck my elbow out again. "Shall we?"

Time to answer the burning question in my mind. Fate had been a snarky bitch to me so far, but perhaps she'd just dropped a present into my lap. I just had to open Autumn up and figure out what her role in saving my land was.

CHAPTER THREE

Autumn

A dizzy sensation swamped me when I took his arm. He was solid and warm when his expression could be carved from marble. I thought he'd be as cool as stone, but the guy was a furnace.

What had he said to those bouncers?

They had looked ready to drop dead when he'd approached. Was Gideon that powerful?

If he wielded so much authority, no wonder he had issues with the land sale. He couldn't just tell them to stop, and they wouldn't do it solely because he'd said so.

I swallowed a wave of nausea.

I probably should've eaten more, but we'd planned to get appetizers after we danced and drank for a while. As the oldest of the group and the most experienced around alcohol, I should've pointed out that food came first.

The music grew louder as we entered. The place was

certainly nicer than any club I'd ever been to, which was very few.

Mirrors and glass on walls and columns reflected soft light. So much black. Any touches of color were a subdued neon along the silver accents. If old money was high-back chairs and floral wallpaper and Victorian-style clutter, then Glitter & Gold was new money. Youthful wealth. It was the bitcoin millionaire who'd remembered his password and pulled all his cash in time. It was the finance bro. It was the "how to become a millionaire before thirty by investing" influencer.

I didn't spot my friends right away, but part of me didn't want to look for them. Sure, I'd urged them to go in without me. But I'd stuck around, waiting, hoping they'd realize there was nothing here worth ditching me for.

No such luck.

Gideon didn't stop to ask about them, and I didn't stop to ask him about them.

A woman with buzzed sides and longer purple-dyed hair on top stopped by us. She was wearing a stylish tux with a gold vest that hugged her curves as she carried a tray. "Are you going to your usual spot, Mr. James?"

"Yes. Bring us a bottle of Rosé Vintage." He directed his gaze at me. In the dim club, his eyes were vivid green, like tractor beams I couldn't escape—if I wanted to. "Do you have any special requests?"

I didn't have to wait at the bar and hope to get noticed in less than twenty minutes? The wait was one of the reasons I liked tending bar at Copper Summit. I made everyone feel seen.

Gideon and the server waited for my answer. I needed food, but I didn't want to be uncouth and ask if they had anything edible. Who knew what I'd get served in Vegas. "A Bloody Mary with extra celery and load up on the olives, please. Make it a whole salad." I laughed nervously. The heat of Gideon's stare was on me.

The server's lips curled into a sexy smile. "Of course."

"Oh—and can I get it with bourbon instead? Do you carry any Copper Summit in-house?"

Her smile dipped. "I'm sorry. No Copper Summit is served on Silver property."

I rolled a *Really?* gaze toward Gideon.

The corner of his mouth lifted. "Give her the Pappy, Sera."

She dipped her head and was off.

"Pappy," I scoffed, failing to be unimpressed.

"You don't care for it?"

I adored Pappy Van Winkle. Daddy had splurged when we were all past the Bailey acceptable age for tasting bourbon and bought a bottle. Copper Summit was an excellent bourbon, but we were just starting to price our bottles in the mid-three figures. "It's just how you casually ordered a thousand-dollar bourbon. For a *cocktail*."

The ghost of a smile was back, but his gaze intensified. "You're mistaken. Sera knows the Pappy I mean is a bottle of twenty-four-year-old family reserve. It's five grand a bottle."

I choked. "What?" Excitement welled inside me until it pushed up through my chest and a smile exploded. "I don't know if Daddy would be proud or horrified that I get to have Pappy in a mixed drink like it's bottom shelf— Oh." Five grand a bottle? "I didn't tend enough bar this summer to afford that." I could afford the whole bottle, but I didn't want to spend my savings on another company's spirits. Both sets of my parents had instilled a sense of fiscal responsibility. My birth parents because of how they'd lost everything, and my adoptive parents because they couldn't help themselves.

"You think I'm putting it on your tab?" His eyes glittered as he considered me. "You're my guest, Autumn."

"Why?"

"Why not?"

There was a why. I just didn't know it yet. My best guess was that he was a predator, and I looked like a scared fawn if there ever was one. Maybe he liked to toy with his kills. Maybe he was planning a bigger humiliation for me than getting rejected for my schoolteacher fashion style. Maybe. But I'd go down drinking damn good bourbon.

"Oh! I like this song." I whipped my head back and forth, my hair flying. An electric dance song pulsed and a roar came from the dance floor.

Gideon had taken his suit coat off and hung it on the hook at the corner booth. The server had offered to take it for him. Was that a thing? His arms were stretched on either side. The Rosé Vintage he'd ordered was a Dom Pérignon. Half of the bottle was gone, and I was on my third bourbon Bloody Mary.

I popped a plump green olive into my mouth. I'd had close to an entire jar of olives, a full bunch of celery, and a pint of cherry tomatoes. Those were a delight to find impaled on a stick in my drink.

I wiggled to the music.

"I should find my friends." I didn't have to yell, this seat was fairly isolated, but I was fueled by Pappy. Still, I could shout, and I wouldn't bother anyone.

The booth had a curtain! When I asked if the seats would glow under a black light, I'd gotten a funny look from Gideon. Was he regretting whatever he'd said to the bouncers?

"Why are you worried about your friends?"

I lifted a shoulder. I wasn't missing them. I had zero messages on my phone. For the first two drinks, I'd asked Gideon about Silver and what his job entailed. He'd told me about upcoming renovations, which was crazy. The casino had opened only five years ago and it was considered outdated?

"They might worry." I took a tomato off the spear.

Guilt was starting to build, making my neck itch, when he pointed to the dance floor. "Is your crew out there?"

I had to lean close to him to see the dance floor. This booth had a view of the whole club, but there were a ton of writhing bodies on the dance floor. I spotted Brittany's topknot. Kaitlyn and Destiny were behind her next to an attractive guy with his shirt half-unbuttoned. He was either sweaty or he had a lot of hair product in. Either one was Destiny's type.

"They're doing well," I said, a bit too chipper.

"You want to join them?" His voice was deceptively casual, but his gaze was shrewd.

"No." The crestfallen feeling had nothing to do with whether I wanted to dance or not. At least I didn't have to lie about that part. I didn't want to join friends who were having a grand time and had forgotten about the friend they'd left behind. "I don't dance. Not like that anyway."

"How do you dance?"

"Privately."

A dark brow notched up.

A fire ignited in my cheeks. "Smaller venues. More subdued music. Like, I'd dance to this stuff at home. I can't just let loose on a dance floor. What about you?" I reclined against the back of the booth. The seat was really comfortable, but I also hadn't eased away from him when I'd leaned over to find my group.

"I don't dance like that either."

I nodded knowingly. "Private dancer."

He chuckled. "No, firecracker. Not privately either."

"Firecracker?"

"Red's a gimme."

I practically preened at the nickname. Gideon James was not the cold man I'd expected. He wasn't warm and fuzzy either, but the alcohol was making me warm enough for both of us. "Cinnamon?"

"Not when you smell so sweet." Then he clenched his jaw like he hadn't meant to say that.

I giggled and took a long drink of my Bloody Mary. I should ask for a glass of Pappy just to savor, but I liked the decadence, like I was wealthy enough to mix the drink with pond water if I wanted. Daddy always joked that was the difference between his generation and ours. There wasn't a bourbon Wynter and I wouldn't mix in our recipes.

"It's my lotion. I get really dry skin." I held an arm up and the room spun. I switched to grabbing another olive instead. "I'm the opposite of a firecracker."

"And what's that?"

I wrinkled my nose. A dud. I wasn't admitting that to the guy all the servers scuttled around. He was like royalty. "You rule this place."

"It's my job."

"My job is to be in charge of twenty-two little humans, but they don't say 'yes, ma'am' or 'no, ma'am' like Sera."

Just then, Sera appeared with another veggie-loaded drink and a small tray.

I laughed. It was more like a guffaw, but maybe the music would drown out the sound. Gideon's gaze was on me, but he didn't roll his eyes like my brothers did when I got a little tipsy and spoke too loudly. "I said your name and you appeared."

Sera's smile was either genuine, or she was damn good at her job. She made me feel special. "I brought the charcuterie tray you requested, sir."

I squealed and clapped my hands. I got salt cravings when I drank. "Yessss."

She rattled off names of meats and cheeses as she pointed to each one, but I didn't care. It could be a Lunchable. I was hungry and the cheese looked delicious.

Gideon slid the fancy wooden cutting board closer to me.

"Aren't you going to have some?" I asked, picking a thin slice of what was probably expensive prosciutto. What were the hard flakes of cheese again? I paired it with the meat.

"Help yourself."

"I've helped myself to a lot." I took a bite. Salty flavor burst over my tongue. My eyes rolled back and I moaned while I chewed.

I was making a spectacle of myself. I wasn't usually this free, but something about Gideon cut through the self-consciousness. He was out of my league, and I assumed he hated my family, me included. If he dropped the bill on me thinking he'd get one over on a Bailey, I could cover it. I hadn't had a treat like this in . . . ever.

I picked up a slice of something that had as much fat as meat and paired it with the hard cheese. I put it on top of the warm toasted bread that also had a fancy name. "Here."

He looked from my fingers to me, then drew his arms off the back of the booth. He twisted to the side, gingerly took the food offering, and put it all in his mouth. The muscles of his jaw bunched as he chewed. How could eating be so . . . masculine?

I was mesmerized, watching his lips. He had a tiny crumb at the corner of his mouth.

I swiped it away, and his pupils dilated.

"Dang. Sorry, I didn't mean to touch you." I finished off my third Bloody Mary to distract myself from the slight scrape of stubble I'd felt. Did his whiskers defy the razor every day?

He chose the combination I'd first selected and held it up to my mouth. Was he feeding me? He gave me an expectant look.

Carefully, I snatched the compilation from him and popped it into my mouth. I might get stuck with the bill. The thought helped dull the thrill. I was not Gideon's type. I swallowed hard.

He hated my family. Remember?

My memory seemed to be a sieve where he was concerned tonight.

"I saw you storm out," I blurted as if to remind him

he didn't like me. In case he'd forgotten. "When you were at Copper Summit last spring."

His eyes flickered. The pupils that had dilated when I fed him were now smaller, more intent. "You caught that."

"I was working in the bar."

He didn't look at me as he pieced together more meat and cheese. He put the combo on a cracker this time. "I didn't realize the bar was open that early."

"We are, but I was doing the books."

He slid his gaze toward me, then back to the food as he compiled another stack. Then he offered me one and made a second for himself.

I popped an olive off drink number four and gave it to him. "I bet this will taste amazing with the softer cheese."

"Olives are your favorite."

"How'd you know?"

A slight arch of his brow brought a sweep of embarrassment. I'd gobbled the olives off my first two drinks. I'd maybe moaned once or twice. If I could've dived headfirst into the Bloody Mary, I would've.

I put the olive on the plate. "They are, but I can share what I like."

"Is that what you teach the kids?"

I nodded. "I think it's important to teach them when to share. Otherwise, it's like a free-for-all."

He paused with the stack of food close to his mouth. "Very true. My class could've used that lesson."

"Yeah, it's much more complicated than we give it credit for. But my students are also older too. It's mostly learning to respect others' property and knowing that you don't have a claim to it just because it's within the school's walls."

He chewed and propped an elbow close to my shoulder. When had we gotten closer?

"How do you have time to do the books when you teach full-time?"

The books for the bar were fairly simple compared to the rest of the distillery. What my brother Tenor did was more like conducting an orchestra with all the moving parts involved in the distillery. The bar was a teeny-tiny part, and I kind of resented that I only got so much say over it. When Wynter worked the bar more, the guys would defer to her. When I brought it up, they'd tell me I wasn't around. I had a full-time job.

I wasn't going to confess any of that to Gideon. "I have summers off. Other teachers can use the money from teaching summer school, and I have an easy second income. Besides, I like working in the bar and creating drinks."

"You like mixology."

I liked control. The patrons didn't knock over their drinks nearly as often as kids spilled leaky water bottles. And when a tipsy customer spilled a drink, I didn't have twenty other students commentating the event and the cleanup. Drunk patrons didn't throw blame around quite as much as eight-year-olds, usually. Plus, tending bar didn't require parent-teacher conferences.

I loved teaching, but I liked my breaks. Some days were exhausting. And just when I was sick of dealing with my brothers, I could go back to school and feel like I had some authority.

"I like creating fun drinks. Wynter and I got into it, but then she moved around. Now she's back, but she's working in—" I was going to say the offices, but that made it sound like the C-suite, which would imply I was just another part-time staff. I sort of was. "She works from home a lot with the new baby."

His expression remained politely interested but, overall, impassive. "So you bartend?"

"I bartend. And do books." I didn't know why it was important for me to include that. He was the CEO of this entire building. Silver was like a small city, and Gideon was the mayor.

I poured drinks part-time and taught addition and subtraction and grammar full-time. I was proud of my work. Both jobs. But next to Gideon, I felt like the girl who'd been left in line when her hotter friends were let in.

"And the books," he murmured and selected another piece of meat and cheese. He held the food up toward my mouth. "A real family business."

I snatched it from his fingers. Surprise flitted through his dark gaze and the corner of his mouth quirked so slightly I almost missed it.

I chewed on my food. Whoever did their purchasing knew what they were doing. The flavor was excellent. Every part of this casino was meticulously run.

What was it like working for Gideon? He looked like he never smiled. Was he a tyrant or a fair boss?

My brothers were amazing guys—excellent to work for and all-around gentlemen. They also bought their own hype and could be frustrating.

"A real family business," I parroted and collected more food. I assembled a crostini, some of the spicier meat, and the smoothest cheese. I held it out for him.

Instead of grasping the food, he circled his long

fingers around my wrist. His tanned skin made my pale flesh stand out.

I watched—gaped—as he lifted my hand closer to his mouth. Then he took a deliberate bite.

He locked his gaze with mine as he chewed.

"Is it good?" I sounded ridiculous, but I had no idea what to say. No man as good-looking as Gideon James had eaten out of my fingers.

Had I fed any guy like this?

He gently took the remaining meat and cheese compilation and brought it to my lips.

Oh god, oh god, oh god. He wanted me to eat out of his hand?

I'd eat off this man's chest.

I overshot my bite, thanks to the bourbon Bloody Mary, and my lips closed around his fingertips. Instead of being a sophisticated and sensual woman, I was a half-lit, sloppy girl.

But from the way his pupils dilated, I wasn't sure he agreed. The idea was heady. Could I, Autumn Kerrigan, small-town teacher, do something that a Vegas CEO as powerful as Gideon James found sexy?

He swallowed, his Adam's apple working up and down, completely mesmerizing, and watched my lips as I finished chewing.

I couldn't break eye contact as Sera appeared to deliver another drink for me, loaded with even more olives than all the others had been.

"You tell me, firecracker. Is it good?"

"Very." My attention wasn't on my taste buds. The green in his eyes caught the dim lights overhead.

He shifted to face me more fully, like he was going to

tell me a secret. "What's it like working for the family business?"

"Tate's in charge of Bailey Beef. Teller's in charge of Copper Summit. Summer manages the Bozeman location. The daily operational and financial decisions are made by them. Larger ones that affect the whole company need all of us. We're the board."

His attention intensified. "And your spouses?"

My excitement swelled. "Tate's wife works with me at the school. We were friends before they married." She wouldn't have left me outside the club. "Wynter's husband runs his own distillery—Foster House."

A dark brow lifted. "I've heard of it."

"Summer's husband has his own successful business. I don't know. Maybe if a spouse wanted to be a part of the company, they'd get hired on." I took another drink and set my glass on the table. I didn't know what to do with my hands, so I folded them on my lap, but with the way I was sitting, the angle was uncomfortable. I looked like I was posing for family pictures.

He took my hand and my heart stammered. His rough thumb stroked over my knuckles. "Maybe what I'm asking, Autumn Kerrigan, is why you're not married."

A thready laugh eked out of me. Gideon James wanted to know why I was single.

Maybe what I'm asking...

It wasn't what he was asking, it was why.

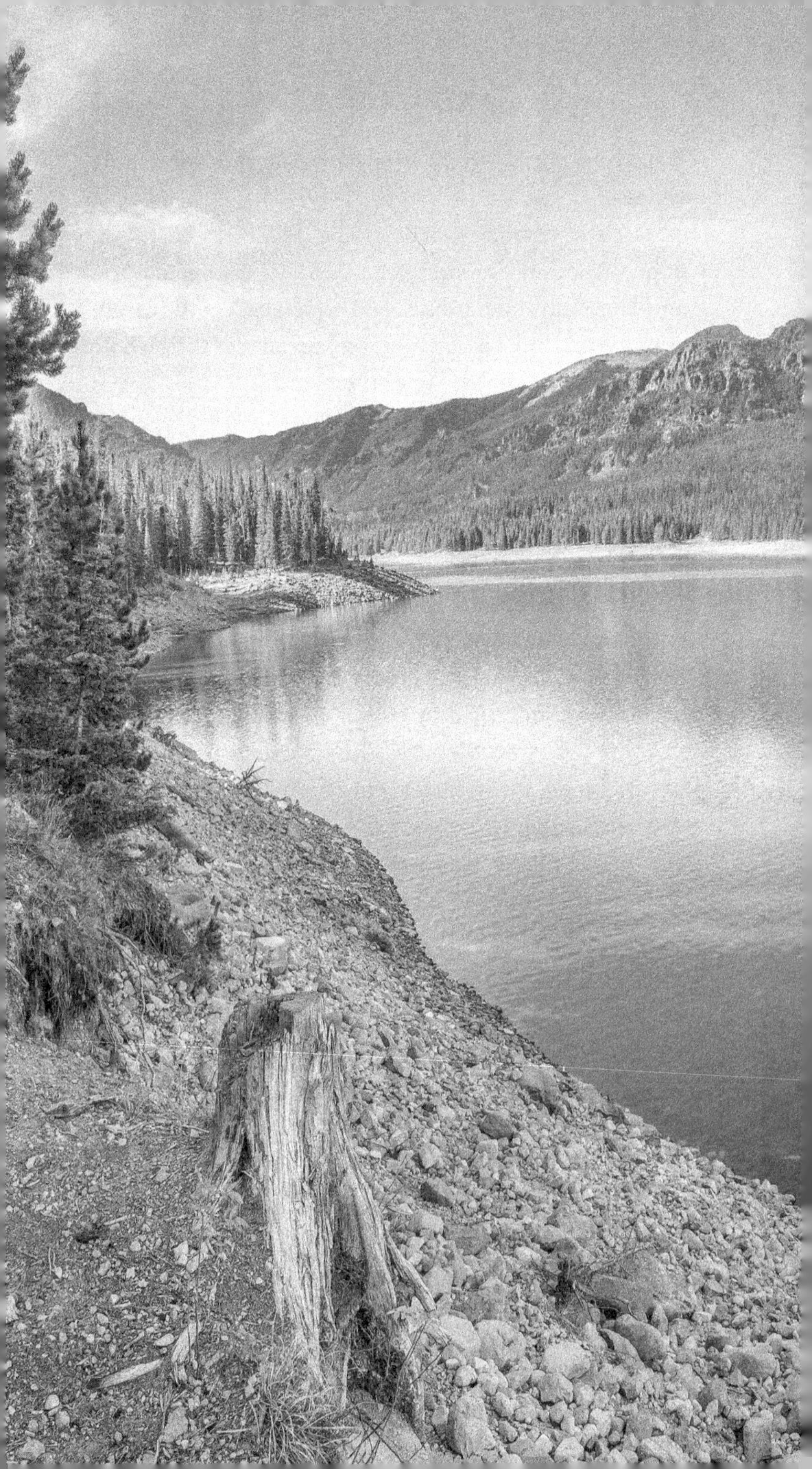

CHAPTER FOUR

Gideon

This morning, when I'd woken up and put myself through my normal five-mile run and strength training—chest and back—nothing could've convinced me this day would end any differently than any other. I'd thought perhaps I'd meet Taya later, and whether we ended up in bed was neither here nor there. No matter what, I'd get up tomorrow, do another workout—legs and arms—and go to the office. I didn't care if it was Saturday or Sunday. I would be in the office.

Instead, tomorrow morning, I'd be waking up married.

Opulence surrounded us. I'd been little more than a distant authority figure in Silver Linings Chapel, but now I could see everyone's hard work firsthand. From the moment we'd entered, we'd been treated like royalty.

The two women working either had no idea who I was or they were pretending not to know me. Unlike the club, I'd never stepped foot in this place except for when it had first opened. When I said my name for the marriage license, neither of them flinched. Confidentiality was required of every employee with the Silver logo on their paycheck, but today, I was incredibly grateful for our diligence.

I had no fucking clue how I would explain this to anyone who knew me, and I would not be telling the truth. The idea of lying skated over my skin, leaving an inky stain. I wasn't a deceitful person, but this was a necessity and I was known for doing what had to be done.

Autumn had the giggles next to me. We'd just said our vows.

Marriage vows.

The younger of the two attendants—Christ, she was probably half my age—grinned at us like this was her favorite part.

"You may now kiss the bride."

Desire wound its way through me, heading downward. It must be the wine. I only drank for business. The stuff had no reason to be present in my personal life. Tonight, the two were combined.

I could kiss my bride. I wasn't usually anticipating a kiss this much, but Autumn's lips were fucking kissable, plump from the way she kept licking them. I'd barely been able to look away from her mouth all night. When I did try to rip my gaze off them, my attention wanted to drop down to her chest. My palms itched to test the weight of her generous breasts.

"A kiss." Autumn giggled, then she looked at me. Her pretty amber eyes widened and she swallowed. All trace of humor was gone, and I got immense satisfaction from the way she couldn't keep her attention off my mouth.

What was this pull between us? It had to be my fury at her and the rest of the Bailey crew.

This was necessary. Yet I didn't need the reminder as I swayed forward. I caught her around the waist, and Jesus, she was as lush as she looked. A guy could lose himself in her body. She had padding in all the right places. I'd never considered myself to have a type, but she was definitely in the running.

Her hooded gaze was on me. "Are we really going to kiss?" she whispered.

"Yes, *wife*."

"What happened to firecracker—"

I cupped her chin and caught her mouth. I barely stopped a groan before it slipped out. Her lips were as deliciously soft as the rest of her. They parted slightly, and I dove in, unable to stop myself. I blamed my recent dry spell.

She tasted better than anything I'd had on my tongue all night. Sweeter than the champagne, more savory than anything on the charcuterie board, and more potent than the bourbon in her Bloody Mary.

Her arms wrapped around my neck and a squeak left her. Dimly, I realized I was tipping her backward. I was bent over her like I was a vampire and she was my virgin snack.

Lust punched me below the belt. I doubted she was a fucking virgin, but my mind continued to veer toward the thought of sex with this woman. I straightened, keeping her hugged close to me. More reluctantly than I would've ever guessed, I broke our kiss.

At our side, the officiant grinned. "Congratulations, Mr. and Mrs. James."

Autumn's eyes flared, the name change catching her off guard. I hadn't put much thought into it—like this whole fucking night—but I was a king at capitalizing on opportunity. Having her go by Autumn James would serve me better. It would keep her family from ripping this marriage apart.

I'd do that myself when I got what I needed.

Autumn

I was married.

Oh god. I was *married*.

Mrs. James.

I had to be dreaming.

Gideon and I hadn't even kissed until we were man and wife. But here I was, draped on him, riding the elevator to the top floor of the casino where he lived.

He placed another soft kiss on the corner of my mouth. Then, the other corner. And finally, in the middle. And when he swept his tongue inside, I felt like I was the charcuterie board. I was the meat and cheese he was dining on tonight. That maybe wasn't the sexiest way to describe the kiss, but he was a good kisser. I'd made out with a few frogs who'd never turned into princes. I knew the difference.

What a crazy thing to do. Married.

Had I drunk too much?

I'd had four . . . five? . . . Bloody Marys. But I'd had

food. And, please. It was bourbon. But the dreamy flush that swept over my body from head to toe, filling me with warmth and amplifying the desire that had been burning since I'd first set eyes on Gideon, suggested that maybe . . . I'd had too much to drink.

When the elevator dinged and opened into a penthouse, Gideon broke the kiss. I blinked, dazed, and faced his place.

"Holy shit. It really is like TV." I crept out of the elevator, getting the sense he was waiting for my reaction. "Look at this place. Don't you get tired of all the light?"

He didn't have blinds on his windows. His home was in the freaking *sky*. Who'd need drapes? The floors were done in tile similar to other flooring in the casino, but there were plush rugs scattered in strategic places—at the entry, in front of the couch, and in front of the bank of windows that let the Las Vegas neon lights in.

So much light.

I turned to find Gideon standing with his back to the now-closed elevator doors, a perplexed expression on his face. "Sometimes," he said.

I nodded. "I bet where you grew up, it was the yard light and the stars. Like our place."

The "our place" started a niggle in the back of my brain. I was married. Where would I be living?

I gasped. "I have work. I have a return flight tomorrow. Work on Tuesday. Monday is a day off school." I gasped. "My friends!"

He cocked a dark brow and all my worries faded away. The man was still in his slacks, his shiny, fancy shoes, and the cuffs of his shirt were rolled up. So. Sexy.

I'd married him. I'd always wanted to get married.

Another giggle left me. Who knew I wouldn't be a blushing bride but an alcohol-flushed one with the giggles?

My family was going to detonate when they heard about this.

A hiccup rocked my body.

Shit. I wasn't a sexy bride. Yet he'd made me feel like one with each kiss.

Gideon's gaze narrowed on me.

I hiccupped again.

"Let's get you to bed, darling."

I shook my head. "No. No 'darling.' That sounds fake as hell."

The perplexed expression was back on his face. "Excuse me?"

"Have you called other girls darling?"

His mouth tightened.

"Right. So if I called you big boy, would you feel a little . . . diminished?"

"That's an oxymoron, is it not?"

"So were they." I shrugged and hiccupped. "If you call me darling again, I'll salt your dinner so bad your mouth is going to feel like the Sahara for a week."

Laughter sputtered out of him. Lines winged out from the corners of his eyes and his smile seemed almost rusty—shaky at first and then so bold it lit up the place better than the Vegas skyline.

His grin stole my breath. This man needed to smile more.

"Come, firecracker. I'll show you the bedroom."

He said "the" bedroom. Not his or ours. Was he avoiding the logistics of how this union was going to work?

Did it matter?

Not tonight.

I toed off my shoes and padded behind him. The floor was cool under my thin socks. I hoped I wasn't leaving sweaty footprints behind me.

"Guest bathroom," he said as we passed a closed door. He hadn't bothered to turn on lights but all the material in this place was so bright it didn't matter. White tile. White walls. Sedate black and silver artwork on the walls. It could be a mausoleum, but I couldn't imagine this penthouse being a home.

He rattled off each room's purpose as we passed closed doors. "Closet, guest bedroom. Second guest room. Office."

The door at the end was open and he stepped to the side to let me in first. "There's a full bathroom to your left."

Again, he avoided putting a claim on the bedroom. I blinked the fuzz out of my eyes. I was buzzing pretty good. Gingerly, I stepped in.

Nerves tightened my belly until I was afraid I'd start shaking.

I'd gone from seeing Gideon in a parking lot and developing a severe case of infatuation to being married to him and standing in his bedroom. How had it happened?

He'd asked why I wasn't married. I'd told him I'd like to be. He'd said all the guys I'd dated must've been idiots. I'd laughed and said, "Why? Do you want to marry me?" A little more back-and-forth, and we were at the chapel.

Now I was here. This room was not like the cozy little four walls I slept in. My bedroom didn't fit much more than my queen bed and a couple of dressers. "I can fit my house in here."

Half of the square footage of the penthouse was in the bedroom. Plush carpet greeted my feet. White, naturally.

"It's spacious," he agreed.

I giggled, but when my gaze landed on the bed, I choked.

"Do you need to use the bathroom first?" he asked quietly.

"Yes, please." I wasn't crawling into Gideon's bed with meat-and-cheese-platter breath.

In the bathroom, I stared some more. I had land, thanks to Daddy, but my house was in town, not far from the school. I'd purchased it myself. I could've afforded a larger place, but I hadn't needed bigger. The bathroom had creaky pipes, the water pressure was variable, and cracked plaster was the main decoration. Gideon's shower could swallow my bathroom in one gulp. I quit counting the showerheads at six. How many sinks did a bathroom need? There was another open door, and when I peeked inside, I snickered. "The toilet gets its own room."

My gaze swung back to the shower. An image of Gideon's muscled body thrusting into a naked woman he had pressed against the wall flashed into my brain. Only the woman was sleeker than me. Classier.

I shook my head. Not now. I was less than an hour into my marriage, and I was not getting jealous.

I should be scared—what did he expect tonight? What would my family say? My work? The entire town? More importantly, what would Gideon think when I told him what I wanted out of this marriage?

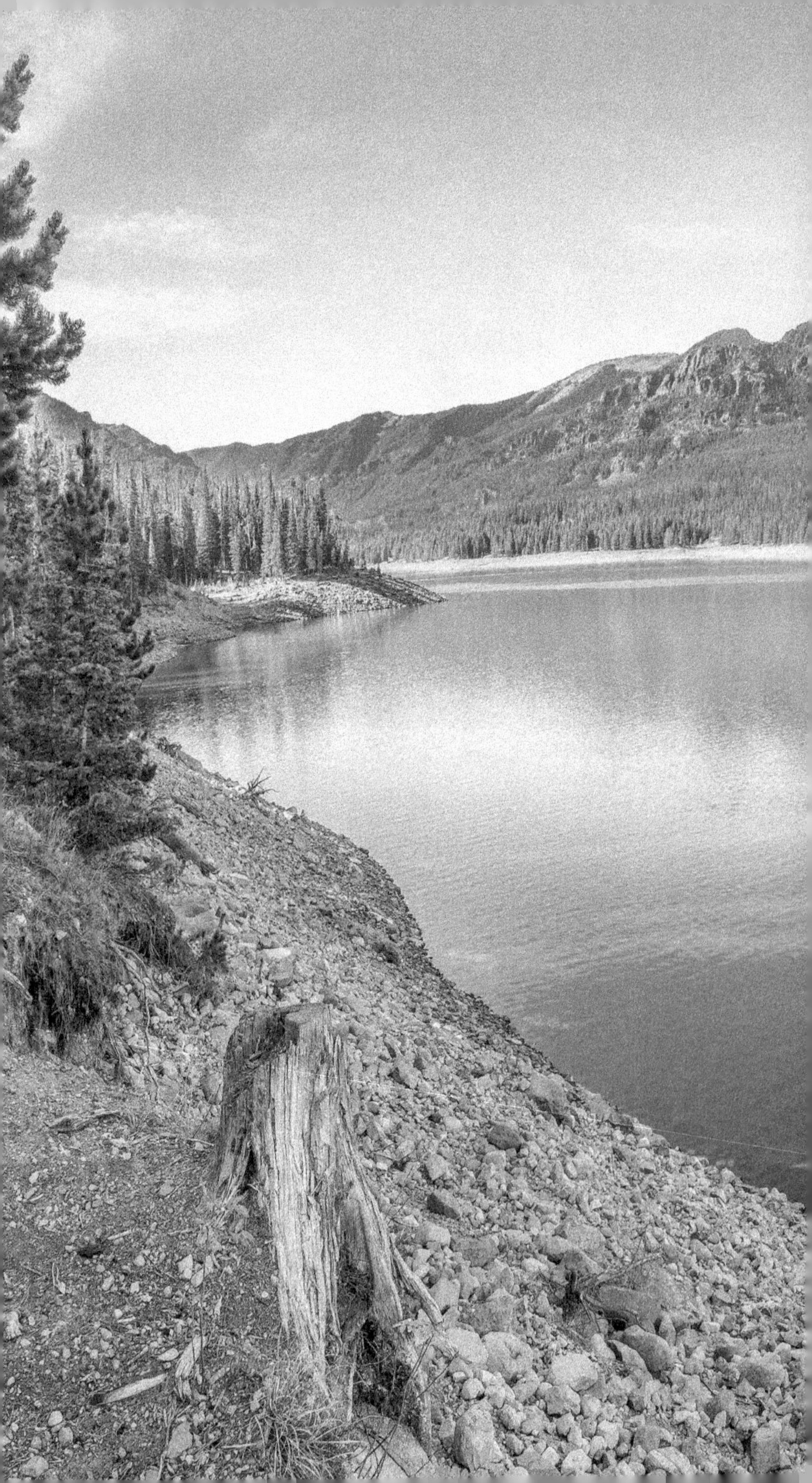

CHAPTER FIVE

Gideon

Autumn exited the bathroom, her hands behind her, smoothing her dress over her leggings. She looked odd in my bedroom. Her reddish-brown leggings ended where her thin socks started and were stark against the pale room. A single flame that warmed up every square inch. The woman didn't bare more than her hands and neck, but she exuded sex appeal that only dunces would miss.

I'd have to be careful. I hadn't married her for physical reasons, and I couldn't let my interest in her body sway my motivations. I pulled the covers back. This was the side of the bed I usually slept on, but she looked ready to bolt as she shifted from foot to foot.

"Go ahead. Crawl in." I knew what she expected. The trepidation and excitement mixed in her eyes.

I had to admit I'd never been with a person so skittish around me.

She tiptoed toward the bed, her gaze flitting from

my face to the covers. She might not be revealing much skin, but her pulse fluttered erratically at the base of her throat. Despite my earlier mental warning, I eyed her ass and the way it rounded when she got between the sheets. When she was settled, I leaned over her and kissed her forehead. Completely unnecessary. She'd already been seduced, and I had the marriage to show for it. "I set a shirt and shorts on the end table to change into if you'd like. Get some rest."

In the ambient light from the window, I could see her pink lips pull down in a frown. Was she afraid she couldn't fall asleep without shades? She'd been practically aghast over the view when my few other guests had gushed about it.

"What's wrong?" I asked, more concerned than curious.

"We aren't— Um . . . You don't want to . . ." Her furious blush was adorable. How could she be so innocent when she didn't mind her family conning land away from an old drunk?

"No, wife." I said it more to remind myself and ignored how easily the word slipped off my tongue. I was a married man. My gut clenched as much as it twisted. "You've had too much to drink. You need sleep."

She blinked slowly, her eyes owlish. Then she sat up, clutching the blankets to her chest like she was nude instead of fully dressed. I'd have offered her the change of clothes first, but I didn't care to risk seeing another inch of creamy flesh.

She pushed her thick hair off her face. "How are we going to convince my brothers not to buy your family's land if we aren't *married* married?"

Cold washed through my insides. I'd underestimated this woman. A mistake I hadn't made . . . ever.

"What?" My voice could've cut glass.

She looked at me like *duh*. "I mean, I want a family. You want your land." She rolled her eyes—*rolled* her goddamn eyes—at me. "Did you think there was nothing I wanted out of the deal?"

"What deal?" I bit out. Family? The thought almost made me heave. Kids?

She finally had the grace to look embarrassed. "I guess I never said it, but then neither did you."

Ice continued to crystallize in my veins. I could lie. Tell her I'd fallen madly in love with her as soon as I'd seen her, but she wouldn't believe it. Not if she didn't buy that I'd swept her off her feet and into Silver Linings Chapel because I couldn't stand the thought of living without her.

Fuck. "How'd you know?"

She chortled, another adorable reaction I didn't expect. "You? Instantly smitten with me? Come on. I couldn't even get *into* the club, yet Gideon James was so taken with a schoolteacher he whisked her off to say vows after a few drinks together? A few drinks that were *not* made with Copper Summit bourbon. Because Copper Summit isn't served anywhere on the premises."

Irritation flared bright behind my sternum and not because she'd called me on my pettiness. "For such an innately sexy woman, you don't think very highly of yourself."

A furrow formed between her brows. "I think just fine about myself, but I'm also realistic. I can't be bothered to dress sexy anymore. That's what my twenties were for—uncomfortable clothes and even worse shoes.

All I caught with that look were mommy-dependent man-children." She wrinkled her nose. "Come to think of it, this look attracts the ones who want to be mothered too."

I almost smiled. This conversation was absurd. "Speaking of mothering—what the hell do you mean *family*?" The edge was back in my voice.

She sighed and her shoulders slumped. "I want a family. If I can't have the loving husband and kids, I'd rather have the kids from a guy who's proved able to look after himself."

I didn't know if I should thank her for the odd compliment or throttle her. "I don't want kids."

Her lips puffed out. "Oh." She looked down at her hands. "Damn." She spread her fingers and inspected the flawless one-carat diamond on her finger. I'd been going to buy her a five-carat ring, but she'd practically gagged. I'd selected a two-carat ring and she'd almost panicked. She'd even insisted one carat was too big, but a guy had his pride. I'd duped her into marrying me—or so I had thought—and the least I could do was buy her a nice ring. My ring matched hers. A simple platinum band with squared edges.

"Maybe I could do artificial insemination. People might assume it's yours."

My mouth curled into a sneer. I didn't want kids, but the idea of another man's baby in her belly ignited a feral response.

I was better than this, and I needed time to think. I wasn't fooling her and the relief was immense. Had I been prepared to sell my soul for the family land?

Yes. I always did what I had to do—run the ranch when my drunk dad couldn't, leave home so I could have a future, and marry a Bailey so I could save my legacy.

Turned out this Bailey was just as determined to create a legacy for herself. "We can discuss this when you're sober. But since you know why I married you, tell me how you can help me stop your family from buying my land."

"My brothers," she said. "We'd have to talk to my brothers."

"You can't halt the sale?"

She lifted a shoulder. "Maybe."

Uncertainty was written through every feature. I gawked at her. "You do the books."

"I do the *bar's* books." Guilt crossed her face.

I'd been had *by a schoolteacher*.

Panic expanded in my chest, squeezing my lungs. The last-ditch scramble to keep Percival in the James name was slipping through my fingers.

"*Fuck*." I stuffed a hand through my hair and paced the bedroom. I'd married the girl who did the bar's books, and her brothers would hate me. They'd close the sale faster just to spite me. "Fuck!"

"Hey," she said in a calming voice that ought to upset me, but my tension notched down. "You don't want kids and I don't have as much power as you thought. That doesn't mean we can't help each other."

I propped my hands on my hips and faced her. "How's that? You're going to ask them nicely after you show up with me as a husband?"

"You're going to Bourbon Canyon?"

"I can't do much from here," I snapped. "We'll change your flight so we can go together."

She ignored my outburst and flicked a finger up.

"Okay, one, asking nicely gets you pretty darn far. And two, I'm still part of the family. We act as a united front. If you're part of the family, they'll listen to you. Or maybe give you a role after the sale."

Fury ramped up my blood pressure. "Golly gee, I can manage *my* land that someone else owns."

"It's not your land," she said bluntly. "That's the crux of the issue, or you wouldn't have me in your bed."

Damn. She cut to the heart faster than any high-level investor I'd met.

She lifted her hands, palms in the air. "Look, it's not ideal, but you and I seem to be the only way we can each get what we want. My brothers have no problem buying the place you think should be yours, but would they hesitate if they were buying it out from under your dad's grandson or granddaughter? Would your dad reconsider if he thought that?"

Her meaning sank in. Her brothers didn't give a shit about me. Even if they were sympathetic to my situation, they had long since decided it didn't matter. We'd last parted ways yelling at each other. They thought they were supporting my delusional dad with his decision.

But if there was an innocent kid, a niece or nephew, who would lose their legacy? Would that make them pause long enough for me to get through to Dad that he was making a goddamn mistake? Would the thought of a grandkid make Dad reconsider?

Was it worth having a kid to find out?

I had ruled out kids to prevent them from going through what I had. But Autumn had a big family. If something happened to one of us, there'd be plenty of aunts and uncles for the kid to lean on.

A child.

A baby.

The image of my mom's smile doused my anger and stabbed right into my heart. She would've loved to have a grandkid.

She was the reason why I'd been determined not to.

But the only slice of heaven Mom loved in the world was getting sold, and if that kid could help me save it?

"You have a deal, wife."

Autumn

When I woke, I smacked my lips together and squeezed my eyes shut. I needed a gallon of water and some fresh fruit ASAP. Between the drinks and the salty food, I was dying of thirst.

I pried an eye open. God, it was bright in here.

The soft smell of laundry detergent mingled with the scent of cedar citrus. Gideon.

I was in his room. In his bed.

I sat up. "Holy crap."

I was married.

Holding up my hand, I squinted at my ring.

Married. With a big dang rock on my finger.

He'd wanted to buy an obnoxiously large diamond. No, thanks. The size of even this ring gave me palpitations. What if I lost it in Play-Doh? I loved the platinum setting. I loved the sparkle.

It couldn't be real.

I blinked out the floor-to-ceiling windows, then

swept my gaze around the plush room with chests and dressers that probably cost more than my house.

The diamond was real.

I rubbed my forehead as the events of the night clicked back into place. The club. Flirting in the booth. Gideon's charm. The guy was smooth, but I spent my day around kids who were afraid to tell me they'd peed their pants when a wet line ran down their leg. I knew all about lying and ulterior motives, though I couldn't attribute all the skills to my current and former students. I'd dated some doozies.

Where was Gideon anyway?

The other side of the bed was smooth, the blankets pulled tight. After he'd agreed to give me kids in exchange for me helping him keep the land in the James name, I'd barely been able to keep my eyes open.

Where had he slept?

Had he slept, or had he roamed this massive penthouse and counted his money?

I swung my legs down. A bottle of water with moisture dripping down the sides was on the nightstand.

For a new husband, he was already sweeter than a lot of the guys I'd dated. Except Mark.

Guess I had a good reason to turn down Mark's offer to go to Spokane. I chugged the whole thing. Then my attention caught on the suitcase by the bathroom door.

My luggage.

He'd had it brought up? How thoughtful, but my friends had to be worried. I shared a room with Kaitlyn. Had all signs of me been gone by the time she'd returned to her room?

I searched around for my phone. I should be rushed, but I couldn't bring myself to be panicked.

They hadn't left the dance floor to see how I was doing.

I chewed my bottom lip. They were nice women, but also younger than me. We were in different seasons in our life. No wonder Gideon had thought he could trick me into marrying him.

My cheeks heated. I didn't have time for embarrassment. I checked my screen.

Kaitlyn: Where are you?
Kaitlyn: Are you okay?
Destiny: Tell me you didn't get stolen?
Kaitlyn: Did you fly home?
Brittany: I'm so sorry!
Destiny: Are you upset? I'm really sorry, babes.
Brittany: We're terrible people. Just talk to us.

I sort of felt better reading their frantic texts. I was also tempted to continue ignoring them, but I couldn't have them calling my siblings. That mess could wait until later.

Autumn: I'm fine. I'm in another room, and I'll be taking a different flight home.

I didn't bother with the specifics. More pressing concerns dominated my attention.

I dragged my suitcase into the bathroom. I washed up, scrubbed my face, and threw on a pair of black leggings with an oversized Copper Summit hoodie. For a casino named Silver, I was decked out in copper. My hair wouldn't be tamed. I pulled it back into a ponytail and looped it so it wouldn't get tangled in the hood.

Okay. I was ready to find my husband.

The butterflies in my stomach woke up.

My family was going to be irate. They wouldn't

believe this marriage. I didn't believe this marriage. But Gideon had been on board, so between the two of us, we had to be a united front.

I didn't find him in the living room, or in the kitchen that looked like it should have a private chef making caviar pancakes or whatever people with personal chefs ate.

Was he still in the apartment? Had he even slept? It was barely after nine. Was he a five a.m. guy?

I was about to go back down the hallway and knock on closed doors to find my husband when the elevator doors swung open to reveal the leggy blond I'd seen walk freely into the club.

She was digging in a bag that was likely as expensive as her glittery tank top looked. Shiny aviator shades were pushed into her blond tresses and she had as much long leg showing under her wrap skirt as she'd had last night. She stepped out of the elevator, still rustling in her bag. "How was the VIP bullshit from last night? I bet it was an investor. They can be such idiots thinking we have nothing better to do on a Friday—"

She saw me. Her mouth dropped open. Then she drew back, disdain taking over her expression. "You can go now."

Why was she here? The answer was obvious, but my confusion remained. Anger was quickly coalescing in its place. I'd been married to the man for less than twelve hours, and he already had another woman in his place. "I'm the one who can go?"

Her crystal-blue eyes narrowed. "Of course you can. I have important business with him and you're just a—"

"Taya," Gideon snapped, and I jumped. That was how I'd expected him to sound last night when we'd first met. Like a furious destroyer. "Don't talk to my guest like that."

She shut her mouth. Her back was ramrod straight, and she didn't look sorry for almost insulting me. "I should've called first." She sniffed, lifting her chin in the air.

"Autumn, this is Taya. She's the chief financial officer for Silver."

Gorgeous, smart, and powerful. And she worked with Gideon. Fucking perfect. I didn't greet her, just did the small-town nod.

Taya looked like she could command a meeting and then run a marathon without being out of breath. Who had legs like that?

She also seethed with rage, ready to bash out the windows, using me as the battering ram. Then all the tension drained away and she smiled sweetly at Gideon. "We were going to discuss the renovations today. Remember?"

I did not like the way she spoke to him.

"Our talk will have to wait." He came to a stop next to me. I didn't stare. I couldn't look gobsmacked in front of this intruder, but Gideon was wearing jeans and a forest-green polo. Nothing like the jeans and polos guys wore around home. Bourbon Canyon didn't sell jeans or shirts that didn't have a Western style. How could a polo look expensive?

Taya tipped her head, her gaze jumping from me to Gideon, down to the fluffy socks I'd put on instead of my sandals, then back to Gideon. "Are you sure?"

She wasn't asking about the delay. She was asking about me. These two had clearly done more than run numbers together. The image I'd had of Gideon in the shower with a model flashed through my head. I wanted to vomit.

I did not belong here. Not with Gideon. Not in Vegas. And not in this penthouse, facing off with Taya, locked into some unknown competition neither of us had signed up for.

Gideon's big, warm hand landed on the small of my back. "I'm sure. I'll be out of the office for a while."

She blinked. His announcement was news to me too. He had said he was going to Bourbon Canyon, but not for how long or when. We still had to work through the logistics of how this marriage and baby-making would work. I couldn't think about the last part right now.

"How long will you be gone?" Her question was brittle. This woman did not like Gideon acting out of character, and even I knew taking time off was not normal for him.

"At least a month," he replied casually. "I need to go out of town. Family emergency."

"What family?" she snapped.

I waited for him to declare that I was his wife, but he didn't. Taya wasn't looking at my hand and his ring finger was behind my back. For whatever reason, he wasn't announcing the happy news. I knew the significance of a month. That was when the land deal was scheduled to close.

"I'll be working remotely. Contact me Monday." He continued to rest his big hand on the small of my back. I tried not to preen. He still didn't claim me as his wife.

"Fine." Taya stabbed the elevator button and spun back to us. "Have you talked to the board?"

"I've told who needs to know. Have a good day, Taya."

Cold fury blazed in her eyes at his response. When the elevator doors opened, she punched a few buttons, glaring at Gideon until the doors closed.

I let out a long breath. "She's delightful. I bet you two have a hot and sweaty work relationship." I couldn't stop the sarcasm from pouring out and started for the kitchen.

"That part didn't happen often." He passed me and went for the fridge. "And it's been a while."

I snorted. "Sure. She has a key to your house to talk about emergency remodeling."

"I'll change the code."

He offered the option so readily I tacked on more demands. "No one else." I hugged my arms around me, suddenly unsure. I was willing to marry him to get what we both wanted, but I wasn't willing to feel like a fool.

"What do you mean?" He shoved his hands in the pockets of his jeans. He wasn't in socks like me, but more casual loafers than what he'd worn last night. His question wasn't casual. I didn't think that was a thing with him. He made it sound calm, but there was always an edge.

"This marriage is monogamous. Full stop. People aren't going to believe us as it is. I don't need to field gossip about you fucking around."

His pupils did that thing again. The way they widened like a predator's was hot. Tingles rolled down my spine. "There will be no rumors. Just as you will also keep your hands and every other part of your body to yourself. For the next month, you're mine. Until I get my dad to switch the land to my name or sell to me—you're mine."

The shivers notched up to ten. I was his. Wait—until

he got the land? Then we were done? *For the next month* . . . I was sinking into a dream. I couldn't afford to lose myself. I couldn't fantasize about Gideon. This was his home. Taya was his type.

"The closing date is in a month," I said more to confirm that was his timeline. It made sense. Why would he want to stay married longer?

Teller had complained to Tate that the delays with financing would leave them closing right before winter. They wouldn't be able to do much until spring, when all the snow we'd get this winter would melt.

He nodded. "Which means we have less time to pretend we're so in love we couldn't help ourselves when we were so close to a Las Vegas chapel."

My heart sank to my socks. I dropped my gaze. A month wasn't long to test the ol' fertility ability. If we were successful, I might be a single mom. Would he fight for custody? Not from the expression when I'd told my end of the bargain.

This is an act. This is an act. This is an act.

"Right," I said, proud of how strong my voice sounded. "You don't leave this marriage without land and I don't leave without a baby. What if that takes more than a month?"

That sounded callous.

His lips thinned at the word baby. "We have a month."

"Biology doesn't always listen to our deals."

"I have an important job," he said with a clipped tone.

"So do I."

"One month, Autumn."

I was raised a Bailey. I should be comfortable negotiating contracts and deals, but that was what my brothers did. Daddy had familiarized me with everything, but I didn't work at the distillery full-time. Gideon's tone was stone. Unmoving.

He'd seen that pathetic part of my life last night. I didn't care to beg him to get me pregnant. "Good thing I've been off birth control for a while."

His pupils flared again. "We have a few more details to hammer out. I notified my lawyer this morning we'll be in need of a postnuptial contract."

"A postnup?" The ramifications of an impulsive marriage were sinking in. Would Gideon have claim to my share of the ranch and Copper Summit? What about the portion of land Daddy had gifted me? Would I lose that?

Oh god, what had I done?

"Does the idea of a postnup bother you?" His expression was glacial and his tone had an edge, so at odds with his more casual look.

"No. I think protection is always good." Why did that sound sexual?

The iciness was gone in an instant, replaced with simmering heat. "We'll each leave this marriage with what we had when we entered it."

Relief cooled the thud at my temples. "Oh, good." I laughed and waved my hand at his expansive living room. "I won't be stuck with half the view of the Strip."

He blinked. Crap. Had I insulted him? He probably liked his view. Maybe it was something girls like Taya gushed about. I missed a neon-light-free view.

"He'll also draw up divorce papers."

Ouch. A little arrow to the heart in case I'd thought that Gideon would ever be smitten enough to marry me after a few hours of Bloody Marys and charcuterie. "More preparation. Awesome."

"Now that the logistics are settled, we can discuss details." His gaze dropped to my fuzzy socks, and I braced myself for the same distaste Taya had shown. The hardness in his gaze softened only slightly. "If I'm going to Bourbon Canyon, I'll have to stay with you. We'll have to tell everyone that we met and fell madly in love."

I could play madly in lust well enough. "Desperately in love," I said flatly, hating the longing deep inside my heart. "Do you think a month is enough time to convince your dad not to sell?"

"It'll need to be enough to make him think I'll move back and have kids." He turned and dug in the fridge.

I stared at the way the denim molded around his ass. I could bounce a quarter off that thing. "Um, okay—about that . . ." This would be embarrassing. "If I do get pregnant, how is that going to work?"

He turned and set eggs and cheese on the counter next to a bowl of tomatoes I had assumed were for show.

"You cook?" I asked.

He lifted his vivid gaze to mine. "I had to cook, or I would've starved."

Sympathy swelled in my chest. His dad was an alcoholic and the whole town knew how bad he'd gotten after Gideon's mom died. "But you still cook?"

"I don't like strangers in my place."

I left my *Really?* stare on him.

The corner of his mouth twitched. "Taya is not a stranger, and she will no longer have access. Do you want an egg wrap?"

My stomach rumbled. "Yes, please."

He got a bowl out from a cupboard in the island. "As for the baby, we won't do anything until you're ready."

I almost sagged with relief. I wasn't ready, and I hated that it was obvious. The baby part? So ready. Last night with the bourbon influence? I would've climbed him like a mountain—three points of contact and one of them would've been my mouth. But in the stark light of the morning? After having seen his ungodly beautiful coworker?

There wasn't enough darkness to make me feel comfortable.

Besides, I remembered this morning. "You will have to sleep in the same bed as me, you know?"

He stopped cracking eggs. "Where do you think I slept last night?"

A tremble racked my body. Fear or desire?

"The guest room?" My voice pitched up at the end. He hadn't slept with me . . . had he? I would've known.

Did I snore?

Drool?

Fart?

"The recliner?" I asked.

"I don't have one."

I craned my head around. The open floor plan taunted me with the lack of a recliner in his place. Would he look nearly as well-rested if he'd slept on the couch that had more angles than cushions?

He'd slept in the bed with me. He'd tried to use me without *using* me, and when he'd been busted, he'd still slept in the bed with me and then offered to make me breakfast.

He selected a tomato and dug out a cutting board

and knife. I almost offered to help, but it was nice to have a guy treat me.

Things between us were fake, but he was making breakfast. No negotiations. He wasn't hyperfocused and overly charming like when he'd broached the impulsive marriage topic. He was in his head, making plans for the next month. The considerate part of him seemed to be unconscious.

I was already having a hard time telling myself nothing about this was real. If I wasn't careful, this deal between us could ruin me.

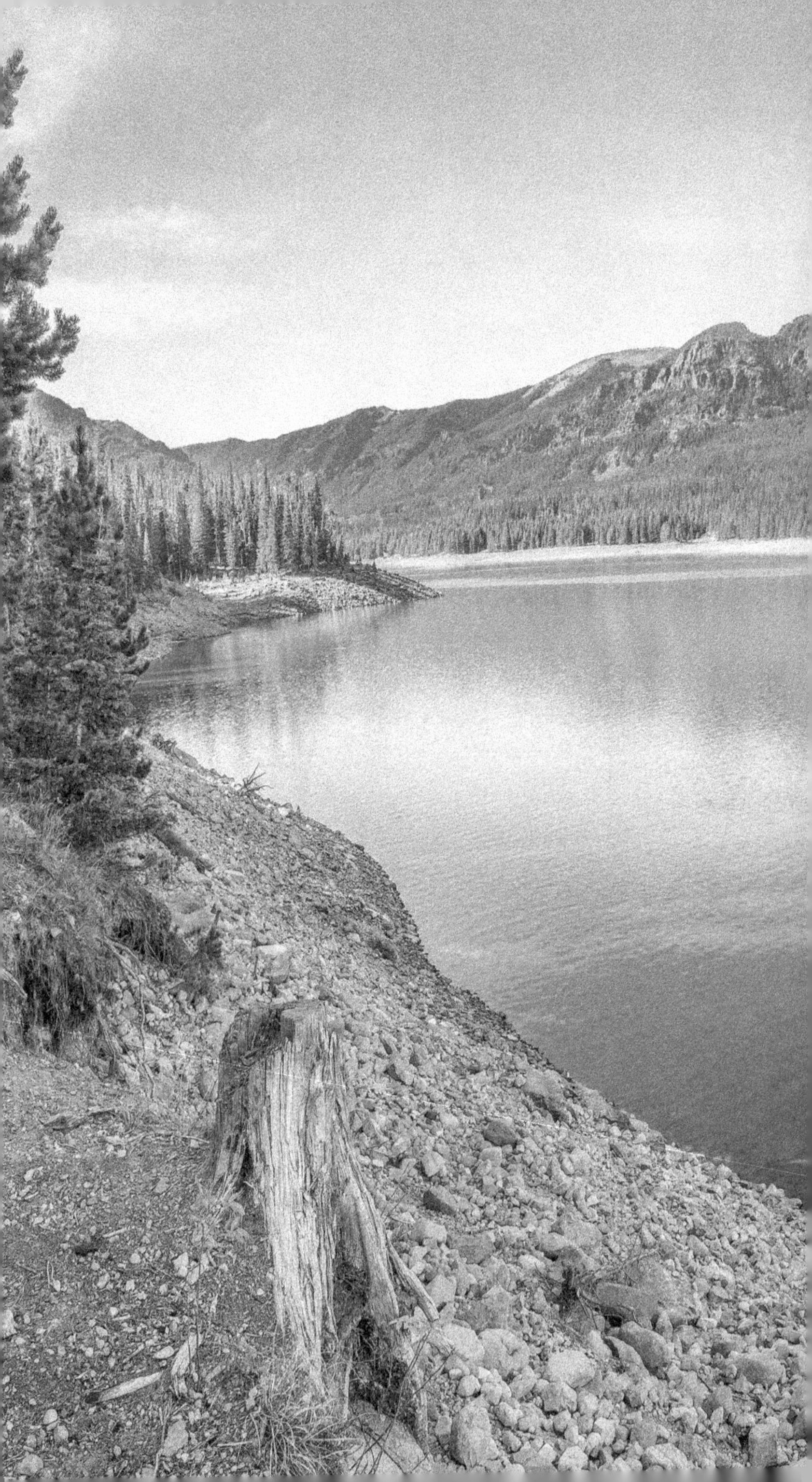

CHAPTER SIX

Gideon

The airplane was about to touch down in Bozeman. My fingers gripped the armrests, my knuckles white.

"Does flying bother you?" Autumn asked. She'd been scanning through movies, not settling on one the whole time. When we'd first loaded the plane, she'd been nothing but a gawking tourist. It only took me two seconds to realize she'd never sat outside of economy on a plane.

The Baileys prided themselves on their humility. They could afford first class. They could afford a private fucking jet. But they were the type of "regular folks" who flew economy.

Autumn had mentioned a private jet co-op.

Fuck the Bailey brothers.

I could've arranged a private jet, but then I might have to explain why I was traveling that way. I might run across flight attendants or pilots I'd traveled with for work before. Talk would get around. The board didn't need to worry I'd gotten married and would run off permanently. Lots of people were lined up and waiting for my job. I was determined to keep my family property and my job. I could get lost in commercial airlines easier.

"No, I'm not bothered by flying," I answered. "I don't like going home."

"Oh."

Too many confessions spilled out of my mouth when it came to her. Like the cooking. I'd seen the sympathy in her eyes. Worse, the understanding. She didn't know me as just some poor kid made good. She'd have heard about my mom. About the way Dad had turned himself over to whatever bottle he could afford. Did she know what school had been like for me? How guys like her brothers had seen right through me? That I'd gone from being a god in Silver to being a nothing in Bourbon Canyon?

I wasn't losing Mom's family land on top of it.

This legacy is yours, Gideon. Four generations to build it, and you're the fifth. Don't let your dad make you the last. My grandfather's words after the funeral were so damn clear.

The plane touched down. Less than six months had gone by and I was back.

Autumn opened her mouth like she was going to say something, then shut it.

"Go ahead," I said, dreading the inevitable inquiry about my childhood.

"Why didn't you tell Taya we were married?"

I'd always thought the idea of women fighting over a man pedestrian, but the baser part of me liked her jealousy.

"I didn't think you'd want word getting to your

family before you told them." Taya would've lashed out, tattling on me to the board. She would have spilled the fact to the rest of the C-suite, and she might've tipped off the local news stations or social media at the least.

I'd been a spectacle after Mom had died. People had stared. Then Dad had drunk. People still stared. And when I'd driven through Bourbon Canyon to meet with the Baileys at Copper Summit, everyone had stared. Only that time it had been because no one knew me. I didn't know which one was better.

"Yeah, I guess that's best. My family should hear it from us." She checked her phone.

She had told me that her friends were hounding her, but I could see the litany of messages.

One stood out. A message from someone named Mark.

"Your friends are worried." And who was fucking Mark?

"I told them I was getting a different flight, so they think I'm pissed."

"What are you going to tell them?" I didn't get the impression she was as close to her friends as her siblings. She got aloof when they were brought up or when she looked at her phone.

"Nothing." She tucked the phone into her carry-on tote. "Like you said, we have to tell our families first."

They'd really hurt her feelings last night when they'd left her outside the club. She'd never tell. I didn't know how I knew, but Autumn had standards and pity to the people who fell below them.

The realization was startling. I was the same.

But she hadn't mentioned this Mark guy. "And Mark?"

The growing pink in her cheeks covered her freckles. "He's, um . . . sort of my version of a Taya."

I did not like the sound of this. "You work with him?" She was going back to work on Tuesday. Today was Sunday. Could she sit out of work for the month?

"We went out a couple of times. Nothing serious." She gave me a sidelong look. "He doesn't have keys to my house."

Still not good enough. "Yet he's still texting you?"

"He's my boss."

"Conflict of interest, isn't it?" How could I get him fired?

"The town's too small not to have workarounds. Vegas is huge though," she said innocently.

My lips twitched. She was like a stealthy prizefighter, getting hits in left and right when I wasn't prepared. "Remember our deal."

"One month."

It was time for us to deplane. I retrieved our luggage. I'd buy anything else I needed. I doubted many suits would be necessary in Bourbon Canyon, so I'd only packed jeans and sweaters.

As we walked through the airport, I tried hard not to admire the architecture. Wooden beams swooped overhead and large windows let in the majesty of the surrounding mountains. Autumn was looking around like she might see someone she knew. I wasn't worried. I hadn't lived in the area since I turned eighteen. I was forty-four.

"My car is in long-term parking," she said.

"Did your friends carpool with you?"

She shook her head, looking straight ahead as we wheeled our suitcases toward the exit. "No. I guess a part of me knew that their reliability only went so far. They joke I'm the mom of the group." I caught her smirk. "I thought any one of them could've ended up married in Vegas."

I bristled under the stereotype. I made it possible for people to go crazy in Las Vegas, whether it was impulsively marrying, trying expensive clubs, or indulging in luxury. I was accustomed to being a nonparticipant.

I followed Autumn outside. Every location had its own beauty, and I'd been able to travel a fair amount during my years working in the world of hospitality. This was the second time I'd been in Montana since I'd left for college, and the same sense of rightness hit me. No matter where I went, the view, the atmosphere, the weather would never feel as right as Montana.

Feelings were deceptive. I wouldn't have a career in Las Vegas entertainment if they weren't.

The temperatures were nice for Montana in October, but the cool hint of a breeze brushed my face, reminding me I was no longer in Nevada.

Autumn dug her keys out and unlocked a small orange hybrid SUV. I reached the liftgate first and opened it to put her luggage in. Then I tossed my bag in the back and held my hand out.

She glanced at my palm, her eyes wide, then lifted her gaze to my face.

"The keys," I prompted.

"Oh." Those pretty pink lips of hers turned down. She tugged on the strap of the purse that had been her constant since we'd met. "Why?"

"We're married. You're not chauffeuring me around." I didn't want to be a wide-eyed spectator driving into my hometown for the second time this year. Bourbon

Canyon had changed, but so much was still the same. More eclectic shops had opened, and seeing them had only pissed me off.

I was sure the Baileys and their damn distillery had made increased commerce possible. Copper Summit offered jobs, drove revenue, and encouraged tourism. The Baileys had contributed to the place where they'd been born and raised. I'd made my gains in a city that didn't need my efforts. When I was done with school, there'd been nothing for me but my grandfather's warning about Percival and working for a dad who didn't listen and didn't care what I had to say. The Baileys had been able to build a bigger empire than what they were born with, and now they wanted what should be mine.

She finally dropped her keys into my hand.

I gave her a nod like she was an assistant who'd just completed a task, but I went to the passenger door and opened it.

She peeked around the back of the SUV. "You're being, like, weirdly formal."

"What do you mean?"

"Loading my bag. Driving. Opening doors. I feel like I'm bringing a prom date home, and he's nervous about making a good impression on my dad."

Goddamn, that hit too close to home. "I'm bringing you home to my father first."

Her coppery brows lifted. "You are?"

"We can stop at your house first. That way, I won't act like such a stranger there after people know." I'd always be a stranger. I'd been one when I'd grown up. Now that I was married into the local elite, I'd be more of an outsider than ever.

Autumn

Seeing Gideon in my house was a mindfuck. Like a lucid dream. A drop-dead-sexy man was roaming the tiny walls of my home. He took up any extra space and made it feel smaller and plainer than ever.

When I'd bought this place, I'd thought it'd be a starter home. I'd meet someone, maybe we'd live there until we built a bigger home. I wasn't keen about building on my property not far from Copper Summit. I should be relieved Gideon wouldn't press me about it like another ex had. Ten years after that guy, I was still living here. Alone.

Except for my cat.

I'd seen Gideon's place, spent the night on a bed that was like a custom-made cloud, and seen a shower that shouldn't be possible. I hadn't used it.

I needed a shower and real sleep.

Being tired didn't mask the observation that the penthouse wasn't made for a family. No one who had kids wanted white anything in their home, professional cleaners or not.

Gideon looked around my living room, his gaze scrutinizing the little fireplace at the far wall.

"I have a pile of firewood behind the garage, just in case."

He cocked a brow.

"If power goes out," I finished lamely. This stilted conversation was a lot like the drive from Bozeman. I'd say something to fill the heavy silence or because I thought he'd want to know some things about me. We had a short window, but we had to be a real couple. He'd only give me monosyllabic answers or that damn brow lift—which was fucking sexy. But then, everything about this man was desirable.

Especially his cooking. I could've orgasmed over those eggs.

He shoved a hand in his pocket. When his back was to me, I ogled his ass. This material had seen very little of the great outdoors and definitely hadn't touched a horse or cow. I couldn't picture this Gideon filling feed buckets for chickens. I couldn't see him waking up early to do chores or even to go for a relaxing ride that didn't include rounding up cattle.

A slight sadness settled over me. I couldn't picture a cowboy hat on his head, dust on his shirt, or the relaxed walk of a guy who loved doing what he loved because he fucking loved ranching. That type of guy was who I'd thought I'd marry, one who wouldn't put an expiration date on my marriage.

I'd always imagined I'd end up with someone like the guys I'd grown up with. Mark was outside of that box, but he was nothing like Gideon. My husband was older than me, and he'd been raised doing the same, but he'd deliberately left it all behind.

Yet he wanted to keep the ranch. That had to mean something, right? Weren't kids more to him than having someone to pass his legacy on to? "We never talked about the specifics of the kids."

"We did, and I said when you're ready." He disappeared into the kitchen.

I took a step to follow, then let my temper take over.

I wasn't some landlord while he looked over the place. "I asked you a question. It's rude to walk out."

One heartbeat. A second, louder heartbeat. He appeared around the corner, his expression neutral. I couldn't interpret the glint in his eye. "You didn't ask a question. You made a statement."

I had to think for a moment. Dang. He was right. "And you're avoiding the discussion."

His eyes barely narrowed, but I caught the discomfort. "I never planned to have kids."

He'd said that, yet he'd agreed to the deal. "You're fighting for Percival, but what happens to it after you're gone?"

His pensive expression amplified. "I never planned to have kids in the immediate future. Biologically, it can happen for decades yet."

Didn't that sound like a dream come true? But he'd cracked the door open to having kids. "If I do get pregnant, how are we going to raise it?"

"It?"

"Him. Her. Himmer?"

"Not very progressive of you, putting the masculine first."

Was he teasing? I couldn't tell, but his lips were pursed like he might shatter if he accidentally smiled. "Herim? Maybe we should come up with a name that could go either way. Sawyer."

"I had a dog named Sawyer."

"I like dogs. Sawyer it is."

A blinding flash of a smile struck me mute. I blinked. It was gone in a millisecond, and he shook his head. "You're unexpected, firecracker."

"Thank you."

He was about to take a step when a "mew" sounded and my tortie, Sprinkles, twined around his legs. She had an orange nose and her mostly black coat was flecked with orange and white. A furrow formed across Gideon's brow. He stared at the cat, who had decided she wanted her scent all over his legs.

"That's Sprinkles. She was found in a dumpster at the school."

That brow lifted, but he continued to stare at the cat. "A dumpster cat."

"The cat distribution system awarded me with a cat as soon as I thought I was ready to have one. A little before, really. I hadn't closed on the house yet, so I had to hide her in my apartment."

He lifted his gaze to me. "You strike me as a rule follower."

"I break them for good reason."

"Those are open to interpretation."

"So are rules."

Another smile ghosted over his lips. "Indeed." He turned, careful not to knock into Sprinkles.

That told me a lot about him.

If he'd been an ass to my cat, he'd have been out on his well-defined bottom. He could suck it on the land sale, and I'd do insemination or embrace my cat-lady life. But he continued to be considerate of her as she followed him down the narrow hall made smaller by his wide shoulders.

Once again, he'd evaded the topic of kids.

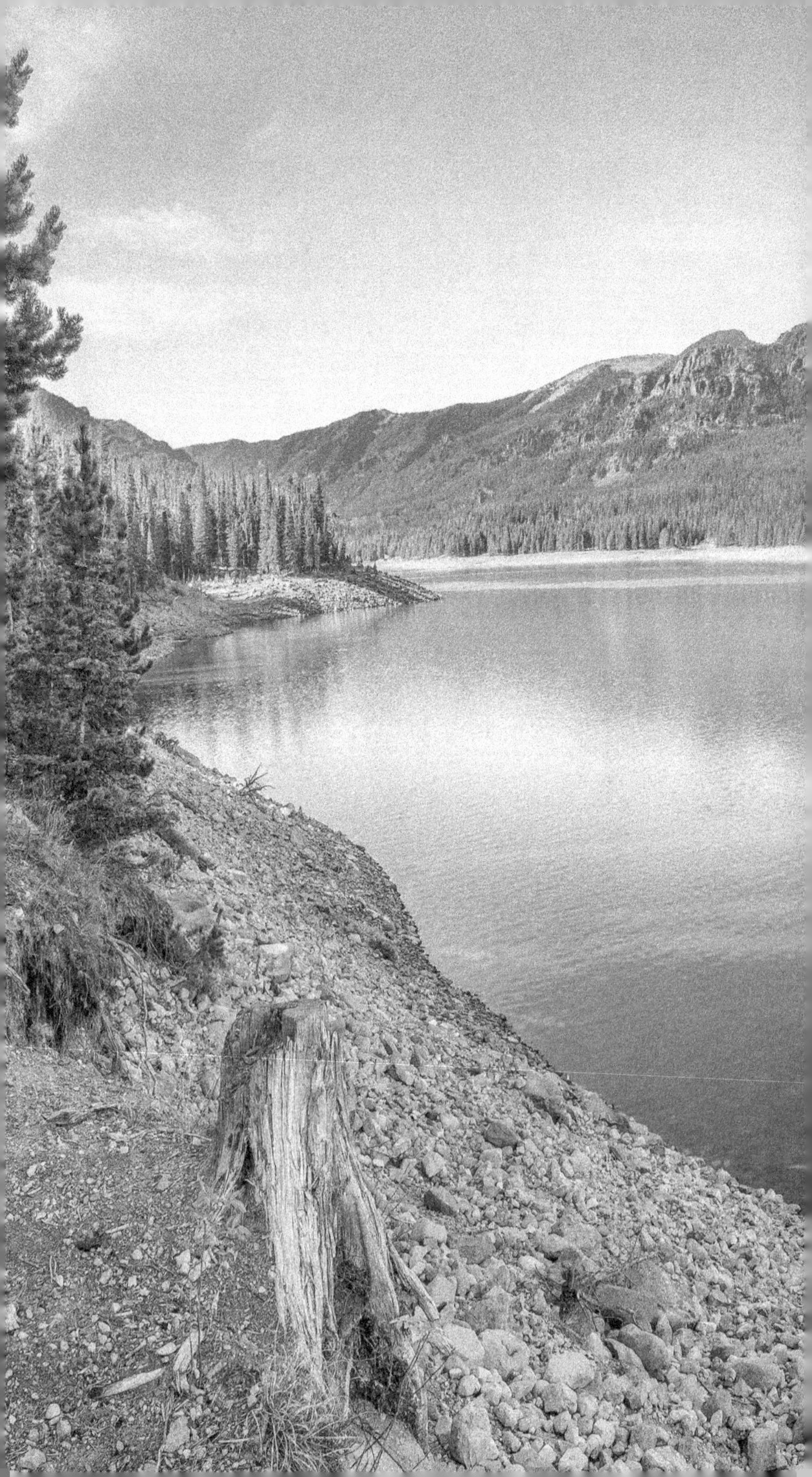

CHAPTER SEVEN

Gideon

I took the last turn to my dad's house. The last time I'd been in town, I hadn't seen him. I hadn't seen Dad for over twenty-five years.

My stomach was twisted in one giant, convulsing knot.

It was mid-October and the green in the area had faded to brown. The grasses were brittle, and the short, bare mountains were the same color. The taller slopes were filled with dark green thanks to the trees dotting the sides. The pastures and fields between us and the horizon were empty of cattle. The dirt that had once been tilled with growing crops had long grown over.

Some of the fencing was new, with shiny wire and metal posts. Why bother when there were no cattle to contain?

As we drove, memories assaulted me. Mom, riding one of the many ranch horses her family had raised, carefree and laughing. She had a favorite, but she made sure we rode them all. She enjoyed having cattle and farming. She'd loved her life. All the way to the end.

Part of me was glad she hadn't seen the accident coming. That she hadn't known she'd be leaving me alone. That Dad would barely survive losing her. Knowing any of that would've broken her big heart.

I concentrated on loosening my grip on the steering wheel. The road wound closer to the house. I hadn't visited Dad, but I'd been on the land. I'd taken a road that overlooked the house. And it'd pissed me off. The place wasn't run down. He'd done some work on it and dammit—I'd been furious.

"Do you think he'll be there?" Autumn asked.

I'd been so angry that he'd kept up the house enough to look decent and then sobered himself up enough to fucking sell it.

"Gideon?"

And then he had the audacity to tell me that he wouldn't talk about the sale on the phone. I had to come home.

"Gideon." A warm hand landed on my forearm and my rising anger dropped like a boulder in water.

My knuckles were white and the speed of the car was creeping up. It wouldn't have mattered that her all-wheel drive handled nicely on the dirt road, I'd land us both in a ditch.

"Do you need a minute before we arrive?" she asked softly.

"No." I wanted to see his face when I showed up with a Bailey bride talking about kids.

My gut heaved again. Kids. I wouldn't think about it yet. How did Autumn know she could have them? How did I? I had enough on my mind. The idea of a baby I was responsible for would have to wait. I had time.

My determination to avoid the topic didn't stop my dick from waking up and reminding me how kids were made. My cock wanted to berate me for not taking Autumn up on the sweetness she had offered last night.

I had never had a hard time being an honorable man until her. After watching her moan over my food this morning, I wasn't sure I'd be able to keep from being rabid when I was in bed with her again.

How quickly I returned to my roots—wild and dirty.

I rounded a curve and the house came into view, dousing my libido. Mom had been so proud of this place. We'd gone from a small, manufactured home to a stick-built two-story ranch house with an attached two-car garage.

So much space, Giddy! Mom's voice was clear as the summer Montana sky. I'd been six. *We can even expand it. Maybe someday you'll fill it with kids.*

My heart twisted as hard as my stomach. Mom had wanted more kids, but she'd hemorrhaged during my birth and doctors had performed a hysterectomy.

I swallowed rising stomach acid. "Home sweet home," I said bitterly.

"I've never been this far onto your land," she said. The awe in her voice made me want to puff my damn chest. "I always thought your place was beautiful when we drove by the pastures."

"He painted." I could tell her everything about the buildings and land. I could tell her that there was an abandoned cabin in the foothills to the north where my grandparents' ranch manager used to live. The old stable and shop were falling down, but a newer shop and barn stood a few hundred yards behind the house. Both had been built by Mom and Dad. The place had prospered after Mom had taken over. Those buildings now loomed isolated against the stark, brown landscape. As if all the life on this place had died with Mom.

I parked by an old, beat-up flatbed truck. The white paint on the front was covered in a thick layer of dust and dirt. I was tempted to turn around and leave. Tuck myself into Autumn's small house and attempt to make babies.

Babies. I could fucking puke.

I didn't have a weak stomach, and I wasn't vomiting in front of my wife.

I opened the door and got out, taking a deep inhale before I realized I was sucking in all the fresh Montana air like I'd been suffocating for the last twenty-five years. Oxygen infused my veins. There was no smell of cigarettes or pot, no scent of exhaust or hot asphalt. I didn't even smell dust. Just pure, fresh mountain air.

A door creaked open. "Giddy?"

I faced my dad, unprepared for the shock. He was older. But where he had once stooped with a permanent grimace on his face and lank, greasy hair, his fist shaking in the air at me while I drove off, he was now hale. He wasn't hearty, but some of the muscle tone that had wasted away when he'd been in his darkest years had returned.

His hair was grayer and thinner but neatly trimmed, same with his salt-and-pepper beard. The mustache portion of his beard was thicker and in a horseshoe shape. His shoulders were rounded but no longer bowed, and his clothing looked clean. The worst shock was the clear gaze.

"Hank." My voice wasn't as strong as I'd intended.

He stepped out farther. The screen door slammed behind him. It'd be an easy fix. I'd helped him repair more than a few doors growing up.

A lump formed in my throat as memories rose from the depths of my brain. Usually, I thought about Mom when I recalled my time growing up. But this time, I could picture myself walking next to Dad as he talked about growing seasons, soil conditions, and moisture levels. I could see him next to me beside one of the tractors, handing me a tool and telling me to try it myself.

The back of my throat burned hot. I refused to recall those times. He'd ruined them all.

He'd ruined everything.

A warm hand slipped around the fingers I hadn't realized I'd curled into a fist. Her cotton-candy scent blew across me, and she put her other hand on my forearm. "It's okay," she said under her breath.

Dad's gaze fell to where she was touching me. Again I felt a resurgence of pride I usually only experienced when it came to my job. I stuffed the feeling down.

"Hank, this is Autumn James. My wife."

I'd be lying if I said I hadn't played out how Dad would react. He'd yell at me like he used to do when he drank the hard stuff. When he had too much beer, he got loopy. He'd think he was charming. When he drank liquor, he turned mean.

Would he collapse from shock instead? Would he be so stunned he'd gape at me and then rage? He'd have to know I was doing this to stop the sale. The easiest part would be getting him to believe my intentions of wanting the family land to pass on to my own family. I didn't have to believe it myself.

I didn't know a damn thing about children.

Autumn's hand tightened around mine. I might've squeezed back. I wasn't paying attention to extremities or how her skin was impossibly softer than I could've imagined.

A wide grin broke out on Dad's face, lifting the sides of his horseshoe mustache. "Hot damn, that's wonderful news." He charged down the porch stairs. When his boots hit the sandy path bordered by dry grass, he opened his arms wide. "Autumn James now, huh?"

"Yes, sir." She crowded into my side, much closer than we had sat on the plane. Her body heat seeped into me, and I got a good feel of her curves from my arm down to my thigh. I could tuck her under me, but as Dad grew closer, she broke away.

I missed her touch instantly.

He encompassed her in his wiry arms. "Sir isn't for family. Call me anything but sir or Mr. James." He stood back. Lines flared from the corner of his eyes, carved deep into his skin, like one of Mom's fans. "Congratulations."

He stepped toward me, but I yanked Autumn back into my side. A clear "no hugging" signal, and maybe an excuse to have her close again. "You're happy?" I sounded dismayed.

Was I?

He laughed. "Ecstatic."

I'd worried about him buying the ruse. Was he delighted because he thought I wouldn't be a pain in the ass anymore?

He clapped his hands together. "A celebration is in order." My veins flooded with dread. He caught my alarmed expression and his smile dipped. "A meal," he clarified.

"That's not necessary," I said at the same time Autumn said, "How wonderful."

She wrapped an arm around my back and hugged me. Hard. "I'd be delighted to get to know you and tell you how your son swept me off my feet."

"He takes after the old man." Dad's eyes twinkled. I wanted to be sick. Whenever the subject came close to Mom, he got melancholy. Then he'd drink until he blacked out.

Autumn giggled and rubbed my back like she could feel the tension vibrating through me. "I'm sure he does."

Dad shook his head, grin back in place. "I jest. It was his mother who had to hit me over the head with a rock to get me to notice more than my own good time. But once I came around, she was the center of my world."

My heart slipped and slid down into my gut. He was talking about Mom. And he was smiling.

Mom had chased him? I doubted it.

He used to surprise her with wildflowers and leave me with grandparents to take her on dates. He was always trying to woo her.

Memories of various bouquets over the years popped into my head, clear as a cloudless sky. I hadn't thought about those since I was a kid. I used to tease Dad when he was stooped in a ditch, searching for the perfect cone flowers.

"We've still gotta spread the news," I said abruptly. "We haven't told her family."

Dad's bushy brows lifted high. "Oh my. There's a story there."

Autumn patted my chest. "Vegas. What can I say? My friends and I stayed at the casino he works at and the rest is history."

His grin remained in place. "When did this happen?"

Autumn stiffened. I was trying to figure out how best to answer, or if I should worry since Dad seemed fully on board, when she answered, "It's our one-day anniversary."

This time I got the satisfaction of his shock. When he slid his almost-knowing look my way, I wanted to pack up my wife and leave. "I don't need to ponder good decisions," I said almost defensively.

She tilted her face up toward me. Instead of wondering what kind of look she was giving me, I tightened my arm around her, dipped my head, and pressed a kiss to her mouth.

I caught her gasp and kept the kiss chaste when all I wanted to do was turn her fully into me and devour that sweet mouth. When I straightened, Dad was watching us, a wistful gleam in his eye that I immediately resented.

A small slice of empathy cut through the negative emotion. I'd been married a day, but Autumn was a real person. I knew she slept like she'd be out for days. I knew that her eyes rolled back when she liked the flavor of something. I knew she had a cat and a cozy house, the first place to make me think there really were homes out there where people could be happy. I knew she took the advice "dress for the job you want" seriously.

If something happened to her, I'd be sad. I'd mourn. Dad had lost his partner. The love of his life. But he'd also been a dad. And he'd failed me terribly.

"Tomorrow night, then?" He rubbed his hands

together. His knuckles were knobbier than they used to be. His shoulders a little more stooped. But his eyes were clear. Bright and lucid. "Is that too soon?"

"Tomorrow." Better to get it over with, but also, I had to know if Dad could maintain this version of himself for more than a day. Perhaps we'd caught him between binges. It had been years since he'd claimed to start his sobriety journey, but I had doubts. Many of them remained. It'd take more than a ten-minute chat to banish them.

He winked at me. "You gonna talk it over with your wife, Giddy?"

"Don't call me Giddy, Hank," I growled.

He laughed, oblivious to my hatred of Mom's nickname out of his mouth. "Sorry, boy."

I cringed harder. Boy. His rampages went through my head.

Autumn rubbed my back again.

"Tomorrow," he repeated. "Invite your family, Autumn."

"Yes, of course." She rested her hand between my shoulder blades. "I don't want to come off as rude, but I want to make sure you know what you're getting into. I have a big family. Just how many do you want to invite?"

"All of them." He waved both hands in the air like he was shooing away a raccoon. "Don't worry about space. I've got nothing to hide and it's all going to be the Baileys' soon."

I jerked like his words were electricity. Wasn't he starting to reconsider? I'd shown up with a wife. If this farce of a marriage didn't work to win him over and get my mom's land in my name, then I'd never forgive Dad.

And there'd be nothing left in Bourbon Canyon that meant a damn thing to me.

Autumn's gaze caressed over my face, and one simple question lingered in my head.

Are you sure there'd be nothing in this town that matters to you?

Autumn

As we were leaving the James ranch, my phone continued to buzz with messages from my friends checking on me. I kept telling them I was fine and that I was home already. Maybe they wanted to hear me say I forgave them, but my brain's realty was taken up by the man next to me.

I was about to turn my phone off when it rang. Scarlett's name popped up on the screen.

Shit.

Scarlett was Tate's wife. She was a fourth-grade teacher at the elementary school, so my fellow travelers were also her friends and coworkers.

What had they told her?

Gideon glanced at me. My stomach did the same little wiggle it had the first time he'd gotten behind the wheel of my vehicle. I was a passenger princess, and it was a nice change.

"My sister-in-law," I explained. The phone stopped, then started again. "Tate's wife."

His gaze went back to the road. "No time like the present."

"I have to invite them to dinner tomorrow, after all." My chuckle was a nervous chime.

I hadn't been too worried about telling the news to Hank James. He'd been nothing but friendly around town, and whenever I had seen him, he'd been helping at a fundraising benefit or with some other town project that needed an extra pair of hands. Hank James liked my family, and I'd expected him to worry more about his son's intentions. He had to know I was not Gideon's type.

It was my family that could tank everything.

I squared my shoulders. I was an adult, and I could make my own decisions. "Hello?"

"Oh my god, Autumn," Scarlett said on a sigh of relief. "Everyone is so worried about you. Are you okay? Where are you?"

I wasn't ready for any of her questions. I needed more time, but things were moving at lightning speed. "I'm in town, actually."

Another relieved exhale. "You're at your house?"

"We stopped in, but then we—"

"We?"

"Yeah, um . . ."

"Did you come home early for Mark?"

I almost asked her who, but right. Mark. "No, not Mark."

Gideon's hands clenched the wheel. He did not like Mark. I couldn't say I was bothered by his reaction after seeing Taya.

"Did you meet someone on your trip?" Her question was full of interest and concern.

"Yes, but he's from here actually."

"Autumn," Tate broke in.

The acid in my stomach roiled. I wasn't ready to face my family. "Am I on speaker?"

"You weren't." Scarlett's tone was disgruntled. "My husband seems to have forgotten his manners."

"Who is it?" Tate demanded.

My heart clawed into my throat. "Tate, listen—"

"The girls told Scarlett you stayed at Silver. What were you thinking?"

The back of my neck grew hot. My brother was speaking loud enough for Gideon to hear. "That I don't need your permission."

"Who is it?"

My brother wasn't a dumb man. He'd been in charge of Copper Summit until Daddy had gotten cancer and couldn't run the Bourbon Canyon distillery or keep up with the ranch. Tate had left Copper Summit's Bozeman distillery and taken over the ranch, but he still thought he was boss of everything, just like he had when my sisters and I had first arrived at the Baileys'.

"Tate—"

"Autumn, you're stalling. I know I won't like the answer. Tell me it's a big damn coincidence, and you reconnected with a guy like Layton Kramer."

"My senior prom date?" My volume pitched up. Gideon's head snapped toward me, but he had to focus back on the road. When his gaze was off me, so was his heat, but I was hot enough with Tate's interference. "He kissed another girl in the janitor's closet while I was in the bathroom."

Gideon's knuckles turned white on the wheel. Was he annoyed with my story, that I was delaying, or was he righteously upset on behalf of an eighteen-year-old Autumn who'd thought Layton could've been the one?

"You know what I mean," Tate said.

I huffed out a breath. I was done with this conversation. "Well, I'm not telling you over the phone. Goodbye, Tate. Sorry, Scarlett."

I hung up just as Scarlett's "I'm so sorry" filtered through.

I puffed a hunk of hair out of my face. I stuffed my phone into the glove compartment.

"That wasn't telling them," Gideon said evenly. "But nice power move."

I laughed, releasing anxious energy. Was I glowing too? Gideon had complimented me. Sure, it wasn't my looks, but I'd take power move in a heartbeat. My brothers often saw that little girl still getting over the injuries she'd gotten in the accident that had claimed her parents' lives. "Thanks. But be prepared for company when we get home."

He slid his dark gaze in my direction again.

. . . when we get home.

I liked the way that sounded. Was he unnerved?

Several minutes later, we were walking into the house. I left my phone in the car.

I trudged to the kitchen. "Are you hungry?"

"Starving."

I glanced over my shoulder, but he was on his phone. So, not one of those innuendo answers. He was legitimately starving. For food.

How bad was it that I was jealous of the phone held loosely in his big hand while he rhythmically stroked the screen with his thumb?

I might have this man's baby. Which meant we'd have to . . .

A shiver worked its way under my skin. I busied

myself with looking in the freezer and the fridge. Gideon stayed where he was, his attention on his phone. I tried not to be disappointed. Maybe it was a good thing that I had regular reminders that this was the equivalent of a business deal.

Back to fixing an early dinner.

The trip had been three days, and I'd planned to get groceries on my way into town after the flight. That was before I'd gotten married and brought a man home.

I had hamburger. There was pasta in the cupboard. I could throw together—

Someone pounded on the front door. Hard.

I whirled around. Smugness infused Gideon's gaze and he tucked his phone into his back pocket. "Ready, *wife?*"

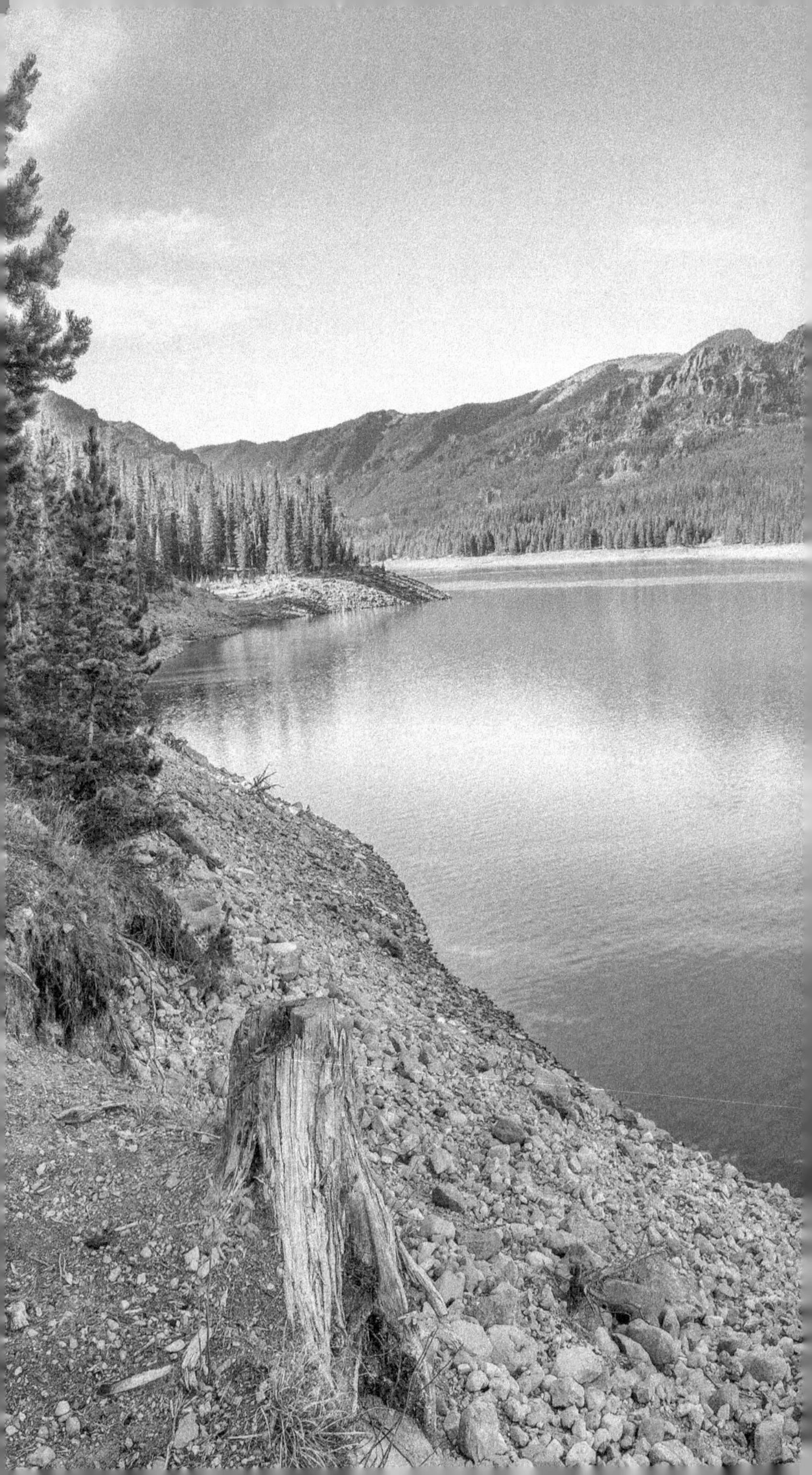

CHAPTER EIGHT

Gideon

I sat on a surprisingly comfortable couch that was way too floral for my taste. Autumn was tucked into my side, her hand back in mine.

I brushed over her skin with my thumb. She was practically shivering as we faced the firing squad of her siblings.

The first demanding knock had been Tate and Teller. Tenor had arrived next. I'd hated facing them at the distillery. I was on Bailey property, but this place was more mine than theirs now.

Just as they'd been getting over the shock of seeing me, Summer and Wynter had arrived with Wynter's husband—Myles—and a baby. Autumn whispered which sister was which to me. Summer was standing next to Tate, the oldest sister, ready to take charge. Myles was currently in the bedroom, changing the baby's diaper.

Wynter hovered in the hallway, ready to cut off a stampede if need be.

She needn't have worried. The guys would try to throw me out of the house, not farther into it.

"Get an annulment," Tate demanded.

"No," Autumn and I said in unison. She smirked at me and I couldn't help a small smile. Our simultaneous answer had turned Tate's face red. The color could've blazed through the man's thick beard.

"Autumn," Summer said, brushing a long, strawberry-tinted lock of hair behind her ear. She looked about the same as she had as a kid but also completely different. I remembered what all the Kerrigan sisters had looked like when they'd first come to town. The way they'd moved, like they'd rather be anywhere else, like they were eternally lost and like they were haunted. Four lost girls.

I wouldn't have paid attention, but Mom had spoken about them. A lot. She'd empathized, and maybe she'd wished she could help. Perhaps it'd been as simple as wanting a daughter.

I hadn't really seen Autumn as often as the others.

A memory jiggled at the back of my brain. She'd been injured. Both Autumn and Summer. Mom had fretted over their recovery. Summer had healed fairly quickly, but Autumn had needed more time.

"Can we talk to you?" Summer's gaze flicked to me and back to her sister. "In private. With Wynter. Maybe we can call Junie."

"Junie will be the only one to congratulate me," Autumn said primly.

"There's nothing to congratulate!" Teller flung his arm toward me. "He's using you."

Autumn rolled her eyes, and damn, I liked when her inner firecracker sparked. "Your faith in me is so appreciated."

I could've snickered. They had no idea how their sister had cornered me just as I was leading her into my web.

"You don't know guys like him. We do." Tate poked the center of his chest.

Autumn wiggled and her back went ramrod straight. I could've done without her hips bumping against mine in front of her brothers. "You've said what you needed to say—"

"The hell we have," Teller snapped. He looked the most similar to Tate, with dark hair. His beard was trimmed shorter. He paced in the small living room, his hands on his hips. He was dirty, like he'd been yanked out of doing chores. "What were you thinking? Were you even thinking? Or did you think a guy like this would really—"

"You'd be smart to shut your mouth right goddamn now." I bit back a growl. "No one talks to my wife like that."

Teller stopped, stunned. Tate narrowed his eyes on me. Summer blinked, then exchanged a look with Wynter. Myles appeared from the hallway, and it was the baby's turn to stare at me.

I didn't look at the little girl with her frilly pants and potbelly. The way she blinked those big, innocent eyes at me was like she was asking if I was ready for something like her. Would I get Autumn pregnant, get my land, and then go back to Vegas and pretend I was single?

A sour taste spread across my tongue. I was ready for everyone to leave. Especially that kid. "We've told you the news. My father's invited you all out for a celebratory dinner. I expect nothing but the same respect you've shown him so far."

"He's still selling?" Tenor asked. Of the three Bailey brothers, he was the most even-keeled. He wore black, thick-framed glasses, had lighter brown hair than his brothers, and didn't sport a beard. He hunched, like he was hyperaware his size might intimidate, or he thought this house was suffocating. And it was, with all of them crowding the living room. He was easily the least hostile of the crew, but I wouldn't put it past him to run me down if he thought I'd hurt Autumn. At least if he did it, I would probably deserve it. Tenor thought before he acted or spoke.

"That remains to be seen." I should get a damn award for keeping the arrogance out of my answer.

Autumn cleared her throat. "Are you guys coming or not?"

Teller still had his hands on his hips, but he was glaring at my hand entwined with Autumn's. Tate had adopted the same stance. Wynter took the baby from Myles and watched us like her siblings.

"I have a question." Summer folded her arms. "What are you going to tell Mama?"

⬥

Autumn

I wanted to squeeze my eyes shut and bury my head in Gideon's strong shoulder. Mama.

I'd been so worried about my brothers and their

reactions. Even concerned over what Summer would say. Wynter and Junie didn't butt in like the rest. But Mama.

She'd be delighted I was married. She'd be just as devastated to think this relationship was fake. She'd be appalled I'd negotiated for a baby.

"I'm going to talk to her." I wanted to clutch Gideon's hand to my chest. Mama had been so accepting of me and my sisters from the start. The last thing I wanted was to feel like I was betraying her trust. I never lied to her. Likewise, I always hid how irritated I could get at my brothers' bossiness.

"And tell her what?" Teller added in a gentler tone than he'd been using. I had Gideon to thank for that. When he'd defended me, he'd forged our partnership. He wasn't some casino god and I wasn't just the mousy teacher. We were a team.

I lifted my chin. "That's between us and Mama. I'd appreciate it if you let me and Gideon tell her."

Wynter bounced from side to side with Elsa. "You'll need to talk to her soon. No offense, Gideon, but your dad loves to share what makes him happy, and if this announcement got him excited, he'll probably tell everyone about this new daughter-in-law."

Hank seemed like a guy who loved to share what delighted him. If he'd been like that when Gideon was growing up, I wouldn't be here right now with a brooding man who was as stiff as a barn door.

I peeked at Gideon and went into instant infatuation mode. Strong jaw. Long, straight nose. Sharp eyes. He'd shaved this morning, but a dark shadow was already dusting his jaw. What would the stubble feel like under my fingers?

I couldn't believe I was sitting so close to him or that

our hands were connected again. I was getting used to touching him, to sitting butted up against him, but at the same time, I'd never get used to it.

But this moment was more than that. He wasn't just some good-looking guy. He had a lot of feelings about his family. His tension around his dad wasn't normal and the comment this morning about learning to cook or go hungry said a whole lot.

Gideon felt deeply. Had anyone witnessed his emotions other than me?

He met my gaze, those feelings simmering deep in his eyes. A slight question was written on his face. What were we talking about?

Oh. Mama. "We should tell her in person. It wouldn't feel right over the phone."

"Then we'll go now. They can leave."

I smiled and patted his arm. "This is all going really fast." He might not be my siblings' biggest fan but this process would be easier if he was a touch more congenial.

"What'd you think would happen when you come back from Vegas married?" Tate held his hands up when Gideon aimed a glare his way. "I'm just saying. We're worried about our sister. That shouldn't be a surprise."

"You're right—maybe I wasn't thinking." I tightened my hold on Gideon's hand to silence the argument I could feel building inside him. "Just like Wynter wasn't thinking when she applied to work for Myles."

Wynter blinked but continued to sway with the baby. She gave Myles a quelling smile. He was frowning, probably over his wife getting called out. Too bad.

"Or," I continued, "I was thinking as much as

Summer was when she left her wedding to stay with Jonah."

Gideon cocked his head at my sister. He wouldn't have heard the story.

"Well . . ." Summer shifted from foot to foot. "I mean . . . I'd just been slapped by my fiancé."

Gideon jerked. The anger radiating off him was almost palpable. A good sign that hearing a guy hit my sister upset him.

"But you didn't want to face us." I'd been a little hurt. I had done my best to understand. I hadn't gone through what she had, and I'd like to think that I wouldn't have dated a guy like her ex, but I'd dated enough duds that I couldn't really talk. "You weren't exactly ready to explain what you were thinking, and we gave you space." I switched my attention to Tate.

My oldest brother smirked. "Can't really lump me in with them since it was all of you butting into my love life that got me together with Scarlett."

He had me there. "You get a pass this once."

Tate's smile was warm, but the concern didn't leave his eyes. "We'll go to Hank's tomorrow, but we're not backing out of the land deal." He eyed Gideon. "That's up to your dad. And I hope while you're here, you realize that he's not the man you think he is. He's not an old drunk."

"I know exactly what kind of man he is."

The corners of Tate's jaw flexed. None of them could argue with what Gideon had gone through, and for that consideration, I was grateful.

"Like I said, that's between you and him." Tate glanced at Teller. "Our end is set, and we're just waiting on the bank. Tomorrow, then. Send us the details and what we can bring. You know Mama's going to want to make food."

He went out the door. Tenor was right behind him, but Teller stopped and faced Gideon. "You hurt my sister and it's not going to matter what you say. We'll bury you deeper than that fancy casino of yours is tall."

He was out the door while I gaped at him. I peeked at Gideon, but his strong profile hadn't shifted. He was tenser with just my sisters left behind.

"Junie's going to lose her shit," Summer said. "Do we have to wait to say anything to her?"

"You're dying to tell her?"

She put her hand to her chest. "I'm dying to tell someone who thinks you're crazy but isn't ready to gut your husband and turn him into bear bait. No offense, Wynter. We didn't have much time before we rushed here."

Wynter patted Elsa's back. "I was in the middle of pumping. She actually had to tell Myles first, but he didn't want to get involved."

Myles shook his head. "I love you like a sister, Autumn, and I disagree with your brothers. I think you can handle your new husband."

The thought made my stomach somersault. I hadn't handled Gideon at all. Eventually, we'd get to that part of the bargain, and we shouldn't wait, or the sale would be final too soon.

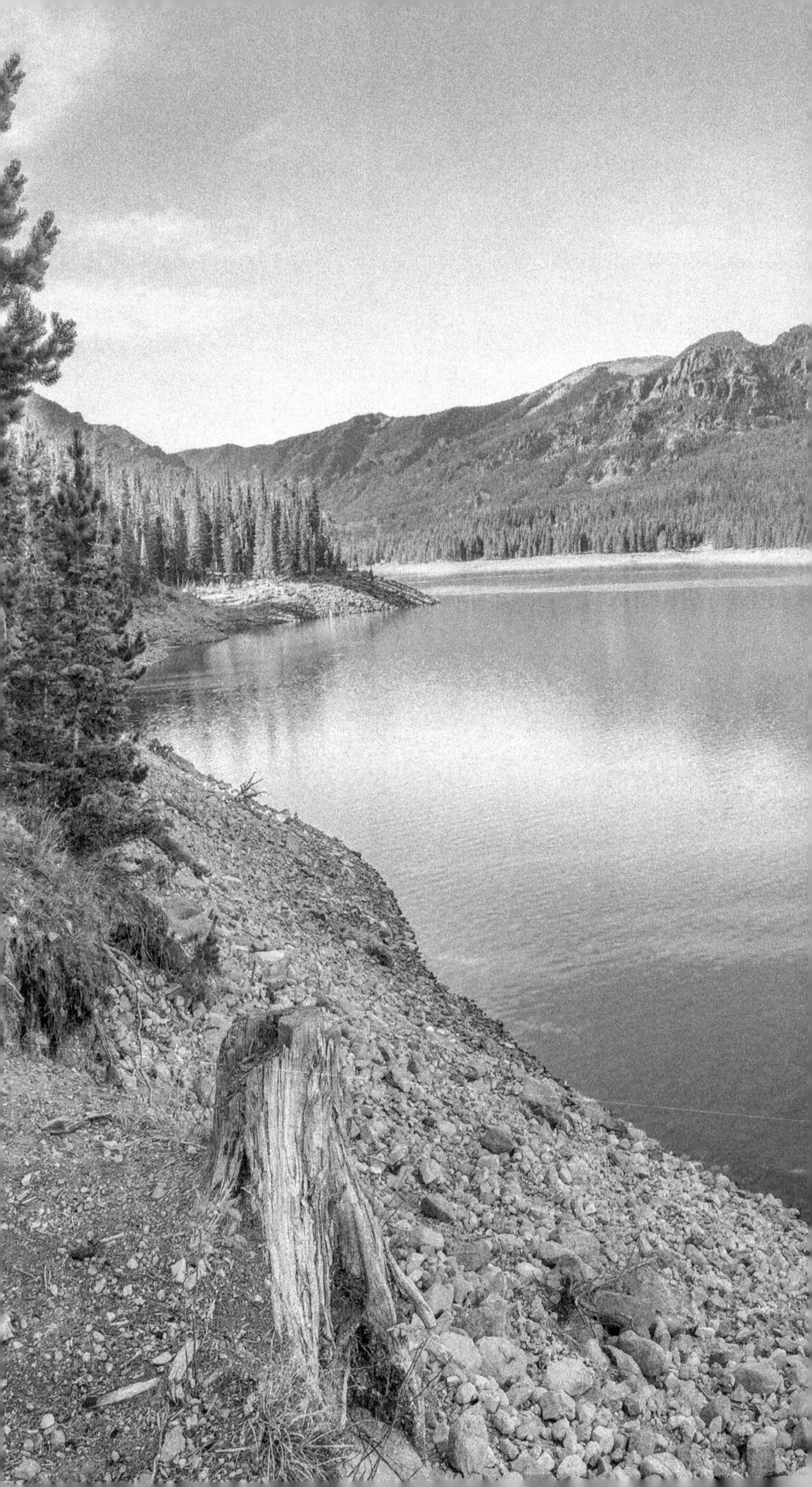

CHAPTER NINE

Gideon

The sun had set, but its fading rays still gilded the structure I drove up to. I never thought I'd willingly be on Bailey property again. The Copper Summit visit had been enough for a lifetime.

From the front, Mae Bailey's house was a magnificent, sprawling log cabin. The main floor had large windows that overlooked the road and the rambling countryside dotted with trees. The picture from the windows would be breathtaking, framing the mountains in the distance and the rolling land in between. The front of the house was the only way to see how massive the place was.

The ground swooped up toward the back, where Autumn parked. From the zero-entry door in the back, it was steps to the garage doors that everyone parked behind. The shops and barns were closer to the house than how my family had situated their property. The view out back wasn't as stunning as the front. It was simpler. It showcased the hard work that backed the Baileys' life. Yet there was undeniable life in that view. A thriving ranch. A place that didn't crumble when the patriarch died.

Darin Bailey had been older than my mom when he'd passed, and from what I'd seen when I first checked up on the Baileys, there'd been some warning. What had Autumn gone through while her dad was sick?

"We can just go in," Autumn said. She'd been quiet since her family had left, growing more silent on the drive out. How worried was she about upsetting her mom?

I'd rather we did this another day. I liked the quiet of Autumn's house. There was a warmth my penthouse didn't have. But we had to get all the family informed. It didn't matter that this day stretched on until it felt three days long.

For the first time, I considered that maybe my idea had been shit. I hadn't liked Autumn because of her relation to the Baileys. The actual person was considerate, though a little devious, and she clearly loved her mom. If there was anything I could respect, it was that.

I got out of the car. Autumn was out before I could get to her side. So much for being chivalrous. She didn't wait on me like . . . It took a minute to think of any woman I'd been on an official date with. I didn't bother to come up with names. The point was, I didn't date.

Autumn twined her cool hand in mine.

"Are your hands always cold?" I asked as I curled my fingers around hers to cover as much skin as possible. She'd warm up faster that way.

"You know what they say about cold hands?"

"Wear gloves?"

She broke into a smile and the tinkling laugh that left her was like harp music. After this afternoon, I liked hearing her laugh.

"Let's go, warmhearted girl." Some tension drained from me. Time to meet Mae Bailey as an adult this time.

When I was a kid, I hadn't given the Baileys much thought. Mama had talked about the sisters. Dad had mentioned Darin here and there. I couldn't even blame them for being the drink of choice for my dad. Bottles with other company names had floated through the house. Copper Summit products were quality, and Dad couldn't waste money on good booze.

I'd talked to Mae Bailey once in my life. At my mom's funeral. Everyone had looked at me with such pity, tears in their eyes, dabbing at their nose and cutting off words when they tried to talk to me. Or they looked through me and saved their condolences for my dad.

Not Mae. She'd pulled out a chair next to me and asked when I had eaten last. I'd told her I wasn't hungry and she'd patted my shoulder. *I know. What do you normally like to eat? I'll fix you a plate. It'll taste like dust, mind you, but I'd love for you to have a few bites. We'll both feel better.*

I'd had a fleeting thought that I didn't care if she felt better, but a larger part of me had hung on the way she doted on me. I'd been an afterthought for a short week, and I hadn't liked that feeling. Without Mom, I was invisible. I'd had no idea it was the beginning of many long years of not being seen, my only use dulled down to my work ethic or my genetics.

Autumn opened the back door and pulled me in behind her. The outside air had a chill to it I had barely noticed until the warmth of the house enveloped me, welcoming me in.

A lump formed in my throat. This was so damn familiar. The scent of coffee underneath a mouthwatering, savory smell. Mae was at the stove stirring something in a pot. My stomach threatened to rumble, but I clenched my abs. I would not salivate in this house.

She glanced over her shoulder. Her hair had thick streaks of gray and she'd pinned the sides back. Her dark eyes held mild curiosity, her aura pleasant.

Autumn hung her coat up and crossed to give her a hug. "Hi, Mama."

"Hello, hon." Mae's smile widened, deepening the grooves around her eyes as she returned the one-armed embrace. I detected a hint of sadness that was achingly familiar. That wouldn't go away. Not when you lost someone so close to you. Mae's kind gaze captured mine. "Gideon, nice to see you again."

She almost sounded like she meant it. I dipped my head. "Mrs. Bailey."

She scoffed. "I might feel the oldest in the morning and at night, but there's no need to throw around the Mrs. Baileys. Mae, please."

"Tate told you we were coming." Autumn didn't pose a question.

"Yes." Mae flicked the burner off. "He didn't tell me why. Just said you'd be stopping by with a guest. Of course, it was the way he said it that made me curious."

Autumn went to a cabinet. "Can I set the table?"

"We're eating?" Weren't we going to break the news to her and leave? I wasn't ready to hunker down with . . . with . . . someone I didn't want to dislike.

"Everyone gets fed when they come to my place,

dear." Mae gestured to the cupboard. "I gather you two haven't eaten yet?"

"We haven't had time for a bite since breakfast. The flight was quick."

In my head, I finished the rest for her. *The flight was quick, but nothing else has been.*

"Autumn will show you around," Mae continued, "but you'll find the plates and cups over there. Peek in the fridge and see what you'd like. Autumn can show you where the spirits are if you're so inclined."

Autumn took after her mom. Unassuming. Sweet. With a spine of steel that caught one off guard.

I did something I hadn't done in a long time. I set a table for more than just me. I didn't have dinner company at my home. Anyone who walked through the door of my penthouse wasn't invited to stay long.

Autumn handed me three plates, each with a different design.

She got the glasses and filled all three with water. "You don't strike me as a milk guy."

"I haven't had milk in years."

She set the water on the table. "Then I have a surprise for you."

I dug through the drawers to find forks. What else went on a fucking table?

My mom's voice drifted through my head. *Forks and butter knives, Giddy. Napkins—I don't want to catch you using your shirt. We're not cavemen.*

With a lump in my throat, I located everything else. When I looked at the place settings, the items were different than anything I'd eaten on recently. Mae's water glasses were plain and sturdy, not sleek and delicate like mine. The plates were older, with faint pictures of flowers. Mine were square and plain white. Also sleek and delicate. But even though I'd cooked only for myself all my adult years, I always set the same items on the table, unaware my mom had created such a habit.

I remained standing. Autumn slid into a spot next to mine. She patted the chair beside her. "You can have a seat."

"Doesn't your mom need a hand?"

"She had us set the table to stay out of her way. But don't worry, once she finds out we're married, she'll give you more work, like mashing the potatoes."

The short spike of excitement was unexpected. I could mash potatoes for Mae.

Goddammit. I'd been around the Baileys for less than a day, and already I was willing to bow to their every wish.

I yanked the chair out and sat.

Mae bustled in and out three times, depositing fried chicken that smelled divine, a pot of the fluffiest mashed potatoes I'd ever seen, and a gravy boat.

I frowned at all her hard work. We were closer to clubbing hours than dinnertime. "Was she planning to cook like this before she heard we were coming over?"

"No, but she has it down to an art. A meal like this is as easy for her as making a sandwich."

When Mae was settled across from us, she smiled at me. "Dish up, Gideon. We don't wait on ceremony."

I dutifully obeyed her. It'd only been a few minutes since I'd chastised myself for doing just that, but Mae wasn't the one buying my family's property.

Once our plates were loaded, Mae sucked her lips against her teeth. She had a knife in one hand and a fork in the other. "Now. Care to share what's going on? I'm wondering if it has to do with that rock on Autumn's finger."

Autumn

I flexed my left hand. The rock in question glinted under the country chandelier. I hadn't hidden it, but I hadn't expected Mama to pay attention to my hands that much before we spilled the news. "We're married."

Honesty was the best policy with Mama. She'd raised too many kids, fostered too many others to be able to get one over on her.

Mama's brows lifted, and her back hit her chair. Her knife and fork were still sticking up. "Indeed."

"Yes," Gideon confirmed, even though Mama hadn't asked a question. I appreciated his steady presence at my side.

"The guys are upset," I said.

Mama inhaled. "Indeed." Her gaze went to Gideon. Then back to me. She took another breath in and cut into her chicken breast. "Seems to be a mighty coincidence with the sale and all."

"Well . . ." I could try *a little* fibbing. "My friends wanted to stay at Silver since there's been news of Gideon in town."

She gave me a knowing look. "I didn't realize it was such big news."

"They're single, Mama. And he looks like that." My cheeks warmed.

Gideon's fork paused over his potatoes. He had to

know how good he looked. Women probably told him all the time. Gushing about it to my mother right in front of him seemed juvenile, and I'd seen firsthand that he preferred sophisticated women.

My stomach growled. I was starving and Mama's fried chicken was one of my favorites. "So, anyway," I said, stabbing my fork into a thigh. "They went into a club and I was hanging out outside . . ." I swallowed as the heat in my face bloomed. *Thanks a lot, embarrassment.* "Gideon happened to walk by."

"You go to the club?" Mama asked Gideon like she was getting to know my husband, but I could tell the question for what it was. A subtle interrogation. *Do you go to the club and party? Do you go often? Are you a party boy?*

"I was meeting an associate." He took a bite of chicken after neatly sawing a chunk off.

The image of Taya walking in when I was denied entry flashed through my head. I blinked at him. "Taya."

He slid his gaze toward mine, his jaw flexing with each chew. A small dip of his head was my answer.

I had cockblocked him.

Then she'd shown up the next morning. With a key to his place.

Acid churned in my gut, and the back of my neck heated to nuclear levels. He'd been planning a booty call that night with a gorgeous woman, and then he'd been waylaid by my dejected ass and opportunity.

Gideon set his fork down and swallowed. He rubbed my back. "Autumn saved me from another mundane night. Talking with her was refreshing."

Some of my humiliation evaporated. He almost sounded believable. I didn't want to miss out on Mama's food, so I'd take it. I'd let myself believe he was telling the truth just this once. I smiled at him, startled to see a pinch of concern at the corners of his eyes like he was asking if I was okay.

"The club has good bourbon," I said. "He got me Pappy."

Mama chuckled. "That's one point in your corner." She set her silverware down. A small furrow formed between her brows. "You'll have to excuse me. You married my daughter after knowing her for one day, and Bailey Beef just so happens to be buying your family land? The deal with which you've openly made your displeasure known? I'm an old country girl. I was born and raised in Bourbon Canyon, but I'm not naive."

Gideon didn't pick up his fork. "I didn't think you were, Mrs.—Mae."

"Autumn's special," Mama said, her tone hard. "She's also not a naive country girl."

"Believe me, I've been made aware," he said wryly.

I bit the inside of my cheek to keep from smiling.

"I don't like sharing my personal life with anyone," Gideon said. "Autumn is officially part of my personal life. I can promise you that I'll do my best to make sure I live up to what she expects of me, and I'll treat her with the same respect and honesty she's shown me."

I stared at him. He wasn't looking at me. Was he uncomfortable with what he'd said? Was he lying?

No, he'd been careful about how he worded his statement. Gideon didn't seem like a guy who made promises he didn't expect to be able to keep.

"I'm glad to hear," Mama said after a moment. "We're a large family, Gideon. It's going to be hard to keep others from wanting to intrude, but I'll respect it as much as possible. I can't speak for my kids. But I want you to know—you're part of this family now."

Gideon stiffened next to me.

Mama picked her utensils back up. "Let's eat before this chicken gets cold. It'll be easier for you two to do dishes before everything hardens on the pans."

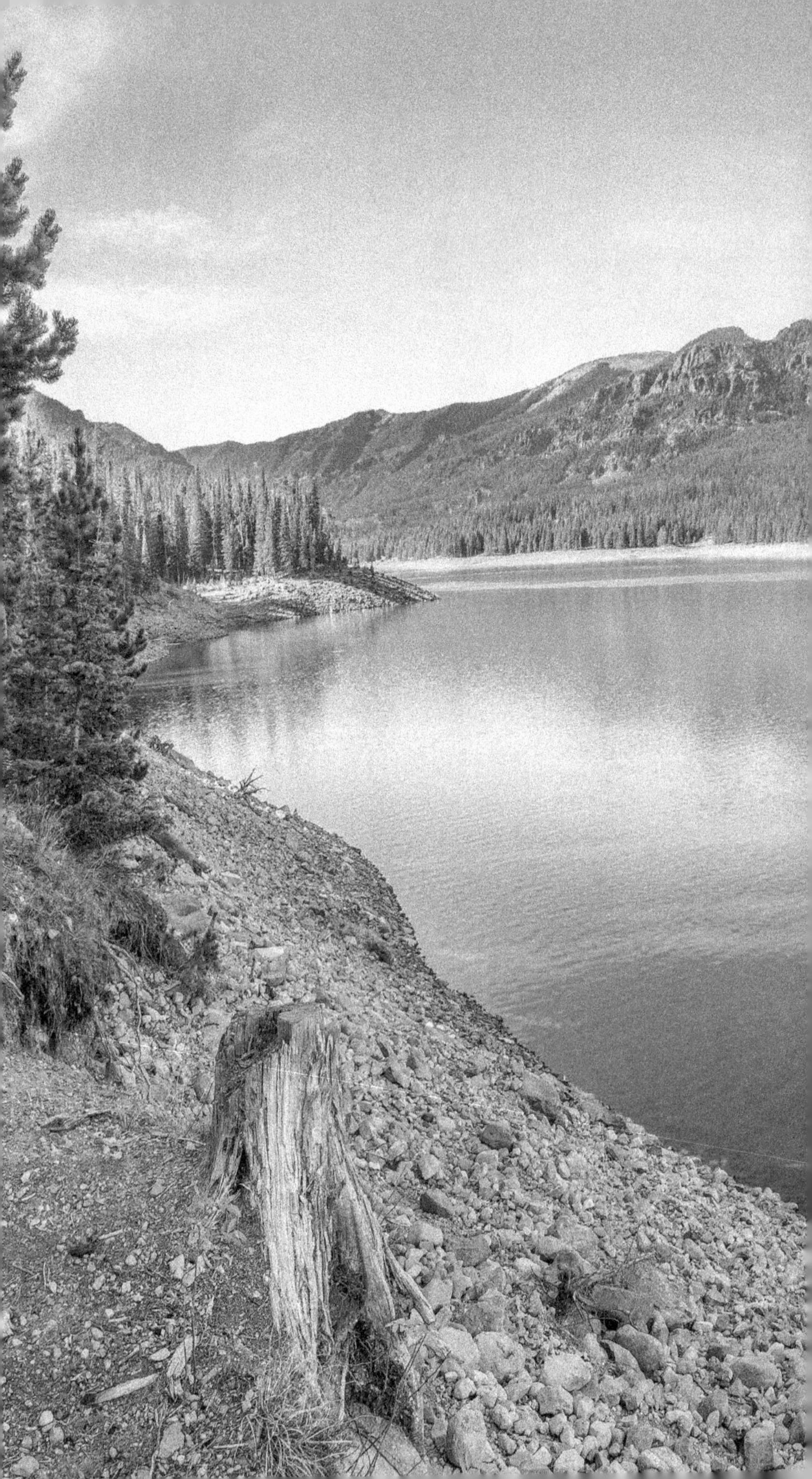

CHAPTER TEN

Gideon

You're part of this family now.

Mae's frank statement echoed through my head all the way back to Autumn's house. Our house? Fuck, I didn't know. This day had been confusing, and I wanted it to be over.

I stopped inside the door from the garage and frowned at the dark little box of a house. The day was over. It was time for bed. She didn't remember me lying next to her last night.

A pressure wound itself around my shins. The cat.

"It's been a *long* day." Autumn flipped on the light. "It'll be so nice to sleep in my own—" Those expressive amber eyes shot toward me. Her pink lips parted.

"Our bed," I said more to see how she reacted. I was not disappointed. The ripe mouth, the way she blushed when she thought of me and the bed at the same time.

She pursed her lips and a worry line formed across her forehead.

Heat coiled in my gut, but I needed a clear head to figure out how to stop the sale. I couldn't get wrapped up in this lust I felt around Autumn, but we also had a deal and I hadn't done my part yet. I didn't want to consider the consequences of having a baby.

The main problem was that getting between Autumn's legs could be detrimental to my clear head. I wasn't sure what the hell to think about kids yet, and I didn't need her soft-in-all-the-right-places body wreaking havoc with my thinking.

But I wanted to fuck her. Badly.

She'd been a rock all day. Facing her family, telling her mama, and cleaning up after dinner. The only time she'd wavered was when she'd realized I was supposed to meet Taya at the club.

I'd meant what I'd told her. Last night had been fun —sitting with a sexy woman who wasn't afraid of what she liked and was proud to share it with others had been refreshing. It was the first night in a long time I hadn't talked solely about my job.

"I have a futon in the office." She took off down the hall. The cat pranced behind her.

No fucking way. I hadn't slept on a floor, futon, pull-out, or in my car since college, and I wasn't doing it now. "We need to get used to sleeping together."

She stopped, frozen.

"Not like that, firecracker." Not yet. As soon as my lawyer expedited my early morning request, I'd retroactively fix the target I'd drawn on myself when I'd married her with no prenup. And we'd have divorce papers just as quickly. I wasn't ready to wade into the mess that was parental rights and custody arrangements. But I also wasn't sleeping on a goddamn futon after slumbering next to her last night. "We'll sleep in the same bed and get used to each other for another night. Without alcohol."

The bloom was back on her cheeks. Would she blush like that after she orgasmed? How far would it spread over her body?

The heat coiled tighter in my gut. I'd sleep with a raging erection all night if I kept those thoughts up.

"It was easier when I didn't know you were in bed with me."

Not for me. I'd caught myself watching her twice. What was it like to sleep with that much abandon? To be sprawled in a near stranger's bed and snooze like it was the safest, most comfortable spot in the world? I paid for an excellent mattress. I had room-darkening shades for the wall of windows if needed. I was regimented about when I had caffeine and how much. Nothing fucked with my sleep, and yet, at best, I could get a few hours of actual rest. Otherwise, a mouse could cough and wake me up.

"I can wait until you're asleep."

She lifted her chin, rallying at the idea of going to bed with me. A guy with a lesser ego might be insulted. Instead, I was amused.

"No," she said, "otherwise Sprinkles will take your spot."

"The cat sleeps in the bed?" I wasn't used to sharing, and I wasn't used to cats.

"Every night," she said, like she was challenging me to cut the cat off. "Didn't you ever have a house pet?"

"No. The dog worked more than I did." Sawyer had passed shortly after I left for college. I suspected Dad had forgotten to feed him. One more strike against the man. "Mom didn't like cats."

She smothered her surprise. Was it unheard of not to like cats? "If I lock her out, she'll yowl at the door."

"She's welcome to stay." Part of me was curious how the tiny feline thought she could rule the bed against two adults.

Autumn jerked her thumb over her shoulder and cocked her head. "I'll use the bathroom first and then . . ."

I punched down my brewing laughter. She was uncomfortable. I was . . . interested. Intrigued.

I never overnighted with a woman. If we ended up in the same bed, that meant we had gone to that bed for one specific reason. I didn't witness bedtime routines. I saw no pajama choices. By morning, I was alone again. Just how I preferred it.

Autumn's butt swayed against the long sweater she had on over her leggings. I'd seen her in all of two outfits, but she'd hidden her ass with each of them.

I ground my molars together. An ass like that shouldn't be hidden. I could quickly become obsessed with the globes of her butt bouncing under the fabric.

Heat circled under my collar. She'd disappeared into the bedroom. I wandered through her kitchen, peeking into cupboards and being nosy in a way I hadn't been willing to do while she watched me.

She had one box of cereal that had collected dust on the top of her fridge. Her eggs looked farm fresh and my damn mouth watered. It'd been decades since I'd had those. The chickens had gone shortly after Mom's death. In the freezer, I had to pause to check out her assortment of ice cream. Rocky road. Tin roof sundae. Chocolate. Mint chip.

My wife didn't just like salty food, she also liked chocolate. I filed that knowledge away like a good husband who might need it to prove her brothers wrong.

They weren't wrong about anything.

I brushed the thought away and went to the hallway closet. It caught me off guard as much as the lineup of ice cream. Tubs of—I leaned into the small, lightless space. Decorations and art supplies. Another bin was marked *Lessons*.

Wasn't there room in her classroom for this stuff?

A door squeaked open and I stepped away from the closet. I gently pushed the door shut, resisting the urge to slam it in a rush to see Autumn emerging fresh-faced from the bathroom.

She was sitting up in bed by the time I entered. Her sweet smell hung in the air. The cat was circling at the base of her feet. Autumn's freshly washed hair was loose around her face and my gut clenched. The rusty halo around her head looked like the most expensive crown a guy could buy, and I'd seen a few expensive ones in my time in Vegas.

She smoothed what had to be a handmade quilt over her lap. "Help yourself to whatever."

There was one thing I wanted to help myself to, but there was a cat in the way. Beyond the cat was a woman who was about to fidget out of her skin. Her fingers worked a loose string on the quilt.

"You're going to unravel that thing."

She looked down and let out a nervous laugh. "Oh, yeah. Wouldn't be the first time. Mama's had to fix a lot of holes I made pulling strings. She finally made me learn how to sew up a patch myself."

A fine scar ran down the side of her arm, just above her elbow. Instant concern propelled me forward. Without thinking, I ran my finger down the uneven white line. On each side of the line were smaller pucker marks. "What's this from?"

Her wide, unblinking eyes were staring at me.

I was tracing her skin. I yanked my hand away. "Sorry."

"No, it's fine. I almost forget it's there. It's from the accident when I was a kid. With my birth parents." She screwed up her face. "It's always weird to call them that, but it's just as odd to say my first set of parents, you know?"

I didn't. I'd lost my mom, but I'd forgotten that Autumn and her sisters had lost a mom and a dad in one fell swoop. "My mom used to talk about you guys." I got lost in the memory. Mom making dinner and bustling around the kitchen while I worked on homework at the table. "She'd tell me everything she heard about the Kerrigan girls."

"Really? I mean, I know people followed our story, but it's weird, isn't it? How we were strangers before yesterday, yet you probably know more of my story than a lot of my coworkers."

"Coworkers like Mark?" The fond memories of my mom evaporated as I envisioned pummeling the unknown man's face.

"No." She frowned, her gaze getting a faraway look.

"I don't think he knows any of it. I'm so used to people knowing that I don't really talk about it." She gasped. "I have to tell him I'm married. I'll have to tell my friends, but I should get to him first. Since we . . ."

"Since you were seeing each other?" My teeth ached from clenching so hard.

"It was barely that. The first date was more of a random meeting in the coffee shop. Then it was like a work picnic before school started, where we kept talking after. The third was official, and then . . . Well, you don't want to hear about that."

"I assure you, Mrs. James, I very much do."

She lifted a doubtful reddish brow. "He asked me to go to Spokane with him to meet his parents."

The fuck he had. I kept my temper reined in. "Spokane is over a six-hour drive away."

"Right?" She puffed out a breath. "An overnight trip at least. He's easy to talk to, but I didn't think we connected that hard. We didn't even . . ." She flicked her gaze away.

"He planned to on the Spokane trip," I said, irritated. My heart rate jumped. What if I'd missed her at the elevator? She'd have returned to Bourbon Canyon and might've taken Mark up on his offer.

"And he probably doesn't even know Mama isn't my birth mom." She shook her head, the damp strands of hair dancing over her breasts.

The knowledge eased the burgeoning rage inside me. "You didn't tell him?" As if I mentioned my parents, living or dead, to anyone.

She shook her head and dropped her gaze.

I sat at the foot of the bed. "It's hard talking about

losing a parent. And you lost two. You were also injured."

Her fingers found the loose thread. I put my hand over where her feet were tucked under the blankets. The cat was passed out.

"Summer and I are the oldest, so we were in the middle row. Mom and Dad took the worst of the impact from rolling, but she and I also got hurt. Summer almost died." A line pinched between her brows. She gestured to her chest. "Internal bleeding."

She'd been through a nightmare and was more concerned about her sister. "This scar isn't from something minor."

"No." She pulled and tugged at the quilt.

Now that I was closer, I could see several patch jobs and areas where seams had been reinforced. Maybe they should've sewn in threads that were tuggable and wouldn't unravel everything.

"My arms and legs got really beat up," she continued. "All the flying around when the car rolled." She spoke like she was trying to be detached but also like speaking about it brought her back. "I was lucky though."

"Is that what everyone told you to make you feel better?"

Her expression wavered before she nodded. "I didn't feel lucky."

"Neither did I when Mom died. It fucking sucked, and it's okay to say it all fucking sucked and that the last thing you felt that day was motherfucking luck."

"Who told you that you were lucky?"

I clenched my jaw. "Everyone. I was lucky I wasn't snowmobiling with her. I was lucky I still had Hank. I was lucky to have her as long as I did. It's all bullshit."

I stood and went to her side. She pondered her quilt like my words were sinking in and she was finally giving herself permission to spin the accident the way it had happened in her head. A horrific event that had nothing to do with luck.

I leaned down to drop a kiss in her hair. Just like when I'd touched her scar, I didn't realize I was doing it until her cool strands tickled my lips. I hadn't planned to lay a finger on her at all, much less my mouth. "Get comfortable, Autumn. I'll only take a minute."

I took my toiletry kit to the small bathroom. I didn't unpack the whole thing. Just like she wasn't ready to have sex, whether she admitted it or not, I wasn't ready to submerse myself into a fake marriage. I couldn't risk forgetting that in a month, this would all be over. I wasn't ready to ask myself if I was okay returning to visit because I had a goddamn kid.

I brushed my teeth and changed into a white shirt and gray sweatpants. Autumn was curled on her side with her eyes closed. I doubted she was asleep, but she was pretending she was.

When I crawled in next to her and was surrounded by her sweet scent, I drifted off. Not even the cat commandeering an entire bed around two adults bothered my slumber.

Autumn

I woke up snuggled into a wall of heat. A warm iron band was around my back and my nose was buried in a hard chest. The comforting scent of cedar citrus filled my nose.

I was cozy as hell. I kept my eyes closed and wiggled closer.

The chest under my face rose. My eyelids flew open. Gideon!

I tried to shove away, but that band around my back kept me in place.

"You need to be getting more comfortable with me, rusty."

The new nickname gave me pause. It also gave me floozy butterflies. "Rusty?"

"Seems more fitting for the morning. Actually, since we haven't had sex, I don't know which nickname fits you better."

I swatted his chest. My cheeks were probably as bright as my hair.

He laughed, a pleasing, deep sound that made me smile.

"I'm not rusty," I muttered.

The laugh turned into a growl but cut off right away. "How not rusty are you?"

I left my hand on his abdomen. Was he hard everywhere? The blanket was pushed down to his waist, so I could answer the question. I stayed where I was. In this position, I couldn't see his face, and I wasn't breathing on him. "Want me to ask the same thing?"

His stomach tightened. "Fair enough. Six months, I think."

I popped my head up, forgetting about the morning breath. "That long?"

His expression was softer, and his hair was tousled. Suddenly, he was approachable. I was married to the guy, but seeing him like this was more dangerous to my resolve than anything else. He was out of my league on a good day. In the soft light of the morning, in my bed, he was intimidating.

I laid my head back down before he answered. I was still cuddled into his side, and I was content to stay there. I was soaking up a handsome guy in my bed while I could. Living the dream while I could.

"At least six months," he reiterated. "I only remember because that matches up with the end of Q1 and I was working more with . . ."

"Yeah." As distasteful as it was hearing about his sex life, I liked hearing that Taya was only when time and opportunity matched up. "No Q2 nookie?"

Another deep chuckle reverberated under my cheek. "The land sale didn't make me the best guy to hang around."

"How kind you are doesn't strike me as a deal breaker when it comes to you."

"You keep mentioning my looks, rusty."

I snorted. "They're that good."

"You also haven't answered me."

Crap. It was my turn. "Um . . . right after the New Year. I tried another dating app last fall, and I thought I'd found someone who was a contender."

"A contender for what?"

"For being a partner. He had a job and his family was nice. He seemed respectful and treated me decent."

"He was a creep?"

I traced my finger over an ab ridge. Was I going to admit this? I hadn't even told my sisters. Hello, embarrassment. "I caught him stroking off to a picture of Junie. It was her magazine interview in *Music Today*."

He went taut under me. "What a fucking bastard."

"Can you imagine how awkward family dinner would be after I knew that?"

"Don't tell me you entertained staying with him?"

"He was trying to defend it, so I told him to print out a picture of his brother and I'd rub one off." I bit the inside of my cheek to keep from telling the rest of the story.

"Don't tell me he called your bluff?"

There went the rest of my pride. "Are you a mind reader?"

"No, I've just seen a lot living and working in a casino for so long."

"People can suck sometimes."

"A lot of times."

We fell quiet, but it was a comfortable silence. Then Sprinkles jumped on the bed and meowed. She marched across the covers and caterwauled in my face.

"Is there a fire somewhere?" Gideon asked. Sprinkles marched up his chest, smothering my face with her kitty pooch as she went. She wailed in his face.

"It's time for her to eat. And we have a party to get ready for." I rolled away and he let me go. Sprinkles sprinted for the kitchen. I scooted out of bed and made sure my loose green pajama pants and my sleepy-cat nightshirt were covering everything.

"Autumn."

I turned before going into the bathroom.

"We're going to have to be intimate soon."

"I know." I did. And the more I thought about it, the more timid I got. The first night with him, I would've spread myself out like one of the buffets Vegas used to be known for. Now, I wasn't sure I could survive going back to my quiet life when he deemed me of no use to him.

Would the sex be worth it? Would that be better or worse? "Thanks for, you know, giving me time."

The look he pinned me with was dark and promising. "The clock is ticking."

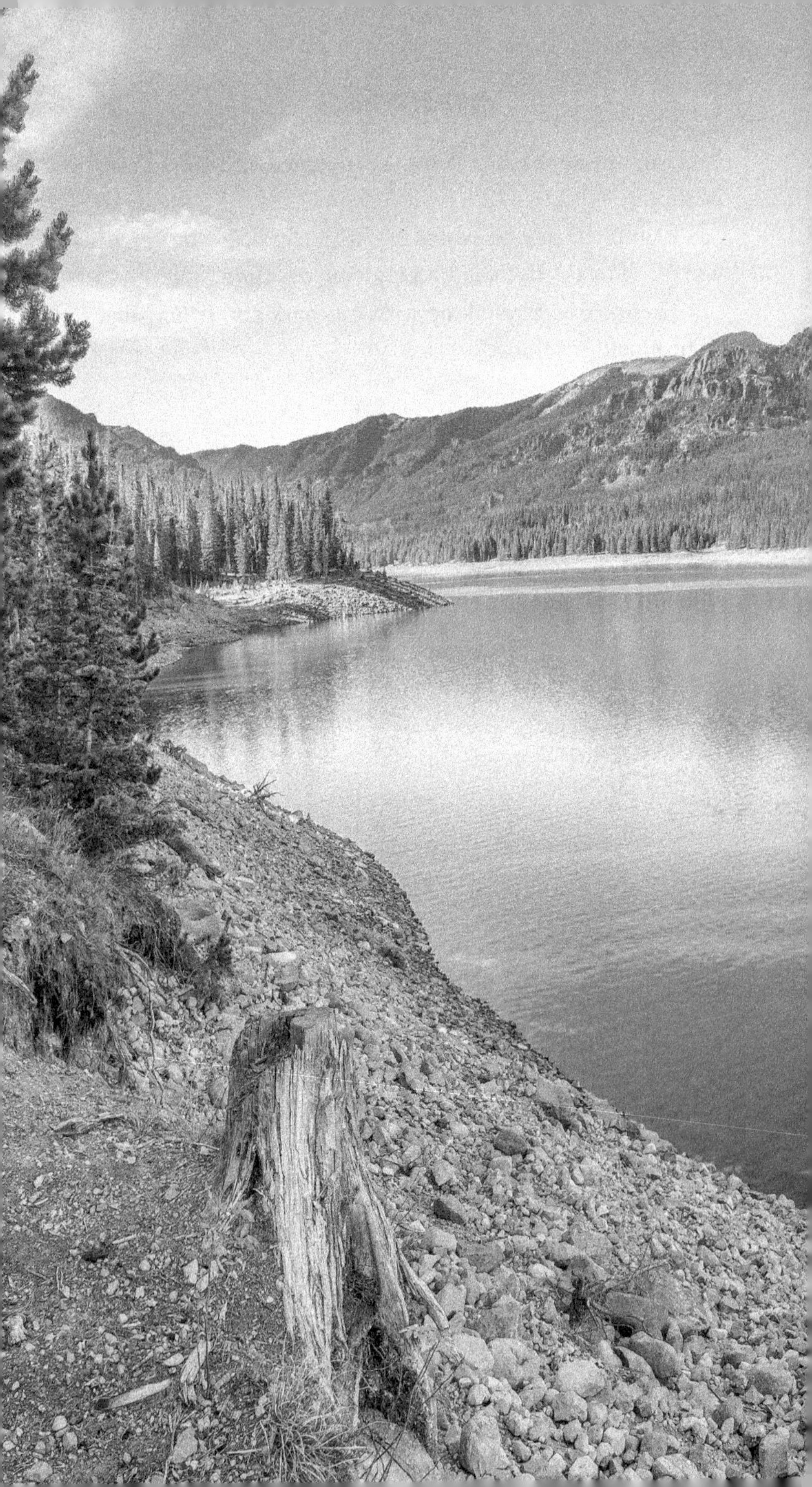

CHAPTER ELEVEN

Autumn

Gideon had gotten a message from his dad that the celebration would start at five. He'd worked at the table all day. I had texted Mark that I'd gotten married in Vegas and would bring in my documents to change everything with HR. Messaging my friends was next. Then I'd shut down my phone. I'd continue dealing with my family's reaction later; my coworkers would have to wait.

It was almost four. We'd have to go to Hank's party soon. I'd suggested arriving early to help his dad and put on a good show of being happy newlyweds. My nerves were a lump in my stomach.

I gently prodded Sprinkles off my lap and rose. I'd spent the day working on lesson plans only because I felt guilty reading while he was working.

I was sneaking behind Gideon when he pushed back

the chair and faced me. The force of his gaze sent shivers whispering over my skin.

"My lawyer has the documents prepared. You can read through them and sign."

I glanced from him to his laptop screen. There was a document-signing program up with a bold yellow button on it.

"This is the postnup," he explained. "Then you can read through the divorce papers, but you don't need to sign them now."

"That was fast," I muttered. I'd had the day off, but his legal team hadn't.

"I don't pay my legal team to drag their feet."

Well. I slid into the seat. He crossed his arms and loomed over me. I'd been exposed to a fair number of contracts through Copper Summit, but always through our lawyers first. I scanned over our information. "Don't you need my property information?"

"I told him all it needed to say is that anything that was ours before marriage is ours after and anything we make or produce or come into ownership of while married belongs to whoever received it."

Meaning I'd have no claim over Percival Farms. I was fine with that. I'd expected pages and pages of documents, but in the end, it was simple. Gideon didn't want me to get anything that was his, and he couldn't claim anything that was mine. He had more to lose when we divorced. But he might not have Percival when we divorced.

I went through the clicks to sign the document.

He leaned over me, his scent washing over me, and clicked on another tab. Divorce papers. He stepped back and took his heat with him.

A chill sank into my bones as I read over more legal jargon. "There's nothing in here about children."

"We can cross that bridge when we know there's a river. If you'd like more time to look them over, I can send a copy in an email."

I let him dismiss the kid topic. For now. "No. That's fine. You can send them when it's time to . . . file."

"We need to get going," he said softly.

I gladly escaped to the bedroom. I changed into a long-sleeved dress with my trusty leggings underneath. I might've picked another pair of rust-colored bottoms because of my new nickname and not just because they looked really good with the blue designs in my favorite pair of cowboy boots.

My heart skipped a beat when I caught Gideon eyeing my legs on our way out the door. But during the drive, his expression returned to his normal smolder. It was his standard CEO look and not a special heat just for me.

We're going to have to be intimate soon.

He would live up to his end of the deal. Neither of us knew if we'd get what we wanted, but we were willing to try.

Was that what I wanted?

Gideon, yes. His perfunctory compliance? No.

I was in over my head.

I was almost glad I had tonight to take my mind off physical activities with Gideon and what he'd think of me.

I *was* rusty. I'd never been a firecracker about a damn thing in my life. I didn't even light them off.

He turned off the main gravel road that led to the long, winding road to his dad's place. I frowned and peered out the window. I wasn't familiar with their land, but this road was narrower and bumpier. It was little more than a dirt path with two wheel tracks.

"Where are we going?" I asked.

"You're going to pick a hole in those leggings."

I glanced down to where my hand was scratching at the seam on the side of my thigh. "I'm nervous."

"I know. You about jumped outta your boots when I put my hand on the small of your back yesterday."

Did he realize how casual he sounded? Did he get more relaxed with increased pressure? Figured.

The road went through a scattering of trees. There was a short approach that led to a wire fence. He stopped, turned around, and parked with the car facing in the direction we'd come from.

"I can do some breathing exercises." I closed my eyes and inhaled—one, two, three.

His heat crowded me before I heard the click of his seat belt and then mine. His fingertips touched my jaw and tilted my face toward him. "I have a better idea."

His mouth landed on mine.

Stunned, I quit picking at my leggings and kissed him back. I twined a hand around the back of his neck. The short prickles of his tightly trimmed hair tickled my palm. His lips were soft but unyielding. I clutched his shoulder with my other hand, fisting my fingers in the material of his expensive polo shirt.

A whimper left me and he deepened the kiss, his tongue sweeping inside. I was twisted in my seat and so was he. The console was between us, but we were wrapped up in each other.

He cupped my face, his long fingers in my hair. His tongue had my sole focus. Where'd this guy learn how to kiss? I never thought about my kissing ability. No complaints meant it was good enough, but Gideon was robbing me of breath. I was running a marathon while he was on a leisurely stroll.

He broke the kiss, only to nibble a path across my jaw. "You taste like sunshine and candy."

I tipped my head back as he kissed a path down my neck. My eyes fluttered open when he bunched up the hem of my dress.

I jerked when warm fingers touched my abdomen. This wasn't my best position. I had a belly and hips. Curvy might be in, but those curves also formed rolls when sitting like this. I wasn't splayed across a settee like a Renaissance model.

A disapproving growl came from him. He brushed his hand up my side to skim underneath my bra, then he cupped a breast over the material. "Does this feel good?"

"Yes," I gasped.

He kissed up my neck and nibbled my earlobe. A shiver rippled its way down my body as he worked his wicked fingers under the cup of my bra.

Oh god. How could getting to second base blow away any other experience I'd had?

"Gideon?" I whispered, but I didn't know what I was asking for.

My breast was free of the material and he stroked my nipple between his thumb and forefinger. In the time since he'd put his mouth on me, a direct connection between my boob and my pussy had formed. A steady thrum pulsed between my thighs, growing stronger and more demanding.

He claimed my mouth again, and again, I whimpered. I stuffed my hands in his hair and held on for dear life. He kissed me senseless. There was no part of my mouth he didn't explore with his tongue. I was his to devour.

When he pulled away, I let out a needy moan and blinked. I should be embarrassed, but damn. Why'd he quit?

He removed his hand and gently tugged my bra cup back into place. Then he smoothed my dress down. Humiliation was creeping up into my stunned brain. Except for some ruffled hair, he appeared unbothered. How could he kiss like that and just . . . stop?

He slid his hand around my neck and stroked my jaw with his thumb. "What's going on in that sharp mind of yours?"

I'd take the compliments where I found them. "You just stopped."

"We have a celebration dinner to get to."

"Right."

Our faces were inches apart, and he studied me. "This isn't a comfortable place to fuck, but don't delude yourself. If we kept going, that is exactly what I would be doing to you right now."

My legs quivered. "Really?"

He leaned in even closer, his breath wafting over my cheek. "I'm dying to know if you taste like cotton candy everywhere."

I groaned. The sounds this man could get me to make. I was a proud hussy.

He claimed my mouth once more for a sensual kiss. "Now, when I touch you, you won't fucking flinch."

He reached over me and buckled me in. He was so efficient I wasn't sure I believed him about losing control if we continued. But before he took care of his own seat belt, he adjusted the giant bulge in his jeans.

He glanced over. I lifted my gaze to his, and I saw it. The incinerating arousal he kept a tight rein on. A tiny flicker in the green mask of his irises.

He looked away and calmly put the car in drive. We bumped back down the road to celebrate our wedding.

What would happen if I coaxed that spark into an inferno?

Gideon

When we arrived at the house, my raging erection finally redirected blood to my brain. The stop had been necessary. My reasoning was practical. It had nothing to do with how hard it'd been not to roll her over and plunge into her when I woke up with her soft body pressed against mine. It had nothing to do with seeing her ass cheeks bounce in her pajama pants.

She hadn't been wearing underwear and thank fucking god she hadn't realized how see-through the thin material was.

Creamy, white butt cheeks that would be perfect to hold on to.

I was getting a hard-on again, only this time I was surrounded by Baileys. But all I had to do to get rid of it was remember her studying and then signing the postnup. The woman knew what she wanted and my wealth wasn't it. My respect for her grew. But then I'd pulled up the divorce papers and I'd gone cold. I'd wanted to shut the laptop.

Those papers marked the end. Wasn't that what I wanted? An end to the sale. An end to the need for this ruse. A halt to the talk about kids and everything a divorce would mean on that front.

I could say for certain that I wanted an end to this damn dinner.

We weren't in the house. I hadn't gone in since we'd arrived. I hadn't been in that place since I'd left after graduation.

The shop that used to hold various bits of broken-down equipment Dad had never fixed had been cleared out and cleaned up.

When had that happened? Definitely wasn't in the last twenty-four hours.

The walls were clear. The pegboard that had held all sorts of tools was bare. Someone had painted too.

Where'd he gotten the money to hire all this out?

Mae had arrived with two men I'd never seen before. Autumn introduced them as Myles's brothers, Cruz and Lane. They were much younger than him, and from what Autumn had told me, while we'd filled our glasses with punch, they'd started working for Mae in the last two years. She'd said they hadn't known Myles growing up and Myles hadn't known they existed.

The rest of the Baileys who'd been at Autumn's house to berate her were here but with their kids this time. I'd sort of met Myles and Wynter's baby, Elsa, but I wasn't prepared to see so many little people. A lanky teen boy made sure a little girl in a twirly dress didn't drag a small toddler outside to get into whatever trouble they could find.

Those kids were Tate's. I didn't care to see him as a happy family man. Just like I didn't want to witness the smitten way he gazed at his wife.

I took another drink of punch. No alcohol. Not in the punch and not anywhere in the shop.

I could start to believe Dad was sober when he acted like this.

I had expected Autumn to mingle with her sisters, but she was glued to my side.

Tate's wife approached us with a pleasant smile. She'd arrived with Tate, and Autumn had introduced her as Scarlett.

I smoothed my hand down Autumn's back as she chatted with Scarlett.

Dad approached. "I hope you don't mind the sandwiches. I thought it'd be easier to throw together at the last minute."

"The party didn't have to be at the last minute."

A flash of hurt faded in his eyes. Right after, a burn ignited behind my sternum. I hadn't eaten yet, but my heartburn didn't care.

"I can still be a little impulsive," he said roughly. "I was happy to have you home and then to find out it was for this." His fond smile was aimed at Autumn.

"I'll be around for a while." Once the land sale was stopped, I was out. The board didn't like their CEO gone for long. They were already sending semi-panicked messages.

"That's music to these old ears." He brushed his fingers down his freshly trimmed beard. The longer parts of his horseshoe mustache blended with the rest of his facial hair. "You two want to come out some night? Just us for a quiet meal?"

I didn't want to see how the house had changed. How he had ruined any memory of Mom like he'd wrecked the ranch she was so proud of. "I'll talk to Autumn."

She turned into me. I was acutely aware of how the side of her breast was pushed into my side. I had almost ripped her damn bra off to get at those creamy tits.

"Hank invited us for supper," I explained.

"Oh? What night?"

"Any night you want," Dad answered. He sounded so damn excited. My heartburn grew more intense.

"We'd love to," she gushed and I didn't think she was doing it for show. "I'm not sure how this week will work though. I go back to work tomorrow, and the music teacher and I will be getting ready for the program Thursday night. I work at the bar on Wednesdays and on the weekends."

She worked nights and weekends? I was prepared to work from her kitchen table during the day, but the disappointment that she'd be gone for some nights increased my reflux.

"I've got meetings Wednesday nights, but yeah, let's plan for another week." Dad's smile was kind.

What meeting did he have? Was he being coy, trying to figure out how long I would be in town? We hadn't addressed the question of where she and I were making our home. I was letting her family think I could work remotely and fly back and forth as needed.

We also hadn't discussed how we'd end this after the month was done. I'd leave and we'd chalk it up to an impulsive move that wasn't practical due to our different lives.

I'd bring that up to her. Later.

She returned his grin. "We'll figure something out. Next week is conferences, and Halloween is next weekend. My kids love stopping by the house to trick-or-treat."

"Oh, the heck," Dad said, and he chuckled. "I never even think of that. Living out here, no one ever stops by."

I expected his tone to make his statement a dig, but instead, all I heard was sadness.

"Same at Mama's," Autumn replied easily. "Trick-or-treating kids is a perk of living in town."

"I'll get to experience that next year, I reckon." He traced his fingers around the inside of his waistband. There was a time when he'd lost so much weight I'd worried those pants would fall right off. The habit of pulling his jeans up must've stayed as he'd put back on much-needed weight.

Then what he said sank in. "You're moving into town?"

He nodded. "That new senior housing place, not far from the elementary school."

I scowled at him. I hadn't thought of where he'd go. Had I thought he'd sell and then squat on the land like he was part of the deal?

Senior housing.

When had Dad become a senior?

My heartburn redoubled. Goddammit. I took a long pull of my punch, wishing there was a splash of Copper Summit in it. Then chagrin set in. I was wishing for a drink at an alcoholic's place. Not only that, I myself lived by guidelines when it came to the stuff. I'd have a drink for business and during social events. Never because of emotion. *Never.*

You're more like your old man than you thought. You need to get outta here, or you're going to end up like him. My grandfather's wheezy words came back to me.

I inhaled, the air like glass. I'd left like he'd said, and here I was, dangerously close to acting like my dad. "It's time to go, Autumn."

I started moving before she did. I slid my arm off her shoulder and snagged her hand. Since I'd caught her off guard, she stumbled when I tugged on her. "Gideon—"

"It's time to go."

"But we haven't eaten."

"Take some to go." I continued pulling her toward the door. A band was squeezing around my chest and the air hurt to breathe. I needed to get out of here. Out of the past. Out of the thoughts of how much I was like the one person I had ever counted on, the one person I had worked so damn hard not to be like. I'd toiled all my adult life to stay away from the place where I'd never measured up.

Autumn yanked on my hold. When I turned to frown at her, I caught the way Tate was scooting around his wife, like he was coming to rescue Autumn. I couldn't keep towing my wife and fighting her and then end up arguing with her family. That wouldn't work.

I pulled her into me and dropped my mouth to her ear. Her body was rigid and her eyes were full of concern, but also annoyance.

I wasn't used to irritation from women.

"I need to leave. We can either bicker with your siblings or make up an excuse. I don't care. I have to leave."

She searched my expression. Whatever she saw made her relent, but only slightly.

Tate approached us. "Everything okay, Autumn?"

I shot him a glare. I'd make sure Autumn was fucking fine.

"It seems like lunch didn't agree with Gideon. Stomach cramps," she whispered loudly.

I'd forgive her for tossing my guts under the bus. I wasn't behaving like a gentleman.

"The house has a toilet." Tate's bluntness wasn't helpful.

"No telling how long it'll last or if it's infectious. We wouldn't want to spread it." She patted my forearm. "Hopefully I didn't pass anything on to him. Lord knows I have a stomach of steel after all my years of teaching. Poor guy. It's going to hit him hard."

She was using diarrhea as our reason for leaving—nonexistent diarrhea—and I was admiring her for it.

Tate's mouth twitched like he knew exactly what his sister was up to. "We'll send you home with some food." He twisted. "Chance, give me a hand."

Autumn

Gideon didn't talk all the way home. He gave me the keys, and I assumed it was to make it look like he really wasn't feeling well. But the whole trip, he was on his phone, clicking away.

When he'd first dragged me off, he'd looked green around the gills. Like he'd seen a ghost right after eating bad shrimp. Meanwhile, my stomach had been rumbling up a storm.

My sisters and Scarlett had packed us a ton of food, and Chance had helped them carry it out. Mama had watched the show, but she'd been looking Gideon's way, her brow furrowed. She must be concerned about him.

I had been too.

Now, I was a little irritated. We'd been home for an hour. He'd ignored the food and was set up at the table on his laptop. He'd called it early on the gathering that was to celebrate us and now he was ignoring me.

I was starving. And I was done waiting for him to interact.

I fixed myself a plate, my stomach growling the whole time. It took everything in me not to ask him if he wanted me to do the same for him. Two could play the ignoring game. I heaped on ham, veggies, Wynter's fruit salad, and the macaroni salad that I was sure Teller had bought from the grocery store and put into a bowl. I even took all of Mama's cookie salad.

Not once did Gideon glance up. He didn't initiate a conversation. He didn't treat me like I'd want to be treated as a real *or* fake wife.

I took my food outside and sat on the front stoop. The day was beautiful. A little cool, but I was still wearing the cardigan I had put on over my dress.

The sun was going down, but I chomped down on my food. I needed the crisp, fresh air to chisel away the resentment I was building toward the absurdly gorgeous man in my kitchen. How could he kiss me senseless and then brush me off like I was nothing more than his chauffeur?

Did I want to have his bigheaded, frustrating babies?

My appetite vanished, but I continued to clean my

plate. Hank and my family had put a lot into this last-minute celebration and I would honor it.

A boy skidded to a stop on his dirt bike. Large chunks of mud dripped off his tires. It hadn't rained in a few days, so I could only imagine where he'd found enough mud to skid around in. "Hey, Miss K."

"Hey, Deon. How's school going this year?" He'd been my student last year.

"Eh. You know."

I did. I knew exactly what his teacher was going through. Deon was an active young man. His brain worked almost as fast as his body, which led to a lot of interesting and occasionally infuriating moments. He was a good kid, but if he'd gone to school in a large town, he'd have had a lot of trouble. Thankfully, in Bourbon Canyon, we could be a little more flexible and creative to accommodate active kids with vibrant learning styles.

"Did you have a good long weekend?" I asked.

He shrugged. "My stepdad worked all weekend."

"That stinks. Does he have to work over the performance?" He was in Scarlett's class and their performance was a couple of weeks after my class had theirs.

Deon nodded and looked away. He adored his stepdad, but the guy did shift work and couldn't help his schedule. "My grandma's coming though."

I almost said which one. Between his parents and stepparents, Deon had a lot of grandparents. He was a lucky kid. "I'm looking forward to it. You guys have worked so hard."

He ducked his head again. His brown gaze lifted over my shoulder and his forehead crinkled a moment before the screen door opened. The corner of the door brushed against my back, but I didn't move.

A wall of heat was between me and the house. I didn't look up. I picked one of the fudge-striped cookies out of the creamy cookie salad and licked the vanilla pudding and whipped cream mix off.

"Who's that?" Deon asked, staring at Gideon.

"Uh . . ." Shit. How did I tell my students? I was bracing myself for work tomorrow, but I'd been anticipating adults.

"The proper way to ask is to introduce yourself first." Gideon's tone was almost disapproving.

My defensiveness rose, uncovering my mischievous side. No one messed with my kids, but Gideon did have a point and the teacher in me couldn't miss a teachable moment.

Deon screwed his face up more. "Huh?"

I put my cookie down. "You say 'Hi, I'm Deon' and stick your hand out to shake his."

The kid eyed me dubiously.

A disgruntled snort came from behind me, and I grinned. Deon was almost as dirty as his bike. The mud streaking up his legs was drying, same with his hands and arms, but there was no way someone was getting out of a handshake unscathed.

"It's okay. He'll tell you who he is once he shakes your hand." I peeked over my shoulder, making my expression as full of censure as possible. "Right?"

Gideon towered over me. His dark gaze was intense and his stance was unyielding. He clenched his jaw once but said, "Right."

Deon shrugged and laid his bike on the sidewalk. He swaggered across the lawn and up the stairs next to me.

He thrust his hand out. "Hi. I'm Deon. Miss K was my teacher."

I clutched my plate. Would he shake the kid's hand? Deon was bold but sensitive. If Gideon was rude to my former student, he'd have to sleep on the lawn tonight.

Gideon shook Deon's hand as if he were a fellow CEO. "Nice to meet you, Deon. I'm Gideon James. Miss K's husband."

"No sh—kidding?" Deon's wide eyes swiveled back and forth between us. "I didn't know you were married."

"Surprise," I said weakly.

His grin spread wide, showing off a missing canine. "Wait—so are you Miss J now?"

"I . . ." Shit. "Yes? Mrs. J." I said it slowly, testing the flow. I'd only ever known Miss K, and it wasn't like I'd had time to rehearse answering to something new.

He jogged back to his bike. The side of my leggings he'd brushed up against was covered in dirt.

"See ya tomorrow, Miss J!"

He rode away. Most kids would drop the missus and call me miss. It was just the different letter I'd have to get used to.

"Why are you eating out here?" His question cut through my contemplation.

"Because the company inside is rude." I plucked my cookie off my plate and took a bite. I didn't bother to finish chewing before I spoke. "You were quick to teach Deon about manners, but you sure sucked at them today." I brandished the portion of the cookie I hadn't chomped off. "Did it occur to you to share why you ripped me away from a party that was partly for me? That had almost my *whole* family there? They all showed, with less than a day's notice, and they even brought food. I ate all the cookie salad, by the way, and I'm not even sorry. You're not the only one who can be thoughtless."

His sharp inhale almost made me cringe. Had I gone too far? I didn't really know this guy. Would he get upset?

"Trust I had my reasons," he said evenly.

I'd slept in a bed with this man twice. I trusted him with my physical safety. I trusted that he'd do a lot to keep his family's land from getting sold. But to trust him around my family? With my feelings? That was yet to be earned. "Why don't you trust me with your reasons?"

Several silent moments ticked by. I ate the rest of my cookie and polished off my plate.

"We each entered into this marriage with our own separate yet related agendas. That doesn't give you access to everything about me, just as I don't expect to have access to all of you whenever I want it."

Ouch. What he was saying was true, but the hurt made my gut twist. I regretted those last few bites.

I wanted kids. I wanted a family. Should I press pause on expecting him to hold up his end of the bargain? I wasn't sure I could help him with the land anyway, and I didn't want my kid to have an emotionally unavailable father. Without kids, I could enjoy this little fantasy until Gideon went back to Vegas. Once he was gone, I wouldn't have a reminder about what a stubborn ass he could be.

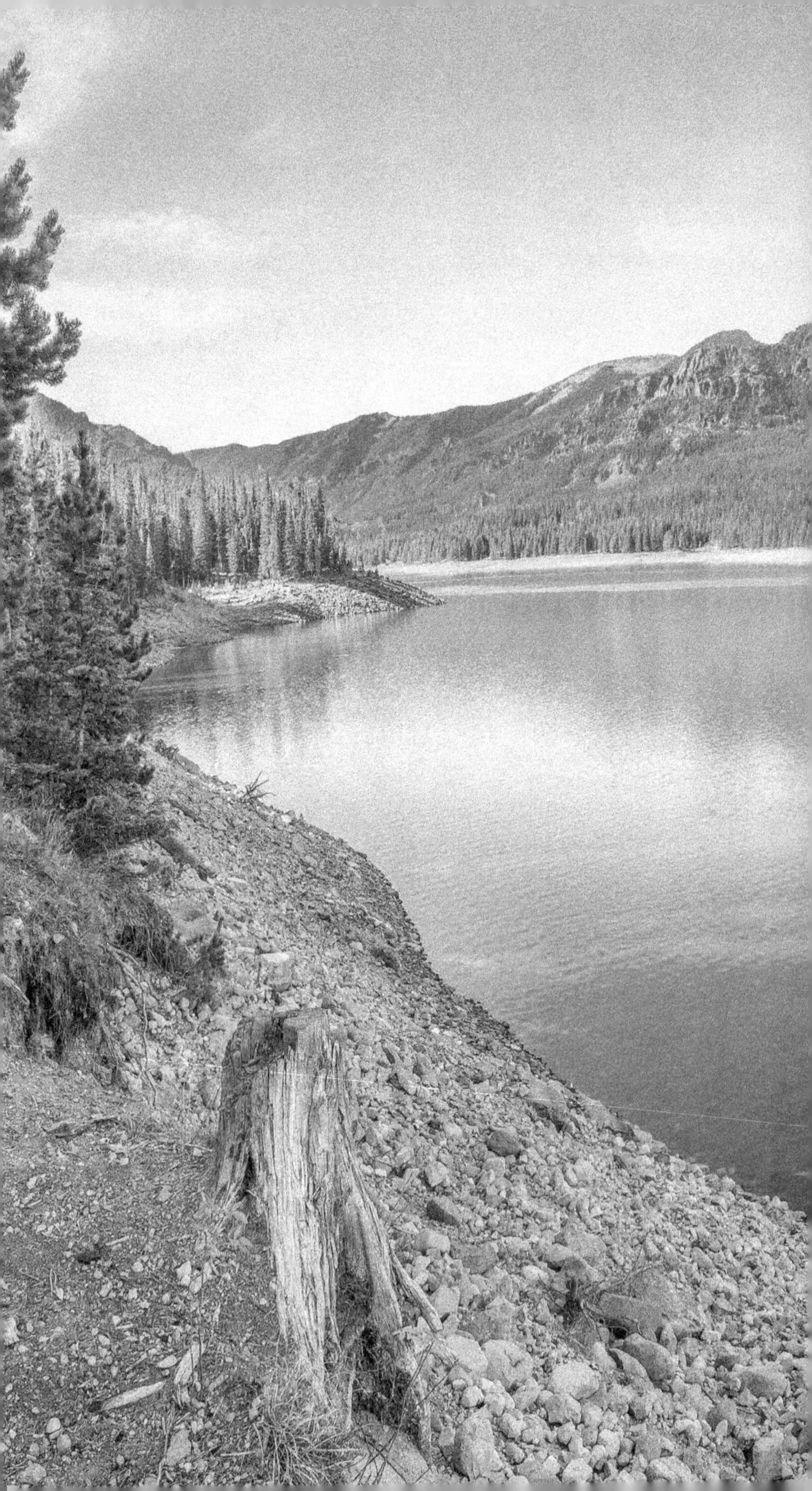

CHAPTER TWELVE

Gideon

I looked out the window and checked the temp on my phone. The weather outside was warmer than the frigid vibes Autumn was giving off. She had gone to work for the day, or so I assumed since she hadn't said a word to me.

After I'd shut down her admonishments, she'd sat outside for another half hour, and when she'd come inside, she'd gotten ready for bed and read until she shut the lights off. I had taken the opportunity to catch up on work. The board was not happy I'd left on such short notice and I had to wonder how many of those anxious texts were fueled by Taya.

I had over five years of diligent service to Silver, along with months of unused vacation. They should know I wouldn't have left without reason. Many of them had known me when I'd worked for other casinos in the Las Vegas area.

I had mollified them for now. Where was my wife? How upset was she? All she had asked me to do was talk to her.

She'd called me rude.

I'd heard myself described in various ways over the years. Hard. Uncompromising. Too demanding.

Not fucking rude. By a schoolteacher.

I let the blinds go. I went to the fridge and dug out the rest of the leftovers. One slab of ham and a bun was all that was left.

My stomach was waking up and my damn mouth was watering. The plate I'd heated for myself last night after Autumn had retreated to the bedroom had made me want to gobble everything up. There wasn't enough remaining for another meal.

I'd seen Autumn packing some in an insulated bag with horses on it this morning. No one in Silver would be caught packing a lunch bag with horses on it for work. She'd probably left me scraps to make a point. She could be rude too. I ate the remnants.

I sat at the kitchen table and worked for a few hours, answering emails and conducting one phone meeting. For my dinner, I found a freezer full of beef besides the ice cream. I made eggs instead. Autumn had plenty of veggies around to make a decent omelet.

The groan that left my mouth when I tasted the farm-fresh eggs was shameful. I sounded like I was getting my dick sucked, which wasn't going to happen after the way Autumn had shut down on me last night.

I scrubbed the dishes with more force than necessary. It didn't matter if she kept her distance. It didn't. Getting her pregnant in a month wouldn't be enough time to change Dad's mind. I just needed him to buy that we'd have kids in the near future.

But that wasn't part of the deal.

A bead of sweat broke out on my forehead.

I abandoned the dishes in the drying rack and went back to work. I stayed at the computer until my shoulders ached and my back protested. I missed my ergonomic chair.

When I glanced at the time, I did a double take. It was after six?

Outside, the sun was dipping toward the horizon.

Where was my wife? School had let out hours ago.

When I peered outside, Deon rode by. He glanced at the house and waved at me. It took me a moment to remember I should wave back. These windows weren't one-way glass, and I wasn't high above the city.

He sped off after I returned his greeting.

Where the hell was my wife?

My stomach growled again. She'd only packed a lunch. What was she eating for dinner? Who was she eating with?

I went to grab my keys to leave, but damn. No keys. No car. I hadn't even considered that when she'd left. If she'd thought of it, she'd left me hanging.

Because you deserved it.

Deep down, I knew that wasn't her. She might've absconded with the food I didn't deserve after my abrupt departure, but she wouldn't leave me stranded intentionally.

I found my athletic shoes that I usually reserved for the gym and changed into jeans and a gray Silver hoodie gifted by the marketing department that I'd only worn once in the years I'd had it. Then I left the house and locked her door. A simple knob lock wouldn't stop a soul, but I couldn't flip a dead bolt without a key. I couldn't wave a card and have it lock either.

Keep the windows and door open, Giddy. I love the fresh air. I shook off Mom's voice, clearer now that I was in Montana, and set out for the school.

I navigated the town like I'd never left. Cars passed and people gawked, but I didn't pay attention.

When I reached the flat, one-level brick school, the doors were locked. "Goddammit." I could see classroom lights on. What the hell should I do? Knock on a window?

A couple of women were coming toward the door, chatting with each other. When they spotted me, they stopped and stared. I gestured to the door, not used to having to ask for permission for entry. I could go anywhere and everywhere in a casino that employed more people than lived in the city limits of Bourbon Canyon.

Finally, the woman with long, black hair pulled into a high ponytail opened the door a few inches. "Gideon?"

"Yes?" I didn't recognize her. I had to be almost twice her age.

Her face lit up in a zealous way that had me taking a step back.

Her companion's mouth fell open. "You're Autumn's—" A high-pitched squeal left her. "Oh my god. I can't believe you two— I mean, it's just . . ." They stared at me some more.

These must be two of the women who'd ditched my wife outside the club. "And you two left her alone in a giant city?"

Their expressions fell at once and their guilt was identical.

"I really didn't think they'd leave her outside the whole night," the one with black hair said.

"She seemed like she wanted to go to the room from her texts," the other said. "I should've seen through them."

"Yes. You should've."

They exchanged a look that shared blame but also *What's with this guy?*

The first woman flipped her dark ponytail over her shoulder. "She's in the gym helping with the set for the program on Thursday."

Right. She'd mentioned evening work obligations to Dad. I'd been too wrapped up in my own drama. I could take a month off and work from home. Autumn's work was different.

"Thanks," I forced myself to say as I maneuvered around them.

"The gymnasium's on the left," one of them called after me, "then a right at the end of the hall."

I didn't bother telling them I'd gone to school here.

I felt like a giant walking past lines of coat hooks that were at chest level and cubbies that hardly reached my shoulders. I didn't bother to look inside the classrooms.

I passed one room and pictured my mom, her hair as dark as the other woman's, talking to a teacher of mine and smiling at me during parent-teacher conferences. When I got to the juncture where I turned right, I caught sight of the library on my left. It had been remodeled, but I could still remember towing my parents inside for the book fair.

My parents. Another memory of Dad had snuck in. I hadn't had many before Mom died, but they were hitting me at the oddest moments.

Like entering the gymnasium and seeing the big stage at the end, the red curtains were open. I recalled standing in the middle, in the back row because I was a tall kid, and looking out to see Mom and Dad smiling at me.

I had been in middle school when Mom died. My chest grew tight. This building held nothing but good memories. The unwanted memories. Because they showed me how far Dad fell after that.

I swallowed the acid eating up my throat. Autumn circled a set of risers with two other people, a woman and a guy who looked to be over fifty. Was that fucking Mark?

Autumn's hair was now back in a ponytail, her shiny, coppery strands reflecting the overhead lights. She wore the same clothing as this morning—a long striped top that was belted at the waist, brown leggings, and knee-high boots.

She glanced over and her eyes widened. "Gideon? What are you doing here?"

The other two stopped to stare at me like the first two women had.

The guy took a step forward. "Gideon James!" His laugh boomed across the gymnasium. Good acoustics. "I bet you don't remember me."

So . . . not Mark.

He looked like any other suburban dad who came to Vegas with his family for vacation.

"You guess correctly." I walked toward the stage.

The other woman's gaze was dancing between me and my stunned wife.

Only the man smiled. "I was the student teacher when you were in fifth grade. Mr. Ellison?"

I peered at him. Years of dust flaked off my memories, and yeah, I did remember a young guy helping my teacher that year. "You loved to play football at recess with the rest of us."

"Heck yeah!" Joy danced across his face. He truly loved being recognized as my teacher. He held an arm out to the other woman. "This is my wife, Kerry. She's the music teacher here. Kerry, as you heard, Gideon was one of my first students." He looked at me. "I thought you were going to be the arm that helped us get to state, but you never played."

The same excuse slipped out of my mouth that had decades ago. "The ranch needed me."

He waved it off. I used to get pitying looks back then. People knew the story of my mom and my dad and knew why the ranch needed me.

"Eh, I realize now that's a common story around here. Congrats on the wedding—uh, marriage." He flashed an awkward smile. "It's going to take some time to get used to changing from Miss K to Mrs. J."

I dipped my head, unsure what to say when I was feeling like a goddamn fraud around people who sincerely wanted to wish us well.

"You here to help?" he asked.

I glanced at Autumn. She'd been watching the exchange, curiosity in her eyes. Now, there was challenge.

"You need a hand?" I aimed my question at her. Why hadn't she asked me earlier? Or at all?

"The kids wanted to do a Halloween-themed music program, but the school doesn't have much for decorations. We bought some, but they don't work with the high ceilings. No one can see them, even if we can get them up there in the first place."

"The janitor found some old plywood and gave us her toolbox," Mr. Ellison said.

"But she has bingo tonight," Kerry added. "So, it's us and some scrap two-by-fours." She propped her hands on her hips. Like Autumn, she was dressed for teaching in knit leggings and a long shirt. "We still have the risers to place and the rest of the props to make."

"Props?" In my day, we sang a few songs and went home.

"The kids turned this into more of a skit," Autumn explained, her cheeks growing pink. "And they were actually getting excited. I couldn't say no. I figured I'd just toss up a quick set."

"It's turned into a bigger production than any of us anticipated," Mr. Ellison finished. He was still in slacks, but his polo shirt was half-untucked. None of them were prepared to build a set. "But we couldn't leave Autumn here to work alone."

They'd get it done, but it'd be late. I could leave, but I'd just wait up for her and get some more work done. I'd wonder how she was doing. How the set would look. My shoulders already ached at the thought of working at the table.

I could still swing a hammer.

I pushed my sleeves up. "Tell me what you need."

Autumn

Kerry had gone and picked up pizza for us. Gideon had slipped her some money without telling us. Judging from all the pizza she'd brought, it had been a lot of cash.

I considered how thoughtful that was way too much. Almost as much as I watched him work. The way he bent and squatted, lining up boards and hammering nails. We didn't have major power tools. Our tool was Gideon.

He'd had a couple slices of pizza, then gone back to work.

I was on my third slice. The ham sandwich and leftover macaroni salad had burned off hours ago, and I was starving. The heat kindling low in my belly said I was hungry for more.

"You have good taste," Kerry murmured. Joseph Ellison was helping Gideon move the set into place so we could hang our decorations off it.

"Thanks. I think the mushrooms are best with black olives."

She snorted and brushed a napkin over her lips when the guys glanced at us. "I wasn't talking about the pizza toppings, Autumn." She rolled her eyes. "I think the smoking-hot husband you brought back from Vegas is a sign of your good taste."

"He used to be your husband's student," I whispered.

"He's definitely not a kid anymore."

"Nope."

All day, I'd been smiling and nodding when coworkers congratulated me. They gushed over his looks and my ring. My hand had been yanked several times so the ring could be inspected. I'd had a minor heart attack when I'd gotten acrylic paint on the diamond.

The kids were the biggest relief to be around. After five minutes and a few questions, mostly about whether I'd won a ton of money in Vegas, my marriage was forgotten.

Now that husband was here. He hadn't told me why, and I didn't care. Seeing him in jeans and a hoodie was all my libido cared about. Waking up to him for the last three days was hell on my hormones.

Kerry gave me a sidelong look. "Is it weird for you? To suddenly be married? I thought you and Mark might have a thing."

Mark—Mr. Knutson at work—had been overly formal with me, only brusquely telling me to give my documents to Kaitlyn.

"Yes." The first honest thing I'd said all day—other than agreeing with Gideon's looks. "It's one thing to get caught up in the idea and another when he's here. In my home. At my work."

The guys were hauling the plywood wall next to the risers, otherwise I would've kept my mouth shut.

She patted my shoulder. "Well, it looks like you got a considerate one."

"It's also weird that people know him." He was still a stranger to me.

"None of us *know* him." She grabbed another slice of pizza. "We've just heard of him," she said around a big mouthful.

Same.

Both guys turned and faced us. Joseph grinned. He didn't have to say how delighted he was to be working with a former student. "Time to hang our colony of bats."

I gathered the cutouts of bats the students had made. Kerry got the tacks and Joseph found some string.

Gideon appeared at my side. I was trying to get a bat toward the top. He slipped the decoration from my hands and stuck a tack in it toward the top. His chest was pressed to my back and his scent surrounded me.

"Thank you," I murmured.

"No problem."

We hadn't had time to talk since he'd arrived. "Why did you come?"

"You weren't home." He said it so simply.

"Okay?"

This time, the line of his jaw hardened. "You didn't tell me why."

"I thought you heard me tell your dad." When his right eye twitched—because he hadn't been paying attention?—I continued. "I'll go to the bar tomorrow after work, and the program is Thursday night. I'll probably stay at school until it starts."

He didn't respond. But he did help put the unexpected set together.

Since I'd lectured him about being rude, I could be considerate. "Would you like to come?"

He blinked. "Sure. Why not?" He made it sound so casual I bit back a smile. I doubted he would've come without an invite, but he sounded like he had wanted to. "I might have to buy a car while I'm here."

"Why?"

"I don't have a vehicle when you're at work."

Oh. Wait— "You walked here?"

"Why wouldn't I?"

"How long did you wait on the curb before you realized a car wasn't going to magically appear?"

His gaze intensified and then the corner of his mouth lifted. "I promise it wasn't more than an hour." He tipped his head. "Would it surprise you I didn't have to ask for directions?"

I snorted. "I bet a lot of women stopped and gave them to you anyway."

His laugh was deep.

I grinned. "I just have to put all my stuff away, and then I can give you a ride home."

He came with me without asking. I loaded my empty buckets that had once held carefully crafted bats and pumpkins my students had worked on all afternoon. Another bucket of staplers, tape, string, and paints was next.

Gideon pushed the cart. In my classroom, I put everything away and he wandered around.

"Is it weird to work in the same place you went to school?" he asked.

"Yes and no. When I first started, it was intimidating to work with people like Joseph. He's always excited when an old student starts working here though."

He roamed through my class. I felt exposed, like I'd lifted my blouse and was flashing him as he strolled through my life's work.

"Why elementary?" he asked.

"I've always liked kids. I watched Mama take care of them my entire life, and I guess I wanted to pay it forward. The high school can get crowded some years, you know, with the middle school stuffed into one wing." Bourbon Canyon was too small for three separate buildings and infrastructure.

He approached. I'd already put my office supplies in their place, but I moved the stapler from one side of the computer to the other.

"That's not the only reason." He stopped at the edge of my desk. I tried to picture him as a little kid, saying Miss K at least three times while leaning over the papers I was grading to get my attention. My heart melted. The cowlick he kept brushed in place, trimmed at just the right length to weigh it down, had probably stood on end when he was young. "Let me rephrase my original question. Why teaching?"

How had he known I wasn't telling him everything? I stabbed at the pens in my penholder until they all sat evenly on the bottom instead of sticking up at different heights. "I wanted something of my own."

"You have something of your own though, don't you?"

I chewed the inside of my cheek. "What do you mean?"

"Your dad gave you all a portion of the ranch."

"Some land," I clarified. "So yes, I get rent from letting my brothers use the pasture, but not much. Most of it isn't fit for livestock."

"You wanted more to call your own."

I gnawed on the raw spot of my cheek. I released my flesh before I could bleed and pressed my fingers into the top of my desk. "I freely admit I suffered from middle-kid syndrome."

He snorted. "There're a lot of middle kids in your family."

"True. But Summer's the oldest of the girls. The guys deferred to her."

He cocked a brow. His expression was a few shades shy of arrogant. "Just because she's the oldest?"

He knew to dig where it was most sensitive. "Yes and no. When we arrived at the Baileys' after our parents' accident, Summer and I were both recovering. I took longer with the broken bones, and I guess I always felt like I was the one they had to watch out for."

I pushed my hands through my hair. Guilt ate at my insides. "I'm really useless to you. God, I should've been less evasive—"

His sharp laugh echoed in the otherwise empty building. "You call the deal you made with me in my bed after our wedding *evasive?*"

"You thought I had more authority over my family."

He let out a long breath, his solid green gaze never leaving my face. "Perhaps we both hoped you did. It's the marriage I need, Autumn. I can commiserate with not feeling heard when it comes to family."

The lonely boy in him had never been louder. What his dad was doing had hurt him. "I wish I could help you more."

"Likewise. The idea of kids . . ." There was a brief glimpse of stark fear.

The dream that I'd be a married mom with a good job took its last breath. I couldn't do that to him. "Don't worry. I'm not going to hold you to it."

"Autumn—"

"No, it's fine. Really. I don't want to get so focused on having babies that I run over people. You've already said you wouldn't ditch a kid, so we'd have to figure out custody. The thought obviously bothers you, so I'm not forcing your end of the deal. The thought gives me the ick."

His brow arched again. "The ick?"

"You'd be surprised how young kids are when they pick up slang. I've learned the floss and heard a kindergartner tell me I'm sus, no cap."

"I have no idea what that last sentence meant."

"The floss is a dance move that I can only do in slow motion before I pull a back muscle. Sus is suspicious. No cap means no lie."

"Was she suspicious of your floss?"

"Basically, yes."

A low chuckle came from him, and his smile would've incinerated my panties right off if it weren't for the heavy topic we'd just discussed.

His grin faded. "Kids were always a thought for the future. And then you proposed the idea. I know I should jump on it, especially if Percival becomes mine." He shrugged. "I don't know a thing about kids."

I held my hands up. "No need to explain. They can be scary. But they can be sweet, and smart, and smelly, but also so witty. Even at eight, they can tell jokes with timing professional comedians would be jealous of. And some of them try so hard to impress you— Anyway. I like my job. I love it. I love teaching in my hometown. I like working at the bar. I get to go home to the ranch and do chores whenever I want. I just have to suck up getting reminded about the touchy clutch in the old front-end loader, and the stubborn gate in the north pasture that has an extra latch, and to take bales from the north end of the stack, as if I hadn't been doing all that since I was a kid too." I shrugged. "It is what it is."

"Which part of the Bailey property did you get?"

"It's gorgeous—on the edge of the forest, and a creek runs through it, but there's also a spring-fed pond, which is why the cattle graze there in the summer. Daddy found a spot that was accessible already and had a good view for each of us. When the sun's setting, it's just gorgeous." I sucked in a breath. His family property would have the same traits. "I shouldn't gush about it. That was callous."

He sidled around the desk until he faced me. "I'd be a coldhearted bastard if I made you quit talking about something you so clearly love."

"I know you're not coldhearted," I said, breathless. He was close. I tipped my head back to look at him.

"How do you know that?" he murmured.

I put my hand on his chest. His heart beat steady under my palm, the rate increasing. "You saved me from humiliation that night." Only a few nights had passed, but it felt like months ago.

"Don't overestimate my good intentions, and I didn't save you." His voice turned hard and displeasure rippled across his face.

"Don't underestimate how much I enjoyed the talking-to you gave the bouncers."

"Don't underestimate how much I like watching you talk about something you're passionate about."

My hand was still on his chest. "And what's that?"

"Your job, your land, your family." He slid his fingers around my neck, and he traced my lower lip with his thumb. "The amber in your eyes gets brighter and outshines all the green. Your cheeks flush, and I start wondering if that's how you look when you come."

Did he just say what I thought—

He dipped his head down and put his lips where his thumb was. The firm press of his mouth increased until his tongue danced at the seam of my lips. I let him in, garlic breath be damned. We'd both eaten the same thing. Probably the only time he and I were on even ground.

He growled and circled his hand behind my neck until he gave my ponytail a gentle tug. As my head dipped back, I opened up to him and he devoured me. Without the awkward angles in the car, we were perfectly lined up. My shorter height only made it possible for him to dominate me. All I knew was his tongue, his heat, his smell, his touch.

He shifted us until my back was to my desk and my ass hit the edge. He didn't stop until I was perched on the edge of the desk. I wrapped my legs around him. The move was automatic, but damn. The impressive bulge that pressed against my center hit all the right spots. My need grew one thousand percent stronger. How had I slept beside this guy and not done anything?

Then he started rocking. If my eyes had been open, they would've rolled back and been lost forever. This guy could make me feel this desperate, this needy, this wanton, and we hadn't removed a stitch of clothing?

The pleasure was already smothering me in the best way until he feathered a hand up my skirt. He stopped to cup my ass through my leggings, pulling me against him until he could rock against my core.

I let out a whimper and he worked his finger farther up. My nipples tingled, remembering everything about how he'd touched me in the car.

Yes.

A jingle of keys and a whistle sounded from outside my door.

I gasped, and Gideon stepped back so fast I teetered

on the edge of the desk. He caught my hand and steadied me until I was back on my feet.

I spun toward the door just as Eleanor, the school's janitor, arrived.

She grinned and gave a big pantomime wave when she saw us. "Mr. and Mrs. *J*, glad I caught you. This must be the mister? I see a little bit of that boy who used to run around here."

Gideon didn't step out from behind me. I could die in a puddle of cringe if I thought of why. But also . . . death by pride. He'd gotten hard for me.

I shook the thought from my head as I smoothed a hand over my ponytail. "Yes, this is Gideon. I was just going to lock up." On a scale of one to ten, I sounded like a six on the guilty scale. Not bad after what Gideon had done to my body.

"No worries," she said. "I saw the light on when I was heading home and thought I'd stop by and put my tools away."

She was territorial over her things. She loaned them out, but she kept an eagle eye on them until they were returned. If it hadn't been for bingo, she would've been directing us.

If it hadn't been for bingo, I wouldn't have seen Gideon out of his suit, working with his hands. If he put on boots and a cowboy hat, my ovaries would combust and the rest of me would turn to ash.

"Yes, we're done." My voice was steadier. "I think Joseph put most everything back in your room."

"Thank you for the use of them," Gideon tacked on.

Eleanor beamed. "Got your hands dirty, then, did ya?"

"Been a while." He was back to wielding his corporate charm. "I appreciate the chance."

"You were always a hands-on kid. I'm not surprised to see you back." She winked. "You two have a good night." She disappeared from the doorway.

"She's lightened up a bit," Gideon said.

I couldn't bring myself to turn around. I'd look at his lips, then his crotch, and I'd probably crawl back on the desk. "She's a gem, but she's only happy like this when she wins at bingo."

His hand touched the small of my back. I jumped. An electric current ran up and down my spine.

"Let's get home," he said.

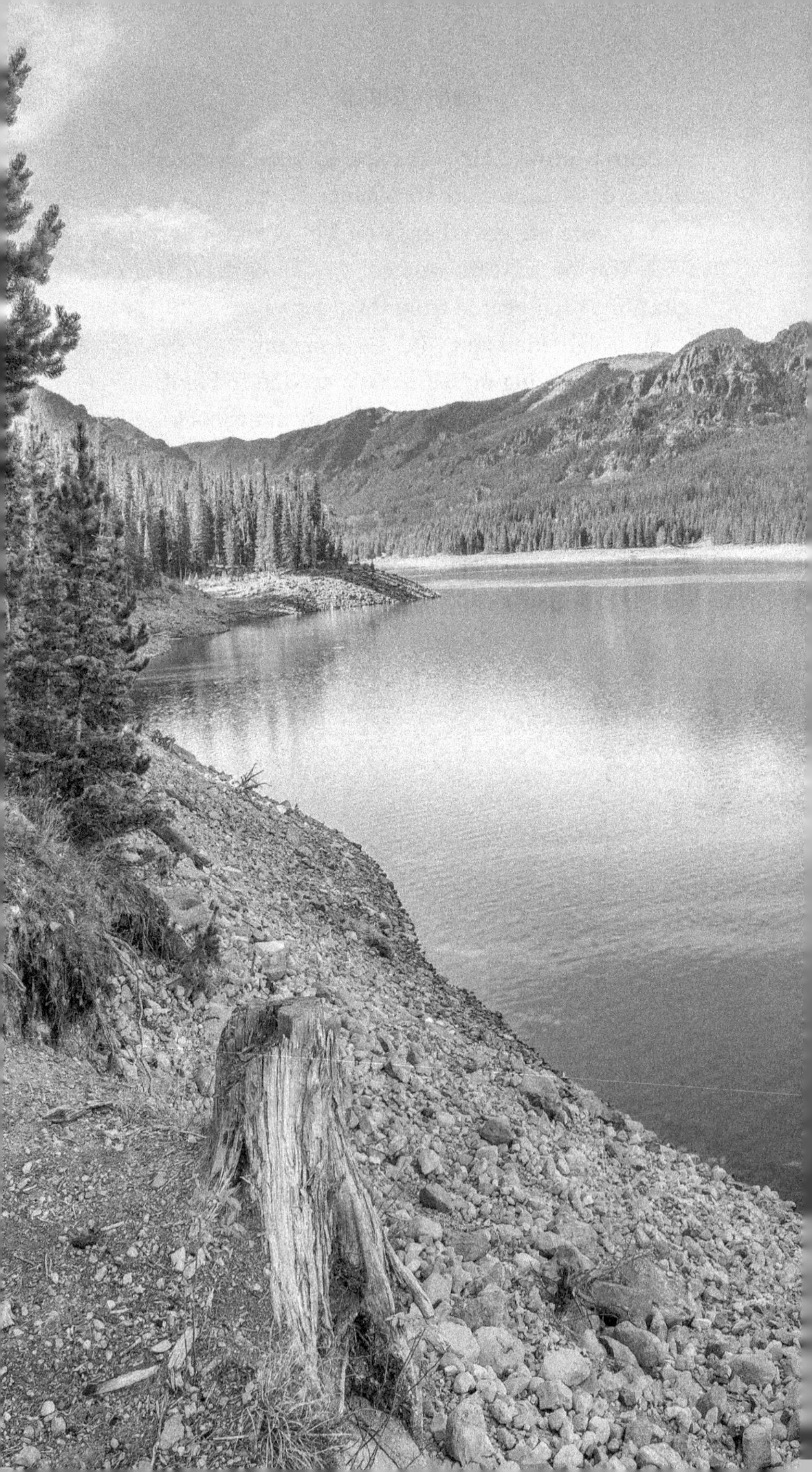

CHAPTER THIRTEEN

Gideon

My erection wasn't going away. I tracked Autumn into the house like a fucking panther. I wanted to get her inside and get my hands on her again.

"And this one time, Eleanor didn't win for over two months at weekly bingo, and me and a few of the other teachers almost gathered a pool of cash to bribe the bar to let her win." She giggled. She hadn't quit talking since we'd left the school. I liked hearing her rattle on, but mostly, I used the lilting cadence of her voice to fuel the desire pumping through my veins.

I kicked the door shut behind me.

She bent to take her boots off. "None of us could figure out how they'd do that. I mean, we'd have to bribe the other players. So then we thought, what if we all go and play and just keep our bingos to ourselves. Would that help?"

She was about to step away from me, but I caught her wrist and spun her toward me.

Her lips were parted when I smashed my mouth to hers. I didn't hesitate to sweep my tongue inside.

Fuck, she was sweet. We'd each taken a mint from the admin office on our way out, but it wouldn't matter if she'd bathed in garlic sauce. I would lick every inch of her up. One thing I knew after that kiss in her classroom—I could not take one more night sleeping next to her without my dick getting itself in trouble.

A needy groan left her. Good, we were on the same page. I lifted her, fucking loving the way she twined her legs around me. This girl didn't hold herself back and I needed her open and willing tonight.

"I'm taking you to the bedroom." I took a step and had to wait until the pressure against my shin let up. Stepping on the cat would kill the mood. "And I'm going to fuck you until my name echoes off the walls."

"I told you the kid thing is off the table."

"It's not about a kid. It's about you and me. Do you want me to fuck you, firecracker?"

"Yes," she moaned as she kissed a path down my neck. Energy knotted itself tighter around my muscles. I was stiff as a board and it wasn't just my cock.

She pulled back, uncertainty in her eyes. "So this is—"

I paused in the hallway. "Just you and me. No deals."

She flicked her tongue out to lick her lower lip. "Might as well, right?"

Did she have to talk herself into it? "Why waste an entire month?" Or I'd fucking explode. Sleeping in her bed, right next to her, for weeks would be sheer torture.

I'd resort to jacking off and lose the control I prided myself on.

Desire lit her eyes and her legs around my hips tightened. "An entire month."

"I'll be inside you every fucking day." I continued to the bedroom. When I crossed the threshold, I aimed straight for the bed—the way she pressed against my erection demanded it, but then I remembered the cat. I kicked the bedroom door shut too.

Crossing to the bed, I laid her down. She dropped her feet from my waist to the covers, but I was cradled in the juncture between her thighs.

I kissed my way down her neck as I tunneled my fingers under her dress to start tugging her leggings down. She gasped and half sat up, knocking her chest against my head. An oomph gusted out of me and I sat back on my knees, blinking.

"Oh my god, I'm sorry." She grabbed my head between her hands and inspected me. "I didn't take any teeth out, did I?"

I never laughed when I had sex, but I chuckled. What an odd feeling—to be so turned on yet find humor in her caring reaction. "No. The only way your tits would make good weapons is if you smothered an attacker."

"I don't know if that's a compliment."

"Trust me. It's a compliment."

Her soft chuckle cut off. She lowered her hands. I almost put them back in place. She reached over to flick on her bedside lamp. Soft light washed over us.

She sucked her lower lip between her teeth, her gaze anguished. "I don't have any condoms."

As blood ever so slowly rerouted to my brain, I understood the issue. She wasn't pushing the baby agenda on me, but she had been ready to have a baby. So, she likely wasn't on birth control.

"I don't have any either," I confessed. How could I have not anticipated needing them?

Because I'd been too obsessed with being inside her. The idea of protection had never occurred to me, baby deal and all.

She eyed me. "You don't have *any*?"

I ran my hands down her—clothed—legs. "I don't walk around the world planning to get into some woman's pants wherever and whenever. I'm deliberate." I was paying for my lack of preparation. Desire built under my skin and only Autumn could sate it. "I can run to a gas station—"

"No." Her eyes grew round as saucers. She gripped me by the shoulders. "We're supposed to be so wildly in love we married right after meeting. Your dad won't buy the family idea if gossip spreads around town that my new husband is buying protection."

From her tone, she was worried the nameless and faceless gossipers would say more, like that I was purchasing condoms to keep from getting my new wife pregnant.

A small glow of disappointment lit in my stomach. She kept her wits about her when I was pawing at her. I was ready to bury myself in her sweet body and she was thinking strategy. She'd been considerate about me and then about my plans.

My ego wasn't usually frayed so easily, but Autumn wasn't swept away by the thought of just being with me.

"I'm sorry." She shook her head. "But no condoms will be bought in Bourbon Canyon."

"No one knows me at the grocery store."

She gave me a doubtful look. "You're right," she said dryly. "No one will notice the incredibly handsome stranger buying Trojan XLs. And absolutely no one, especially not the older employees who've worked for *decades* at the store, will put two and two together when they hear that Gideon James is back in town and married to a Kerrigan."

The way satisfaction rolled over me when she said my full name was all-consuming. I wanted my name on this woman's lips, only I'd rather she was breathy and moaning it. "What, then? We have those Trojan XLs shipped to us?"

Her hands were propped on the bed, but she lifted her shoulders. "I guess."

"I'll run to Bozeman tomorrow."

"I can walk to work."

"No. I'll drop you off." A reminder clicked in my head. "Shit. I have a meeting right away. I can drop you off and then run to Bozeman. Maybe I need to buy that pickup."

Her mouth twitched like she was holding back a smile. And yeah, the idea of planning a condom run around work meetings to run a half-a-billion-dollar casino was absurd.

"Mrs. James, there is nothing funny about our lack of protection."

She pinched her finger and her thumb together. "It's a little funny. You're planning to buy a vehicle so you can buy condoms."

Kissing her told me it'd be worth it. Protection wasn't happening tonight, but I was a resourceful man. I gripped the fabric of her leggings and tugged. "There's plenty we can do in the meantime."

"Oh," she squeaked, going tense. "Um . . ."

I paused. "Do you want this?"

"Oh my god, yes. But can we shut the light off?"

No fucking way.

Yet I wanted her to be comfortable with me. Only minutes ago, she'd twined her body around me like I was a pole and she was a Vegas stripper.

I claimed her mouth again and eased her to her back. "I want to see it all," I said against her lips and skated my hands over her sides and down her torso. "Every last inch."

"I don't think—"

"Good. If you're thinking, I'm doing it wrong." I kissed her again, taking my time plundering her mouth until I earned that little whimper and she went molten in my arms.

Her legs relaxed and her knees fell to the side. Instead of stripping her down and getting to business, I rocked against her, loving how she automatically tipped her hips up to meet me. I wedged an arm between us and drew her knee out, getting her used to being spread out before me. Then, I worked on getting her top over her head.

Her bra was plain and white and trimmed with lace. A simple, perfect wrapping for spectacular tits. I tugged the straps down her arms and freed her globes from the material. Her breasts popped out, her nipples pearled and begging to be sucked.

"Fuck me, those dusty-pink tips make my mouth water." I caught one just as a shudder of self-consciousness was closing her expression. As soon as my lips touched her skin, she arched into me.

"That's it," I murmured and gave each side some

much-needed attention. I kneaded her flesh, licking and sucking her nipples and getting her as pliant as I wanted her.

When a needy "Gideon" left her mouth, I worked my way down. I rolled the leggings off and tossed them to the floor. The damn things had been blocking heaven for far too long. Her underwear had come off with them. I faced a nearly naked Autumn. Her bra straps held her arms in place. Her round tits were peaked with tight buds and her legs were spread. The most erotic image I'd ever seen.

Vulnerability shone in her eyes. I was completely dressed, which was a good thing. If my cock wasn't trapped in place, I'd blow. One brush of the bedding and I'd be coming all over it.

She tried to close her legs, but I put my hands on her thighs. I was staring, but how could I not? "You know what I see when I look at you?"

The rawness in her eyes was back. I didn't like it, but I had to make damn sure she knew what she did to me.

I traced a finger over a long white line on her thigh. Just like her arm, small white pockmarks dotted each side. From staples or stitches? Maybe she'd tell me someday.

I looked her right in the eye. "I see a pussy begging for my tongue."

Her breath hitched.

"I see how fucking wet I make you." I dragged a finger down her seam. She rocked into the touch. "That's it. Let your body tell me what it wants." I reversed direction. She was hot and wet and I knew she'd be fucking tight, but I'd find out soon enough. "I see thighs that I want clamped around my head." I pushed her legs farther apart.

"Gideon," she groaned. But she was no longer tense.

"Everything I see makes me so fucking hard it hurts. Now I need to know how you taste." I wedged my shoulders between her thighs and licked through her small patch of trimmed curls to her clit.

Her hips ratcheted off the bed. I used the moment to tuck my hands under her ass and pull her as close to me as possible. I licked down her seam and back up to her clit. Her moans filled the room. I stroked and sucked, giving her clit even more attention than I gave her nipples. She would get close, her body would get taut and I'd back off. Maybe I was being cruel, but I didn't want this to end. I'd waited all of four days for Autumn and it felt like a goddamn eon.

"Gideon," she panted. The need for release was in her voice. Her heels were digging into my shoulder blades, but I could spend an eternity buried between this woman's legs.

I was being selfish, and for once, I didn't care. I took what I wanted because she was giving it to me.

Finally, when her legs were shaking from the vibrations of her body, I threaded a finger inside. Hot, wet heat squeezed around me. If this was my dick, I'd never make it beyond one thrust.

This time, the groan came from me. "Goddamn, you're fucking tight, just like I thought." And I was back at her clit.

A rush of heat exploded against my face.

"Gideon!"

The bed shook as she came, hard and loud. I continued lapping at her until she came down from her high and sagged against me, too boneless to do anything. I pulled away and kissed a path up her stomach. She twisted her hands in my hair, keeping them there until my hips were nestled back between her legs. My jeans were a barrier, but her heat enveloped me.

"You're going to get your pants dirty," she murmured.

My erection was painful. The seam of my pants was cutting in, but I didn't want to ruin the moment. She had the sleepy, well-fucked look going on and we hadn't officially had sex.

"I don't care." Her breasts were pressing against my chest. My heartbeat hammered in my groin, but I was content. Strangely satisfied with only getting her off.

She started lifting my shirt. "You need—"

"I got what I needed."

Confusion scrawled over her features, but I lightly kissed her mouth. "This isn't quid pro quo. I can wait."

What I couldn't say was that I wanted to hold her. I couldn't verbalize that this had been the most intense sexual experience of my life and my dick was still firmly zipped in place. My world was already disrupted. I needed an anchor right now. I needed to have her in my arms. After getting married, seeing my dad, and tasting Autumn, I needed to feel like I wasn't the only one whose world as they knew it was slowly crumbling around them.

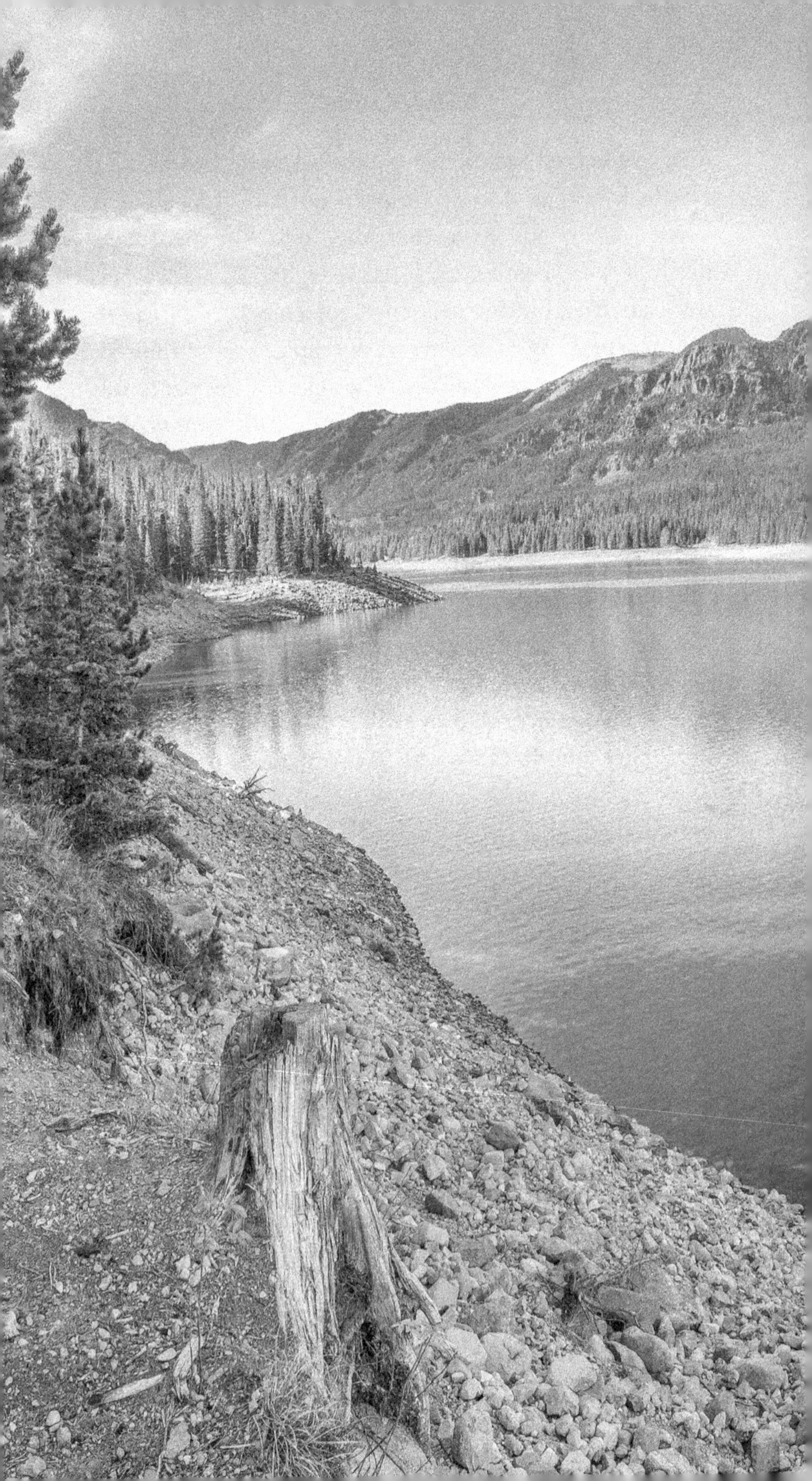

CHAPTER FOURTEEN

Gideon

I was going to run out of time to get the condoms.

Last night, she'd curled up in my arms, and I listened to her even breaths. It'd taken me another hour to fall asleep.

This morning, my pesky erection had been demanding either relief or medical attention, but Autumn had had to get to work. I'd dropped her off at school. She'd shyly given me a kiss before she'd gotten out of the car. And then I'd returned to her dining room table for my meeting. A meeting I'd thought was about approving the renovation schedule and costs had become a not-expected chastisement for interfering with the bouncers at Glitter and subtle prying about why I'd returned home.

If they were so concerned about a family emergency, I wouldn't tell them I was married. I should be flattered they were worried I'd pull up stakes and leave, but at the same time, I was irritated as hell. Getting pestered was what I got for years of diligent service.

The irony chafed. The board worried about my absence when few of them actually lived in Nevada. Or if they lived there, they were at their second or third homes around the world. I blew out a hard breath, wishing I could shut my laptop and make the condom run now that the board meeting was over, but Taya was still on the line.

"Can we switch this to camera mode?" she asked from the other end.

"Is it necessary?"

The silence on the other end told me no. Taya wanted to make this call personal, but I no longer had personal business with her.

"Very well," she said. "Are you ready to tell me what's really going on?"

"I've said all there is to say."

"Gideon." She used the same tone when she cozied up against me in Glitter & Gold. The sultry way she said my name let me know she was thinking of sex.

Every time I thought of sex, I saw Autumn spread out before me, her legs wide and her pussy glistening. I heard her screaming my name and felt her tremble around me.

My erection was returning. "Taya, do you have a handle on the next meeting?"

"I . . . Yes?" My abruptness must've thrown her. "We're reviewing Q3 reports from the marketing team, so—"

"Good. Have Grant write up a summary for me and I'll review it before the weekend. Otherwise, you know how to reach me." I clicked off before she could argue.

I pinched the bridge of my nose. I wasn't acting like my usual self. I'd never cut Taya off when it came to work and I'd never shirked my duties, even if they meant monotonous meetings with data that made my eyes burn.

But I had a family emergency. I had to buy condoms.

I pushed away from the table. Sprinkles pounced, jumping on my lap and curving her tail around my forearm. I paused for a moment and scratched behind her ears. Her purr ignited, and I rubbed her head too. She stood on her hind legs and propped her front paws on my shoulder. I let her sniff my mouth, give me a head bump, and then she jumped down.

She'd done that a few times while I was working. I didn't hate it.

I grabbed the keys and left. It only took five minutes to get to the tractor supply store. In Vegas, I had a personal assistant I called when I needed clothing. I couldn't be bothered to shop. If I had to, this type of store was more my style. Everything I could need under one roof—tools, snacks, and clothing.

No condoms. I checked.

I bought a ball cap, mostly for camouflage. Some of the older workers were not so discreetly gawking at me. Next were more jeans and sweaters. I grabbed a couple of shirts. When I passed by a rack of heavy-duty socks, I selected a few pairs.

An older woman with graying brown hair stopped by. "Oh, we have a basket for you."

I was about to say I didn't need one, but my arms were loaded. "Thanks."

She held the plastic container with handles while I

dumped my pile inside. "You could use a cart. I'll get one for you."

"Oh no, you don't have—"

"The boots are right behind you."

"Excuse me?"

She smiled, her soft-brown eyes twinkling. "You're clothing yourself head to toe. Figured you'd want some boots."

I turned. The aisles of work boots, cowboy boots, and loafers that weren't far removed from slippers were to my left and right. Had this place expanded since I moved?

Boots. Did I need boots?

My phone buzzed. I mentally sighed. Fucking work.

To be sure it wasn't Autumn, I checked who the caller was.

Hank James.

I stared at it as it buzzed in my hand. What did he want?

Anxiety burned in my stomach. The last time he'd called was to tell me he was selling. What shit news would he give me now?

"Hank," I answered.

"Giddy." His greeting was like old times, like when he'd come home after moving cattle all day. I'd been too young to join him, so I'd spent the day closer to the house, helping Mom.

"Don't call me Giddy, Hank."

"I have a long stretch of fence that'd take me two days," he continued like I hadn't said a thing. "Care to join me? Many hands make quick work."

His enthusiasm didn't irritate me like normal, but

that wasn't what I was caught on. "Why are you fixing fence if you're selling?"

"I'm not selling garbage."

"Aren't they going to do more planting than ranching?" The purchase might be going through Bailey Beef, but Dad had said they wanted the property to raise some of their own grains for Copper Summit. There was some acreage that we'd used for growing grains for our own feed. The rest was better for ranching than farming.

"Eh, that's what they said, but this fence is an eyesore."

"They can fix the eyesore if they want to buy it."

"I'm not selling garbage."

He'd been fine with running it down in the first place. Percival Farms was dead because of him.

"It gives an old man something to do," he said simply.

He'd gone from doing nothing to doing nonsense. "What do you think you're going to do when you move into a smaller house? You're not even going to have a lawn."

There was silence on the other end.

I'd get nowhere yelling at him. Maybe the best way to dig into his brain and figure out why he had to sell so bad was to get my hands dirty. "I'll be there in forty-five minutes."

"Hey, that sounds great. I'll get some sloppy joes ready. We can have a bite before we go out."

The other end went dead, and I rolled my eyes to the ceiling. A skylight hovered overhead and crossbeams lined my view. A nest was plastered in one corner. I hadn't heard a bird inside. How old was that nest? The concept took my mind off my infuriating father.

The lady returned with a cart that had a squeaky wheel. "Here's your cart, sir. Can I help you with anything?"

I scratched the back of my neck and considered the aisles. "No, thanks. I'm just going to pick out some boots."

"We have some good winter coats too." She smiled before she wandered away.

Coats? I wouldn't be staying that long.

One month. The sale would be final in the middle of November. I'd need a goddamn winter coat. It wasn't like I was giving up all my plans and moving back.

Autumn

I went outside for my afternoon break. Normally, I'd catch up on some work or grab a quick snack, but I needed space and fresh air. One of the kids had been crop-dusting me all day with his gas and the air freshener was starting to give me a headache.

Summer: I'm going to Copper Summit tonight. You gonna be there?

Wednesdays were slow nights, and I could get the books done. I hadn't planned differently. But I was married now, for the next month at least. Gideon had been home alone all day.

He wasn't a dog. He could care for himself. I hadn't gathered the third-quarter numbers for the guys. If I waited much longer, Tenor would dig into my books, and when he did that, he rearranged things the way he preferred them. He'd never admit he thought his way was better when my process worked just fine.

I chewed on my bottom lip. **Yes, but I'll be later than normal. Gideon's picking me up after work.**

I thought the next message was Summer's reply, but it was Junie. **WHAAAAT?**

This couldn't be the first time she had heard about my marriage. **I texted you.**

My phone started ringing. Summer's message popped through before I answered. **I'll pick you up from work on my way to the bar.**

I wanted to walk out the door and find Gideon waiting for me after school, but I had to answer Junie, or she'd relentlessly send messages. I put the phone to my ear. "Hi."

"What the hell, girl!" She half sang her shout.

I winced at her volume. "It's been five days."

"I know! I've been avoiding my phone and social media."

"Too many kissy-face pictures with your boyfriend?" A site had just reported that Junie had started dating another up-and-coming country star. He was considered a heartthrob if you were into the reformed-player type. The only problem was that, according to the media, he wasn't reformed.

"They always get my bad angles."

Junie had no bad angles.

"So. You're *married*!" she screeched. "I Googled him."

I waited. "And?"

"Tall, dark, and brooding? He looks pissed all the time. I like it."

I laughed. "Well, you're the only one."

"How'd Mama take it? Oh god, tell me everything."

"I'm on break. I only have ten minutes." I checked the time on the phone. "Eight minutes."

"Talk fast."

"I went on a girls' trip, met him at the casino he works at, we got married, and now the guys are pissed at me. So are Summer and Wynter." Mama saw right through the whole thing, but I didn't mention that part. "Mama's chill. You know how she is."

Junie snorted. "That's how I can tell we're not blood-related. Okay. You married sex in a suit. Now what?"

"I . . . don't know." My time was ticking down, but Junie was excited for me. She was thrilled in a different way than my coworkers. I could probably tell her everything, and she wouldn't bat an eye. She'd keep my secret. Summer and Wynter would too, but it was like I'd already lied. Fessing up would somehow make me feel worse. "I wanted to start a family right away, but I don't know if that's going to happen."

"Autumn." I rarely heard Junie so serious. "Having kids is your dream."

"I don't think it's his though."

"Oh. Wow. I mean . . . What are you going to do?"

"We'll talk it out. It's been less than a week." We'd already talked it out. A month wouldn't be enough to keep him from turning pale whenever babies were mentioned. I couldn't keep telling half-truths. The guilt would gnaw right through my stomach. "I really hate to cut you off, but I have to go back in."

"Autumn."

"Yeah?"

"You sure you're okay?"

After last night, my body was singing, and I was half terrified that he might consume me again. He'd only used his tongue and a finger. When he got his whole body involved, I might not survive. But also, no. I wasn't okay. I had a husband I didn't really know. I had a sham marriage that I wanted to be real. And I had a family that didn't buy that a guy like Gideon would hopelessly fall for me. All I had were my fantasies.

Junie was probably sold on it the most because she wasn't around to see the odd couple Gideon and I made. The casino CEO and the schoolteacher.

I turned the question around on her. "Are you okay?"

"Hmmm. How about we both tell each other we're fine and keep lying to ourselves?"

My sister wasn't one to admit when she was struggling. That she'd said this? "Junie."

"I'm fine. Glor-i-ous! *Mm-wha*." She made a kissing noise. "Keep me posted on the baby drama."

I'd get no more out of her. She could close down harder than my brothers. "Love ya, June."

"I love you so much I'll write you into a song."

"You write heartbreak songs."

She was laughing when I hung up. I considered Summer's message again. She probably wanted to get me alone, and after the turmoil of the last several days, I could use some sister time. I called Gideon. This was the first time I'd ever called or messaged him. We'd been married for five days, and this was a first.

"Gideon." He sounded out of breath and a rush of wind came over the line.

"Hi." Where was he? I didn't have much of a yard, but maybe he was enjoying the weather on my lawn. "I have to do books at Copper Summit before I bartend, and Summer said she could pick me up on her way there. Do you mind?"

"No." A grunt sounded, but it wasn't his. "Hank, I said I got it."

"You ain't done this in a bit, Giddy." His dad's voice filtered through the line.

"Don't call me Giddy, Hank." His response was more automatic than hostile, like the last time they'd had the same interaction.

I had to get back inside, but I couldn't cut the conversation short yet. "You're with your dad?"

"Fixing fence. Can I pick you up at Copper Summit when we're done?"

Did I want to see a dirty, sweaty Gideon? "Of course. I'd better get back in, but hey, have fun."

"It's a blast," he said grimly before he hung up.

I typed Summer a quick **Sure** and then rushed inside. I'd get some sister time and then see my husband. I just hoped the month I got with Gideon wouldn't be cut short over some fence.

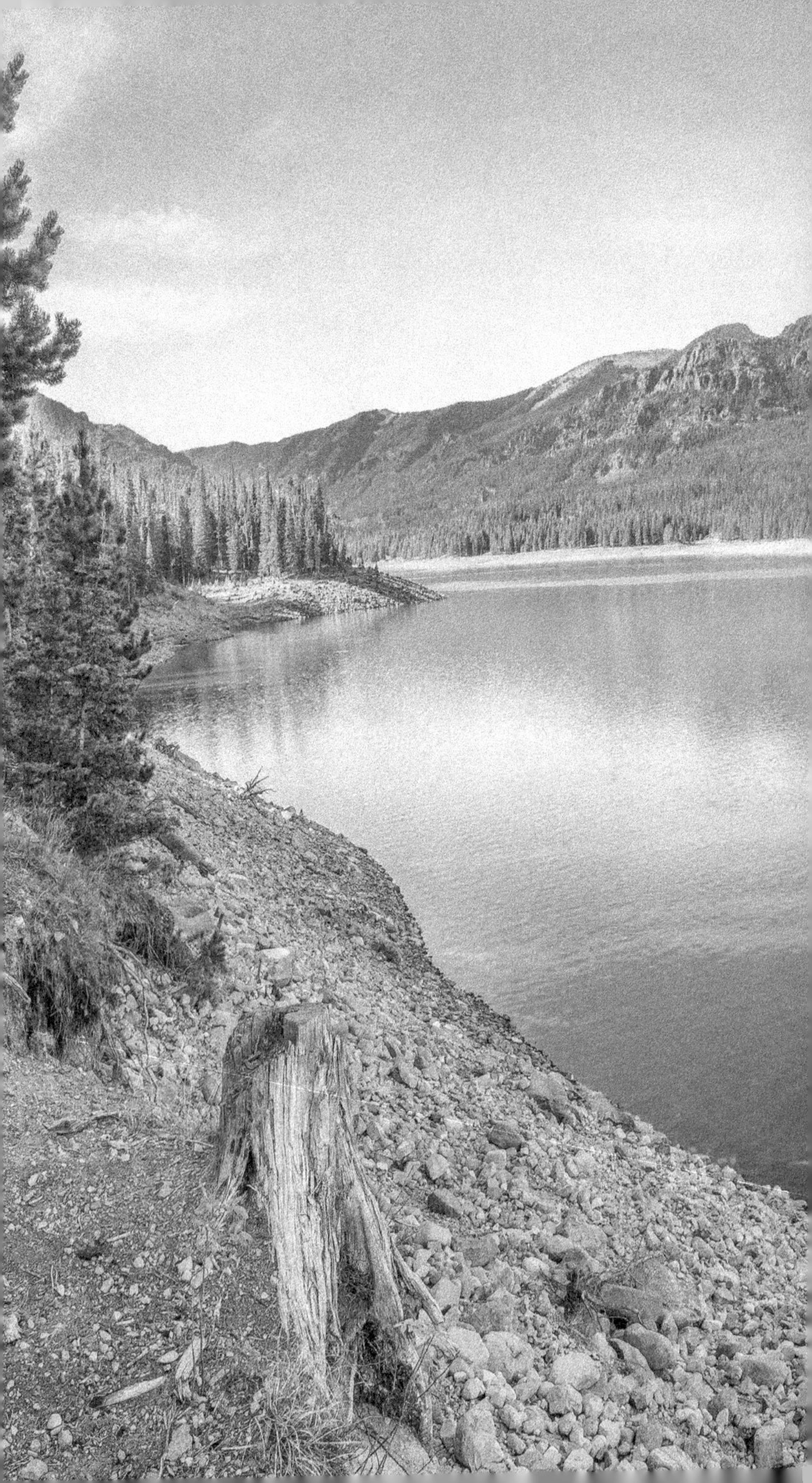

CHAPTER FIFTEEN

Gideon

It'd be a beautiful fucking day if I weren't so annoyed. Only a few fluffy white clouds littered the sky. The light wind blowing over the rolling brown hills kept me from getting too hot, but it was too cool to strip down to my recently purchased shirt. I kept the new army-green hoodie on. I'd already gotten a hole at the bottom from some rogue wire.

I was fighting heartburn from the sloppy joes and cherry Kool-Aid Dad had packed. My taste buds had been delighted with the nostalgia, but my gut had gone into panic mode.

"It's fence," I said through gritted teeth. We'd been at this for hours. "The method of fixing couldn't have changed in twenty-five years."

Sweat trickled between my shoulder blades. My new ball cap was already dirty. So was the rest of me. We were working on a two-hundred-yard stretch of metal fence posts that hadn't been touched since I'd probably been the last one to stretch wire. But no, Dad wanted new posts swapped out.

I shouldn't complain. He'd at least bought more metal posts and hadn't decided to upgrade to thick wooden posts to impress the Baileys. I still didn't understand why the hell we were doing this anyway. Dad could sign the papers and leave everything as is.

"I'm not sayin' the method's changed." To give Dad credit, he looked heartier than he had all day. The cool temperature pinkened his cheeks, his hat shaded his eyes, and the wrinkles that had formed since I'd left town gave him a rugged air instead of a tired one.

I ignored the stark relief in my chest that he was looking better each time I saw him.

He shrugged. "I'm just saying that we don't have to rush."

I took off my cap, pushed a hand through my hair, and stuffed the cap back on. "They could erect another casino in the time it's gonna take us to finish this stretch."

"I'm sure they'll hire you to run that one too."

I couldn't decipher his tone. Snarky? Disappointed? Crestfallen? "It's not like I'll be rebooting *my* farm if you finish the sale."

"You sound a lot like your grandfather right now."

"Is that a bad thing?"

He straightened. His expression was the most serious I'd seen it since I'd gotten home. "It is if you're spewing his poison."

"He was dedicated to this place. And to Mom."

"Is that how you remember it?" He peered at me, intent on my answer.

"I remember he was around when you weren't." He hadn't been able to help physically, but he'd imparted his wisdom to me.

Sadness filled his gaze. "At least he tried to build you up instead of tearing you down. Not that I agree with how or why he did it."

"What's that supposed to mean?"

He shoved his hands into the pockets of his tan Carhartt jacket. "What is it you plan to do? Quit your big-city job and come back to farm and ranch? Autumn can get a job anywhere, but there are no casinos in Bourbon Canyon."

Irritation heated the back of my neck. "I know that."

"Then Autumn's moving? Mae's going to be sad to see her go."

I stomped to the bed of the pickup. He had a different vehicle than when I'd moved, but this one wasn't much newer. Which piece of farm equipment had he sold to buy it?

I grabbed a new post. Only a shitload more to put up. "We haven't decided yet."

"I heard it's a mighty nice patch of land that Darin left her."

I hadn't seen it yet. "Yeah, it's nice."

"Gideon, what are you doing?"

I knew what he was asking. He was thrilled about Autumn and that I was home, but the alcohol hadn't burned away all his brain cells. "Trying to save a family legacy."

"But you no longer have yourself to think of. You're partners. She has her own family. Her own hopes and dreams. You can't railroad them because your grandfather tied your worth to some dirt."

Some dirt? This was home. This should be *my* home. "The sale would've broken Mom's heart."

Those wrinkles of his carved deeper with his frown. "Giddy, I did the best I could."

"Don't call me Giddy, and you didn't do a thing. Did you even care for the animals after I left?"

His brows crashed together. "Of course I did."

"So the dog died from old age? Same with the chickens?"

"The dog got cancer and I gave the chickens away. What did you think happened?" Realization dawned on his face.

Aw, hell. I hadn't expected to feel so fucking guilty today. I was the one missing work to fix fence for no damn reason.

"Look," he said, deflated, "I didn't say my best was a lot. I'm not making excuses, son. I failed you. I failed this place. But I'm trying to do right."

"By selling?"

He let out a long sigh. "Your mom didn't have life insurance. I couldn't run a farm and ranch. I've sold things off over the years to support myself. It's time for retirement, and I've got nothing."

The chafing around my neck intensified. The empty shop and cleared-out barns weren't all from fueling his alcoholism. But his alcoholism was why he'd had to start selling off useful items to start with. "You've been living off what you sold?"

Shame filled his eyes, and he nodded.

"You can sell to me."

His jaw went tight. "I don't go back on my word."

"Hank, I'm family. You can change your mind for family."

He peered at me. "Can you?"

What'd he mean? "Grandpa instilled a strong sense of honor in me."

Dad's parents had been more interested in going south for the winter than visiting their only grandchild. Mom's parents had been all about passing on lessons of family and fortune.

"I was afraid of that." Before I could ask what he meant, he checked his beat-up black watch. "I've gotta head into town."

Dad and my grandfather had never gotten along. There was no point in bickering about a dead man.

I looked down the long stretch we had yet to get to. This fence was another kick of irony. My grandfather would approve of how much nicer it looked. Why was Dad leaving before we were done? What had happened to working until the sunlight was gone?

"Can you come back out tomorrow?" Hope filled his eyes.

The burn of guilt was back. He wanted to spend time with me. "I don't know. I'm a little behind at my own job after today." The words tasted sour as I said them.

"Well, I guess I'll be out here no matter what." He stooped to pick up the wire spreader.

I sighed. "What time?" I put the posthole digger in the bed of the pickup.

"Eh, midmorning?"

"What happened to 'when the sun's up, we're up'?"

"I can be out here at dawn, but I doubt either of us want that."

I thought of how the grass would glisten with dew. This time of year, frost would make the strands sparkle. A quiet I hadn't heard the entire time I'd lived in Las

Vegas would drape over the countryside, and it'd be peaceful. Just like now. Only the breeze and the birds filled in the silence when we weren't talking.

I missed that. "Midmorning, then," I said gruffly.

The smile that graced his face was like a hot pack on my conscience. He liked being with me.

Yet he wouldn't sell Percival Farms to me.

Autumn

I tapped through spreadsheets, compiling data for the last month and the previous quarter. The bar in Copper Summit only had three customers, and they were having a drink by the windows that made up one wall. Wednesdays were typically quiet nights, which was why I preferred to work them. I could get some extra tasks done.

Summer and I hadn't talked much beyond idle pleasantries on the drive here. She had gone up to the office Teller had readied for her. She was still the manager of the Bozeman site, but she worked remotely. When she had to travel for work, Jonah and their dog went with her.

A large shadow loomed over me. As big and quiet as it was, it had to be Tenor. I saved the cash flow report. "What's up?"

"Got a minute?"

"I was just getting ready to send you last quarter's reports."

He had a tablet under his arm. He pushed his glasses

up. "About those, I was talking to Tate about how to boost bar sales during our slow months—"

"Why Tate?"

He cocked his head. "Why not Tate?" he asked carefully.

"I run the bar, Tenor."

He nodded, but the corners of his jaw flexed. Tenor was mellow, but he hated explaining himself. "I don't see you as often as him. We like to talk about the ranch and distillery."

And make decisions about them between themselves.

"We don't want to bother you when you're working," he added.

"It's literally my job."

"You have a forty-plus-hour-a-week job that takes precedence over this place."

"I've juggled both for years."

He lifted a heavy shoulder. "Exactly. Anyway, when you and Wynter come up with holiday specials, we think you should aim for three to four new cocktails, with a few that can make an annual return."

It wasn't a terrible idea, but with Wynter being a new mom, her time would be more limited. "I'll talk it over with her."

"Teller thought December would be a good time to start."

Which meant that was what Wynter and I would do. "Three to four Christmas specials, coming right up."

He narrowed his eyes at the bite in my tone. "Okay. I'll, uh, let you be." He started to circle around the bar and head for the entry into the main part of the distillery.

"Sure. Just let me know what else you and Tate decide about the bar."

He paused and glanced over his shoulder. I got a small nod from him and then he was gone.

I'd been a little catty, but seriously. Tenor never stopped in to chat about his ideas. Just to order me to complete them.

I punched through the rest of the reports. Summer breezed in, rubbing her hands together and adjusting the neckline of her cowl-neck cream sweater. The offices upstairs could get cold with the old windows.

"So. You ready to talk about what happened the other night?" she asked.

I'd almost forgotten about the way we'd left the party and how unwilling Gideon was to talk about it. Last night had kept my thoughts occupied since I'd woken this morning. Teaching multiplication tables when I'd rather dwell on the possessive sounds he'd made was hell on my concentration.

"He's still adjusting to talking to his dad again." I wasn't going to tell my sister I didn't know. I had no idea why Gideon had pulled us out of the shop with no warning, and he had made it clear he wouldn't tell me about it.

I could get angry. Or I could enjoy waking up in his arms while he was in my bed. Option two, please.

She leaned on the bar and put her chin in her hand. "Are you ever going to tell me what's really going on?"

I sighed. My sisters and I were close. We weren't secretive—until we were. For years, Summer hadn't told us she'd broken up with her high school boyfriend right before he'd gotten drunk, crashed his pickup, and died. Only recently had she opened up to anyone about it, starting with Jonah, her ex's brother and now her husband.

Before that, Wynter had gone to Colorado to low-key stalk her husband. He'd been a foster kid at our house when we were little. She'd only told us she was in Colorado for work, not why.

Who knew what Junie was keeping to herself. She was all up in our business when she had time, but when it came to sharing what was going on in her life, she wasn't specific.

I could throw all that back in Summer's face like I had when she'd confronted me with the others. Yet I couldn't deny I needed to talk to someone. My husband was giving me all sorts of feels. He was standoffish but unexpectedly thoughtful. He blew my mind in bed but asked for nothing for himself. And now he was helping his dad, but he hadn't sounded thrilled about it. Yet he'd skipped a day of catching up on a demanding job to do it. I didn't buy that it was only to get into his dad's good graces to influence the sale.

I made my decision. "If you tell any of our brothers, I'm going to fly to the other end of the world and live there forever."

Her light brows notched up. She hated flying. My threat was a personal blow, but I meant it. Our brothers would drive Gideon out of town if they knew why he'd married me. It wouldn't matter that I had wanted something out of the deal.

Something I wasn't going to get.

I punched the button to shut off my tablet screen. Inventory would have to wait for the weekend.

I glanced at the guys by the window. They weren't paying attention to us, and their glasses were still full. "We made an agreement," I said quietly. "We agree to marry and look happy so his dad will change his mind and think we're having lots of little James babies to pass the land down to."

She was quiet for several heartbeats, her keen brown gaze scrutinizing me. "What do you get out of it?"

I appreciated that she didn't assume I was so smitten with the man I'd do anything, that being on his arm was enough.

Even if that was the case.

"Uh . . . I wanted a baby."

Her strangled gasp grabbed the attention of the customers. She turned her back to them and crossed her arms. "Autumn," she hissed. "What the hell—" She shook her head. "Never mind; that makes a lot of sense, really."

Should I be insulted? "Yeah, well, it's off the table." She kept quiet, waiting for me to answer. The truth piled on the end of my tongue. "One, we haven't done it yet."

Sympathy welled in her eyes and my nape prickled.

"I was drinking the first night, and he didn't want to take advantage. Then he realized how nervous I was and said we had time for me to get used to him. It didn't take long for me to notice how weird he gets about the idea of a kid."

"I imagine. He's not planning to move here for this charade, is he? The sale will either go through or be done in the middle of November. He'd be faced with abandoning a kid."

"No, he's not staying." A little fissure in my heart opened. This was the risk of enjoying the dream. "The divorce papers are ready to go when he is."

"Autumn," she said flatly.

"Whatever. I don't want to make babies with a guy who isn't sure he wants them. I don't mind helping him stop the sale." At her censuring look, I rolled my eyes. "Yes, okay? I like having him around. Can you blame me? Waking up to that every morning? It hasn't been a hardship."

Her lips quirked. "It is nice to open your eyes to someone you want to climb on top of with every heartbeat."

"Almost TMI." Though her feelings for Jonah were no secret. "He helped put the set together for the music program tomorrow night. And he's fencing with his dad today."

"I'm sure I don't have to tell you this." Her tone said I'd hear it anyway. "But he's been gone since he graduated. He doesn't know his dad sober. You and I don't know his dad drunk. Hank James is just a pleasant guy we see around town."

He'd always say, "How are the Bailey girls today?" when he passed us on the street, and he'd always end chatter with, "Tell your folks hi from me, will ya?"

"Gideon's going through some things emotionally, and he doesn't strike me as a guy who's usually in touch with his emotions."

I ground my teeth together. I couldn't argue.

"I'm worried, Autumn. I can see you really like him, and the way he looks at you and how he defended you the other night is the only reason our brothers haven't dumped him in some ravine."

"I'd like to see them try."

"It'd be a show for sure." She sighed. "You're getting attached, getting your hopes up that this marriage will be real, and he's not looking beyond whether his dad will sign the papers."

"I'm not getting my hopes up. Divorce papers, ready to go, remember?" I couldn't forget. Because of those, I wasn't thinking about what it would be like to wake up, smile at him, maybe have a morning orgasm, and then sit at the table over our orange juice and eggs and talk about the upcoming day.

I wasn't thinking about what it would be like if he hung up his clothes in my closet. Sure, we couldn't make room for much, but there could be space. I wasn't thinking about upgrading to a place with more bedrooms and a bigger garage. That pickup he mentioned buying would be parked by mine. Would he understand that I didn't want to build on my land? Would he be bitter if he couldn't live where he was raised?

"I can see the hearts in your eyes," Summer said. She gave my shoulder a squeeze. "Just keep talking to me at least, okay? You and Scarlett were there for me when I thought Jonah and I were done. And Wynter's not a stressed-out new mom anymore. We're all here for you."

"No, I can't tell Scarlett. I can't expect her to keep something like this from Tate."

"Talk to Wynter. She needs some juicy drama to fuel her marketing inspiration."

Wynter was head of marketing for Copper Summit, and now that she was back to work full-time, she was supercharged with ideas.

We already had a virgin drink in the bar called Fool's Gold. I could just imagine what Wynter would come up with. *My sister's marriage is fake, but our bourbon is not.* Or would she name a new line Summit's Impulsive Blend? A Vegas Wedding Special Barrel? Copper Summit Split?

A few more people walked in. Two of them were parents of a student I'd had a couple of years ago and then another guy I'd gone to high school with.

They sat at a table on the opposite side of the room from the guys by the window. After I finished taking their order and preparing their drinks, a few more people walked in. We usually got a Wednesday night after-church rush before closing.

Summer tapped me on the shoulder. "You sure you're okay if I take off?"

"I'm fine. Gideon will be here soon."

She didn't look confident. "Okay, but I'll have my phone on me. Call if you need a ride."

"He'll be here."

"He is here." A deep voice broke in.

I turned and blinked. A guy with a dusty navy-blue ball cap stood behind me. An olive-green hoodie clung to his broad shoulders, matching the piercing green eyes. "Gideon?"

"You expected someone else?"

Summer's stare bored into me. Yes, I was gawking at the man I'd married.

"God help me if you have boots on." My mouth was dry, and my pulse was speeding up. My body knew exactly how this man could make me feel, but seeing him all countryfied was giving me palpitations.

He frowned at his footwear. "They're new, but they don't look like it after today."

I leaned over the counter. He was wearing black square-toed cowboy boots, also as gritty as the rest of him. I groaned. "It's even better than I imagined."

Summer choked behind me.

Gideon leaned forward and gave me a peck on the lips. My eyelids fluttered shut like it was my first kiss ever. The pressure of more eyes on me poked into my skin. Was this for show? Or did he want to kiss me in public for more reasons than to cement the idea we were a real couple?

"I'm dirty and irritated," he murmured against my lips. The brim of the hat shaded his eyes. "This is what gets you?"

My heart thumped a steady beat against my ribs. The guy was fire in a suit. So damn good-looking. But all scruffed up, with his five o'clock shadow showing through the sun- and wind-burnished skin? Be still my raging hormones.

"It makes you look less like you want to punch everyone," Summer said. "Except now, you look like you want to punch them and then run them over with your tractor."

"Accurate," he replied. "Present company excluded," he finished, tipping his hat.

Aw, he wanted Summer to know he wasn't insulting her.

"Don't be so sure. I'll be a pain in your ass if I think you need it." She knocked on the counter. "I'll get going, then. Call me if you need anything."

I said goodbye to her, and when I looked back at Gideon, he was watching me with those hooded, intense eyes.

There went my butterflies. "Okay, I'm irritated about my brothers keeping me out of their brainstorming for the bar. Why are you irritated?"

His eyes narrowed. "You need to tell your brothers to

knock it off."

"I do."

"Use the same authority you handled me and Deon with. Pretend your brothers are just third graders who don't listen well."

If I did, I might start giggling, but also . . . I talked to my brothers like a younger sister. Maybe I needed to bring more of my teacher persona along for the conversation. "You have a point. Enough about me. Why are you upset?"

The glower returned. "Hank's work ethic has changed to whatever, whenever. He's fixing fence that doesn't need to be repaired. It does, but not by him. And he stopped right in the middle, claiming he had to head to town."

"Just like that?"

"He didn't tell me his business, nor did he tell me why he won't sell to me, other than he lumps me in with some city slicker who'll hire out a ranch manager."

"At least you're a local boy."

He slid onto a stool. "Meaning the town won't like it if I hire out a ranch manager?"

I put a large ice cube in a squat glass and dug out my special bottle of bourbon. Autumn's Summit.

His gaze landed on the bottle. A dry chuckle escaped him. "It never dawned on me before. There's one for each of you."

"I thought you banned it from Silver's premises."

He took a sip, his jaw moving as he rolled the fluid over his tongue. His throat worked with his swallow. "I make it my business to know my competition." He studied the fluid in the glass.

I laughed. "You didn't know I was staying at the Silver last weekend."

His burning gaze flipped up to mine and held me immobile.

"You knew?"

"I wanted to be notified if a Bailey ever came into the casino. I'd be remiss if I left the Kerrigan sisters out."

"You were watching me?" I picked up a rag and swiped at the bar. The butterflies went dead silent. Mortification did that to them. "Our meeting wasn't a coincidence?"

"I wouldn't say that. Like I said at your mom's, I was heading to Glitter anyway. Running into you in the elevator was still mildly surprising."

"Huh." I should be creeped out. Scandalized. But the sense that we'd been entangled since before we'd met was calming. It gave me hope I shouldn't have. This was exactly why Summer was worried.

"I have some bad news."

I stopped wiping the counter. "What?"

"I didn't have time to get to Bozeman. The good news is that the next drink on my tongue will be you."

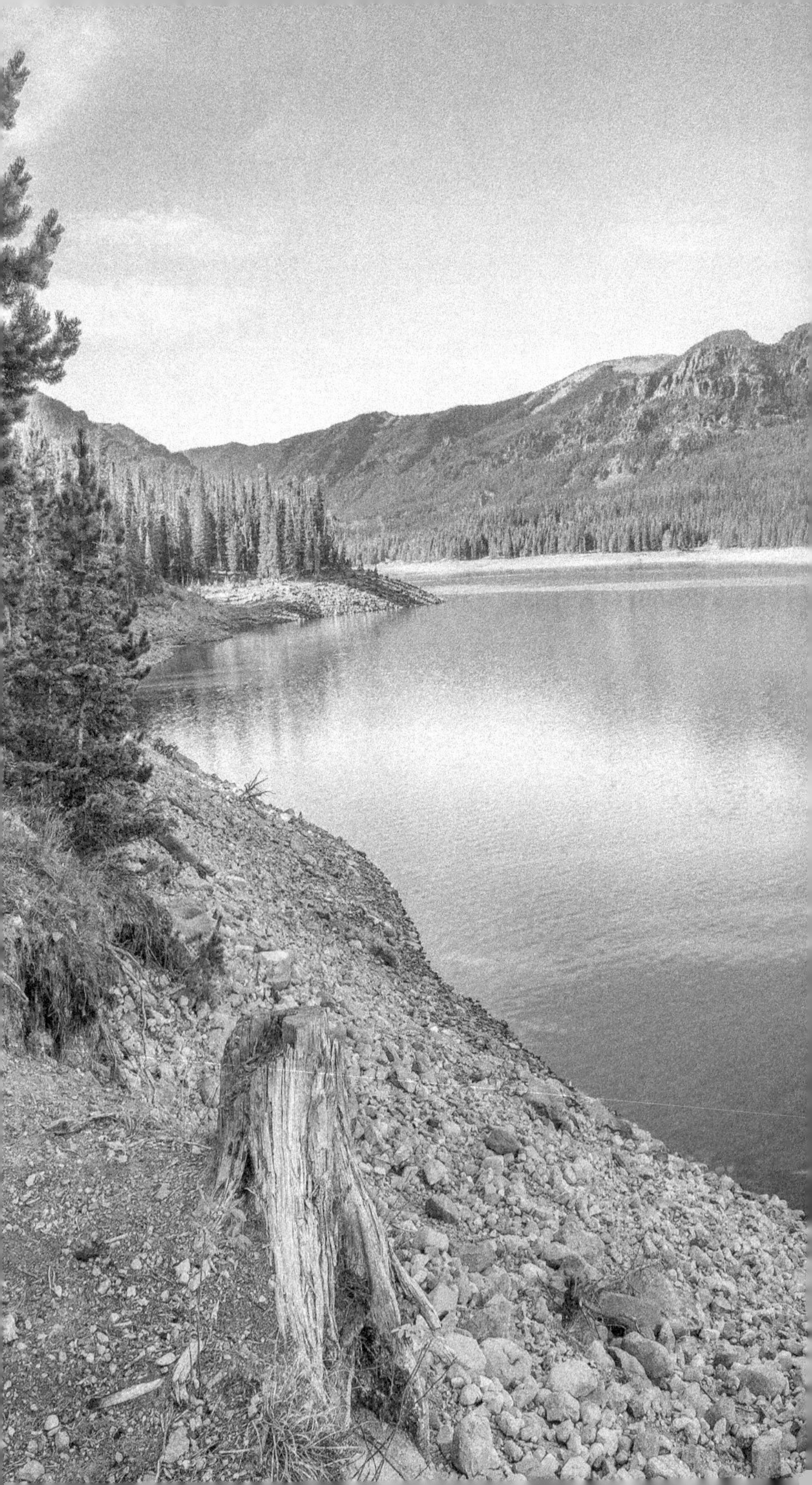

CHAPTER SIXTEEN

Gideon

I swiped sweat from my brow and put my ball cap back on my head. Today was cloudier and cooler than yesterday. I might need to break out that new coat if I kept coming out to help Dad. "I've gotta get going."

"Gotta date with the wife?" Dad picked up his small tool bag and went to the pickup. We had finished, but he'd mentioned going all the way to the tree line to make it uniform. He'd also said that he wanted to go through the old stables that had been used by my grandparents when they boarded horses. He thought some of the gates could use new hinges and a few boards needed replacing.

"It's a valid reason for stopping." I was baiting him, and he gave me that infuriating, aloof smile. I was too stubborn to ask outright why he'd cut yesterday short. "Autumn's class program is tonight. I helped her and the other teachers make the set."

I was just shy of boasting like I was a little boy who wanted his dad's approval. But also, I was proud of that damn set, and I wanted to see it in action. The physical work was different than the paperwork I normally did. Silver ran on my authority, but I hadn't put one screw in place. I hadn't even hung the pictures in my penthouse. I hadn't even picked them out.

"That'll be fun. I always enjoyed watching you squirm up there."

"I didn't squirm."

"Please," he scoffed. "You hated the spotlight."

I still did. I'd grown up with people watching me, and it had never been for a good reason after Mom was gone. "You got everything taken care of?"

"Go ahead." He waved me off. "Tell Autumn I said hi."

We'd driven separately, so I hopped into Autumn's car and took off, bumping down the path to the road.

After I reached her house, I ran through the shower. I almost chose slacks and a polo, but I paused. This was a Bourbon Canyon Elementary School program. I picked jeans and one of the nonhoodie sweaters I'd purchased at the tractor supply store.

Before I left, I stopped at her fridge and frowned at the contents. We needed groceries.

We.

I closed the door. I should've taken care of the food situation this morning.

I checked the time. I had to go. Autumn had said there was plenty of seating, but I planned to sneak in and sit in the back.

When I arrived at the school, I parked and thought of what Dad had said. I hated the spotlight. But as I got out and walked toward the front double doors of the school with the other parents, more memories assaulted me.

I was growing used to it in the four days since I'd been in town. I remembered Mom and Dad dropping me off at the front. I'd run in and they'd park. When it was time to sing, I'd look for them in the crowd. Mom would always give me a little wave and Dad would have that twinkle in his eyes and a secret smile playing on his lips. I could never tell if he was laughing at me or if he was proud.

I remember the answer being important, but I'd never asked.

In the gymnasium, a ton of plastic folding chairs were positioned in rows, an empty aisle running down the middle. They were already filling in.

I put my head down, wishing I'd put on my new, clean ball cap. I could use the shade of the brim. People glanced at me, then murmured to each other as I made my way to the far back corner of the gym.

Autumn was nowhere to be seen.

A man with a sweater over a collared shirt was talking with parents and grandparents. I tried to scoot by, but he cut me off. "Good evening. Thanks for coming."

"Evening." I tried to take another step.

"I'm sorry, I thought I was getting to know everyone's family. Which student is yours?"

While I was glad the school watched over the kids, I didn't like being stopped or questioned. "I'm here for a teacher."

Realization dawned and his professional politeness died. "Are you Autumn's husband?"

This must be Mark. He was maybe in his midthirties, dressed in the slacks I had bypassed, but overall, he was a decent-looking guy. I could see why Autumn would date him.

I disliked this man. "Mrs. James? Yes."

Annoyance flickered in his gaze. He didn't care for how I'd phrased my answer. Good. "Right, Mrs. James. Congrats on that. The name change is taking us all some getting used to. Welcome." His smile was forced.

I nodded, squeezed his hand harder than I should've, and left him behind, grateful I'd made time for the performance if Mark was lurking around.

People filed in. An older couple I'd guess were grandparents took the chairs next to me.

"Our grandson is so nervous for this." The woman beamed at me. The apples of her cheeks glowed under the fluorescent lights. "Do you have one performing?"

A beat of longing tugged at my heart. No. I had no one. I was forty-four and had no performances to go to. "No. My wife's the teacher."

She blinked at me. "What teacher?"

"Autumn." Her expression remained blank. "Autumn Kerrigan, now James."

The man looked over from the other side of his wife, squinting his pale-blue eyes my way. "You the James boy?"

I hadn't been the James boy for a long time. "I am."

"Oh!" The woman brightened. "It's been forever since I've seen Hank around. How is he?"

Stubborn. Frustrating. Happy, and I didn't know why. Content, which irritated the hell out of me. "He's well."

She patted my arm. "Good, good. I like hearing that. He's been through so much."

I ground my teeth together. *He'd* been through a lot? And he had these people's sympathy?

"Congratulations on the wedding," she gushed. "Autumn is such a nice young girl."

"She is." When it came to her, I didn't feel like I was talking about a stranger.

The kids started filing onto the risers. I got one last smile from the woman who grated on my nerves for having the gall to care about my dad, then we both focused on the performance.

Autumn and Kerry helped the kids get into position, scooting from side to side until the kids were in single file on each of the three levels.

When the kids were situated, she went to a stand-up microphone. She had her hands clasped in front of her, and her smile was wide and genuine. "Welcome, everyone." Her smooth voice carried through the room. Everyone settled, including the kids. "This year's third-grade class has been working so hard on this performance for you. I'm super proud of their efforts, and I know you're going to love it. Now, without further ado . . . enjoy the show!"

She stepped to the side. The lights were dimmed, and Kerry hit a button on a stereo system. Haunting music poured out of the speakers.

The singing was light at first, hesitant. Their voices grew stronger. Kids searched the audience for their parents like I once had. Between songs, a few of the kids did a little skit that included the bats attached to the backdrop. They rushed back to join in the next song.

"Aren't they cute?" the woman next to me whispered.

I nodded, surprised I agreed with her. Their effort

and enthusiasm wove through the program. Tonight, I was around more kids than I had been in my entire adult life. I never noticed children, and the thought of them didn't factor into my plans or ideas for the casino. We catered to the over-twenty-one crowd.

Autumn's life was so much different than mine. We'd grown up very similarly, both had experienced tragedy, but she'd surrounded herself with youth and excitement and unbridled energy.

I was surrounded by concrete and steel and people looking for an extreme escape. There was no learning going on in Silver. No thoughts of the future, only the present and the pleasure that could be had.

When I looked back on my career, I had spreadsheets to show for it. Reports. A casino with its doors still open—no small feat. But when she looked back, she'd see hundreds of kids she'd influenced. Kids like me who'd grown up and attained powerful positions.

I didn't even mentor up-and-coming corporate wannabes. I left that to another team. I wanted to do my job and build my own empire so I could secure my family's fortune, so to speak. But in the end, I had nothing of my own. Autumn had individually touched so many people's lives.

I swallowed hard as the last string of music blared through the speakers.

My wife was pretty goddamn amazing.

I looked forward to tonight as much as last night. I'd get her home nice and early. Her back would be on the mattress and my face would be between her legs for the third day in a row.

My phone buzzed.

Son of a—

As the students filed off the stage, I peeked at my screen. Hank.

What the hell?

I silenced it. He was probably going to ask me to help him with the bullshit projects in the stable.

A moment later, my phone started buzzing again. I stared at the thing. He never called more than once in a row.

Parents were filing out. The woman who'd chatted with me gave me a goodbye wave once she saw me with my phone. I nodded at her and her husband.

Damn. What if something was wrong? I answered. "What's going on?" The irritation came out like it usually did when I dealt with him.

"Giddy, I'm sorry to bother you."

"Don't call me Giddy." A small jump of alarm crawled around my throat. He sounded frantic. "Something wrong?"

"My truck died, and I have a meeting. Can you give me a ride?"

Not even I had meetings at eight at night.

Something tickled the back of my mind, a factoid I should grasp that might be important, but irritation smothered it. "Shouldn't we be concerned with towing your pickup to a shop?"

"I'm going to miss it entirely. Is the program done?"

"Yes."

"I'm a quarter mile from the highway."

"I'm still at the school. I haven't even talked to Autumn yet." She was laughing with a group of parents and little kids. Mark hovered nearby with his own group.

She glanced at me. I lifted my chin, and she gave me a little wave. A little girl blatantly stared at me with big eyes. I gave her a wave too. The way Autumn smiled in response lit up the gymnasium more than any of the lights could.

"Do you think you can get me in the next fifteen minutes? I'm usually really early, but someone else will have to set up. This way, I'll only miss a few minutes at the beginning."

I did quick calculations. Picking him up, bringing him to town, going back for the pickup and towing it after dark—it'd be a late night. Autumn would have to work in the morning. I wouldn't be able to keep her up.

It'd be best to drop her off at home so I could be Dad's errand bitch.

He had no regard for me, my life, or my time. He'd managed to cost me two workdays fixing fence for no reason. "I can give you a ride home. I don't know what is so important to you at eight at night that both Autumn and I have to—"

"I really need to go tonight. The urge has been . . ." He sighed. "It's my AA meeting, Giddy. Alcoholics Anonymous."

Autumn

Hank hobbled into the Lutheran church, his shoulders stooped and his head down. Streetlights and the dashboard lit Gideon's face. His jaw was carved from granite and the green of his eyes was uncharacteristically dark as he watched his dad disappear into the church.

I'd seen the exact moment Gideon's expression had gone stark. He'd been talking on the phone, his brows drawing closer together, and then the lightness I'd caught when he laughed during the skit was gone. He was the guy I'd met in the elevator in Las Vegas.

"How long has he been in AA?" The meetings were in a local church and I'd seen the signs posted, but they were such a constant, I didn't ever think about them or who might attend them. To me, Hank was just a friendly face around town. The stories about his drinking were from so long ago that sometimes it felt like Gideon was talking about a different Hank James.

Gideon's jaw turned impossibly harder. "I don't know."

"It's a good thing though. Right?"

He finally tore his eyes away from the brick building. "He said he's been having a hard time. That this week has been really hard." He scratched his jaw, the scrape of his fingers loud against his whiskers. "Yesterday, he quit early to go to town. I didn't figure it out. He went to town for a *meeting*." He worked his jaw. "Two days with me, two meetings."

I put my hand on his forearm. He was tense there too. "He's taking care of himself. He has measures in place. He'll be okay."

"I never really believed he was sober."

I pressed my lips together. He said it like a confession, raw and ragged.

"I didn't believe him. In fact, I was goddamn upset at the idea that he might have gotten sober well after I was gone." He snapped his mouth shut like he was afraid to keep going. "Why now? Why not when I was a kid? Why not when he had to sell off the cattle? The equipment? All of that could've gone toward his damn retirement."

"I don't know, Gideon, but from what I've seen, alcoholism and addiction make the rules long before the person ever does."

He glued me in place with his hooded gaze. "How do you know that?"

"I hear a lot from the kids and their parents. And yeah, when I was new, I got so distraught when a kid made a comment about a parent being in jail for drugs. About five years ago, a mom caught me after school. We talked for almost two hours about her experience with addiction and recovery. For some reason, she needed someone to hear it, and I was that person. She said her addiction makes all the sense in the world, but it doesn't make sense at all."

The hard muscle under my hand finally relaxed.

He pinched the bridge of his nose. "He said the meeting would take about forty-five minutes to an hour. Want to steer the pickup while we tow it?"

"You think this is going to tow his pickup?"

"Is there twenty-four-hour towing in Bourbon Canyon?"

"I'll just call Teller."

His arrogant lips were flattened in a line. "I'm not calling Teller."

"Tenor?" At his silence, I thought for a moment. He wouldn't let me call Tate either. "Myles just bought a pickup, but he and Wynter were going to Denver for the weekend. There's Jonah Dunn, Summer's husband. Do you remember him?"

He thought for a moment, his eyes getting that faraway look that happened when he delved into the past. Jonah would be a little younger than him.

"Somewhat," he said.

"I think you two would get along. Neither of you really smiles."

The firm line of his mouth finally gave way to a small smile. "Fine. I'll concede to a brother-in-law." His phone buzzed. He frowned while he read the message. "Dad said one of the guys will hang out with him until we return if we're late."

"Okay, I'll call Jonah."

"I can take you home. You don't have to be with me for all this."

"It's okay. This is an exciting night in my world."

The corner of his mouth tipped up. "That's nicer to hear than you'd imagine. I've gotten reports of terrifying nights out in my line of work."

"Does all this seem boring?" I bit the inside of my cheek. I didn't need the confirmation.

"It's refreshing, Autumn. I never hated the small-town life. I only hated mine."

He was returning to the part of his past that wasn't a good place. His dad had measures in place, but Gideon didn't. I had to get him out of that headspace. "You know what the difference is between tonight and nights like this when we were younger?"

He shook his head.

"We're towing a vehicle instead of getting it stuck."

He barked out a laugh. "Too true. Give Jonah a call. I need to get this done so I can show you how not boring the small-town life can be."

"Oh, I think you've given me a couple of glimpses."

My cheeks grew hot and warmth bloomed between my thighs.

"I plan to give you more than a glimpse." He leaned over the console. "Because I didn't meet Dad until ten this morning so I could run to Bozeman and get some condoms."

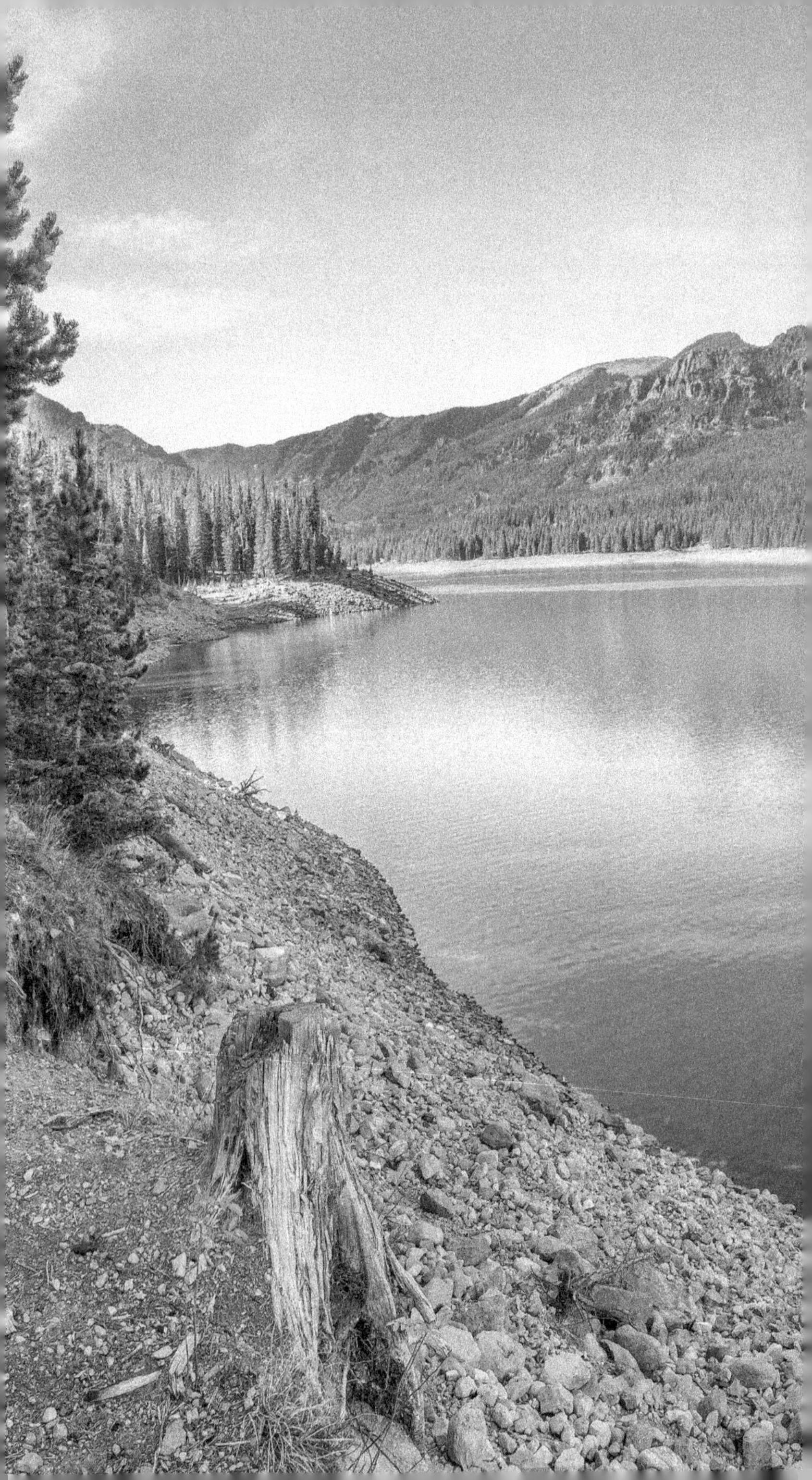

CHAPTER SEVENTEEN

Gideon

I entered the house. The cat was on the couch. She blinked at us, then closed her eyes and went back to sleep.

Dad was safely home. His pickup was in the shop he'd had the party in, only there were no tools other than what was in the bed of his pickup. Jonah and Summer had left.

Jonah hadn't said a word about the sale. He hadn't said much at all, just gotten to the task at hand. The guy was different from what I remembered. He was younger than me by a few years, but he hadn't been the bearded, quiet man then. Autumn had told me about his accident and the death of his brother fifteen years ago, and I could see how it'd changed him. Taught him to seek peace in his own head. I knew the feeling.

Now, I had Autumn home, but I couldn't put those condoms to use. I was dirty and had grease stains on what had been my good casual clothes. Autumn was as fresh as a daisy. Her cheeks were pink from laughing with Dad.

My chest grew tight at how easily they had chatted. Dad hadn't talked about his meeting, but Autumn had told me that was a thing, hence the anonymous part.

She gave Sprinkles some scratches and got a trilling sound in return. I could bend this woman over the couch, and I wouldn't care what an eyeful the cat got, but I didn't want to mark that creamy skin with the grunge from earlier tonight.

"I gotta shower."

"Okay. Leave your clothes outside the door and I'll put some spray on them."

"You don't have to do my laundry." Other people had been doing my laundry for years. It was one of the perks of living on the premises. But not Autumn.

"You can't grow up a Bailey and not learn how to get grease stains out. It's fine, and don't worry, it won't be a regular thing." She smiled, but it slipped immediately.

I was about to ask her what was wrong, but the *regular thing* part of her comment stood out. Our relationship was scheduled for mere weeks.

"Go ahead and clean up," she insisted, skipping past the odd silence. "I'll find us something to eat."

"Thanks." We only had about three weeks left. Did I want us to be longer?

I pushed a hand through my hair. It didn't matter. Without Percival, I had no ties to this town. Entertaining thoughts of a lasting relationship wasn't fair to Autumn.

My grandfather's low growl rose in my head. *A man's*

worth is in his name. Percival is no longer your last name, but it's alive in the land. Don't let your dad destroy it.

I shook off the memory, exhausted at still being torn between my grandfather and my dad after all these years.

Besides, I had to shower, and then I had to bury myself in my wife.

I folded my clothes outside the door for Autumn. In the bathroom, I turned on the faucet and stepped under the frigid spray. I needed the cold shock after tonight. Once the water warmed, I let it pour over me and scrubbed myself off. This was my second shower of the day, and I needed the reprieve of this little curtained cove.

So much had changed since I'd left. Was it me who'd altered the most? Or Dad?

When I'd left home, Dad hadn't had to worry about feeding me, though he'd quit long before that. Had he noticed I was even gone? Maybe not as much in the years he was drinking.

Seeing him reminded me of the good times, and I hated it. Those days had been me and Mom, but now memories of Dad were invading my brain. Was that what it had been like for him? Had I been a walking, talking reminder of the life he used to have, the one he'd lost when Mom had died?

No wonder he'd let me go without a word.

What had made him sober up?

It sure as fuck hadn't been me.

I flung the shower curtain back and pressed a towel against my face. Autumn's sweet scent glided into my nose on a deep inhale. The tension from my earlier circle of thought drained out of me.

None of that mattered anymore. All I had to worry about was a quiet night with my wife.

I stepped out of her bathtub/shower combo. How quickly I had adapted to one showerhead. A delicious cinnamon smell was drifting into the bathroom. After throwing on a T-shirt and an old pair of black basketball shorts that proved I wasn't always a slacks-and-loafers guy, I went in search of my little teacher and the source of the sweet smell.

She was at the stove, her hips swaying. Her phone was on her dining table by my computer. A twangy country song came from a small speaker by one of the cupboards. This was the private dancing she did. I was glad it was all for me.

I went behind her and slid my hands around her waist. She jumped and giggled, looking over her shoulder. "You just appear, don't you?"

"It's a handy trait when you're the boss." I eyed the french toast she was cooking. In another pan was sausage, and she had a bowl of eggs already whisked together sitting on the counter. "You didn't have to go through all the trouble of cooking."

"I don't know if you noticed, but we don't have many takeout options in Bourbon Canyon."

"That was the one thing I never looked back on when I moved."

She glanced over her shoulder. "You looked back though?"

"A few times," I admitted. If anyone else had asked, I'd have denied it. "College was easy. It was new and I had something to focus on, and there's a lot to do in Vegas."

"But you got homesick?"

"Yes. There're always people. To go from barely seeing Dad to having roommates and classes full of more people than my entire high school? A vast change. Then I got a place of my own with a buddy, but he worked nights and was gone a lot."

She flipped the two pieces of french toast. "And you were back to being alone."

"Sometimes my grandpa Percival would visit, but he'd rant up a storm about how Dad was mismanaging the farm and what a drunk he was. Then he got too sick to travel." The relief I'd felt had filled me with shame. My grandfather hadn't realized that he was also detailing all the ways I'd failed. I didn't share his last name. I hadn't gotten Percival. I couldn't help Dad. No matter how much wealth I accumulated, it wasn't Percival, and Grandpa Percival didn't care, wasn't even proud. The thought filled me with dread, like he was going to return and indict me all over again.

"You two were close?"

"Yeah." I thought for a moment. "In a way. His health didn't allow much, and he and Dad never got along. So our visits were short." And filled with Grandpa Percival's anger. "At least he called a few times when I was in college before he died. Dad never reached out." Not for a long time. By the time he had called me, I'd bottled up so much resentment I disconnected midring.

She looked back again. "That must've hurt."

"Yeah," I said gruffly. At the time, I hadn't realized how much I'd dwelled on it. "I can only guess that when he started calling was when he got sober. I'd been gone for almost ten years by then."

"Do you think he wanted something?"

"Since I was working my way up the casino and hotel

management chain, I assumed he wanted money. I didn't have to look very hard to know how bad the farm and ranch were doing. But he never asked." Unlike Grandpa Percival, Dad hadn't demanded anything of me during those calls.

Mom's voice rose in my head. She'd cut off Grandpa Percival during one visit. *You leave him be, Dad. Giddy's going to make his own legacy.* Her voice had been light, laughing, but my grandfather had shushed her and kept recounting the Percival family history.

"Did you keep in contact with anyone after you moved?"

I buried my nose in her hair, grateful to leave that memory behind. She'd let her hair down, and I toyed with the coppery strands. "Not really. My other grandparents all passed away before I left Bourbon Canyon."

She dug the two slices of french toast out and transferred them to a clean plate. She set the spatula down and faced me. "Your dad might've been reaching out because he felt ready to face his failings."

A hot wave of resentment wound its way up my neck, but she flattened her hand on my chest.

"I'm not saying that negates what he did. I'm saying that he loves you. He failed you, and you feel like he's failing you again. But he loves you."

"Are you saying I should forget everything?"

"No, I'm saying don't let the terrible experiences erase the good in every memory. Not for his benefit, but for yours."

Any response I had stuck in my throat. The way I wanted to heave suggested I'd do nothing but sputter if I tried to talk. The past was mixing with the present. Dad's easy acceptance of me when I was a kid compared to my grandfather. Dad had done the same with my job, with Autumn, and with the way I treated him. Regret was replacing a small portion of bitterness, and goddamn, I was not ready for that.

She scrutinized me. Was she guessing how I would react? I didn't even know.

"Can you check the sausages, and if they're done, will you cook the eggs? I have some more french toast to batter." She patted my pecs and turned away from me, giving me much-needed distance.

Before I'd returned to Bourbon Canyon, I would've sworn all my memories of Dad were bad. Now I was seeing a different side of him, and it was difficult. My resentment had built up so strong, solidified so hard, that I'd been ready to use an innocent woman to get what I wanted.

Autumn might be innocent, but she was smart. Once again, she'd said something that tilted my world and made me look at my past differently.

Autumn

I had worried for several minutes that my comments about Hank were deeply disturbing for Gideon. I thought he'd close in on himself again, but he loosened up, and after the first groan over my french toast, I knew we were in the clear. As we ate, he asked me about the music program and the skit and how I thought it went. Now, he was helping with cleanup and dishes.

Some of my single friends had their wedding plans.

They lived for the day. But this was what I had dreamed of. Domestic bliss. We'd cook together and clean together and just talk. Not every night of course, but regularly. Just like this.

Would I miss this or the bedroom activities more when he left?

"Do you have another program coming up?" he asked.

I shook my head and loaded the dishwasher with detergent. He was behind me and his gaze was a brand on my ass. I'd miss that too. He made me feel sexy. I was his only option at the moment. He was a man of his word, but I wasn't complaining. "No. I'm going to help Scarlett with hers."

"You're not helping the friends who ditched you." He ended with a growl.

I tossed the detergent back under the sink, started the dishwasher, and rinsed my hands off. "I know you don't like them, but they're just young. I might've done the same thing at their age."

His gaze challenged me to admit the truth.

I sighed. "Fine. I'm a little salty, but it's a small town and I work with them. Besides, it's hard to be upset when I got on an elevator with this moody CEO who wanted to trap me into a marriage for the horribly *selfish* reason of saving his family's land from getting sold to this big land baron family."

His lips quirked. "They're into running moonshine too."

"Not since Great-Grandaddy Bailey."

He laughed and crowded me into the corner of the counter. "I feel like some of that rebelliousness rubbed off on you."

"I'm adopted."

"The trait is that strong."

His mouth was close. He was hovering over me. The low desire that had been simmering in my body all night cranked up a few notches. "The natural Kerrigan stubbornness might've been able to flourish in the Bailey household."

"The moody CEO might've been attracted to that smart mouth." He traced my bottom lip with his thumb. "And a few other things." He trailed his fingers down my neck and over my breasts, softly cupping one side before moving farther down. He bracketed my hips with his hands.

I curled my arms around his neck. Disbelief rocked inside of me like it had been doing since I'd said my vows. I had Gideon James in my kitchen. I liked waking up to him. I liked chatting with him. I liked the Gideon who helped his dad, the one who joined me at school for special projects and the guy who helped cook breakfast for dinner with me.

He lifted me onto the counter.

I let out a squeal. "I'm too heav—"

"Don't you dare finish that." He planted his mouth on mine, and a second later, our tongues were tangling.

He wedged between my legs, and I hooked my feet around his hips.

He kissed along my jaw to my ear. "Fuck, you taste sweeter and sweeter every time."

"It's the syrup." I shoved my fingers into the strands of his already-dried hair. When he'd walked out of the bedroom with wet, spiky hair, I'd taken a mental snapshot. Just another way he was making my list of requirements for the guy I did settle down with impossible to meet. Gideon was ruining me for anyone else, one casual look at a time.

"It's not the fucking syrup," he growled, dropping to his knees. "It's you." He tugged at my leggings. I had to lift myself off the counter so they could slide down my legs. He took the underwear with them too. The hungry way he eyed my pussy went on my list.

Yes, that. I had to have more of that. "Again? Aren't you tired of, you know, doing *that*?"

He'd said he had condoms. Had he forgotten them in the car? Giving me daily oral sex wasn't part of the bargain.

The dark look he gave me stole all my questions. "Which part would I tire of?" He leaned in and licked through my seam.

My body went into autopilot. I leaned back on my hands and widened my legs. If he got tired of oral, a part of my world would permanently dim.

He caught my gaze and slicked a finger through where he'd just licked. "Do you think I could get tired of the way you get wet for me?" He pushed his finger inside and I moaned. "Or those sexy fucking sounds you make?" One thrust, then two, and he withdrew. I nearly combusted when he put his finger in his mouth and sucked my wetness off. "Maybe you're worried I'll get tired of having your flavor on my tongue or hearing you scream my name when you're coming."

I nodded because I couldn't form words.

"My sweet little firecracker, I'm never going to quit craving you." He tongued my clit again and didn't let up. I let my head drop back and held on.

The desire inside me built, growing impossibly larger. I gave myself up to him, something I'd been doing since we met, and slammed into my peak. When I careened over, fireworks went off behind my eyes. "Gideon!"

He increased the pressure and added a finger. I could feel myself squeezing around him and my climax got stronger—it'd be his cock next and this was already overwhelming in the best way.

"Fuck, Autumn."

I was barely aware of him rising. I opened my eyes in time to see him ripping the corner off a condom packet with his teeth at the same time he was shoving his shorts down.

I was wet and dripping, and if I was supposed to be embarrassed, I couldn't bring myself to care. His erection popped free, straining between us. He was big, his length lined with veins. I wrapped my hand around him, absorbing the heat and strength in my grip. He jerked under my touch, and the empty condom packet fluttered to the floor.

"Remove your hand, firecracker, because I need inside of you right fucking now."

I took my time taking my hand off him. I wanted to play, but the promising look he gave me said I'd have plenty of time later. He shoved the condom on and notched himself at my entrance. I held on to his shoulders, loving the pressure of his almost intrusion but also needing so much more.

"Gideon?"

A tremor ran through him like he was holding back for me. "Yes?"

"I want you inside me."

Resolution lined his face and he thrust in.

I gasped at the sheer pleasure, the feeling of fullness,

of how overwhelmingly large he was, but also at how I adapted to fit perfectly around him.

He tipped his forehead against mine and rocked into me until he was seated all the way in. "*Fuck*." A little withdrawal and thrust. "Fuuuuck." Then his mouth was back on mine, consuming me.

I tasted myself, blended with him, and mixed with the way he was moving in me—I was lost. My arousal was a wall cloud, expanding and growing, preparing for another storm. With each thrust, my overly sensitive clit rubbed against him and tossed fuel on the inferno raging inside of me.

He matched the rhythm of his tongue with his hips. Our first time together was as groundbreaking as I hoped it'd be. This would be how he completely ruined me for anyone ever again.

I was nearing another peak, ready to explode, but a faint thought in the back of my head rose. What if this was real? What if he was really into me and not just an opportunist?

What if—

I veered toward the ecstasy stacked in every facet of my body. No. This was now. I would not allow myself to consider a future with this man. He'd told me what he was after, and it was not a wife and kids.

I would be left with the memories of tons of orgasms, not a broken heart.

Gideon

. . .

I could barely hang on until her walls clamped around me, convulsing. She ripped her mouth away from mine. "Gideon! Yes!"

I held her tight. My hands imprinted on her hips as I gripped her through my peak. I had to squeeze my eyes shut at the pleasure detonating inside me.

"Fuck." My vocabulary had shrunk to one word. "Fuck, fuck, fuck," I chanted from between clenched teeth.

My orgasm wouldn't quit. I shook and hung on to her. She was my lifeline, the only way I'd remain upright instead of taking both of us down. I would not interrupt the best sex of my life by dumping myself and my partner on the floor.

Her cries had quieted by the time I started coming down from my climax. She buried her face in my chest, her sides heaving. I was breathing like I'd sprinted around the block a few times.

What the hell was that?

I'd fucked her against the counter. I liked sex, and I hadn't thought it'd be bad with Autumn, but I'd had no idea it'd scramble my brains like a carton of eggs. Orgasms weren't that powerful.

I pried my hands off her soft skin. She still had her shirt on. My shorts were around my ankles, and I just wanted to carry her to bed and hold her until my world steadied back into orbit.

She fisted her hands in my shirt and inhaled. "Wow."

I didn't have the energy to chuckle. I wanted her naked and in bed. I had the energy for that. "Yeah."

I lifted her from the counter. She curled around me like we did this all the time.

What if you could?

No. This life wasn't for me. I was coming to terms with that. Just like I was facing the reckoning of my past.

I stepped out of my shorts and walked bare-assed to her bedroom. Thankfully, all the blinds were closed. The whole neighborhood would've seen what was my private show. All mine.

She nibbled along my collarbone. My erection decided it didn't need to wane. I was hard again and ready to go. Maybe because it'd been so long, but I didn't think so.

Something about Autumn called to me on a level I'd never experienced before. If I was smart, I'd pack my shit and get on the first plane to Las Vegas. I'd reconcile myself with the sale of the land and go about my business. I had a fantastic fucking job and an extravagant place to live. My savings and investments made me a rich man. The place I'd tried to forget for a couple of decades didn't matter. But I didn't put a stop to this. Maybe some part of me was as weak as my father, giving in to earthly temptations.

I spotted the open pack of condoms and was grateful I'd bought the biggest damn box the store had.

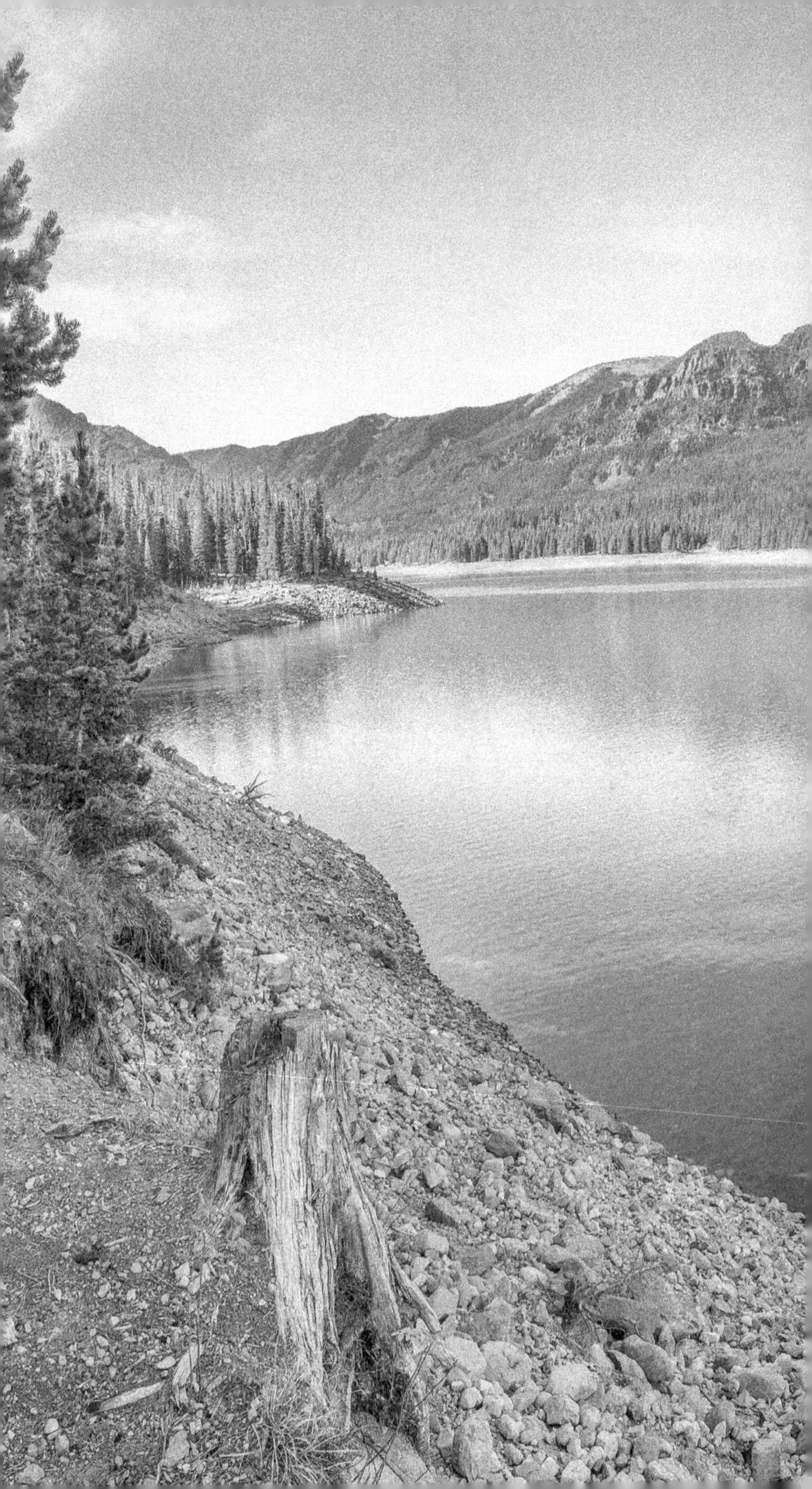

CHAPTER EIGHTEEN

Gideon

While it was clear my wife liked her job at Copper Summit, I wished she'd quit now so we could go home and I could get between her legs again.

I was a man obsessed. She'd barely been able to pry herself away from me to go to work yesterday. Now, it was Saturday night. I was semi caught up on work—after sating myself in my wife—and was actually enjoying the evening. Autumn laughed and joked with her customers. A few of them talked to me. Since the only open part of Copper Summit was the bar, and the entire site was a distillery, I was safe from being around Dad.

He'd called yesterday, asking if I wanted to help with bullshit projects. Regardless, I almost said yes, but legitimately, I'd had meetings and reports to get to my assistant to type up for next week's meetings. I'd also needed space from him.

Autumn was more than a nice distraction. She was

my focus. I was unsure about Dad, I didn't know what he'd do, and I wasn't clear on how I felt about home, him, and everything else.

"Voilà." Autumn slid a clear glass mug in front of me.

I frowned at the white frothy drink with a sprinkle of cinnamon. I'd already had a concoction that included Scarlett's lemonade, a light, fruity cocktail that was outside the realm of anything I normally drank. This was out of the entire universe. "A bourbon milkshake?"

"No." She laughed, then paused to consider the idea. "You know, that might work and appease Teller and Tenor's desire for more limited-edition drinks. I'll have to brainstorm with Wynter." She tapped the glass. "You're the guinea pig. This is our annual bourbon eggnog. Wynter and I switch up the recipe each year, but it's pretty much on me this year."

"I've never had eggnog."

"It's delicious, I swear."

"Raw egg with my drink?" I said dubiously.

"We use pasteurized eggnog. It's safe, I promise."

I took a drink. The play of spices hit my taste buds first. Cinnamon, probably nutmeg, maybe ginger, and something else I couldn't identify. Smooth bourbon fused with the creamy flavor. "It's good."

She grinned, pride shining in her eyes. "I added ginger and cardamom this year. Mostly, we just add a new spice each year and take one off." She leaned on the bar top. "We learned the hard way we can't veer too far from the traditional eggnog flavor. Peppermint nog was an epic fail."

She looked over my shoulder and straightened. "Teller, hey. Everything okay?"

"Can't I have a drink and talk with my sister?" He

pulled a stool out, keeping an empty one between us. He fit in with the clientele in a green-plaid shirt, blue jeans, and cowboy boots. His dark hair was almost shaggy, but his beard was trimmed. "James."

"Bailey," I greeted in return. I wasn't dressed much differently. But not because I wanted to blend in. My attire just made sense. Made it look like I was accepting this new marriage and new life . . . in a place where Dad wouldn't be.

"She's testing her new concoctions on you?"

He was joking, but he was also diminishing her job. The bar was an advertisement for the distillery. Autumn did ground-level marketing for the company. People didn't just come here for the drinks. They came for that ambience, and also for the employees who served them and added pleasant conversation to cap their day. "Good thing you have such a savvy sister when it comes to mixing drinks."

Teller's brows drew together. "I didn't say she wasn't."

"But you didn't say she was."

He pushed a hand through his hair. "It's been a long fucking day, James, and now you're telling me I'm a shitty brother."

"You're not a shitty brother." Autumn set an empty squat glass in front of Teller. "You're bossy, stubborn—which I've heard is a family trait—and you tend to treat me like an annoying little sister. Sometimes, I wish you took me as seriously as you take yourself."

If I smiled, I'd look like I was gloating, but pride rang through me. She hadn't flinched away from the topic. Maybe she'd told him before and it'd run off him like rainwater, but this time, she had me to corroborate it. He pondered her as she grabbed a bottle from the top shelf, Copper Summit Gold, and poured two fingers for Teller.

He spun the glass in his hand. "Is this about what Tenor brought up?"

Autumn glanced at me like she was seeking permission to stand her ground. I put as much encouragement in my gaze as possible. She said, "It's about Tenor discussing it with Tate first, and then you, and then telling me like I'm just another employee and not part owner. I've taken over running the bar, but it's my and Wynter's area of expertise. Would you two discuss marketing campaigns without her?"

Teller frowned. "You already have a job—"

"I have two," she said firmly. "And it's my decision to decide if I'm overwhelmed or not. I'm not an injured kid anymore. I realize it's inconvenient that I'm not around Copper Summit as much as you guys are, but you can call, text, or email."

"Shit," Teller grunted. "I didn't realize it bothered you so much."

She rolled her eyes. "You did, but you weren't taking me seriously."

Teller rocked back like she'd hit him. "Fair enough. I'll make sure Tenor and I come to you first."

Autumn dipped her head, gratitude and relief in her eyes.

Teller pinned me under his gaze. "You're trying not to laugh."

I didn't hide my snicker.

"You wouldn't laugh if she called you out."

"She's put me in my place a time or two." I took a sip of my boozy, creamy drink. The flavor was growing on me. It'd become my favorite fucking drink if it irritated Teller.

"I'll encourage her to do it more," he grumbled.

She went into the storage room, came out again with a couple of new bottles and started restocking the bar. Was she purposely giving me and Teller space? Or was I invading her work and expecting her to cater to me instead of doing her job?

Teller rotated his glass on its edge. The air between us wasn't strained, but it wasn't light.

I should stay away from the sale topic, but I didn't. "Did you ask Hank to fix fence?"

Teller continued swirling his glass. "He asked if we'd mind. I figured he wanted to keep himself busy before the holiday season."

I pushed the words back. I was not going to ask the significance. "What about the holiday season?" Lost that fight.

"His charity work?" He took a long sip, glanced at me, and did a double take. "You don't know about the charities?"

Other than what I'd heard the Baileys mention, no. I didn't know a lot about what Dad was like since I'd left. "We don't talk."

He wiped off his mouth. "I don't get that. I talked to my dad every day until he died."

"Did he get drunk every day and ignore you? Forget to buy groceries or treat you like hired help that didn't get paid? Did he yell at you for five minutes straight when he was the one who'd spent the grocery money on beer?"

Teller's jaw tightened.

"Did he neglect everything that meant anything to you until it died?"

I got a small shake of his head as a response.

"I don't have to mention the sale on top of it all. He drank away everything else, and he's selling what should be mine, what my mother wanted to go to me. So excuse me if I'm ignorant about what he does for charity."

"He plays Santa at the senior center," Teller said. "He'll dress up for the school's field trips when they sing for the residents. He works at the food pantry year-round. It's usually only open once a week, but between Thanksgiving and New Year's, the office hours are three days a week. Then there's the toy drive. I heard he can wrap a mean gift."

"I wouldn't know."

Teller's right cheek twitched and he took a big gulp that was more like a shot.

He polished off his drink and glanced at Autumn like he was making sure she was still across the room. "The man you know isn't who the rest of Bourbon Canyon know, and I think once you understand that, maybe you'll understand his motivations. What you experienced was wrong. But if you truly fell that madly in love with my sister, and she was suddenly taken from you, would you keep your shit together? Or would you lose it until the pain dulled enough to face it?"

That'd never happen. I'd have to fall in love first. "I was a kid."

"I know." His voice was soft, compassionate. "I'm just saying you might understand him. Look, no one knows why he's not turning Percival over to you. I looked up what you're worth. God knows you can pay him for it. Maybe it's pride? He doesn't want to live off the son who didn't have a chance to live off him? I don't know. No one does. But reminding him of every way you hate him probably isn't going to soften him up to stop the sale."

I didn't hate my dad. That was part of the problem. "And you'll go through with it if he does?"

"Better us than some rich out-of-stater who doesn't give a shit about Montana and thinks the local residents are quaint and disposable little peasants."

I didn't want to see Percival going to some stranger either. I didn't want hunting cabins built, and if I heard the word "rental" thrown around in regard to the property, I'd burn every structure down. Pretty rich coming from a corporate city guy like me.

In Bourbon Canyon, I wasn't as much that person as I had been over a week ago. Each step I took in town shed one more layer of polish. "I'll agree with you on that."

He shrugged like it didn't matter. "How are things with you and Autumn?"

I drank a mouthful of eggnog. Fucking hot. That wasn't what her brother wanted to hear. "She hasn't kicked me out yet."

"You also haven't moved in."

What'd he mean by that? How would he know? Had he gone into her bedroom and seen my suitcase open on her dresser? Had he judged the new clothing that I hung on a folding chair next to it?

He was trying to trip me up.

Autumn breezed back, dropping off glasses from the customers who had just left. Only Teller and I were left in the bar.

He pulled Autumn in for a one-armed hug. He'd

darted in for that comment and was jumping back out of range. "I'm going back to the office to work a little more. You mind locking up when you leave?"

She patted his back. "Will do. Love you, big bro."

"I know you're testing products," he grudgingly admitted. "You do good work. But you're still my sister and I'm gonna give you shit." He started to walk away but stopped. "Oh, and I only take myself that seriously because I'm a big deal."

She snorted and flicked a rag at him. He danced away, smirking, then he disappeared from the bar.

I helped her wipe down and put the dishes away.

On the way out of the bar, she flipped off the lights and locked the door to the outside, but she led me through the entry into the main distillery. A little store was on the far end, tucked into a corner next to another wall of windows that opened into the still room.

Autumn caught me looking. "You haven't seen the rest of Copper Summit, have you?"

Surprised I was interested, I shook my head. "No, you mind?"

She hooked an arm through mine. "Only if you promise not to zone out when I geek out." She towed me to the windows. Giant copper-and-steel stills filled one end of the room. A small ladder led to a platform between some squat but still quite large tanks. The ceilings were high and the walls were a mix of cinder block and rock, much different than the rugged wood and rock exterior that made the place look more like it belonged in the mining industry. Metal piping ran between the pots and stills and a maze of plumbing trailed down from the ceiling and up from the floor.

"The mash tanks are the short tanks. Let's go in so you can smell them."

"I've never been asked to smell something by a woman."

She grinned. "Who better to do it than your wife?" She tugged me toward one of the mash tanks. Inside, a yellowish mix was bubbling. The sight reminded me of soggy cornflakes. "The yeast are busy at work. When we were younger, we called the bubbles yeast farts." She hovered her hand over the top of the suspension. "You can smell it better from here and feel the heat."

I sniffed. A fruity, bready smell hit my nose, much stronger than the warm-grain scent of the rest of the place.

"It'll create fewer bubbles each day," she explained. "And it'll get browner. Then we call it distiller's beer and it gets piped to the distillation tanks, where we'll turn it to moonshine, basically, and then distill it down some more."

I'd been raised mere miles from this place and I'd never gotten a tour. I'd been in the grocery store or walking downtown and heard tourists exclaim how cool Copper Summit was. I hadn't thought much about it back then. Copper Summit was just another thing I'd left behind.

She led me to the stills. "Do you know how many gallons of bourbon we can get from five hundred gallons of distiller's beer?"

"What happens if I'm wrong?"

She hummed. "You don't like being wrong, do you?"

Not at all. "Fifty gallons?"

"One." Her smile was the nerdy kind she'd warned me about. She was in her element in the distillery. And in the school. She was lucky to have more than one place where she excelled. Bourbon Canyon provided both of them.

There was nothing here for me without Percival Farms.

"How many gallons in a barrel?" I asked to keep my mind from mulling over how I'd made my place in Las Vegas.

"Fifty-three, but we never get out that many gallons."

"The angel's share?"

Her eyes lit at my very limited knowledge of distillery terms. "Every year we age a barrel, we lose a percent of the product, but you also get to extract more of the flavors and sugars from the wood."

"Kind of weird to think you flavor your alcohol with wood."

"Oak, specifically, but we like to play around with different oak varieties." She shrugged and looked around, her fond gaze taking in the building. I could see it in her eyes. To her, Copper Summit was a work of art, but it was also comfort. It was passion. It was home.

She'd never leave. I'd never stay.

"The other buildings on-site are the barrel houses. Those are better to check out during the day." She led me back toward the main entry. "Copper Summit also employs its own delivery drivers. Daddy was really proud of that."

"Lots of jobs."

She beamed. "It's a small but tight team. We can't say we're like family since I can't call other employees a stubborn ass like I do with my brothers. But we have full-time positions other than my siblings." She turned back toward the windows. By the far wall were three computer screens and a U-shaped desk piled with papers and folders. "We track everything. Temperatures, yeast strains, the types of grains and how much— Tenor loves to dig into all that."

"What about you? Do you stick to the bar now?"

"Daddy made me do my share of tossing around fifty-pound bags of grain, but no, I don't do that anymore. I'd be charging into a well-choreographed dance the distillers have going on."

She'd grown up with her family's legacy, yet she'd chosen another profession. She had three older brothers and an older sister. Kind of like a monarchy, she would've been too far down the line to have much authority.

"You were okay with knowing you weren't ever going to be in charge?"

"Oh, yeah. It's still ours."

Her words echoed in my head. All the kids at the party Dad had thrown would learn exactly what Autumn and her siblings had. If we had kids, the same would happen. Their roots would burrow deep in the Bourbon Canyon area.

But we weren't having kids.

"The bottle line is on the other side." She pulled on me again, her hand still in mine. "We can peek in, but it's not exciting. Just a small assembly line where bottles are filled, sealed, labeled, and packed for shipping. The trucks go in and out that side too."

She hit a switch. Lights flooded a plain room whose centerpiece was the metal bottling line. A long carousel traveled much of the length. At one end were nozzle heads to fill the bottles, then more silver knobs and moving parts to cap and label them. At the end was a place for crates and boxes.

"Which sibling oversees this?"

"Teller. He's in charge, so he gets the boring stuff. Tenor's his backup, but he prefers to crunch numbers all day. Tate helps out, but he doesn't like to make Teller or Summer feel like he's watching over them. Junie might not physically work on the premises, but she coordinates with Wynter for commercials and radio spots."

This whole building was a small ecosystem that took from its surroundings and gave just as much back. According to what Teller had said, Dad was giving back too.

I wanted Percival Farms for myself. I wanted it kept in the family. I'd focused only on what I wanted, but I'd never considered how I'd give back. Contributing to the community hadn't been one of Grandfather's lessons. As I was standing here, gazing at what was only one part of the Bailey empire, I struggled to come up with a good example of what I had to give.

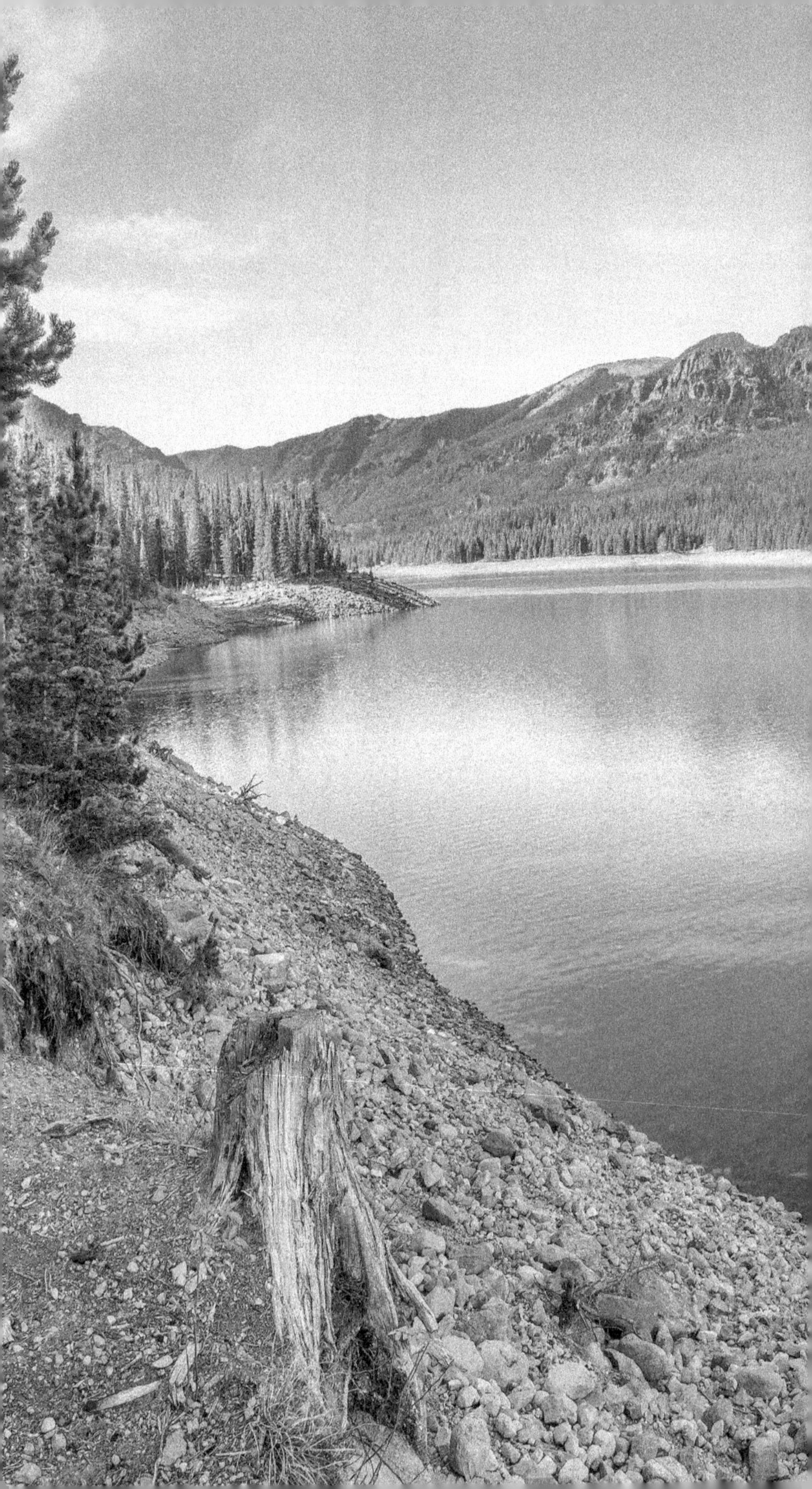

CHAPTER NINETEEN

Autumn

A knock at my classroom door jerked me out of my stupor. A common occurrence in the last week. How long had I been staring at the wall of pumpkin cutouts with each kid's favorite fall memory written inside while I'd been lost in thought about my homelife?

I blinked at the door. School had let out an hour and a half ago, but I'd stayed late to grade since my productivity at home had tanked. Most everyone had left. Except Scarlett.

She wore an amused smile and crossed her arms over her pumpkin cardigan. She wore it every year in the week leading up to Halloween. "I feel like I can tell what you're thinking about since you returned from Vegas. Or should I say who?"

She would be right. Gideon was on my mind all the time. And when I was home, he was inside me. All. The. Time. It was glorious.

I woke up to his cock. I went to bed with it. And many times, I'd even showered with it. Last night, for dinner, he'd had me first. The meat loaf had gotten overcooked.

I grinned. "Can't help it."

She wiggled her finger at me. "Tate would dry heave if he saw you right now."

My brothers would not like to hear what I'd been getting up to with Gideon. "I might have to gush to him to make sure."

Tate hadn't contacted me since the party where Gideon and I had left early. Teller had probably passed on our exchange at the distillery. Other than that, my brothers were steering clear of me. Good.

A little scrape of indignation chafed the inside of my chest. Were they digging in their heels and going through with the sale without even asking my opinion?

Since when had they ever asked for my opinion?

But I was *married*. To the man they were personally upsetting over the sale. Me. Their sister. Wasn't I more than business?

"Uh-oh." She crossed to my desk and pulled up a yellow wobble stool that looked like a giant board game piece with a broad base and wide seat. She sat on it like a pro, without tipping from side to side as she gained her balance, probably because she had some in her classroom. "Now, what thought is going through your head?"

"It's nothing." I shuffled the math papers I should've been done correcting. "What are you doing here so late?"

"Tate took the kids to your mom's place, and they won't get home until later. I thought I could get some lessons outlined so I can relax a little for Friday."

Halloween was this Friday. No one was getting anything done. The school had their fall festival and the kids could get dressed up. There was an art fair in the gymnasium and families were invited for the last two hours to tour the projects and have hot chocolate.

"Mama will send you home a plate of food."

She put her hand on her stomach. "I'm counting on there being dessert too."

I laughed. "There will be. If Mama doesn't remember, Tate will."

She put her elbow on the edge of the desk. The chair was so short her head barely reached her hand when she rested her chin in her palm. "I take it it's going well?"

"So well." A heat wave crept up my neck. "I really like him, Scarlett."

"I hope so. You married him." There was a slight question in her tone.

"I know you don't think it's real." It felt legitimate. Each day that went by, my dream was becoming more of a reality. I liked going home to him. I loved waking up to him—and that was before he made me orgasm before work. But the calendar continued to tear a page away with each day. Slowly, we were creeping up to the closing date.

I didn't want to wonder if he was waiting to go back to his plush penthouse and his runway-ready CFO and fuck buddy. That wasn't part of my fantasy. Neither was him unpacking that suitcase of his and actually hanging something up in a closet. As long as he kept folding his clean laundry right back into his suitcase, I had no delusions.

"I think . . ." She ran her lower lip between her teeth. "I think your brothers are terrified it's not real. They see you as the little sister they were supposed to protect. I see you as a smart and savvy woman who might drool at the sight of Gideon but would see through a facade."

I stiffened. Scarlett was also intelligent and observant. I couldn't tell her about the deal and ask her not to tell Tate. I wasn't risking the only chance Gideon had, and I refused to put that kind of strain on my friend. "We must look like an odd couple."

I was plain; he was a god. I was short; he was tall. I was wealthy in family connections, and he isolated himself. How could we be truly in love when he ran a company that earned over a million a day, and my late nights were filled with paste and construction paper?

Sympathy registered in her eyes. She sat back and wobbled intentionally side to side on her stool. "You two look adorable and I wish you knew it."

I stuck my tongue out at her. Not even my students did that. "You're supposed to say that. You're my friend."

"Do you think I feel like I belong next to Tate? The CEO turned single dad mountain man?"

"He's a rancher. And you're gorgeous." I knew how she felt. We rocked the same style and it normally didn't bother us. But we were only human.

"Good thing the cows don't care he's grumpy half the time."

"He's grumpy because he's not with you."

Her expression went dreamy. "Yeah." She blinked, back to the mild teacher I knew. "He is worried about you, and it's because he doesn't trust Gideon, not you. I'm staying out of it, but I'm worried about you too. Why don't you talk to Tate?"

Why didn't Tate talk to me? "I don't think it'd help." I might as well sidle up to the wall and have a long conversation. If Tate didn't want to budge on anything, he wouldn't. And since he was head of Bailey Beef and this deal was going through the ranch, then his mind was made up. He was the oldest. He'd always been in charge. Teller and Tenor would follow his lead.

She put her hands up. "I'm not going to wedge myself in the middle. Just know you can always talk to me. I won't go to Tate with everything."

I lifted a brow.

She rolled her eyes. "I do keep some things from him."

I kept the brow arched.

"Fine. I'm an open book with him, okay? But I'm still here for you."

"Thank you." I had been hesitant to be my usual self with Scarlett, unsure of what she'd report to her husband.

"What I really came here for, other than a check-in, is to see if you were going to be home tomorrow night for trick-or-treating."

"Of course, why wouldn't I be?"

"Maybe you have a hot date? Or maybe you'll be in flagrante?"

I laughed. With the way Gideon and I had been all week . . . "I'm not going to be doing it when kids are ringing my doorbell. I haven't really talked to him, but I'm sure he's fine with answering the door a hundred times in two hours."

Teachers' houses were popular stops on the Halloween route.

"Only a hundred?" She let out a wistful sigh. "I miss that. No one comes out to the cabin, and I don't blame them. It'd eat up half their trick-or-treating window."

"You're bringing the kids by?"

"Most definitely. Brinley got a taste of the candy last year, and she's been talking nonstop about it."

"I can't wait."

She rose. "What are you going to be dressed as this year? Or is your after-school costume a surprise?"

The air in my lungs froze. My costume. I had purchased it months ago, and I'd been preparing for Halloween, but the idea of wearing it around Gideon hadn't set in. I had a costume I wore at school and then I switched out to surprise the kids when they came by the house. "Uh . . ."

She tilted her head. "You're wearing your costume for trick-or-treating, right?"

"Oh, yeah. Of course."

Her eyes narrowed. "With your makeup?"

"Not at school." We weren't allowed to have face paint at school.

"You know what I mean. Around *Gideon?*" she taunted, like a kid on the playground. "Or are you *scared?*"

"No?" My voice pitched high. "I'm still dressing up."

"Good," she said with false innocence. The hint of gotcha was in her voice. "See you then."

"Bye-ee." My grin faded as soon as she walked out.

Great. My trick-or-treating costume.

For school, I'd learned to wear something that was comfortable, and I had a rotation of clothing and headbands. Black shirt and slacks and a headband with ears—kitty cat. Brown shirt, brown pants, and a headband with even bigger ears—fox. A dress and leggings with a red cape if it was cold out—Little Red Riding Hood.

Tomorrow, a purple dress and a green scarf. With my red hair, I could pull off a decent Daphne from *Scooby-Doo*.

If only I was wearing that for tomorrow night, but my other costume was too uncomfortable for a full day of teaching. I couldn't be Daphne at night too. Every kid that came to my house would be expecting something different. Not only would it be embarrassing to have kids repeatedly ask where my second costume was, but then I'd have to explain why if Gideon overheard.

And if any of the trick-or-treaters found out what my trick-or-treat costume was supposed to be and I didn't wear it? They'd never let me live down the irony of lying.

Gideon

My wife was standing at the threshold of the living room, her cheeks bright red, and it wasn't just from makeup. She wore red shorts with suspenders, a yellow shirt with an obnoxious white collar, and a blue bow tie. She had her hair bundled under a black bowl-cut wig and a yellow-and-blue beanie plopped on her head. A long nose was strapped around her face.

"Is sexy Pinocchio a thing?" I folded my arms. Through the picture window in the living room, I could see a group of kids rushing down the sidewalk toward the house. They needed to slow down so I could take in the picture in front of me.

She shot me a mock glare, but a smile played along her lips.

Laughter bubbled in my chest, but I held it in. "Remember, I'll know if you're not telling the truth."

Her flush deepened. She looked so damn cute and on the verge of a nervous breakdown, but her gaze was obstinate. "They were out of sexy nurse costumes."

A chuckle left me, turning into a full belly laugh. The doorbell rang, and she scurried past me.

"Trick or treat, Miss K!"

I turned when I heard Deon's voice.

"I mean, Mrs. J," he amended.

"It's okay." Autumn dished out candy to the four boys on her stoop. "Everyone's still trying to get used to it."

"I like your costume! Pinocchio!" another boy shouted. "Does the nose grow?"

I snickered and she shot me a hard look. "No, but I don't lie anyway."

"Hey, Mr. J, why aren't you dressed up?" Deon called.

Autumn put the orange candy-filled bowl under her arm and waited for my answer. My retribution for laughing at her.

It was disturbing how badly I wanted her to keep those suspenders on in bed. "I don't dress up."

"Why not?"

"There's no trick-or-treating where I live." Perhaps in some neighborhoods, but not in Silver, I left it at that.

Deon grimaced like he couldn't imagine living in such a dystopia. "Bye, Js!"

He darted off with the rest of the boys.

I took the bowl from Autumn as she shut the door. "I have no idea what any of them are dressed as."

"Deon's a wrestler. I can't remember the name, but there was just a movie about him. Caleb's Iron Man, José is Spider-Man, and Lakin looked like some vaguely familiar anime character. I think I heard him say he was going super saiyan."

"What's that mean?"

"I've been told over the years, but my head spins, and I start getting fandom terms mixed up. I think it's like superpowerful."

More kids piled onto the stoop. The sounds of them arguing over who got to ring the doorbell came through the door.

Autumn put her hand on the doorknob but didn't turn it. "I'd better wait, or I'll upset the balance."

The doorbell dinged. Sprinkles was nowhere to be seen. I couldn't imagine a rescue like her sticking around for the chaos that was doorbells and handing out treats.

Every time Autumn answered the door, cheerful shouts of "Miss K" and "Mrs. J" would ring out. Autumn would chat with each kid and their parents, and even more kids would peek in at me, shamelessly curious. Many of them shouted a greeting.

I couldn't walk through the hall of Silver and get this many greetings.

While Autumn doled out treats, I marveled over how good those absurd shorts made her ass look.

During a lull, she shoved the bowl into my arms. "I've got to go to the bathroom."

Panic crowded inside my chest. "Wait—what—how many?" My desperation reached new heights when I counted only about ten pieces left. "What if I run out?"

"Two pieces each." She disappeared down the hallway. "There's another bag in the cupboard by the fridge," she called.

The doorbell rang and I froze like a deer in the middle of an interstate.

It rang again and someone shouted, "I already pushed it" on the other side. If they pressed the button again, Autumn would think I couldn't handle this simple of a job.

I opened the door to find three little wide-eyed girls staring up at me.

"Where's Miss K?" the tallest one asked.

Another girl elbowed her. "It's Mrs. J now."

The third bounced up and down, her fluffy skirts shaking. "Trick or treat!"

I wasn't about to announce Autumn was in the bathroom. "She'll be back."

Three tote bags loaded with candy were thrust toward me. At the end of the driveway, two adults waited. One had a mug.

A faint memory curled through my head. My mom laughing with my dad. "I bet there's more than hot cocoa in those cups," she had said about a group of dads going through a neighborhood with their kids on Halloween.

I hadn't known what she'd meant at the time. We had covered the same part of Bourbon Canyon each year, and always the nursing home where both sets of my grandparents had spent their last days.

The nostalgia was heavier than normal. I gritted my teeth together and diligently counted out two mini chocolate bars for each girl.

"Thank you!" they belted in unison before running toward the sidewalk.

The parents lifted their mug toward me. I dipped my head. I was about to shut the door, but another group was making their way toward me. Two adults and three kids.

Shit. I would have to get another bag. Did I shut the door? Tell them to wait? Ruin Autumn's reputation by giving them only one piece of chocolate?

The boy who sprinted up the steps seemed vaguely familiar with his height and how he carried himself, but with the white-and-black makeup on his face, I couldn't place him. A little girl skipped up the steps behind him, and a toddler was rushing to catch up. The parents didn't hang back either. The stoop wouldn't be big enough for all of them.

The older boy grinned at me. "Aunt Autumn always has the best candy."

My stomach knotted. Tate's family. I glanced over the boy's head to find steady brown eyes watching me. Tate wasn't dressed up. He wore a Copper Summit hoodie and a ball cap. He'd look like any other guy if it weren't for the beard and the way he carried himself. His stance said he was in charge. Always.

"Chance, right?" I caught Tate's surprise in my periphery. He must not have thought I'd cared enough to remember his kids' names.

"Yep." He grinned. "I'm Beetlejuice tonight."

"I'm a pincess," Brinley announced.

What was a pincess? How did I make conversation with a kid when I couldn't interpret their words? Then she dipped into a curtsy.

Oh. "Do you have a castle, princess?"

"Nuh-uh."

The littlest one, Darin, shoved between them and darted past me. I just watched him run. He yelled some word I couldn't make out.

"Darin," Scarlett and Tate called. Scarlett tried to crest the stairs. She was in a yellow dress that I should be able to place, but my knowledge of children's characters was sorely lacking. The two older kids wouldn't budge for her.

"No worries." Autumn appeared. She had Darin on her hip. "Let me grab the second bag of candy. Come on in."

Tate watched me, evaluating my reaction.

"Autumn's house is usually our last stop," Scarlett explained, sounding almost apologetic.

"By all means." I stepped to the side. Chance and Brinley charged in.

Scarlett scooted past me.

Tate managed not to shoulder me, but he looked like he wanted to. "James."

"Bailey."

A trio was coming up the sidewalk, two adults holding a baby in a bumblebee costume. As they got closer, I recognized Myles and Wynter.

Autumn had failed to mention Halloween was a goddamn family reunion.

"There's Uncle Gideon," Wynter cooed. "Can you wave to Uncle Gideon?" I was pinned with big blue eyes surrounded by dark lashes. Elsa's puffy black antennae flopped around when she waved.

Uncle Gideon.

Uncle.

Goddammit, these kids were my nieces and nephews. Four of them. I'd never thought of them like that.

When we got a divorce, I'd go back to being nothing but a stranger. I should feel relief, but it was slow in coming.

Autumn returned with Darin on her hip. He was holding her costume nose. "Hey! Come on in." She set Darin down, took the nose from him, and grabbed the bowl from me.

I was pressed against the open door while Wynter and her family filed in and went toward the kitchen where the others had gathered. Autumn's ass was facing me while she helped Darin dump the candy into the bowl.

She handed the empty bag to Darin. "Can you go throw this away for me?"

"Kitty?" Darin asked.

"No, she's hiding." She tapped the bag. "Garbage, please."

He toddled toward the kitchen. Chance was dumping his candy out on the table.

Another group of kids came to the door. I stayed with Autumn as she went through the trick-or-treat routine. Whatever was going on in the kitchen was a ritual I had no history with.

The street was quiet. Shadows of kids flicked door to door down the road, but no one was making their way toward our house.

Autumn didn't leave the doorway. "It's tradition for Chance to trade out the candy he doesn't like."

"Because you carry the good stuff?"

"It helps I like it too." She took a piece out of the bowl and opened it. Instead of popping it in her mouth, she fed it to me.

I caught the tips of her fingers and she giggled. Chocolate exploded on my tongue. When was the last time I'd had a candy bar?

She tucked her hand into mine. When we turned,

Wynter was watching us. Now that her jacket was off, her Bavarian barmaid outfit was clear. Her pale hair was braided down each side. Myles was dressed like me and Tate.

"Is that how disgusting Myles and I are?" Wynter asked Tate. He just grunted.

"We haven't done it under Mama's roof," Autumn retorted.

"You have no proof," Wynter said smugly. She bit her lip. "All right, fine. I don't lie very well. Do you still have adult treats?"

"Of course." Autumn dragged me into the kitchen. She went to the cupboard she kept her spirits in and took out a bottle of Copper Summit Gold. I took out six glasses to keep myself from having to make small talk with guys who either didn't like me or didn't know me.

"None for me," Tate said. "I'm driving."

"Same," Myles added.

"He likes when I'm the one who gets tipsy," Wynter whispered to Scarlett. Tate winced.

I tried not to laugh. Enjoying this interaction wasn't part of the plan. I wasn't kissing Bailey ass to get my land back. But their family chemistry was infectious. It was hard not to get drawn in.

It was also hard not to make comparisons to my own experience and come up so damn short.

"Scarlett, are you Belle with your Beast?" Wynter asked.

Scarlett blushed and the way she looked at Tate was full of adoration. "He's going to build me a library."

Tate gave her a heated look in return. Any more of this shit and the room wouldn't be kid friendly. But then, the kids were probably used to this. Same with the adults. It was me who wasn't.

Tate leaned against the counter next to me. "Jonah said he helped you tow Hank's truck last week."

"Yep."

He nodded. "You guys have been busy with fence."

Defensiveness prickled along the back of my neck, but he sounded more like he was attempting conversation than digging for information. "Did Hank show you?"

"He's been telling everyone who'll listen that you've been out there with him."

Acid flared up my throat. "He's exaggerating. It was barely two days."

"He likes having you around, but you never said if you were moving to town."

First Teller. Now Tate. I glanced down to the bedroom. Good. The door was shut, but my suitcase was around the corner anyway. "I guess we'll have to see." My gaze followed Autumn as she ran to answer a knock on the door. Darin was on her hip again.

Myles lingered by us. He was holding Elsa while Wynter bent over the table with Scarlett, Brinley, and Chance sorting candy.

"Myles works from his home not far from Mama." Tate said it like a challenge. "Foster House is in Denver."

Another point made. "The casino isn't like that."

"I still fly to Foster House," Myles said more conversationally, "but soon, my brother Lane will be training on-site. In a couple of years, he might be there permanently."

Meaning Myles found running a company from

another state had its challenges, and he thought it was ideal to have the boss there full-time.

"I hired a manager," Myles added as if trying to keep from taking sides.

"I am the guy the board hired to run the casino."

"Autumn's not going to move," Tate said only loud enough for me and Myles to hear.

"Then don't give her a reason to."

He drew in a steady breath. Myles tipped his head down.

"It's not up to me, Gideon. If we don't buy that place, and if your dad doesn't sell to you, then who'll buy it? Some Hollywood asshole who doesn't give a shit about Montana or that land's history."

Clearly, having an outsider buy that place was a general concern with everyone. "Its history is *my* history. My great-grandfather worked his ass off to secure that place after he lost everything else." My grandfather had told me the story many times.

"Then we can't have it going to some bastard who's going to parade their rich friends through—or worse, turn it into a rental and ruin our property value."

I took a long sip of my drink. The heat of the alcohol burned down my throat, giving a place for my rising anger to latch on to. Awareness crept in. I was getting upset and savoring the flavor of alcohol on my tongue.

No. I put the glass by the edge of the sink. Tate's words were exactly what Dad had worried I'd do. "I'm not some rich prick." I kept my voice low.

Tate shrugged. "In the end, it's your dad's decision. Don't take your anger out on my sister."

"I don't think that's what he's doing with her." Myles smirked.

Tate shot him a dirty look. "Don't do that to me." He held his hands up. "Can we call a truce? At least for tonight? My kids love Halloween, and it's Friday, so we don't have to rush them to bed. I'm also not above a steep candy tax, and I need to see what Brinley has to pay with."

Wynter was digging in another cupboard. She withdrew a bag of freeze-dried yogurt bites. "Aunt Autumn came through again. Lucky Elsa."

I had wondered who the hell would eat those.

Autumn lifted her head from where she was recording the candy count with Chance. "There's too much competition for the funnest aunt. I have to stay stockpiled." She smiled at me, and she looked so damn happy surrounded by kids, my heart twisted like a dishrag.

I worked in a place where people went to *escape* this. I made it happen for them. But this was the first time I'd wondered why anyone would want a break from this kind of life. And that was terrifying.

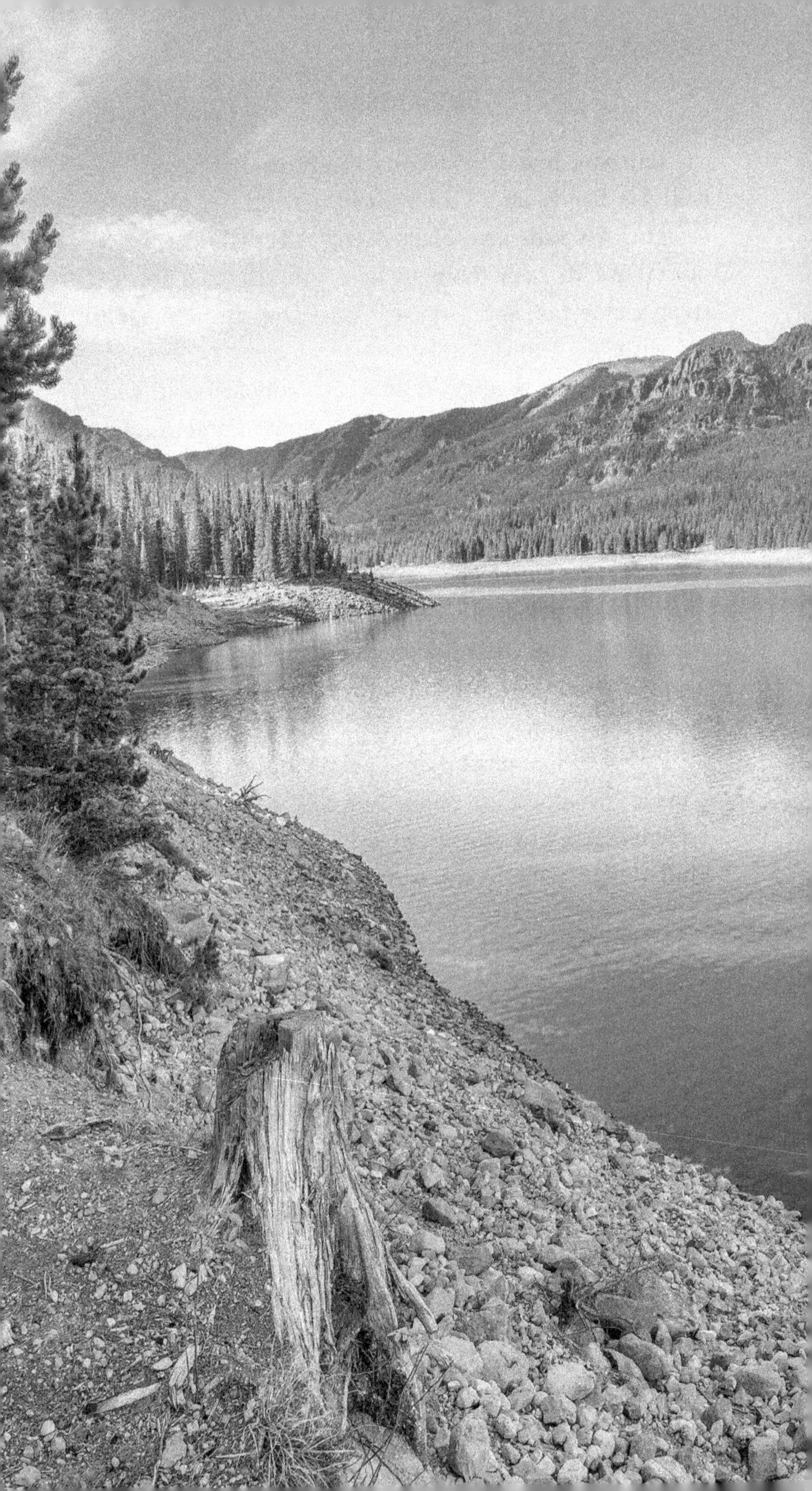

CHAPTER TWENTY

Autumn

Last night, after a short, hushed conversation with Tate and Myles, Gideon had grown ever quieter. We'd had amazing sex after everyone had left, and we'd both had way too much fun with those ridiculous suspenders, but I hadn't asked him what was bothering him. I didn't think he'd lash out like last time, but it was unlikely he'd tell me.

This morning, instead of waking up to an erection pressing against my ass, the other side of the bed was empty. Frowning, I rolled up. The bedroom door was shut, and it was after nine. He'd let me sleep in?

I got out of bed, cleaned up, brushed my teeth, and found a pair of fluffy emerald-green leggings to wear with a thick, gold knit sweater that covered my ass. Though I was less concerned about covering my butt when Gideon seemed to like having it in his face.

Tingles spread through my body like they usually did

when my mind wandered to sex with Gideon. I ignored them and pulled my hair into a loose bun on top of my head.

I found my husband at the kitchen table in a white T-shirt and gray sweatpants, looking like he could command a boardroom from the weight rack at the gym. The candy from last night had been cleaned up. All the types Chance hadn't liked were in the Halloween bowl by the door. I'd been able to hand several pieces out before I'd shut off the porch light to end trick-or-treating, but I had half a bowl left.

Gideon was staring at the computer screen and he'd moved the chair next to him out. Sprinkles was sprawled on that chair like she'd graciously given up the fight to sit on his lap.

"Morning," I said. I hovered a few feet away. I didn't want him to think I was snooping on what he was working on, but also because we didn't do kisses good morning. We fucked. I curled into him before we went to sleep, but he didn't press kisses into my hair. He didn't hug me just because. If we touched, it was foreplay.

For the last week, I hadn't questioned it. I enjoyed the hell out of the orgasms I was getting and seeing Gideon was a giant bonus. But . . . the intimacy was lacking, and really, there was no reason for it to be present. Didn't mean I didn't wish for it, but perhaps having another small line drawn was a good, constant reminder of what our arrangement was—convenient.

"Morning." He glanced over. His gaze raked down my body, leaving a trail of smoldering arousal, then went back to the screen.

"Did you eat yet?"

"No. I'm not hungry."

"I shouldn't be hungry. I think I ate half the candy aisle before bed." I tried to keep it light, but a part of me was feeling a little dismissed.

His brow remained furrowed as he stared at his screen. He had to be catching up on work. He never mentioned friends. Even with Taya, he'd mentioned a casual, very occasional connection that sounded more functional than emotional. He was alone, but for a little while, he had me. I didn't like seeing him disturbed and locking it away.

I folded my arms, hugging myself. The urge to cross to him and nuzzle his hair was strong. "I know you probably don't want to talk about it, but do you think you should?" I crept a step closer. "Something from last night is bothering you. Was it Tate? Something he said?"

I hadn't needed to eavesdrop to know Gideon and Tate had gone a round about the sale, but they'd acted like they'd come to a temporary truce. Gideon had sat next to me as I'd laughed with the kids and helped count and sort their haul for the night.

He tapped out of the screen on his computer and reclined in his seat. "Everything Tate said, yes, but that's nothing new."

His gaze shifted to beyond me. I looked over my shoulder. The kitchen sink.

I tried to picture what he was seeing. The dirty glasses from last night hadn't been put in the dishwasher because the washer needed emptying first. By the time my family had left, it'd been late, and not only by the kids' standards. When faced with going to bed with Gideon and his talented tongue or doing dishes, there would always be one clear winner.

He didn't speak. His phone buzzed and he frowned at the screen. Then he put the phone facedown on the table. He stayed quiet a few more moments.

Okay then.

I went for the fridge. He wasn't going to talk, and it was none of my business.

"I want to show you something," he said. "Let me get dressed."

"I haven't eaten yet. Can I pack something to take with us? Or are we going somewhere with food there already?"

"No food." He closed his laptop, gave Sprinkles a little scratch, and rose. "Pack whatever you'd like." He brushed past me on his way to the bedroom, leaving a cold draft behind him.

The cat got attention, but I didn't.

I shouldn't take it personally, something was clearly bothering him, but the lingering hurt wouldn't listen. I busied myself with breakfast and made a couple of quick peanut butter and jelly sandwiches. I had them packed into little baggies by the time he reappeared in the kitchen, dressed in the country-boy style that went straight to my libido. He even had a ball cap tucked on his head.

When his gaze landed on the peanut butter and jelly still sitting out, he blanched. "I hope you didn't make one for me."

I held up a sandwich bag. The one I'd made for him.

"I can't stand PB and J."

"Oh." Crestfallen, I dropped the baggie onto the table. "Sorry. I didn't know."

"Shit. It's not a big deal."

I wasn't so sure.

He scrubbed a hand down his face and clenched his finely stubbled jaw. "Are you ready?"

"Um, sure." I left the sandwiches behind.

This wasn't the normal, confident Gideon. The only thing I'd seen shake him was the talk about babies. He'd been around a ton of kids last night. Was there a link?

I loaded into the car. When he pulled out of the garage, I dug my sunglasses out. The direction he went was toward his dad's place.

I never tired of this drive. The landside might be different shades of brown instead of green, but with the blue sky and wispy white clouds, it was still gorgeous. The mountains in the background were already snow-tipped, but the trees remained a dark green to add a pop of color.

His family's land was a lot like the portion Daddy had gifted me. I hadn't shown Gideon yet, and I wasn't going to bring it up today. The idea of taking him out there seemed like rubbing salt in his emotional wounds.

I wished my brothers would change their minds, but Hank didn't seem like he would.

We passed the turn for the house. I craned my head to look back, but I didn't ask where we were going. We were still on James property.

He slowed, eventually turning off the road onto a little grass patch by a fence. The tire tracks continued on the other side, following the adjacent fence line over a rolling hill.

"I'll get the gate." I had my hand on the door handle when he curled his fingers around my forearm.

"No. I got it."

I had never been the lone passenger and sat out opening the gate. He got out and sauntered to the chain holding the gate shut. His big body bent over, working on loosening the metal hooks. He looked like he belonged. A born-and-raised country boy, which he was. Did he realize how easily he slipped back into the role he'd been raised doing?

When he climbed back in, the smell of cold sunshine followed him.

"We're going to get snow soon," I murmured, more to make any sort of conversation.

"Yeah. It's November now." The overtones were ominous.

It's November now.

Kind of like *Game of Thrones* and their winter tagline. November was here. Bad things were coming.

He left the gate open since there were no cattle in the pastures. We bumped over the hill. Up ahead, a small drop-off loomed. The tracks veered to the left, but Gideon pulled up parallel to the small crevice in the land.

A creek had slowly carved its way through this shallow draw to drain into what would likely be a pond at the lowest point until the countryside swooped back up. The pond would probably be as dry as the creek bed. We hadn't had a lot of rain this fall, but it'd be a good pasture to turn the cattle out in for the early summer. Winter runoff would fill the pond. A nature-made water source.

My brothers could expand Bailey Beef and utilize the pastures that weren't farmland. If Gideon got the property, would he do the same? Would he leave all the decisions up to a faceless ranch manager while he never stepped foot on Percival for another twenty-five years?

I was about to tell him it was really pretty out here

when he got out of the car. The hill we'd crested was behind us and blocked the road. It looked like there was no civilization for miles, and truthfully, there wasn't much. Another ranch bordered the field on the other side of this one, and if Gideon could go straight through, he'd reach his dad's house, but I doubted the path would handle a vehicle.

I climbed out. "Did you used to ride horses to get out here? Or four-wheelers?"

His back was to me as he looked over the crevice. He didn't reply.

I tucked the hurt away as I came to a stop next to him. My soft gasp carried away on the wind. The other side dropped lower than where we were standing, and on the edge was a neat little white cross. A bouquet of dried flowers shook in the breeze.

Jenni James had died when she'd rolled her snowmobile.

I put my fingers to my mouth. Tears pricked the backs of my eyes. "Oh, Gideon. I'm so sorry."

He propped his hands on his hips and aimed his gaze at his boots. "She died in November."

Would he shrug me off if I tried to hug him? He vibrated with *leave me alone* energy.

I gave in. If he pushed me away, so be it, but he shouldn't be on an emotional island right now. He likely hadn't had many shoulders to cry on when he was younger. I wound my arms through his and around his waist. It was like embracing a wooden pole. A breath later, he wrapped his arms around me. I didn't have to look up to know his gaze was stuck on that white cross.

"He set the closing date for the month we lost her." Grief outlined his every word.

"I'm sorry."

I felt him nod more than I saw it. "It's no less than I should've expected."

I kept my cheek tucked against his strong chest. His heartbeat was strong and steady, but even that sounded mournful under my ear. He was entwining himself in his pain. Had he ever processed his emotions, or had he locked them away? Had he considered that others around him were processing their own gut-wrenching feelings?

"Can I play devil's advocate?" I asked.

Tension radiated through him. "As long as you're ready to hear me disagree."

"The first thing I wonder is if he has his own grief journey." I tipped my face up to him. His gaze didn't soften. "That's what the funeral called it when Daddy died. Our individual grief journey. I would've rolled my eyes if it hadn't resonated so deeply with me."

His hold around me tightened. I pressed my cheek back against his chest.

"Like Wynter," I continued. "She couldn't be around when Daddy was at his sickest. It was too much like sitting in that car waiting and knowing our parents were dead. The way she avoided the house was hard for my brothers to understand. It wasn't hard for me." Because I'd been in that same car. "It makes me wonder . . . maybe in a way that doesn't make sense to us, or at all, but for your dad . . . I wonder if it's his way of respecting what she left him with."

He went rigid again. "She would not think he was respecting her."

"I'm throwing it out there. People don't always do what makes sense when they're hurting. I see it in the kids, and honestly, I don't think we grow out of it like we think we do."

"What do you see in the kids?"

"The ones who hurt the most lash out the hardest—at others or themselves."

His stomach clenched. He was struggling, but he also wasn't trying to leave. Did it surprise him to think that his dad was probably still destroyed about his mom?

"Have you ever . . ." His chest expanded with his inhale. "Did you ever go back to where it happened?"

I didn't have to ask him what "it" was. Or where. "Yes. All of us went when Summer got her license. Mama used to take each of us aside and ask if we needed to visit our parents' graves or the site. We all said no." My laugh was dry. "But one night when I was, gosh, fifteen, we were all helping Wynter through a storm—she hates them. I mean, none of us liked them after that night, but it's *a thing* with her, you know? Anyway. Summer had the idea. It's twenty miles away, in pretty rural territory, because we were out camping. We never told Mama."

"Why?" He started stroking my shoulder.

"Who can say. Maybe we thought she'd say no. Or maybe we were scared we would crash and break the Baileys' hearts. Sometimes, I think she would've offered to come with us, to drive us even, but we wanted—needed—for it to be a sisters' thing. As far as I know, that was the only time any of us have been there." Once was enough, and none of us could probably explain why. I looked up at him. "Is this the first time you've returned?"

"No," he said softly. "I used to come here a lot as a kid. Dad lost his shit once when he found out I took the four-wheeler—I think he was actually scared the same thing would happen to me—so after that, I had to ride Cray-Cray." The corner of his mouth tipped up. "That was Mom's horse. I heard her tell Dad once that his real name was Crazy Bastard, but by the time I was ready to ride, he was old and mellow."

"I've known a few animals that could be called Crazy Bastard."

"This is the first time I've been here since I left home. I used to sit out here for a while and just wonder..."

He didn't have to tell me what went through his head. The what-ifs.

What if she'd survived? What if nothing had happened? What if he had died instead? His dad? And the questions. How would things be different? Would they be better? How could life be worse when the people you loved most were gone? I'd had similar thoughts.

In my case, my sisters and I had been placed in an excellent home and the Baileys were now our family. We'd become Baileys. We'd only kept our names because we'd had so little left of our parents, and there'd been a ton of changes already. In Gideon's case, he *knew* that things would have been better with his mom. He'd have been happier. His dad would've been healthier.

I rubbed his back. "I have a blanket in the back of the car. Let me grab it. We can stay a while."

"Don't you have to restock the bar and work tonight?" His expression was tight, like he was afraid I'd say *oops, you're right*.

"That's one of the perks of being one of the owners. I can stock whenever the hell I want."

Gideon

We'd had to give up sitting outside. If we weren't moving, it was too chilly out to sit on a blanket on the ground.

I swung the car around and opened the hatch. She laid the seats down. I was sitting up, reclining against the front seat. She was curled into my side.

We weren't having sex. This was full-on cuddling. Something we only did in the dark of her bedroom. Something I otherwise never did. With Autumn, I could have her plastered all over me for the rest of the day. Tomorrow too.

A few minutes ago, I'd gotten a surprising text from Tate. It wasn't the call I wanted, but at least it hadn't been Taya. She kept leaving me messages to call her. If what she had to say couldn't be texted or emailed, I didn't need to hear it. I had to keep things professional.

I showed Autumn the message.

Tate: We're doing grid moves this week. If you think you can still stay upright on a horse, we could use a hand.

"Grid moves?" I asked Autumn. "Is that a new term?"

"I don't know. Tate started using it when he took over. He's got books for his books."

"When you say things like that, I feel like Tate and I could actually get along."

She giggled. "You'd either be best friends or mortal enemies. Do you know how he and Scarlett got together?"

"He demanded she date him?"

"He agreed to the local bachelor auction fundraiser."

I'd have loved to see him paraded in front of a bunch of women and sold off, but Autumn's tone made it sound like the fundraiser was a light, fun time. "Since when does Bourbon Canyon have a bachelor auction?"

"I don't recall when it started, but I knew Scarlett had a thing for Tate. Summer and I suspected Tate felt the same. Scarlett was Chance's fourth-grade teacher, so they knew each other."

"So you encouraged Scarlett to bid on him?"

She shook her head, her smile mischievous. It was one of my favorite looks on her. "We invited her to the auction, and we bid without telling her it was her name we were bidding under."

"You bought your brother for your friend?"

She grinned. "The rest is history. All of us pitched in. Summer had to bid crazy high. He was a hot commodity."

Instead of being disgruntled at how amazing everyone thought Tate was, I chuckled. An entire family pooling money to help their loved one find love.

What would it be like to have a big family like that? To have all that support when things went to shit? To have someone to celebrate with during the good times?

College graduation had been just another day, only one without classes. I'd had no one to tell when I'd gotten my first real job. And when I'd landed the role of Silver Casino and Hotel CEO, I'd treated myself to a dinner out. Then I'd gone home alone.

The emptiness inside me turned restless. I was married into that same family, but I doubt they'd celebrate me. "Are you going to buy a significant other for Teller and Tenor?"

"We might have to." She brushed the backs of her fingers over my cheek. "Are you going to help my brothers move cattle on Monday?"

"I'm curious to see if they plan to get me trampled and call it an accident."

"That's dark." Yet she was grinning. "You might have to dust off those country-boy skills to keep up."

"They'll keep up," I growled. It'd been more than a few years, but fencing had come back like I'd been doing it around Silver my entire adult life.

"I wish I could see it."

"I'll just be another guy on a horse."

"You're not just any guy."

When she said shit like that, my chest threatened to puff up. She didn't drop superficial compliments on me like other people had my whole career. When she said something, she meant it.

My wife was generous, realistic, and honest. Traits that'd make returning to work difficult.

A few strands of her hair escaped her bun. I let them slip through my fingers. The color was bright against the bronzed skin of my hands. "Why can't you witness me be a superhero cowboy?"

"The fourth- and fifth-grade music programs are this week. I usually help, and now I'm on the hook because their students wanted to do skits at the last minute."

"They guilt-tripped you?" I asked lightly.

"You could say that. Scarlett and Joseph aren't upset, but I said I'd help. Joseph would help anyway, but since he helped me, I owe him." She hooked my hand and threaded her fingers through mine. "I'll miss you being a cowboy, but you have to promise me something."

Sitting with her, across from the place my mom had died and where my dad must still stop by and pay his respects, I was ready to promise her the world.

"If Mama offers to cook for everyone tomorrow night, you need to stay and then bring a plate home for me."

"How do you know I'll be invited?"

"She'll make sure you're there. In her eyes, you're family."

My heart constricted and pain radiated out from my ribs. I wasn't family. I only had Dad and he'd never been there.

But he had tried . . .

I shook the thought off. He wanted to foster a relationship and I wanted him to get his head out of his ass. The Baileys were my in-laws for only another couple of weeks.

My gaze landed on that white cross and the flowers that weren't very old. A tangle of emotions swelled in my chest. Dad had never talked about Mom after she'd died, and I didn't speak with him enough to know if he did now. My grandparents had been gone for years. Dad was the only one who knew where Mom had died and would care enough to maintain the cross and flowers.

Was Autumn right? Was this sale a way for him to purge the grief he'd been hanging on to? Those emotions that had driven him to drink? He had AA, but then, after every meeting, he went home to an empty house that used to be filled with love and family.

He'd promised Mom 'til death do you part. After

that, he'd had nothing to hang on to. I hadn't been enough then, and I wasn't sticking around now.

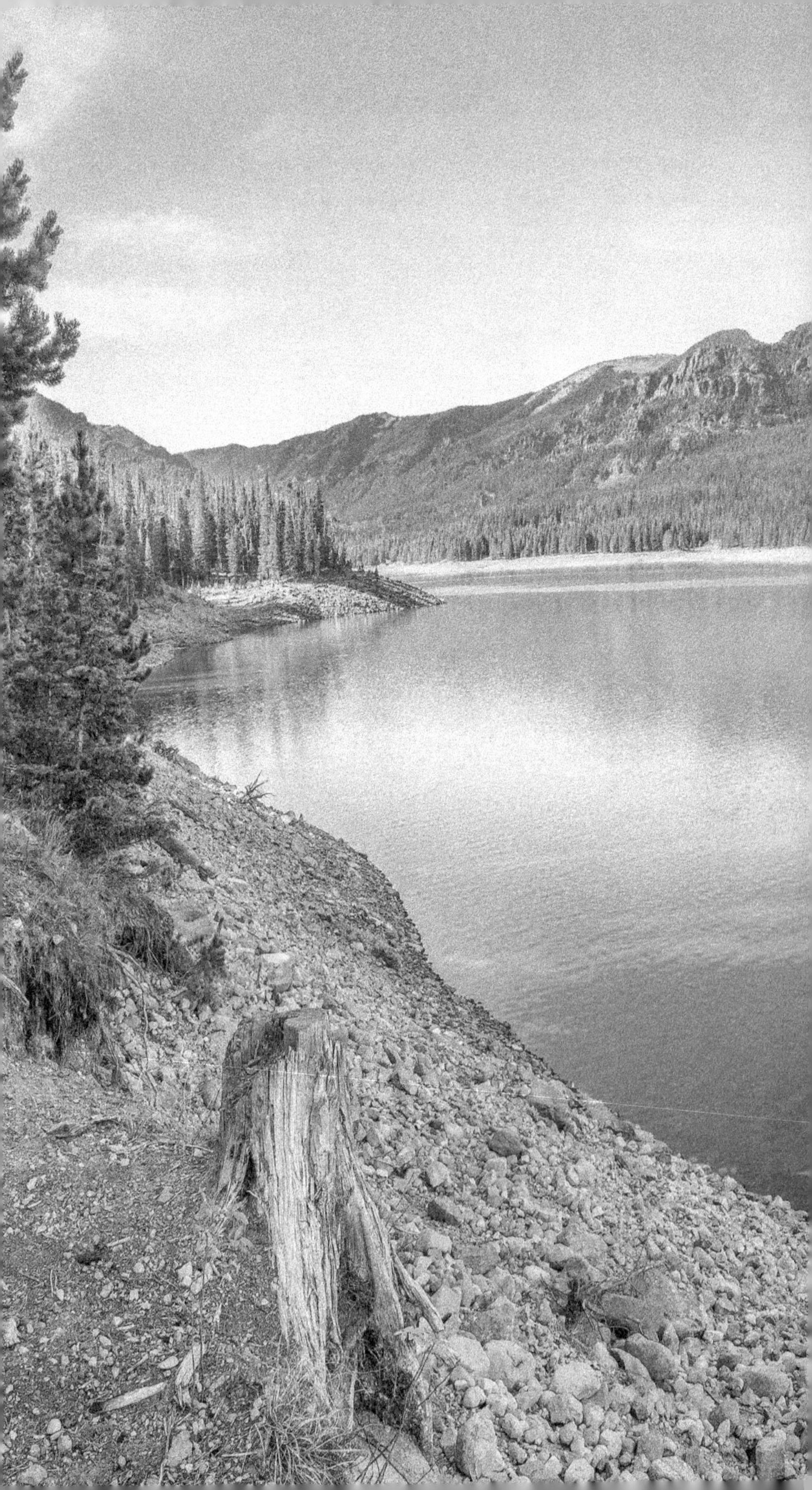

CHAPTER TWENTY-ONE

Gideon

Yesterday, I'd gone to the tractor supply store and picked up thick work gloves and a cowboy hat. I was wearing everything I'd bought to the Baileys.

This morning, the light hadn't yet crested the horizon when I'd coasted down the Baileys' drive. Scarlett had said she'd pick up Autumn for work and give her a ride home. I'd been half tempted to buy a pickup yesterday so Autumn wouldn't have to beg rides, but she'd shut me down. I'd been telling myself for nearly two weeks that I should buy a vehicle to make it easier on us.

What are you going to do with a pickup in Vegas?

I had no answer to that question. I could sell it. Hell, I could give it to Autumn as a parting gift. *Here're divorce papers and a new truck for your time.*

The idea rested like lead in my gut. Maybe if I knew

whether Dad would pull back at the last minute, I'd have a more optimistic response.

I parked by the house like Autumn had told me to do and walked down to the barn. The crisp, cold scent in the air propelled me back to an earlier time when I was saddling the horses to move our own cattle. When I was younger, I had been stitched to Dad's side. By the time I'd been a teen, I had been running the show. Dad would pretend he was in charge, but I would have everything ready. Unlike the Baileys' property, ours wasn't big enough to require overnight cattle drives. Mom and Dad had made a long day of it, and I'd loved each moment.

Part of that joy rose up from a long-locked-up memory. I had loved long days working with cattle as much as I had loved harvesting from sunup to sundown. Sometimes, I'd been alone in my own head, but then afterward, I'd join in the chatter with my parents. What went well? What could we do better? What needed fixing? I'd feel like a grown-up, and when I'd talk with my grandfather afterward, he'd beam and nod.

Farming's in your blood. The outdoors is in your blood. Trust your gut.

Later, before I graduated high school, he'd said similar things. *This place is yours. You know your dad won't do what needs to be done. He's going to run Percival into the ground. My father scraped his pennies together and bought that land after everything had been taken from him and his family. Don't let your dad take this from you. Start by scraping your pennies together.*

My grandfather's voice was echoing louder than it had in years. Those memories were why I was here today. If Dad heard about what I was doing today, he'd know I wasn't some city asshole who wanted to claim a tax deduction and walk over the locals. I was a local, goddammit.

Tate and Teller were loading horses into the silver horse trailer attached to Tate's pickup. Tenor was tossing coolers into the back seat. Pails and Rubbermaid bins were piled by the front of the horse trailer.

The wind buffeted my face. A few flurries fell from the sky.

Myles appeared next to me. "I guess it could be colder."

I almost didn't recognize him with the tan cowboy hat on, and I hadn't even noticed him following me. I looked back. Wynter was dressed in jeans and boots, a beat-up tan jacket zipped to her chin. Her own black cowboy hat was pulled down low and her blond braid was tucked into the collar of her coat.

"Got the baby here too?" I asked.

Myles grinned, but his indulgent gaze was on his wife. "No, Elsa's going to be with Mae all day. You should see how giddy Mae is about that." His gaze lifted to two men pulling up in a pickup with another trailer. "You met my brothers, Lane and Cruz, right?"

They had been at the party Dad had thrown. "Briefly."

"Since Wynter's going to boss us around," Cruz said to me, "you might want to ride with the other guys. Four and four."

I nodded and jumped in to help load the gear.

Tenor worked beside me, directing where everything got stashed and stored.

"You sure it's only a day trip?" I asked.

A horse from the trailer whinnied and one of the

geldings getting loaded up in the Fosters' trailer answered. A chorus of whinnies went up.

Tenor grinned and pushed his thick-framed glasses up. "When Tate took over, he got us signed up for a pasture management program."

Teller walked by and grunted. "Talk about a fuckton of fencing."

Tenor nodded. "We made smaller pastures and we move them more often. This way, we're not as reliant on hay during the winter and the pastures have more time to rest."

"Which means more vegetation." *I might've read up on a few ranching-related topics while I was in Vegas.*

"Yup. Plus, Tate couldn't be moving cattle for days at a time anymore with Chance, and now that he has three little ones, he certainly isn't going to leave Scarlett days at a time." His grin widened. "And we're all getting older. Sleeping on the ground in the cold and heat is a little harder than it used to be."

Made sense. Tenor must be in his late thirties. Except for Myles's brothers, we were all either pushing forty or well past that birthday.

"Disappointed?" Tenor adjusted the brim of his cowboy hat. "Or are you dying to get back to your plush bed in the city?"

Autumn wasn't in my plush bed in the city.

Teller walked by in the opposite direction. "Just so you know, James, we're taking bets on how long you'll last in the saddle."

Tenor snickered and continued loading supplies. Thumps and bumps of metal from the horses moving in the trailer filled the air. Just because the last time I'd ridden a horse was probably before Lane or Cruz had been born didn't mean I couldn't handle the entire day in the saddle. And I'd prove it.

Autumn

When I got home after work and after prepping for the fourth-grade music performance, the house was dark. Gideon's laptop sat closed on the kitchen table. The satisfaction I got from that was supreme. In Vegas, I bet no one in that casino would believe he could take a break from work that long.

My smugness took a dip when I realized he always had his mind in the game. He'd gone to help move cattle, but he probably had an ulterior motive.

I rubbed my suddenly tight gut. I hadn't eaten. Tomorrow night, Scarlett planned to order pizza. I was rummaging in the kitchen when the garage door opened and closed. A minute later, Gideon stepped through the door with two plates in his hands.

"Hey," he said in a low timbre that chased the chill away and warmed me from the inside out.

"Hey."

A cold draft wafted in with him, and I caught the scents of horse sweat, crisp fall air, and dirt. His hair was smashed down from his cowboy hat, and he was dusty from head to toe, but it was his gaze that gave me pause. A slight twinkle shone from their depths and it was the most relaxed I'd seen him . . . ever.

Even after sex, he was never boneless like me. He had a constant tension radiating through him to match the way his mind was constantly working. These days I assumed the land sale was occupying his thoughts, but before me, before this, his regular job probably took up the majority of his brainpower. Today, maybe it was the cowboy boots that gave him an easy, rolling gait, but the constant tension across his shoulders was gone.

He shoved his laptop aside—also satisfying—and set the plates down. "Mae already had your plate prepared when we returned."

But he'd come bearing two plates. "Haven't you eaten?"

He shook his head. "I knew you and Scarlett wouldn't be working too long, and I didn't want you to wait." He went to a drawer by the sink to dig out two forks.

He'd been riding all day. Whenever I'd helped move cattle or had been around when my family was done for the day, they piled around the table and barely remembered how to eat like civilized beings. "You didn't have to."

His direct gaze caught me. "I know. Sit."

I did as he said. Mama had made a ground-beef-and-pasta dish that was cheesy and creamy. A perfect meal for people who'd been outside all day.

After the worst of our hunger was sated, I peeked at the way the muscles in his jaws bunched when he chewed. My fingers itched to ruffle through his flattened hair. The look was different on him. It softened the edges of his sharp, professional persona and the jaw carved from stone.

"How'd it go?" I asked.

He pushed some pasta together, not seeming to mind all his food mixed. Was it just when he was extra alert, like meeting Mama?

Mama had piled both of our plates high. I would have enough for lunch tomorrow, but Gideon was almost done. "Good." He took another bite.

I kept eating.

His fork clinked on the table. "Actually, it was really fucking fun, and I'm a little pissed about it."

"Oh?" I turned in my seat to face him.

He shoved a hand into his hair. Clumps stuck up between his fingers and stayed mostly in place when he removed his hand. "There were a couple of cows in the brush and I chased them out. Do you know how long it's been since I've done that? Since I've done any of this?" His jaw clenched. "I loved every part of it. Those days when Dad and I used to move cattle? I don't remember those fondly. But today . . . I remembered when Mom used to be with us."

"And the fun came back?" I asked quietly.

He stared at his mostly empty plate for a minute. "Yeah."

When he returned to eating, I swiveled back to my food. "I am glad you found the joy again."

He grunted, likely thinking about how it might be the first time since he'd left town but the last time for the rest of his life.

I put the wrap on top of my plate and put it in the fridge. "Don't worry about tomorrow night. Summer's bringing Chance, Brinley, and Darin to Mama's, so we don't have to rush. Scarlett wants to order pizza."

"Got it." He rose, but didn't move. "Is Mark going to be there?"

I blinked. My thoughts had been consumed with Gideon. People still congratulated me on my marriage. I'd almost forgotten that I'd been on a few dates with Mark. "No. He's steering clear of me."

"Good." He took his dishes to the sink. "I'm going to shower."

His jean-clad ass had my rapt attention as he sauntered down the hallway and disappeared into the bedroom. He'd had fun and he was pissed about it. That summed up his mood.

I sighed and went to the bedroom. I'd clean up in the bathroom after him.

A few minutes later, he was done, exiting the bathroom with nothing but a towel wrapped around his waist. The scruff on his cheeks was longer. He hadn't shaved yesterday or today.

I grabbed my pajamas and scooted around him. This bedroom was tiny when he was in it.

He grasped my elbow and spun me toward him.

"What's wro—"

He smashed his mouth onto mine. The kiss was immediately all-consuming. His whiskers brushed my skin, sending rivulets of tingles down my body. I shivered, and he hugged me closer to him. My arms were crushed between us, but I still had a hold on my pajamas. I couldn't drop them if I tried. They'd have gotten caught on the thick erection pressing between us anyway.

He pulled back enough to say, "I missed you today."

"Mmm. It's been a while since I've helped. Tate tries not to do it over weekends all the time."

His gaze bounced between my eyes. "I kept thinking how sexy you'd be out there with your boots and cowboy hat." He pressed another kiss to my lips. "I kept wondering how much your tits would bounce when you rode."

The tingle turned to a full-body shiver. "Mr. James, did you give yourself an erection on horseback?"

"Yes. That was fucking irritating too. Good thing I had to go flush out the cattle right then."

"I like where this is going, but I've gotta use the bathroom."

Another kiss before he let me go. "Okay, but I'm not done with you."

I scurried into the bathroom. I clipped my hair up and ran through the shower. I was about to crawl out of my skin with anticipation when I exited the bathroom. The overhead light was off. Only the glow from the lamp on my nightstand lit the room. The door was closed to keep the cat out.

Gideon was stretched out on his side of the bed, making my queen look like a twin bed. The towel was piled on top of his privates. His long legs, dusted with dark hair, were crossed at the ankle and still so damn muscular even as he slumbered.

I huffed out a quiet laugh. He must be exhausted. He'd been up before dawn, which at this time of year wasn't as early as he was used to, but he hadn't been behind a desk all day.

I left the door shut so Sprinkles wouldn't wake him. I shut the light off and crawled in.

Heat emanated from him. Should I cover him up, or would he get too hot?

I lay back.

"I said I wasn't done with you yet."

I jolted. "Geez, you scared me."

His deep chuckle resonated between us. "I might've been dozing, but a full day in the saddle isn't enough to keep me from you."

His compliment warmed me. "If you're tired, you can sleep. It's okay."

"Autumn, turn that damn light back on so I can watch your tits jiggle when you ride me."

I choked on a squeak. "I'm not riding you with the light on."

We'd done a lot. He'd seen it all. But he was usually the one doing the work. I was like an enthusiastic bystander who loved the orgasms.

"Autumn," he growled.

My breath hitched. Was I really going to chicken out? He knew what I looked like from so many different angles.

I flipped the lamp on. We were bathed in weak light.

He tossed the towel off him, and his cock strained long and proud toward his belly. "Climb on."

A condom sat on the end table by him. I reached over him, but he caught my arm. "Not yet. I need to feel you first."

The need in his voice was enough to get me to straddle him. He really wanted to see me astride him. I'd been on top before, but it had been an in-the-moment thing. Not the beginning, middle, and end.

He was tired, but like he said—not tired enough to skip this.

Who was I to deny him?

I adjusted my legs on either side of his hips. My pussy was right on him. Since we were touching, I could feel how wet I was from the slickness between us. I rubbed back and forth.

A deep groan left him. "Fuck, you're like soaked velvet. Just fucking hot and soft."

He gripped my thighs, but he didn't move me. My breasts swayed as I leaned over and stroked myself up and down his length.

"Fuck," he said from between clenched teeth. His body was taut, but I was turning to liquid. "You're so goddamn wet for me, and I've barely touched you."

As if he needed to rectify that, he palmed my breasts. The strength in his hands, hard and unyielding, was always gentle enough to keep from hurting me.

"Christ." He retrieved the condom. "I'm not going to fucking last."

He ripped the package open with his teeth, but I took the rest from him.

"Let me do it."

His gaze promised retribution for slowing down the moment. I wanted to savor his attention. My insecurities were gone. How could they bother me when simple dry-humping got him this worked up?

I sat back on his thighs and took my time rolling the condom down. His cock twitched under my fingers, and he massaged my thighs. I gave his erection a few lazy pumps. His gaze was on my hand, then on the junction between my thighs, then back to my hand.

"Get on, wife. Show me how you ride."

My chest grew tight. Wife.

I shifted and placed him at my entrance. Then I sank down. Slowly. With each inch, he balled up with tension, his knees bending behind me. He rolled up slightly.

When I was fully seated and so damn full of him, I

rocked to adjust to his size. "You're so big." I might sound like I was in a porn, but I was telling the truth. I'd thought penises like his were a fantasy. It was like I'd special ordered him. Give me an almost perfect husband to test for a month.

"Jesus." He crunched up, gripped my ass to grind me down onto him, and tongued a nipple.

A long, needy moan left me. "Gideon."

I didn't have much room to move, but I did. He loosened his grip and lay back. "Fucking ride me, firecracker."

I tipped my head back, my hair brushed against my lower spine, and I stuck my chest out. I increased the pace and my breasts swayed, then bounced, just like he wanted.

"Fuck, yes," he said tightly.

I was ready to ride him for as long as he wanted, letting my climax build and stall. I could control the rise in this position. But then he ran his thumb across my lips. I licked it. Heat filled his gaze a second before he dropped that thumb and stroked it across my soaked clit.

Oh god. I gasped and had to tip forward. He was working my clit as I rode him. The sensations were too much and then he used his other hand to massage a nipple.

"Gideon," I whined.

"Say it again."

"Gideon." I was getting out of breath. I was fighting off the climax, wanting this to last longer, but it was impossible with him.

"What else can you call me?"

My mind was too focused on my center to work.

"Gideon."

"What else, rusty?"

Right. Nickname. "City boy?"

"What else?" He eased the pressure on my clit. I wanted to cry. I had to come. I needed to.

A tremble racked my body. I was on the precipice, and he was keeping me there.

"What else, wife?"

I never called him anything else, but I knew what he wanted. "H-husband."

The calloused stroke of his thumb was back. The storm inside me reached a crescendo and explosions detonated behind my eyes. I flung my head back, crying out something unintelligible.

He rolled up, grinding into me, his hips bucking as he came. I wrapped my arms around him, and he buried his head into my chest.

"Fuck, Autumn."

When I crashed down, he caught me. I was limp. He rolled us to the side. No one would guess I wasn't the one who'd spent the day on a horse. I let him slip out of my body. The baggy end of the condom dragged against my thigh. He glanced between us and his expression shuttered.

What did that look mean?

I was about to snuggle into him when he reached over the edge of the bed and grabbed the towel.

We silently cleaned up. I waited until we were both back in bed before I turned out the light. When it was dark, I could cuddle against him since we often woke up that way. But tonight, there was a weird distance between us since we'd climaxed together.

Had I done something wrong?

Was I overthinking it all? He had to get up early again tomorrow and miss more work. Maybe he was stressing.

The thought didn't seem quite right.

"I'm sorry I won't get you pregnant." His words were quiet in the dark.

Surprised, I stared at the dark wall. He had drawn away because of me? "I understand." Since he was vulnerable, I could expose myself a little more. I might've ranted about how I wasn't naive, but at the same time, I was. "It was silly of me to think you'd plant the seed and move on as if you gave zero fucks." He'd care deeply about a kid. Was that what scared him?

"A lot of guys do."

"Not you."

"No. I couldn't. You'd be a good mom."

Heat poked the backs of my eyes. I wanted a family, but I didn't want to sacrifice who I was. I wanted what my parents had had. Mama Starr and Daddy Bjorn had been committed to each other. He could've left Mama Starr with four young kids. Same with Mama Starr. But they'd stuck together through the hard times until the end. Not only had they been each other's support, but they'd kept the gravity of our situation to themselves.

Then there were my Bailey parents. So damn dedicated to each other. A solid foundation. Yes, I wanted kids. But I wanted a partner in life more. I wanted someone to share laughs with, someone to vent to, someone to commiserate with. I wanted that support. To be loved for me.

Could I be a single mom? Yes. And I'd probably be a good one. I was fortunate to have a huge support system. But that was only a part of my dream.

"Thank you," I said. Was this one of those times I should tell him the same? "For what it's worth, the fact that you care means you'd probably be a good—"

"No. I wouldn't. I'm too much like my dad."

"Gideon." I was reaching for him when he rolled over, giving me the broad, shadowed expanse of his back.

"Good night, Autumn."

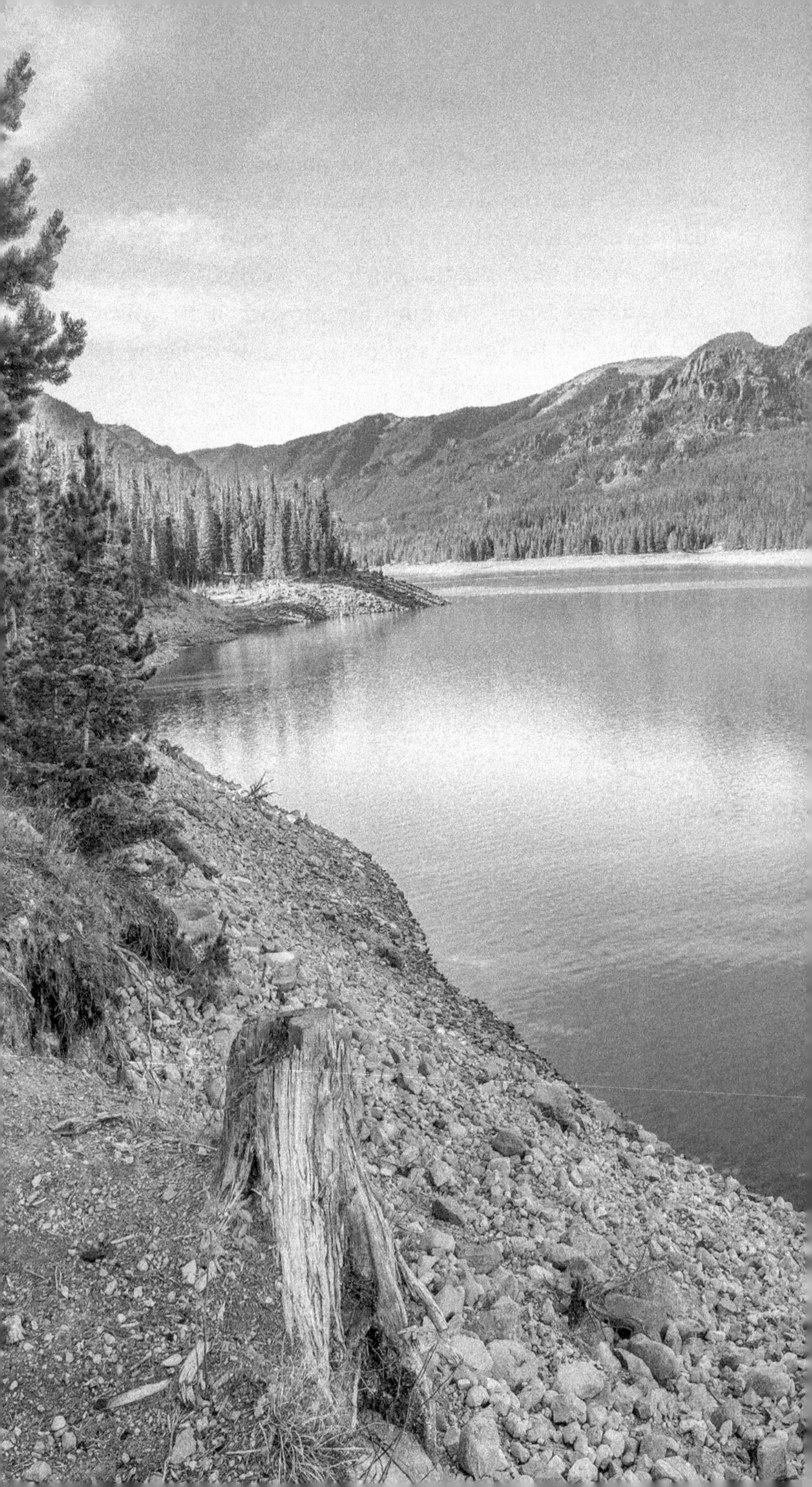

CHAPTER TWENTY-TWO

Gideon

I staggered toward Mae's house. My legs and ass—hell, my entire core—were sore in a way they hadn't been in my entire memory. I was both stiff from the previous day and sore from a fresh ten hours in the saddle. The pastures today had had a lot more brush, and a couple of those infuriating hunks of living leather liked to hide.

Tate slapped me on the back. He was just as uptight when he worked, yet there was a casual air about him now. He was serious, diligent, but the ranch was his element. It was likely the same at the distillery. It'd been me and the sale issue that had made him tenser than normal.

I had that effect at my job too.

Except for today. No one had treated me differently than anyone else. When a cow had charged through a copse of trees and I'd gone in after it, getting bitch-slapped by dried branches, they'd had a good laugh. And likewise for me when it had happened to them.

Tate said we'd be done tomorrow. One more day. Then I'd have work from sunup until sundown at my laptop. As if on cue, my phone buzzed. I checked the message just in case it was from Autumn. She'd sent one earlier, saying the plan for the pizza party was still on and she'd be home late.

The new message was from Taya. **Seriously. Can you just fucking call? It's sort of about work.**

Sort of about work? That was new, but it still didn't answer why she couldn't email. Since she'd given me a tidbit, I gave her a partial answer. **I'm wrapped up in something. I'll call when I can.**

I tucked my phone in my pocket and followed the crew inside. Myles and Wynter weren't out today. Scarlett had brought the kids to Mae's. When the door opened, the shouts that came out sounded like ten kids were in the house instead of three.

"Grandma?" Chance said, his voice cracking. I barely remembered that age or the whole puberty thing. My mom had just died and the time period was a fog of doing what needed to be done with an increasingly self-pitying dad. "Where do you want this?"

When I entered and the crowd cleared, I found Chance helping Mae put food on the table.

She waved us in. "Come, come. The little ones were ready to charge the table. Chance would've led the way."

Yes. I recalled those days. The constant hunger among the dwindling supply of groceries. Roaming the kitchen while my stomach gnawed at me. And then waking up, only to scrape the remnants of peanut butter out of the jar to cobble together another PB&J.

When Mom had been alive, our kitchen had smelled like this—savory meats and spices. Our house had been warm like this. Though with only three of us, there hadn't been this hustle and bustle.

This was . . . nice. A lot nicer than coming home to a dark apartment lit by the Vegas skyline.

I took off my cowboy hat and shrugged out of my coat. Both looked like I'd been wearing them for years instead of days.

Mae sidled up to me, a bowl of steaming peas in her hands. "Do you mind if I make a plate for your dad? Would you be able to drop it off?"

Confusion sparked before my natural resistance to seeing my dad followed. Since we'd helped him the night of the AA meeting, I hadn't seen him. "You don't have to. I'm sure he's eaten already."

I had no fucking idea.

Her smile was kind, but a hint of obstinance glinted in her eyes. "I made a ton, and with the leftovers from last night, I'm going to be eating pasta and pork chops for weeks. I can also send leftovers for you and Autumn for lunches." She squeezed my elbow. "Come. Let's eat."

She hadn't taken my subtle no for an answer. I'd get a shitload of food and that would be that.

I sat at the empty seat at the table by Tenor. Teller was across from him. Tate and Chance were closer to Mae, who was flanked by Brinley and Darin. Cruz and Lane took the seats at the end by me. Dishes were passed counterclockwise and I filled my plate. Tate updated his mom about the day, and Tenor and Teller joined in with a story or two to make her laugh. I laughed along with them.

Then Tate asked Chance about school. The other

guys peppered the kids with questions. Teller bet Brinley she couldn't eat more peas than him. She won, but I suspected Teller threw the game.

When was the last time I'd smiled this much? I was nothing but a spectator, yet I felt like part of the group. When the meal wrapped up, I helped clear the table and do the dishes.

Mae dug various plastic containers out of the cupboards and filled those along with a thick paper plate. "Thank you for doing this, Gideon."

Lane clapped me on the back. "She says it like you have a choice."

"Hey now." She shot him a playful glare. "Don't be selling my secrets." She patted me on the shoulder. "Tell your dad I said hi."

I only nodded, dreading the task.

I left on a wave of "See ya tomorrow" and "Bright and early." I tossed my cowboy hat in the back seat. The food in my stomach molded itself into a bowling ball. How the hell did Mae talk me into this without really discussing it? My headlights lit the familiar stretch of road. A few snow flurries melted on the windshield. They were supposed to add up to nothing, but then later this week, we'd get measurable snow.

The house came into view. A porch light shone in the dark along with the glow from the living room. I parked in front of the walk and stared at the food containers. I'd get this over with and leave. I got out. When I reached the front door, I hesitated. The old wood smell of the porch surrounded me, along with the crisp promise of snow on the breeze. Nostalgia poured into my brain.

"Mom! Dad! Pickles had kittens!"

Pickles had been my favorite barn cat. She'd disappeared one day, and we'd assumed she'd become food for a larger animal. I'd been distraught, and Dad had taken me fishing.

My throat grew thick. Those memories did me no good. I rapped three times on the door. It swung open on the last knock. The door didn't make a sound. He'd fixed that too. He was fixing everything but the relationship between us.

Dad's lined face looked older with his hat off. His hair was trimmed short and mostly gray. He kept his mustache and beard trimmed. I'd gotten much of my looks from my mom, but I could see myself in the sweep of his shoulders and the shape of his face.

"I was wondering if that was you." His gaze dropped to the plate.

"Mae claims she made too much food."

His eyes lit up. "Did she now?" He turned away and left the door open. "Come on in."

"No, I gotta—"

"That Mae. She's a good cook." He looked over his shoulder as he went up the stairs. "You eat yet?"

I was still holding the food. I'd be a real dick if I just left with the goods.

Stepping over the threshold, I steeled myself against the feelings washing over me. "Yeah," I said gruffly.

The smell was different. I had prepared for a stale-beer smell. A dried, dead yeast smell that was so unlike the thriving fermentation scents of the distillery. Instead, I was hit with a soft cinnamon aroma, so faint it was barely noticeable. The carpets were the same, everything I could see was the same, but it was . . . clean.

I hadn't grown up in filth after Mom had died, but

we hadn't been worried about total cleanliness. Things had been grungy. It was one of the reasons I'd been drawn to my immaculate penthouse.

"I had a light dinner," Dad said, taking the stairs up. "That's about all I have these days."

He went to the kitchen and I followed. The living room hadn't changed other than a couch that might've been new ten years ago. Same with the recliner. A flat-screen TV was newer, but still a few years old. He had a show paused. On the far wall was our old family picture. Look at all of us smiling. Memories of that day threatened to intrude. I blocked them out.

I shifted my focus to the kitchen. Nothing had been updated in the kitchen other than the appliances. What had he sold to pay for those?

A tiny tendril of shame spiraled through me. Would I rather he squat in a house with no working fridge or stove and threadbare furniture that smelled like bachelor funk and stale beer?

Maybe I would've said yes weeks ago, but for the moment, I was more grateful that he'd kept the house in fairly recognizable condition. I was glad he'd had things to keep him afloat until he had to make the final decision to sell. Him wanting to move to town wasn't my issue.

He got a second plate and fork out. Then he filled a mug from a drying rack with some coffee from a pot and sat at the table. "There's no way I can eat all this." His chuckle was self-deprecating. "I don't require too much these days, but sandwiches do get old." He made a delighted noise. "Pork chops! Want half?"

"No, thanks. Save it for lunch tomorrow." He was only going to eat half a pork chop? I studied him with a more critical eye. He was healthier than I'd seen him last, like I'd thought when Autumn and I had first stopped by, but he was no longer a towering man. The years of alcoholism might've done their damage, but he also wasn't farming and ranching anymore. He was just existing in a house that used to be filled with love and laughter.

"You've been helping the Baileys?" he asked around a mouthful of food.

"For a few days. Figured it didn't hurt to show them I'm not some city asshole."

"Not all city folk are assholes."

I grunted. "A lot of them are."

He chuckled and stabbed a hunk of fried potato. "Same with country folk."

An easy silence fell between us. When we'd been replacing the fence, he'd filled in the silence with chatter about who was doing what, where my old classmates had moved to and what marriage they were on, and what businesses had come and gone in the time since I'd moved. Before, when he'd been sick, he used to rage about the market price for grains, the diminishing returns for ranching, and the expense of equipment and repairs.

Without his resentment or the work around the place, what did he have to talk about?

"You doing any more work on the shop or fencing?" I asked because speaking was better than realizing how little I knew my dad these days. He wasn't the same hurt and angry man I'd left behind.

"I'm replacing a few posts here and there."

I waited as he took a few more bites and made a delighted noise. The question burning on my tongue spilled out. "Are you the one keeping up the memorial where Mom died?"

He stalled chewing, then swallowed hard. "Yeah," he said gruffly and wiped off his mouth. "Yeah, I figured I'd better get out there one more time, you know, before the snow flies."

Before he'd be considered a trespasser.

"After the closing, I'll continue sprucing up her grave. You should see how big the trees at the cemetery have gotten."

I didn't give a fuck about the trees. I wouldn't be going to the cemetery. My only memory of that place was Mom's burial. My grandparents hadn't had a service, so there'd been no need for me to return for that.

Time for a subject change. "Tate said you help at the food pantry."

He paused briefly while sawing a chunk of his pork chop. "Yeah. I had to use it enough, thought it was time to give back."

"You had to use it?"

He shrugged. "Happens when you mismanage your business." He stuffed a bite in his mouth and chewed, his expression introspective. "I'm glad I made it until your grandfather passed. He would've been delighted to see me in line for some canned goods. Just another way to point out how I'd ruined everything."

The sympathy that rose was surprising. "You two talked after I left?"

"I wouldn't call it talking. He wheezed and I listened, like always. Out of respect for your mother. Like always." He studied his food, his brow furrowed and his expression heavy. "Ya know, I was never cut out for this life."

"You were born and raised on a farm."

His smile was understanding. "A small one. My parents never took on more than they could handle and they were never interested in expanding. They each liked their jobs in town. I had to work for the farm, but I also got to do my own thing. Then I met Jenni." The corners of his eyes crinkled with his smile. "This was her place. The whole operation was her family's, and it was either jump in with both feet or leave her behind. She couldn't leave." His smile faded. "Well. You know which I chose."

And then when she'd passed, he'd been left with a business that included both farming and ranching. Percival was more than a hobby. This place had to become his life.

"Why didn't you ramp down?" Surprisingly, there was no judgment in my voice. "You could've sold off the herd, leased the pastures, even the farmland, and then you could've gotten work in town."

He rewrapped the plate. Only half the food had been eaten. "In the end, it was my decision." He spoke deliberately, like acknowledging his role in everything was critical to the conversation. "At the time, I got a lot of pressure from your grandparents."

"Mom's parents?"

He nodded. "Percival was everything to them. Your grandpa grew up hearing the story and getting told about legacies. Their pride was strong. So damn strong." His gaze fell to the laminate of the table surface, sadness and regret in his eyes. "I was already panicking about how I would do all this on my own. Jenni and I could barely handle everything when her parents had to step down."

"You were struggling?" I had never thought to ask

these questions before, but then he'd never seemed ready to answer them before.

His features pinched. "You'd never know it from how she acted, but yes. We were struggling."

My hackles rose. "Are you blaming Mom?"

A long sigh left him. "After all this time, maybe a little." He put a hand up. My building ire must've shown on my face. "I take plenty of blame, but back then, the two of us should've been more of a team. I was treated like the hired man instead."

I recoiled. I'd felt the same from him after Mom had died. Yet he couldn't put this all on Mom when she wasn't here to defend herself. "Why didn't you hire someone?"

"I wasn't fit to be a boss. I followed Jenni's lead. And when she was gone . . ." A heavy sigh left him. "I wasn't fit for much."

He acknowledged all the troubles so easily now. "I went to Vegas to earn enough money to buy Percival."

"Your grandpa told you to."

Astonished, I gawked at him. "How do you know that?"

"He told me." The muscles at the corners of his jaw clenched. "Several times. He boasted about it."

Dismay settled across my shoulders, heavy and dark. "That's why you're not selling to me."

"No, Giddy. I'm selling because we all should get to live our own lives."

He said it so simply, as if I should understand. "Nothing about that answer explains why you wouldn't let me even make an offer. Percival should be mine. It's my life. It's *my* family legacy."

"That's your grandfather talking."

"Mom wanted me to have it."

"She wanted you to have choices. She wanted the world for you."

"Percival is my world and you're locking me out of it!"

Solemnity lined his face. "Your world is that amazing wife of yours, but all I hear is you putting some old blathering of your grandpa's before her."

"Autumn is none of your business," I growled. Fuck this. Dad refused to hear me, and I was done. I rose. "You have two weeks to understand that you're severing everything between us. Again."

I stormed out of the house. He didn't run after me. Or call my name. He sat at the table and let me leave, just like he had all those years ago.

Autumn

It was another quiet Wednesday night at the bar. Gideon had helped move cattle for the last three days. He'd dropped the car off for me and said Tenor would give him a ride to the bar after they were done.

Last night, he'd returned home with a dark cloud over his head. I had seen it in his eyes and the way he'd moved his body. I'd asked if everything was okay, but he'd just said the day was fine, fun even, and that he was tired. Then he'd fucked me into oblivion before we'd made it to the bedroom. After we'd been in bed, he'd sunk deep into contemplation and hadn't shared his thoughts with me.

We were just over the halfway point of our short time together.

A couple of guys waved to me as they walked out. The whole distillery had been quiet this week with all the bosses out except for Summer. She covered for Teller and Tenor, and Wynter's team was used to her working out of the office much of the time.

I peered out the window.

Summer tapped on the bar top. "Are you seriously that lonely without him for three nights?"

I scowled at her. "I haven't been without him for three nights. Besides, you're just as bad."

"My marriage is real though."

"Ouch."

She lifted a shoulder. Her verbal hit had been intentional. She was testing me. "I heard about Halloween."

"I'm sorry, I should've called and invited you and Jonah over. I was panicking about dressing in my Pinocchio costume around Gideon."

"Don't worry about the invite. We were at his parents' new place. I swear they acted as if they'd never met the Jonah who hands out candy."

"Has he ever?"

"Good point. Probably not. Anyway, was Gideon horrified about the long nose?"

"It was the suspenders he was fascinated with." To distract from my blush, I took out my notebook and wrote down some ideas I'd had for new cocktails. We had frozen huckleberries on hand, and I wanted to make more syrup for flavoring.

Summer leaned over and spied on my writing. "So it's like that."

"I don't know what you're talking about." I couldn't meet her eyes.

"You're obsessed with him." She sat back on her stool. "I'm worried about you. Hank shows no signs of hitting pause."

"I know."

"The marriage arrangement hasn't changed yet?"

"No reason to." I continued scribbling. I needed to make more candied cherries and lemon wedges. I'd gotten behind on the stock since I'd been wrapped up in Gideon.

"Remember when you told me to talk to Jonah?" she said quietly. "I think you should do the same. You care for him."

"What would I talk to him about? He married me as a last-ditch effort. Yes, he's helped his dad and the guys, but nothing's changed."

"You don't know that. A lot might have changed for him."

"What if it's like cosplaying to him? I'm nothing but a distraction, and you know what? I'm okay with that." I was a way for him to pass the time and get laid while we were pretending to be married for a month. I was fine with that. Whenever I dreamed of more, I pictured the divorce papers.

"What if you're not just a distraction?"

Then what? "And he'll live happily ever after with me while my family works what he thinks should've been his? While they till up the memories he has of his parents when they were happy? When he has to ask permission to pay his respects at the place where his mom died?"

She winced and sympathy filled her expression. "You

know he'll be able to go out there whenever he wants for that."

"For *that*, Summer. The place where he grew up. The home he thought would be his forever, to pass down to his kids."

"Which you said he doesn't want."

She wasn't taking it easy on me. "I said he's weird about them." I sighed. "Why would he want to stay married to me when I'm nothing but a reminder of why he doesn't have anything?"

"You know you're not."

I knew that. Would Gideon think that way? "Did you come here to shit on my time with him? I know you don't like him."

She stiffened. "How much I do or don't like him depends on how he makes you feel and how he treats you. I couldn't give a crap about him otherwise."

"Well, I do. But I'm being realistic. His life isn't here, and it's not looking like it'll ever be. He knows it. I know it. We have a deal. You all keep treating me like I've got no brain when it comes to him. Let me have this fantasy, okay? I like pretending I have a sexy husband who can't get enough of me."

Her exhale was quiet. "I'm sorry. It's just that you have such a big heart. I hope he doesn't break it." She pushed off her stool and came around the counter. "You forgive me for being a pushy older sister?"

I hugged her. "I'll be salty about it for a while."

"I expect no less. Need help with anything? I'm not leaving until your man gets here."

Headlights flashed out the window. I tucked my notebook away. "He's here. I've gotta clean up yet." I'd spent tonight chatting with customers and talking to

Summer. "Thanks for staying with me." Whenever Wynter and I worked the bar, the rest of the family watched over us so we weren't alone. All the customers had gone by now.

The door opened and Gideon stepped inside. He was in one hundred percent cowboy mode. A lunch bag was tucked under one arm and a grocery bag hung from the same hand. He took off his cowboy hat. His gaze landed on me first and warmed. My belly flipped in response. Would I ever get used to his focus being on me? I'd been twined around this man last night and for so many nights before that, and I still couldn't believe this was happening.

He glanced at Summer and gave her a nod, then his gaze was back on me.

I loved my sisters, but this never happened. A guy never gave me more attention than Summer, Junie, or Wynter. They never dismissed my sisters like Gideon did, like he absolutely had no interest in them.

"There it is," Summer murmured, turning her back to Gideon as she gave me a quick hug. "Like he wants to eat you alive. That isn't pretend." She pulled back. "I'll lock up on my way out."

Gideon set the grocery bag on the counter. His water bottle was inside, but there was also an old-school green Stanley mug. He took it out. "Mae wanted to send some hot chocolate home. She said you like it for breakfast."

I'd take Mama's hot chocolate any time of day. "Did you eat yet?" My stomach rumbled. I'd eaten Mama's leftovers for lunch today and that'd been hours ago.

"No. I figured you hadn't either, so I asked your mom if I could take food to go." He was subdued again, but he was still thoughtful. How could I not get too wrapped up in this guy? He didn't have to hang out with me, but he chose to anyway.

"Long day?"

"No." He continued to unload the containers of food Mama had packed. Fried chicken, a couple of twice-baked potatoes, and green beans she'd canned from the garden this summer. I had helped. "Today was easier than the rest, and all the cows are closer to home for the winter. I promised your mom I'd wash and return all the containers."

Warmth settled deep in my bones. His respect for Mama only added to how much I wished there could be more between us. But like I'd told Summer, I had to be practical. "You know that's her way of getting you back out there."

The corner of his mouth lifted. "You'd think she'd be tired of hosting everyone for a huge meal every night after babysitting all day."

"No, she's in her zone. She loves the chaos." I grabbed a couple of plates from a little-used cabinet in the corner where we stored our holiday cups and glasses. It wasn't unheard of to bring family parties to the bar after hours.

"I can't imagine."

"I'm sure your house was quieter than mine when you were young. I don't think three sisters and I caused as much noise as three boys."

He doled out food and I got us a glass of water.

As we ate, he told me about how he and Teller had had to stop and fix a flat on the horse trailer first thing this morning, and then how he'd found a calf with an issue in his hoof. He'd stayed with Tenor until the vet could get to them. When he talked, his voice was light and his eyes danced, like when the kids at school would tell me about some cool thing they'd done over the weekend. Did he realize the way he talked about the last three days was vastly different than when he discussed his work with the casino?

When he mentioned Silver, he turned serious. Almost grim. Silver was nothing but business. There was no passion. Did he realize he'd rarely talked about Silver in the last week? The most he'd said was that he had to answer some emails or that he had a meeting he couldn't get out of. He'd never chatted about his coworkers, and he definitely hadn't brought up Taya.

We finished eating, and I started cleaning up. I ran soapy water into the sink, but when I turned, he took my place and started rolling up his sleeves.

"You've been working all day." I still took the opportunity to admire his strong forearms.

"So have you, and you've been waiting on people all night."

"It's not bad. Wednesdays are regulars. Our neighbor Jason is nearly to the point where he pours his own drinks. He'll even wipe the bar down if I turn my back on him."

"Good. I'm glad you have customers like that."

I got another rag and cleaned up the tables and the bar top.

"Wait on that. Sit." He was almost done washing the containers.

"Why?"

The look he gave me was pure CEO. He didn't want an argument. I took the stool I'd sat in to eat.

He dried his hands and reached into the lunch bag. The baggie he withdrew was full of large stuffed olives.

"Olives?"

"You devoured them the night we met. These are stuffed with blue cheese. I didn't expect to find them in the fridge, but Mae said she gets them for you."

"We've been known to make a fancy Bloody Mary or two."

"It's my turn to make a Bloody Mary, this time with Copper Summit bourbon."

My interest piqued. "You're waiting on me?"

He searched the little fridge for the mix. "I'm serving you."

"Mr. James, are you trying to get me drunk?"

His expression turned knowing. "I don't have to get you drunk to get what I want."

The thrum started between my legs. "And what is it you want?"

He speared the olives and rested them across the glass's opening. "I want you to relax and tell me about your day."

"Nothing was different about today than any other day." This was different. Right now with Gideon was not a normal part of any day outside of the last few weeks.

He pushed the glass over and rested his hands on the table. "Autumn, you've been grilling me for three days about moving cattle and how I felt about it. You rarely talk about your job."

Was he keeping me from asking him deeper questions about how he was feeling? Like what had been bothering him last night? "I'm just a teacher, and I'm not supposed to talk about the students."

"Yet the house is full of lesson plans and sample Thanksgiving crafts. You can tell me about those."

"Handmade turkeys are so last century. I'm trying to

figure out another way to make turkeys that doesn't take two hours."

"Good start. Tell me more."

I snatched an olive and popped it into my mouth. "That's just it," I said around the mouthful. I was full, but I'd down anything he made me. "You run a casino that makes how much a year?"

"That doesn't matter."

"Three hundred and fifty million. I looked it up." I swirled the sword of olives in the liquid. "I know teaching kids is important, but everyone's been to school. Everyone knows what teachers do."

"I want to hear what you do."

"But for how long?" Had I really asked that? I shoved another olive in my mouth.

He waited. I took a drink. How had that question slipped out? Dammit, Summer. She'd gotten it in my head that I could talk with Gideon, tell him I was falling for him—I'd crashed hard when I'd first seen him—but I was veering out of my fantasy world.

"What do you mean?" he asked when I swallowed.

"Nothing. I just don't see how my day compares to the casino or even what you've been doing all week."

"You grew up doing the same."

"You're right. I ran a local casino when I was eight."

Humor lightened the green of his eyes. "I happen to find smart-asses sexy."

"How convenient you're married to one."

He smiled, but it faded. The grimness returned.

"Do you want to talk about it?" I asked softly.

He pressed his hands on the counter and cocked a foot back. I braced for him to tell me that whatever he was feeling was none of my business. "Your mom had me take a plate of food to Hank last night."

No wonder he'd been in his head when he'd come home. "I don't think she meant to meddle."

He cocked a brow.

"She's usually there for us, but she's not intrusive. She probably heard about how you worked with him for a few days and then helped tow his truck."

"But she knows he's still selling."

I phrased my next words carefully. This topic was a sticking point and I knew where his opinions rested. Still, it needed to be said. "Being on speaking terms with your dad doesn't necessarily hinge on whether he sells or not."

His gaze went hard. "It does."

I nodded. I hadn't expected a different response. "How'd it go?"

"He said something I can't figure out, and he expects me to know what he meant." His flinty gaze was aimed out the wall of windows. "He said he's selling because we all need to live our own lives."

"What's that mean?"

"Exactly."

His dad had been telling him over and over again that he would continue with the sale. "He's pretty determined."

"Yeah."

I swallowed hard. My drink was forgotten. "Are you going to stay until they close?"

His eyes sharpened. "Why wouldn't I?"

A little glow that had nothing to do with the Bloody Mary ignited inside me.

"I still have time to get through to him."

The spark died. Right. The land came first. That was his priority. Convenient distraction, that was me.

"Autumn."

I was glowering at my drink. I lifted my gaze to his.

"I'm enjoying my time with you. But when this is over, don't take it personally. I'm not good for marriage."

He'd been pretty fucking good for the last couple of weeks. I had two more weeks with him and I didn't want to cry or beg. "I'm just going to miss you. That's all."

An exhale gusted out of him. "Fuck, Autumn. I'm going to miss you too. The thought of going back to my life . . . it won't be as easy as I thought it'd be. You're a special person. Any guy would be lucky to have you."

A murderous expression flitted through his eyes. I blinked and it was gone.

The guy would have to want me first. And then I'd have to be into him. That seemed like an impossibility with Gideon in front of me. Long after he was gone from my house and his scent had been washed from the sheets, would I be able to meet another man and not compare him to Gideon?

Instead of moving my life forward when I'd married him, I'd stalled out. By saying my vows, I'd screwed myself out of the future I wanted.

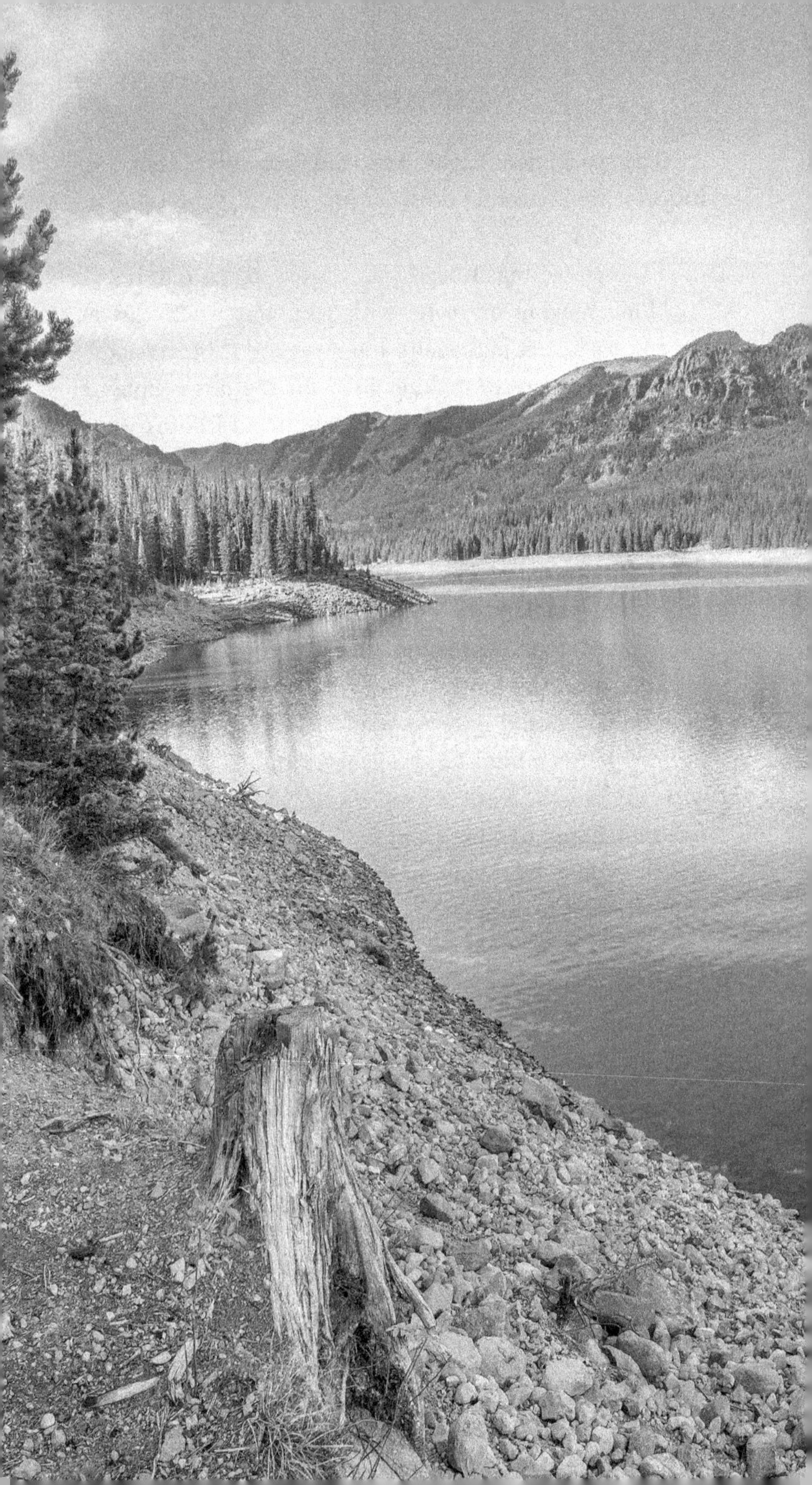

CHAPTER TWENTY-THREE

Gideon

Something about today had felt heavy from the beginning. Now Autumn had hit me where the center of my emotions churned. This damn marriage. How wonderful these two weeks had been. How fast the next two weeks would go.

And admitting that any guy would be lucky to have her pissed me the hell off. My vision tunneled to black and I wanted to smash every glass within reach.

I wasn't sure she'd respond, but then she rolled her eyes and took a swig of her drink. "Funny how I date only the guys who disagree."

"You've dated boys, rusty. A real man will know what he has. Just like a real man knows when he'd be a shit husband and an absentee father."

She studied me. I regretted my choice of words. "Is that why you don't want kids? You wouldn't be around for them?"

We'd go with that. "I know what it's like. I can't do that to a kid even if you swear you're okay with not having me in the picture."

"Because you'd know."

I nodded. "There's no way I can be a decent father when I'm in another state working twelve hours a day."

She tilted her head, the hint of melancholy not leaving her gaze. "You're a good man, Gideon James."

My self-consciousness was unexpected. "I'm not."

"You are," she said in a singsong voice. "And I should say any woman would be lucky to have you, but I want to stab that bitch with this skewer."

I laughed and all the tension drained away. "Now that that's out of the way, tell me about your day."

She didn't roll her eyes, but she wrinkled her nose. Did she really think I wouldn't be interested in her day? That I would think the work she did wasn't important?

"The biggest drama of the week isn't actually kid-related," she said with a smirk. "It's the mystery of who's eating the break room yogurt."

I cleaned up the mess I'd made while she told me about the stolen yogurt, the new playground equipment the school was hoping to buy, the different types of fundraisers they were doing to pay for it, and how she had one little girl in class who'd talked with a posh British accent for an entire day last week.

I loved hearing about all of it. I hung up the rags like I'd seen her do the other nights she closed. She packed up all the clean containers.

"I'll get the lights and then we can go." She disappeared into the back room to get her purse and coat. The room went dark, the only glow coming from the security lights in the main entry.

When she came out, I pulled her toward me. "I haven't gotten a kiss yet."

She tipped her head back. "I thought Mama's fried chicken took priority."

It was good fucking chicken. The best I'd ever had. All week, I'd eaten like a king, but no food was worth going another minute without tasting my wife.

"You thought wrong." I took her coat and purse and tossed them on the counter so they weren't between us. "I didn't kiss you when I first arrived because I would've kept going and your sister was here."

"What about now?"

"I don't see anyone else." I wasn't gentle when I caught her mouth. I also wasn't planning to stop at a kiss. After the heaviness of our earlier conversation, after the way this whole damn night had burrowed into my mind and whispered questions I couldn't answer, I needed a release, and I couldn't wait until I got her to the house.

One of those persistent questions popped into my head. *Do you really think you can never have this in your life again?*

The jumble of questions that had been daunting me for days poured in.

Isn't farming and ranching in your bones?
Don't you miss this? Won't you miss it again?
Why don't you want to stay?
Why can't you be good at marriage?

I had to silence that unknown voice. Where the hell was it coming from?

I pressed her against the counter. She wouldn't want me to strip her down. This was her family business and she prepped food at the bar. But I needed more. Everything was right with the world when she climaxed with my name on her lips.

I tore my mouth away and kissed a path down her neck. "I'm going to bend you over this counter."

She arched into me. "Now?"

"I had to watch you eat those olives off the spear without jumping you. Yeah, right fucking now." Wait—I hadn't been working in an office all day. I'd been outside and on a horse. "Do you want me to shower first?"

"You smell like horse and fresh air. What kind of Montana girl would I be if that turned me off?"

She was so damn perfect. I spun her around. "Put your hands on the bar top."

She did as I ordered and ground her ass into me. I yanked my wallet out and retrieved a condom. I was never unprepared around this woman.

I unzipped my jeans just as she shoved her pants down. Her shirt fell over her bare ass and I growled. "Quit hiding your butt, rusty. It's a shame."

She glanced over her shoulder. "There's a lot of it."

"Fuck yeah, there is."

I didn't plunge into her. As desperate as I was to get as much of her as I could before we went our separate ways, I couldn't use her. She had to want this as bad as me. I circled my arm around her waist and tunneled a finger through her wet seam.

"You're already soaked for me." I ripped the condom open with my teeth and shook the wrapper off.

She wiggled her hips. "What are you going to do about it, cowboy?"

The guttural sound that left my mouth couldn't be described. I'd been called a lot of things in my life.

Labeling me a cowboy should have been absurd, but something about it set my world back on its axis.

Lust pounded through my veins. I wasn't used to this, wanting to be fused with someone else so badly I rarely had a thought that didn't include her. Could I just return to Vegas and go back to business as usual?

The question didn't need an answer now.

Maybe you're afraid of the answer.

Anchoring myself back in the moment, I thrummed her clit. Her body went liquid. She was all mine.

This lack of control was why the next two weeks would go by too fast, yet not quick enough. I had built a nice, controlled existence that no woman could threaten. Autumn dismantled my restraint with no effort at all.

I thrust into her. This was paradise. This was like finding an oasis when I'd been living in the desert for twenty-five years. What an accurate damn analogy.

"Fuck, Autumn. You're fisting me so fucking tight."

I was rougher than I'd meant to be, but she was strong, meeting me with each push, bracing herself and stabilizing us.

Another goddamn analogy I didn't need. I planted my free hand next to hers. She was warm and wet and I could barely hold back my release.

Headlights swung into the parking lot.

She gasped and almost jerked away, but I held her tight.

"They can't see us," I rasped, not knowing if it was fucking true. I continued to pump into her.

"It might be one of my brothers." She kept pushing back into me.

"Then you'd better explode quick, firecracker," I growled.

The vehicle drove through the lot. Her gaze was on it, and so was mine. She was tightening around me, her walls fluttering. She was close. I licked the shell of her ear. "You're such a good fucking girl. You're going to do what I say and you're going to come."

She moaned and a rush of heat enveloped my hand.

"You're going to come, and you're going to shout my name." I thrust hard and turned her face to the side. "Because I need to hear it."

I would not leave this bar without her coming all over me. After telling her I would make a shitty husband, I would not walk out without us being spent and satisfied. After admitting I'd miss her, but I'd still leave her, I *would* follow through on this tryst.

The pickup was parking. Her breathing quickened.

"You're my good little wife, aren't you? You're mine."

"Yes!" Her walls rippled and her cry echoed off the walls.

I had to get one more cry from her. I angled my hips up and slammed into her while I ruthlessly stroked her clit.

"Gideon! Yes!"

Only then did I let the lightning bolt inside me loose. Energy coursed from the base of my spine and straight out of my cock. "Fuck!"

I had to grip her hips to keep myself upright as I emptied into her.

The headlights flashed off. Long before I was ready, I pulled out of Autumn. I tugged her leggings and underwear back in place and straightened her shirt, then I tucked myself in. She'd be mortified if anyone caught her with her pants literally down.

A shadow approached the door of the bar while I got my dick zipped up.

She patted her hair like she was afraid she had bed head when we'd done it standing up. "I can't believe—"

The door swung open. I couldn't make out which brother it was. "Autumn?"

"Tate. Hi." She scrambled to grab her coat and purse. "We were just walking out."

Tate paused. He was outlined by the security lights pouring in from the opening to the main entry. "Is that Gideon with you?"

"Yeah." She couldn't sound guiltier. I bit back a smile. "He brought me dinner and now we're leaving."

"Thanks for your help this week," he said. He'd told me that every day. His olive branch, maybe, but I didn't care. I was less hostile toward the Baileys. Like they'd said, it was Dad's decision. The Baileys would do right by the property, but it was Dad who shouldn't fucking sell.

The invite to help with cattle was a strategic move, exactly what I would've done in his situation. "Don't mention it."

Awkward silence fell.

"I don't want to turn on a light, do I?" Tate asked cautiously.

"What?" Autumn said, her voice pitching up. A nervous laugh slipped out of her. "We're *dressed*."

"To be fair, we never undressed," I added. Autumn stiffened even more, and I clamped down on a laugh.

"That doesn't make me feel better." He stuck his

thumb toward the main entry. "I told Teller I'd stop by and take a look at some info on a new grain supplier."

"Yeah." Autumn nodded enthusiastically. "Okay. We'll, uh, just head home. Like we were doing before you arrived."

Tate's chuckle filled the air between us. "Good thing Daddy never caught you with a guy in high school, Autumn. You lie like shit."

He walked off, still laughing.

Autumn swatted my gut. "You did *not* help at all."

My laughter finally broke out. This moment was nothing I'd ever thought would happen to me. Getting busted having sex where we shouldn't? I'd been rigid about my various and sporadic interludes over the years. I should be as horrified as Autumn, but I wasn't.

Tate could've chewed into Autumn, and I'd have defended her. This could've tanked any progress we'd made. But he'd treated her like an equal, just like he would've if he'd walked in on one of his brothers.

So maybe this fake marriage had helped her a little too. I couldn't give her the picture-perfect family she wanted, but I'd helped improve her image with her brothers.

Or the thought was complete bullshit. Either way, we still had a couple of weeks together.

My wife's cheeks were flushed deep enough to see in the dark. "Watching you squirm is almost as fun as watching you come, rusty." I quickly washed my hands. "Come on. I gotta get you home. I need to shower. And then I'm getting between your legs again."

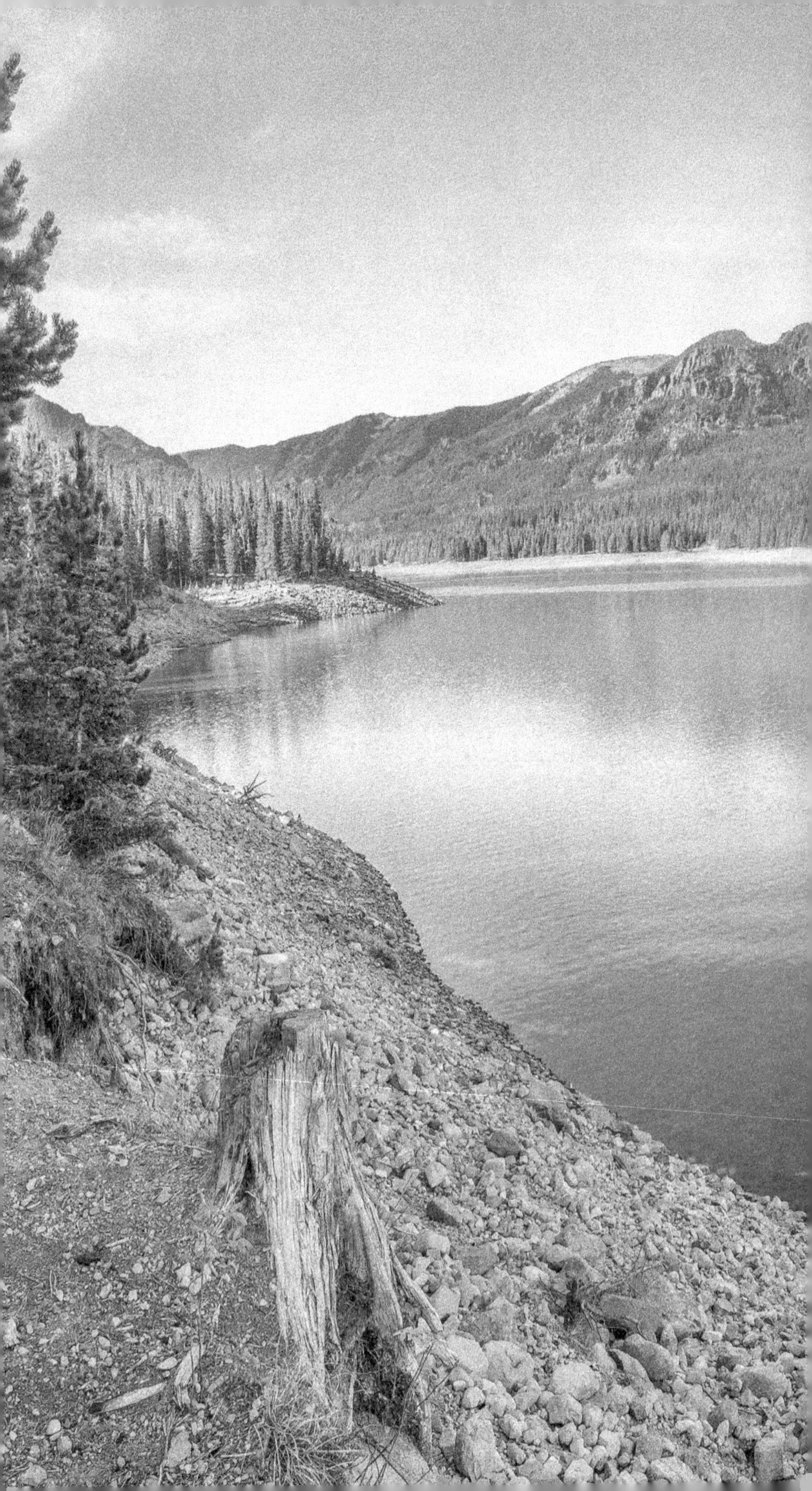

CHAPTER TWENTY-FOUR

Gideon

My inbox was a nightmare. I rubbed my eyes. Some lingering stiffness remained from working outside for three days, but it didn't compare to the way my body wanted to revolt after sitting behind my laptop yesterday and today.

I groaned, rolled my neck, and rose. I paced the kitchen and out to the living room. Sprinkles was curled in a ball on the couch, nestled in the blue fleece blanket Autumn curled up in when she was grading papers. The cat lifted her head and mewed. I scratched around her ears. Sometimes, she sat at the table in the chair next to me and snoozed.

"Was I too boring for you?"

She tucked her head back into her paws and ignored me.

A ping sounded from the kitchen. My goddamn email. I'd turned notifications on. I'd been restless today, drifting off when I was supposed to be paying attention in a meeting.

The newest email was from Taya. Normal reports to prep for next week's meetings.

Meeting after fucking meeting.

I rubbed the back of my neck. I owed Taya a call. She'd been patient and she'd said it was about work, in a way.

I called her, putting the speaker on so I could continue pacing.

"About time, Gideon," she said, annoyance ripe in her tone.

"I'd apologize, but you've noticed I've been working the entirety of my leave."

"Which is for . . ."

"Something that's almost taken care of." That was all she'd get. "What'd you need to talk about?"

She sighed. "Gideon. What's changed? You were rude to me at your place, I can't get back in, and now you take two damn weeks to return my call."

"You tried getting into my apartment?"

"I worked late one night and thought I'd crash there. Imagine my surprise when my code didn't work." Hurt lined the sarcasm. "Anyway, I'm just confused. You stand me up for a VIP visit, then there's a redhead in your place, and now you've been gone for weeks. The board keeps asking me if I'm confident you'll return, and honestly, Gideon, I have no idea. Before that morning, when I walked in on whatever that was, I'd have told them you were never leaving."

I kept my personal life to myself. I wasn't giving Taya an explanation, but I couldn't deny I'd hurt her feelings. Her confusion was also valid. Before I'd met Autumn in that elevator, I'd have said I'd never ditch work for a month. But my business wasn't settled. "Something came up and it's private."

"Right." A brisk exhale gusted over the line. "Whatever."

"Is this something that can wait until I return?"

"I should've let him hunt you down. Then *he* could get frustrated and give up."

I rubbed my temples. I didn't care either way.

My silence must've told her to keep talking or hang up. "You remember Harold Washington?"

He was an early-stage venture capitalist. His thing was to invest in a new business, usually a casino or hotel or combo, and then, when the profits were good, pull out and invest a portion into another business. He had his wealthy fingers in a lot of pots. My bosses had approached him for Silver, but he'd been entering into a deal on a high-rise in Phoenix at the time. But he liked to stop in and chat with board members when they were in town. I'd been to many networking events with him. "Yes, I remember Harold."

"He wants to start a new investment group." Excitement pitched her voice higher. "He wants you and me on the team."

"He offered us a job?"

"Not just a job." She spoke faster. "He told me his plans for a new hotel and casino. On the Strip, Gideon."

Prime realty for a hotel and casino in Vegas. "But Silver's doing well." I felt like a dunce. I should be getting as thrilled as she was. Working with Harold would change my career, supercharge it. I was doing well as a CEO. I had a nest egg I could retire off of now. Add a little risk and Harold's innate business savvy, and I'd be fly-to-space rich. I wouldn't have to grind away twelve hours a day, seven days a week.

"Silver isn't ours," she said succinctly, nailing exactly why I should be drafting my resignation letter.

Silver wasn't mine. I ran it like it was. I worked like the place was Percival Farms and my grandfather was in my ear telling me how I'd be letting down generations if I failed. But it wasn't mine.

And that money in my accounts? The funds I had squirreled away? I might not get the opportunity to spend them on my family's land. Sure, I could buy or invest anywhere, but this would be an opportunity to build something with people I respected. With individuals who weren't family but who also didn't block me out.

"Anyway, Harold gave me permission to tell you. He didn't want to track you down in Montana."

"And you were afraid I wouldn't return."

"All this is unlike you," she agreed. "Look, I know he could find someone else, but you and I make a good team."

She said it with such confidence I nodded. We did work well together. Neither of us had attachments, we kept the endgame in mind, and we let pride interfere at the right time. With my experience as CEO and hers as CFO—we would make a strong team.

A sour burn wicked its way up my throat. "When does he want an answer?"

The closing date was ten days away. I wouldn't have to choose if given the chance to do both—buy Percival and invest with Harold Washington. I could have it all. But I'd have to leave Bourbon Canyon. Which I was doing anyway.

"I told him how long you were planning to be out and he said he wants to meet with you when you return. It also goes without saying . . ."

"Keep this between us." The board respected me, but Silver was their gravy train. If they thought I was jumping ship, they'd replace me in a heartbeat. Loyalty ran stronger up the chain than down.

"Exactly. I love my job, but can you imagine? I could look at a place just like this and say I own that." She sounded wistful, but my chest constricted.

I rubbed my sternum. What the hell was wrong with me? I'd stayed in Bourbon Canyon for barely three weeks and I was sad to leave it behind? To leave a dad who'd rather teach me some mysterious bullshit lesson than just be honest with me? To leave memories that were better left in the past because they did me fuck all now?

To leave Autumn?

The ache behind my ribs grew stronger. "I'll be back soon. We can talk then."

She hung up. I stared at my phone. Regret that I'd called her sank into my gut.

An investment group. I had my own investments, but nothing like what Harold would dabble in. He had an enviable business sense that I'd be a fool to say no to.

I scratched the back of my neck. My laptop sat open on the table, its screen dark, taunting me. I should get back to work, but I went to the living room and sank onto the couch. Sprinkles woke up, stretched until her back arched and quivered, then she sauntered onto my lap and curled up. I put a hand on her warm fur.

My yes should be instant, but I was nothing if not

prudent. I'd give the idea a proper amount of time to marinate, then I'd decide.

Autumn

I'd wrapped up my last parent-teacher conference. Mine tended to run later. I loved to talk and some of my kids' parents had concerns that I couldn't bring myself to cut short or put off. Tonight, I was only wrapping up forty-five minutes late, but thankfully, it was the last set of parents who went over by half an hour.

The number of people roaming the halls had diminished. I'd texted Gideon that I was done and packed my stuff. When I was shrugging into my coat, Mark appeared in the doorway.

He shoved his hands in his slacks. "The snow's falling pretty heavy out there."

I'd been watching it while chatting with students and parents. "Snow day tomorrow?"

His smile was small. "Maybe."

This was the most he'd talked to me since I'd returned from Vegas married. I flung a scarf around my neck and his gaze landed on my ring.

"How's married life?"

"Good." Soon to be over. The backs of my eyes burned. I blinked. Where had that reaction come from? I'd known how this would go.

But last weekend had been more of the weekend before. Gideon had come with me to the bar. He'd sipped a drink while I'd worked and done inventory and finished expense reports. Last night, for my Wednesday shift, he'd brought me a meal from Curly's—with extra buns because I'd said I liked them.

But . . . there was something different. I couldn't put my finger on it. He'd kept me too busy between the sheets—and on the kitchen table and in the shower—to ponder it too much. He'd opened himself up to me, but it was only a crack. I wasn't getting further in, and the depressing truth was that there was no reason to. He worked at home all day, and at night, he lost himself in me. Wake up. Repeat.

If I hadn't had conferences tonight, we'd be doing the same thing. As it was, he would pick me up, take me home, and before I got my coat off, he'd be on me. I shouldn't complain. It was Gideon. Out-of-my-league Gideon James.

How could such spectacular sex leave me so empty?

"Good to hear." Mark let out a nervous chuckle and walked several steps into the room. "I was afraid I was moving too fast, asking you to visit my family, but I guess I wasn't quick enough."

"It did feel a little sudden," I admitted. "But Gideon and I . . . we just clicked." I picked at the hem running up the side of my gray slacks. Was someone going to jump out of my supply nook and yell "liar"?

"Someday, maybe I'll be so lucky." His gaze dropped to the floor and he nodded. "I'm happy for you though. Maybe a little jealous of the way you've been floating through the halls."

My laugh rang empty. Just like I'd be shortly. Soon, I would be explaining Gideon's disappearance. *He had to return to work. We'll try distance.* Then . . . *Distance didn't work. We tried. Turns out we have to consciously uncouple.*

Fuck. The plan had been a lot different on the front end. When the little girl with big dreams inside of me had thought I'd get my conventional fairy tale after an unconventional beginning.

A tall, dark shadow appeared in the doorway. Gideon glowered at Mark.

"Speak of the devil," Mark said easily. "I was telling your wife that one day I hope to be as lucky as her."

Gideon's gaze turned assessing. He must've heard the loneliness in Mark's voice. If I hadn't met Gideon and decided to go to Spokane with Mark, we might've gone all the way to the altar—the old-fashioned way. But ours wouldn't have been a sweeping love story. We'd have been friends who had sex to scratch an itch and fulfill our life goals.

Wasn't that an empty life too?

Gideon allowed a hint of a smile to show through. His peace offering. "Go to Vegas and give it a shot."

Mark's chuckle was good-natured. "That might be what I'm doing wrong. Glad you got here. I didn't want to end the night digging anyone out."

"The snow's getting deep, but if you have all-wheel drive, you should be okay."

Mark ducked his head. "The weather guy says the wind's going to pick up. I think we're all hoping for a snow day."

"Since tomorrow's Friday," I said, "that'd be perfect timing."

"A long weekend." Mark nodded again. Was Gideon's towering presence making him nervous? "But the snow is going to decide that." He clapped his hands together. "You two take off. I'll lock up."

"Thank you." I scooted around him. "Have a good weekend."

Gideon gave him a parting nod and then we were walking out. Gideon put his hand on my lower back and guided me all the way to the front door. He'd parked right in the middle of the drop-off area. Normally, that was a no-no, but it was late, and with the heavy clumps of flakes falling in my hair, I didn't care.

In the car, I buckled up, but he didn't drive away. He was scowling out the windshield. Was he upset about Mark?

"Everything okay?" I asked.

He blinked like I'd bopped him out of a trance. "What's this about a snow day?"

Had he been planning to tell me something else? Our time was so short I doubted it was anything critical. "Well, this white stuff outside—it's called snow. And when there's a lot of it, we sometimes have to cancel school. But it has to be a lot, Mr. Casino. Not a dusting."

The corner of his mouth kicked up. "I have a special punishment for smart-asses."

And I was firmly in my dreamworld for the night. Maybe for the whole weekend. "Promise?"

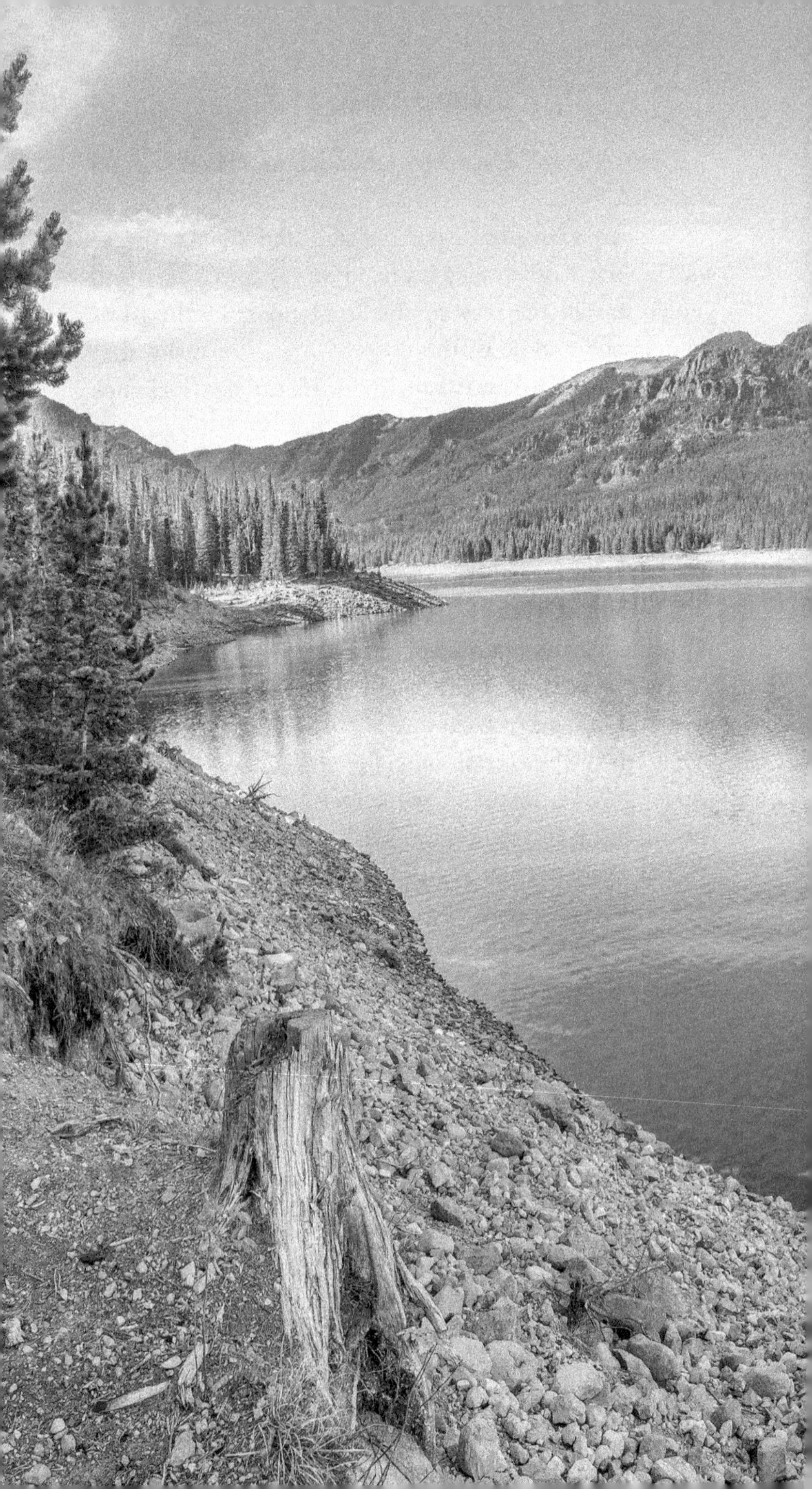

CHAPTER TWENTY-FIVE

Gideon

Friday had turned out to be a snow day. I had worked at the table while Autumn had listened to an audiobook and graded papers. The wind had tormented the outdoors until after sundown Saturday afternoon, so we'd stayed in. This morning, the gusts had died down and the sky was partly cloudy.

We were still in bed. Autumn was sprawled across her side. Half a butt cheek was hanging out of her pajama shorts and her legs were tangled in the sheets. She'd kicked the rest off.

I still envied how she could sleep with abandon. There'd been only a handful of times I could remember sinking into a deep sleep like her. Most of them had taken place in the last few weeks—when I'd worked with Dad and when I'd helped move cattle.

I stared at the ceiling. Cool air drifted in from the old windows. Heat was pumping out of the vents around the room. I kicked the rest of the blankets off. Autumn murmured and buried her face farther into her pillow.

I would be leaving in three days.

Rolling up, I let my gaze stroke over her ass one more time before I went to the bathroom to clean up. I could make breakfast, but a restlessness had settled into my bones. There was a pile of snow against the door and garage to be moved and a sidewalk that needed to be cleared.

I had no snow pants, but the snow removal shouldn't take that long. I put on jeans, a shirt, a sweater, and the heavier coat I'd bought. I dug out gloves and a stocking hat and went through the garage.

A snowblower was parked in the far corner. Next to it was a gas can that looked fairly fresh. Of course Autumn would take care of her equipment. She was a Bailey.

I punched open the garage door and stepped outside to form a plan. The cold blew into my lungs, stealing my breath. *Fuck.* I was a Montana kid. I would get used to the temperature.

I squinted against the bright morning sun. The whole driveway was covered, but a drift had formed on one side that'd hang up her car. How long had it been since I'd moved snow? Seemed like this whole trip had unlocked a time capsule of experiences.

The snowblower started right up. After a few moments, I was clearing a path down the middle of her driveway and blowing a stream of snow onto her yard. The garage door of the house beside Autumn's opened and a guy came out, flanked by two lanky sons, all dressed in better winter weather gear than I had.

He waved. I returned it and kept going. More neighbors popped out. The storm had died down and it was time to make everything passable. As I worked, a sense of satisfaction settled around me. We all had our parts and I was included.

When I was growing up, I had to run the tractor with the bucket. Mom would push snow with the blade on the four-wheeler, and Dad would get as many chores done as he could while we cleaned snow. It had gotten to where I would look forward to snow days.

How was Dad doing? He had no equipment in the shop anymore, but I hadn't gone into the garage.

There was no reason for me to care. He wasn't worried about me.

I wheeled the snowblower into the garage and killed the engine.

But how was Dad doing? That old house was drafty. He'd kept it up, but a ton of expenses had been spared when it was built before I was born. The place needed new windows, a new roof, and probably some gas and a match. Start over.

Which was what someone else would be doing with the place. Whoever the Baileys chose to manage the farm. Probably someone local.

"Are you almost finished?"

I spun. My very own ranch snow bunny was standing in the opening of the garage door. I was surrounded by the smell of exhaust, but I knew her cotton-candy scent well enough that she didn't have to be close for me to smell it.

Her hair was stuffed under a blue knit hat with a fluffy white ball on top. Her yellow scarf matched nothing, especially not the grungy tan work coat she was wearing over her bibbed black snow pants. She was cute as hell.

"Yeah, I'm about done."

Her pants swished as she crossed toward me. She frowned at my jeans. "Aren't you cold?"

"I can't feel my legs anymore."

Her eyes widened. "Go inside and warm up."

"I'm good. You forget I'm a local boy."

"You're usually the one who forgets." She retrieved the wide snow shovel leaning against the wall.

I was stuck on her casual comment. "I've never forgotten where I'm from."

She blinked at me, eyes wide. "You're right. Sorry."

"No, you meant something."

Scraping the concrete with the shovel, she didn't answer right away. "You haven't forgotten, but you don't exactly want to remember." She ran her lower lip through her teeth and her breath puffed around her face. "But it's okay. I understand."

She did. So why wasn't it comforting to hear? She wasn't begging me to stay. Even if she did, I wouldn't. She wasn't hanging on me until I left. She was living up her month of being married. Just like she'd said she would do.

I should be doing the same.

We worked on cleaning off the steps and sidewalk. When we were done, she stored the shovels. The snow wasn't good for making snowballs, but I grabbed a loose chunk and lobbed it at her torso. It splattered in a weak shower of flakes.

Her mouth dropped and a scandalized expression filled her features. "You did not start that."

I picked up another from the bank of cleared snow.

"Nope." I tossed the second chunk. It shattered against her coat.

Her lips flattened into a line, but her eyes? Pure mutiny filled them. "Did you forget I have three older brothers?"

I'd been counting on it.

My firecracker launched herself at me. I was hit with a sweet-smelling bundle before toppling backward. I landed with an oomph. Laughter burst out of me, mixing with her giggles. Cold seeped through my clothing, but her heat chased it off.

"You think you can take me?" I flipped us. She was fully covered except for her face. I didn't have to worry about her ass freezing off like mine.

Her laughter grew louder. The whole neighborhood was probably watching us. She grabbed a handful of snow and spritzed me in the face.

My girl fought dirty. I pushed up and yanked her with me as I went. She wobbled on her feet and I bent to throw her over my shoulder.

"Gideon!"

I smacked her ass and her laughter turned to a squeal. The neighbors were witnessing more than they'd bargained for, but I didn't care. I was frolicking with my wife.

Reality sank in.

I was having fun. With my wife. *Playing in the snow*.

Who did I think I was? A real married man, ready to settle down and watch everything I wanted become someone else's?

The writing was on the wall. In only days, it'd be on the contract, making my childhood home someone else's. Was there a point in prolonging the inevitable? I'd had enough discomfort growing up. I'd also had an email from Harold asking me if we could meet this week. Of course, he'd asked about Wednesday. The day the deal was final—both the sale and this marriage.

I had been going to dump her in a snowbank, but I slid her down my body instead. My decision was made. "I have to leave early."

Her smile froze, then melted like I was a toxic flame. "Oh." She placed her gloved hands on my shoulders. "Okay. How early?"

"Tuesday." The rest of the story piled in my head, ready to spill. I should've told her last week, but I'd thought a concrete decision would make itself clear. I wasn't ready to leave Silver. But I also wasn't ready to leave Bourbon Canyon. In business, that sometimes meant you had to do what you weren't ready for. There was no other way to grow. In this case, there was no other way to move on but to actually move on. "I called Taya last week to hear what she had to talk about."

A delicate brow arched. Did I spy a hint of jealousy? I missed the laughs and the smiles from only a minute ago.

"There's this guy." I was a massive dick. The sense I should've told her sooner was strong. Why? This was my job. My life. A major decision that was only mine to make. Since I wasn't married for real. "We—Taya and I —have done business with him before through Silver."

She tucked her chin into her scarf. Her freckles were stark against her reddened cheeks.

"He's starting an investment group and he wants us to work for him."

"You and Taya?"

I nodded. The emotion I'd first thought was jealousy

turned to disappointment. "One of his first major projects is a casino. At least three of us will be involved, but it'll be ours."

"Yours?"

"He wants to meet on the same day Dad closes on the land. Fitting, isn't it?"

Her breath puffed out. "Yeah. It is."

I hated myself for ruining her mood. "Since you work during the day, I'll hire a ride to the airport."

"No. I can take you. I'll find a sub." She stepped away. "We'll have to find a way to, uh, celebrate. The end." She grimaced. "I didn't mean it like that."

"I know what you meant," I said softly. We'd failed, but in this moment, it wasn't the unfulfilled bargain that felt like the failure. No, that was my plan to leave town. "We did a thing."

Her laugh was faint. "We get points for trying."

"Let's at least do lunch before the flight. And then you can drop me off at the airport." Were there any other ways I could stretch out my time with her? Reverse the clock altogether?

"Right. It's a date." Her smile wavered. "Our first one."

My month was coming to an end, and I hadn't taken my wife out on a date. We'd been to places. We'd been together the whole time. But there'd been no official outing as a couple to enjoy being a couple.

"Yeah. A date." One date with Autumn would never be enough, but if this trip had taught me anything, it was that I couldn't have it all.

I stared at my phone sitting on the table. Autumn was working. I had the whole day to myself, but my laptop was closed. After a morning of answering emails, scheduling my flight, and arranging a time with Harold, my concentration was shot.

Except when I'd finished work, my mind had turned to Dad. Had he gotten all dug out? Should I tell him I was leaving? Did he care?

I hit Dad's number on the phone. I put it on speaker, but I kept my ass in the chair.

He answered with a "Giddy."

"Don't call me Giddy." Why did he always sound so happy to hear from me? "Did you get the snow cleared okay?"

"Oh, yeah. Tenor came by with his tractor. Got me unburied lickety-split."

My normal resentment toward the Baileys wasn't there. "Good. That's good."

"How about the newlyweds? Did you get dug out?"

My heart twisted. It'd be a relief when I no longer had to lie. Dancing around the truth was exhausting. "Yeah, we got the place cleaned out yesterday."

"Good."

The line went quiet. I could let the awkward silence stretch, or I could cut the idle chitchat. "I'm leaving tomorrow. So this is your last chance to reconsider."

"You're leaving already?"

"Something came up at work." Another waltz around what was really going on. "I have an important meeting on Wednesday."

"Oh." Disappointment rang in that one word. "Do you and Autumn want to come over for dinner tonight?"

"We can't tonight." I had no good reason not to,

other than I should talk to Autumn first. But I wasn't going to see him again.

He'd offered dinner before, and I'd never taken him up on it. He also hadn't pestered. After the way our last visit had gone, it was probably for the best.

"Well," Dad continued, sounding deep in thought, "maybe when you get back."

"I'm not coming back." The finality made me stand up and start pacing. "I've gotta figure out how this is all going to go with my job. My bosses don't like me being away."

"And Autumn? Is she going to move?"

No. She wouldn't. I stopped at the sink and stared out the window at her backyard, blanketed in white. "We'll have to see. She doesn't want to."

"No, I can't imagine she does." If disheartened had a sound, it was Dad's tone right now. "But I respect that you're not pressuring her to change her life. That makes me glad."

He'd be disappointed if he saw through this marriage. Another round of silence fell and a tiny spark of guilt flared in my gut. An entire month and nothing had changed between us.

An entire month and it had gone by in a blink because of Autumn.

Fuck. Enough of this. I didn't owe him an apology or an explanation. "See ya when I see ya, Hank."

His chuckle was dry and lined with regret. "You said the same thing when you moved away."

I frowned. I had?

He remembered? He'd been sprawled on the couch, sleeping off a bad night. I hadn't bothered sneaking out the door.

"I just hope it's not another twenty-five years before I see you again, Giddy. Have a safe trip."

My irritation was as hot as a brand. Was he trying to guilt me? After what he'd done? What he was doing? "I plan to have a nice life. Goodbye, Dad."

I punched the screen to disconnect and stomped back to the window. I'd have a nice life. I'd have it all. I'd take the millions I wasn't spending on Percival Farms and invest it somewhere. I'd be able to buy whatever land I wanted, wherever I wanted.

I could have it all.

And I'd start by telling Autumn I didn't want this to be the end of us.

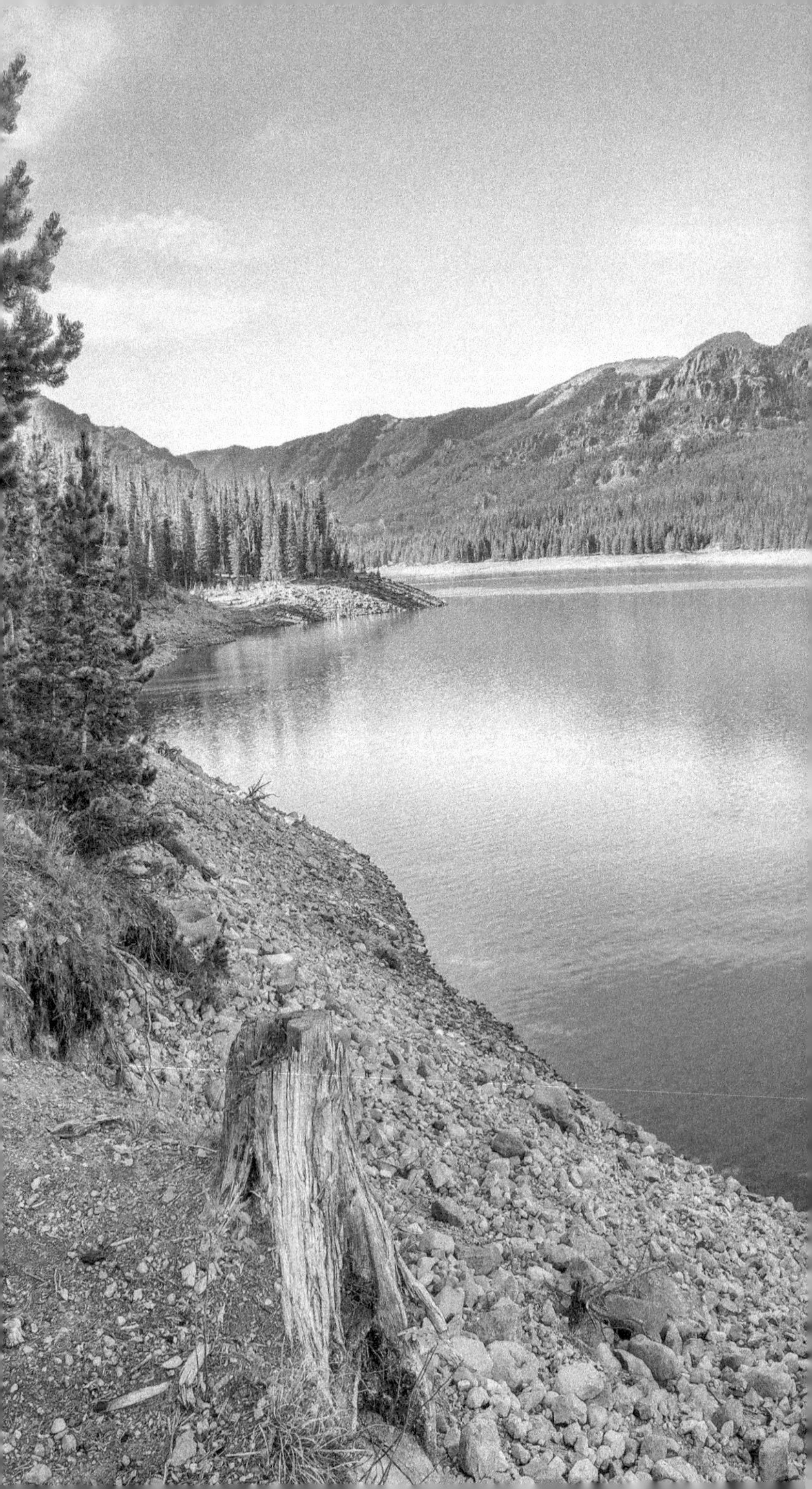

CHAPTER TWENTY-SIX

Autumn

The bustle of the restaurant around us had a corporate vibe. Women were in power suits or skirts, trendy footwear, and stylish blouses. The men looked much like Gideon had when I'd first met him. Not as good-looking, of course. Meanwhile, I was in jeans and rubber-soled boots that were really snow boots but could pass for odd loafers. My sweater was cable knit and made with almost black yarn flecked with color. It looked a lot like my cat, actually.

Gideon was back in his crisp jeans, a long-sleeved shirt that he'd wear when he was working but didn't have to be on video. He didn't have on a coat. Where he was going, the temperature would be thirty degrees warmer. He'd shoved everything in his suitcase.

The tinkling of glassware and forks on plates was all around us. The clientele was corporate, but the place had a rustic style with wooden beams and exposed brick walls. It was trendy, no matter the crowd.

I studied my menu. My hunger had been absent since he'd dropped the news he was leaving early. He had a possible new job. A new venture. He'd return to Las Vegas and create that legacy that was so important to him.

And I'd return to my job. To my little house. I would be content in life. I had prepared for this. I wouldn't cry. I wouldn't beg. This was the end and I was ready.

But I might get another cat. What were the odds there'd be another in the dumpster at school?

"Have you decided what you're having?" Gideon asked politely.

"I'll probably have the club sandwich." What were the chances I'd walk out without wearing part of it on my sweater?

When the server appeared, Gideon put down his menu. "We'll both have a club sandwich. Can she get an extra olive on top?"

The server grinned and gave me a look that said, *Aren't you the luckiest girl in the world?*

If only she knew. I returned her smile. I'd had my time to be lucky. Today, I'd be strong. My future was the same as my past before Gideon, only I wouldn't be waiting and wondering if my Prince Charming was on his way. I was okay being single. I was okay not settling. I had my jobs and my family.

When I glanced back at Gideon, he was studying me, a crease along his brow. "Everything okay?" he asked.

A tiny fissure in my determination formed. I sewed it up as securely as the quilt on my bed. No emotions were going to ruin my last hour with Gideon. "Just fine, you know, for a first last first date. Or is it a last first date? First and only first date?"

His expression went flat. "Does it have to be?"

"Excuse me?" I'd talked myself into a circle. What had I been trying to say?

"Does this have to be our only date?"

Confusion swirled my thoughts into a flurry, just like a snow globe. "What do you mean?"

"I mean we can still see each other."

I stared at him. He wanted to keep seeing me? My hope shone through that mental crack I thought I had repaired. No. It wasn't possible. We lived in separate states. "How would that work?"

"I have a lot of vacation."

"Unless you take this new job."

His hard jaw made a return. "I'll be one of the bosses. I'll get time off."

"Oh." No more words came to mind.

"We're good together, Autumn." The sincerity in his gaze devastated me.

"We are good together." But that wasn't the deal! Our bargain had a defined beginning and a definite end. Gideon was the fantasy I got to live and then remember forever after.

If I kept seeing him? That would be my dream come true. Except our castles were over eight hundred miles apart. I wasn't a princess and he wasn't royalty.

He put his big hand around his ice water and slowly turned the glass. "Is this like asking you to go to Spokane and meet my parents?"

"Mark didn't have divorce papers drawn up on our third date."

Gideon winced. "Yes. The divorce."

Exactly. "How would that work? We divorce and then start dating?"

"If that makes you more comfortable," he said cautiously.

More comfortable? Did he realize the walls I'd had to build around my heart because of those damn documents? Did he know that every day was a pep talk so I wouldn't fall faster and harder for him?

"Autumn. You're upset."

My chuckle came out reedy. "You've caught me off guard. The end has always been tomorrow, and now I have to suddenly shift my thinking."

"You don't need to decide immediately." He continued spinning the glass. "I just thought . . ."

He thought I'd jump at his offer just like I'd leaped into bed with him. Just like I'd said an exuberant yes when he'd claimed we should get married.

So why wasn't I?

He set his glass upright. "I thought you had enjoyed the last few weeks like I have."

Despite the conflict raging inside me, a tangle I couldn't sort, I warmed at his confession. "I absolutely did. I'll never get rid of those Pinocchio suspenders."

Heat infused his eyes. "You'll have to pack them." He cleared his throat and the spark of desire was gone. "If you come visit."

I'd be flying to Vegas. For a booty call. "A long-distance relationship."

"They're done by couples everywhere."

Junie had tried. Three of her last four boyfriends had cheated on her. Logically, I knew Gideon was right, but Junie was my only exposure to long-distance dating.

The server appeared with our sandwiches. I smiled at

Gideon, unsure of what to say. *Yes, absolutely? No, it'll never work? Can I think about it?* Nothing seemed to fit the moment.

Wasn't that the issue? I wasn't ready to give him a resounding yes.

We couldn't talk and eat, and each of us seemed to need the reprieve. I had to work out my feelings, and with each delicious bite, my decision grew clearer. When it was time to go, he paid. His hand was on the center of my back as we exited the restaurant into the cold air.

Too soon, we were at the airport. The plan was to drop him off at the departure area. I wouldn't walk in. There'd be no tearful goodbyes. Our deal would be done. Neither of us had gotten what we'd wanted, but we were adults.

I should be rejoicing. I should be readying myself to jump onto the sidewalk and kiss his handsome face off. If I said yes, it'd only be a matter of time before we were together again.

Celebrating was the last thing I wanted to do.

Gideon pulled to the curb behind a line of cars. He'd been driving all day. This car felt like it was his. But then, he'd never gotten a vehicle of his own. Bourbon Canyon had always been meant to be temporary.

He got out and unloaded his luggage from the back. It'd been so easy for him to pack. Until lunch, he'd been planning to leave.

He *was* leaving. His plans to return were nebulous at best. Little more than good intentions.

The sight of him standing by his shiny black suitcase, scrutinizing me with his vivid green gaze, kept the words I wanted to say firmly on my tongue. His breath puffed around him, but he stood like it was a warm summer day instead of a chilly winter one.

I closed the distance between us and curved my hand around his neck. He bent and I rose on my toes. Our lips met and that familiar sizzle of electricity passed between my skin and his. I didn't deepen the kiss and neither did he. He hugged me to him but loosened his hold when I pulled back.

His brows knit together. "Why do I feel like that was a permanent goodbye?"

"Because it was." There. I'd said it. Until this moment, I hadn't known if I'd be strong enough.

Emotions filtered through his expression. Disappointment. Hurt. Confusion. He gave a single nod. His jaw worked and he looked across the cars streaming around us and parked in the lot behind me. "Why?"

His voice was hoarse. He was crestfallen, and I wanted to hang on to that. He wanted more. But there would only be less.

Gideon had encouraged me to stand my ground with Tate. It was because of that I'd have to speak up for myself again.

The chill crept into my bones, thanks to the weather and the conversation. "You'll return to your job, maybe transition to a new one. I'd come out during Thanksgiving break, maybe Christmas. Would I fly out over Presidents' Day?" I shrugged. "You might fly out, but I doubt it. Your dad hurt you a lot. Anyway, we'd talk about work and superficially about my family. Then we'd have sex." Desire flared in his eyes. I almost wavered, but that spark was exactly why I had to continue. "I wouldn't be more than Taya to you."

He recoiled. "Taya? What does that mean?"

"We might not work together, but we'd fuck and then go our separate ways. To our separate lives. Only coming together for a release."

Understanding filled his gaze. He clenched his jaw and looked down. "I would like us to be more."

"Would you really?" Tears threatened to well, but I sniffed and let the cold air freeze them in place. "You never unpacked, Gideon. I realize we had a deal that ended with you leaving, but you lived out of your suitcase. You borrowed my car as if even *renting* one was too much commitment. But worse, you never talked to me. I'm no closer to knowing the real reason why you don't want kids than when I first asked. You didn't talk to me. You only gave me a part of you, and that's what I can't stand for. But one thing I realized about me is that it isn't just the kids. I want the partner."

His gaze swept our surroundings once more. His cheeks were tinting pink from the cold, giving him the appearance of being upset. The sad thing was, he wasn't really upset about my rejection. He didn't understand where I was coming from.

"You never asked to see the land Daddy gifted me. That place means the world to me, just like your home meant to you. Yet you never saw it. You asked me about work, but only to distract yourself from your feelings." I shook my head and sniffled. "I want a guy who'll stay with me even if we lose our house and have four little girls to take care of. I want a guy who'll be by my side through the decades. I want a guy who won't leave me until he physically can't stay anymore." I lost the battle against the tears. I'd gotten two sets of parents who'd shown me exactly what I dreamed of. I fought the urge to dive into the car, soak up the warmth of the heater, and drive home so I could hide under my covers with my cat until the alarm went off for work tomorrow. "You don't want to be that guy, Gideon."

"Autumn." My name came out strangled.

"Did you ever tell your work you got married?" When he glanced away and his Adam's apple worked up and down, the stabbing pain in the walls of my chest made it hard to breathe. "Taya?"

The shake of his head was barely noticeable.

None of this was real and I'd been right to protect my heart. Didn't mean the hurt was any less. I started backing up. The tears were going to come fast and hard.

He took a step, but I put my palm up. I should've had my gloves on, but my skin could be as exposed and raw as the rest of me. "Good luck with . . ." The investment group? Taya? Your life? "Everything. Just have your lawyer send me those divorce papers."

With that, I dove into the car and left him on that cold sidewalk. I dared to peek in the rearview mirror. He hadn't moved.

But he would. Montana wasn't his home.

Gideon

The view was stunning. I stood in front of floor-to-ceiling windows that created a rustic yet elegant frame around the mountain scenery. The caps were tipped with white, the snow continuing all the way down to the sprawling countryside.

You don't want to be that guy, Gideon.

The visceral reaction when she'd said those words had been staggering. I never yelled, but I'd been about to holler, *Bullshit! You're the only one giving up on us.*

How could that be true when I was boarding a plane soon?

The absurdity. Autumn was nothing like Taya. I was friendly with Taya. Physically and intellectually, we were compatible, but the absence of a spark was noticeable. Hence why we'd never been more than casual and occasional bed partners.

I gripped the handle of my suitcase.

I want a guy who'll stay with me even if we lose our house and have four little girls to take care of. I want a guy who'll be by my side through the decades. I want a guy who won't leave me until he physically can't stay anymore.

Autumn didn't talk a lot about her birth parents. She'd been young when they'd died, but she knew enough to admire her father's connection with her mother. Darin and Mae's relationship had been the envy of Bourbon Canyon. Apparently, it still was.

Bitterness raged through me until the taste of metal coated my tongue. The Baileys and their happy fucking family.

For a few fleeting moments, I'd been part of that family.

Autumn was wrong. There was too much between us. This could work.

I'd return to Vegas, hear what Harold Washington had to say, invest in a business that had a chance of being around long after me—

I'm no closer to knowing the real reason why you don't want kids than when I first asked.

Fuck. How could I discuss something I didn't know myself?

Percival's your legacy, Gideon. It's for you and your children. My grandfather's words were etched in my psyche. They'd formed me. I'd dedicated my life to working for that place. I could afford any price Dad asked. I'd kept my anger buried deep, knowing he wouldn't just sign over what should rightfully be mine.

The farm and ranch were no longer mine. Today, I'd failed on both accounts.

And I felt no different. Just another day.

Those kids I didn't want to think about happening? Didn't matter now.

My shoulders tightened. I rotated my head from side to side, stretching my neck. I'd get back to my plush office chair.

My back started to ache too. Fuck.

Maybe I needed to play more golf.

I hated golf. People said the best networking took place on the golf course or the tennis courts. Whenever I heard that, frustration would well over. I'd grown up on the back of a horse. I'd sprinted across open fields. Heaven had been my backyard.

I hadn't known a similar feeling until I'd sunk deep into Autumn. Until I'd woken up with her in the morning and known I'd go to bed with her at night.

"Look, Mom. Mom! Look." A little boy skidded to a stop next to me.

"Yes, Caleb. I see it. Be careful." His mom's voice was harried. She had a stroller with a googly-eyed little baby. A guy trotted behind her, various bags hooked to limbs. A duffel was around one shoulder. A tote with giraffes on the side hung from his other shoulder. A camera bag wound his neck, and a backpack poked up from behind him.

"Excuse me," the mom said breathlessly, gripping her boy by the shoulders. "He's excited for Disney."

The boy tipped his excited gaze up to me. "Are you going to Disney?"

I blinked at him. Was he asking me? I looked like I should be on that golf course. His dad dressed like he could step off the plane and into the line for the roller coaster in loose tan pants, white athletic shoes, and a shirt with some football team logo on it. Maybe from Vegas, but since I hadn't been able to play in high school, I'd quit following football.

Since Mom had died, I'd quit a lot.

"No." I spun on a heel and walked away. It was rude, but the seemingly happy, completely standard family had me suddenly and irrationally irritated.

Good thing Silver catered to a more adult crowd.

Only I might not be at Silver that much longer.

A few minutes and one frustrating TSA line later, I was at my gate. I continued to stare out the window at the white plane ready to take me away from my home state.

"We're pleased to announce boarding for the following sections . . ."

I would be one of the first to board. But I didn't move.

I was returning to everything I knew. Everything I'd worked for. I took my ring off and stuffed it in my pocket. I did not need to explain my marriage, or the dissolution of it, to anyone.

Only the reason why I had worked so hard was gone. And so was Autumn. All I had left was . . . my career.

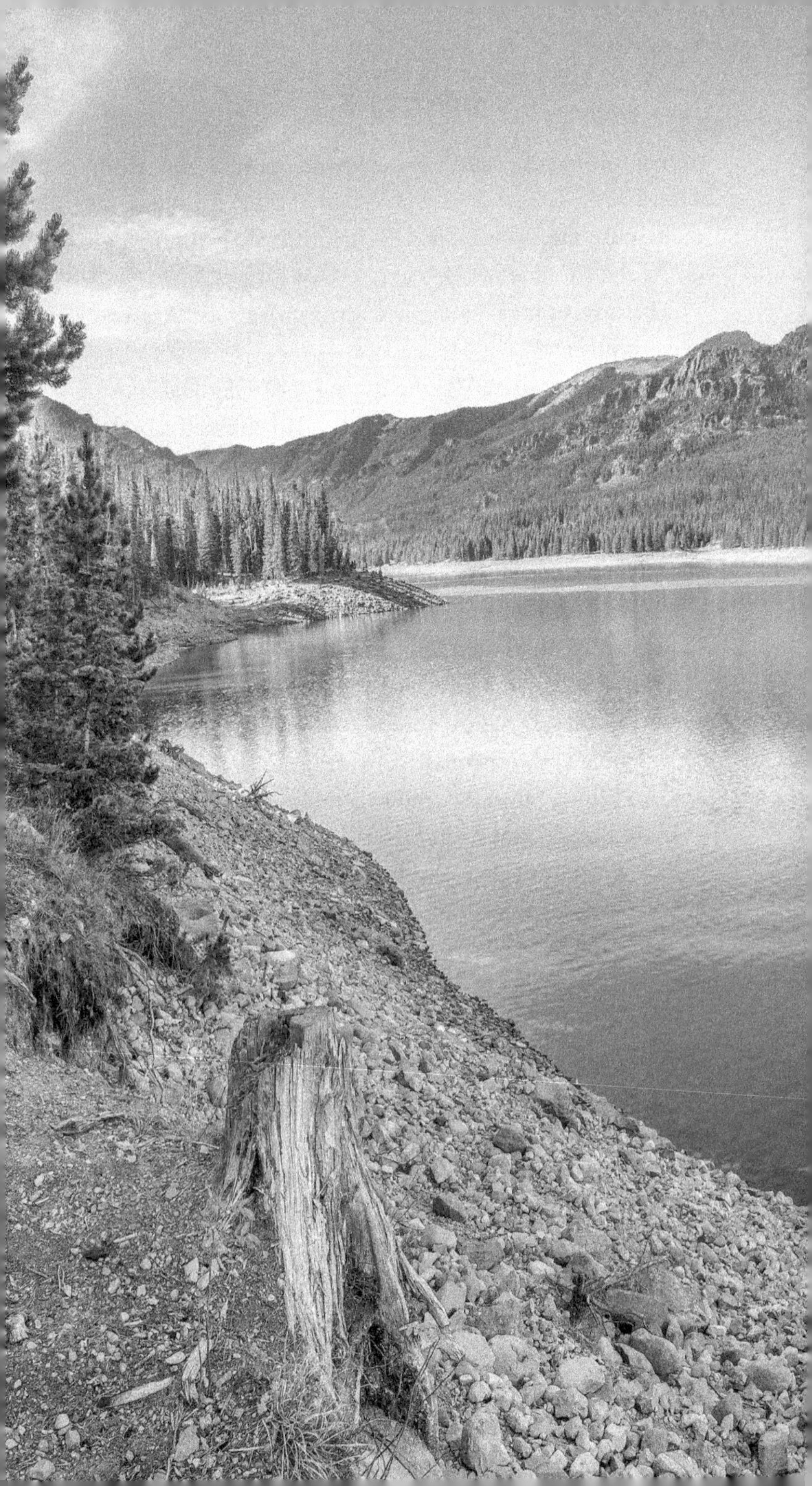

CHAPTER TWENTY-SEVEN

Autumn

I was curled up on the couch with my throw blanket over me. My Friday nights since Gideon had left consisted of my cat and a crime show. I'd started with a rom-com and had immediately backed out at the first smitten smile from the hero to the heroine. I couldn't do it. Give me a stern British detective and a murder.

If the setting was overseas, I wouldn't have to risk characters visiting Las Vegas.

I stuffed my spoon into my ice cream. I was hitting the hard stuff tonight. I doubt I'd be able to touch a Bloody Mary or eat an olive for weeks. Months probably.

Years?

Nah, that was too pathetic.

Yet, if I never drank another Bloody Mary or had one more blue-cheese-stuffed olive, I'd be fine.

My doorbell rang. I frowned at the picture window. Dangerous hope rose in my chest. Had Gideon returned? Had he bought a car and made the drive to Bourbon Canyon to declare his love for me?

Right.

"Quit crying in your drink and open up!" a woman shouted from the other side.

Junie?

I nudged Sprinkles off my lap. She grunted and stretched. I rose and went to peer out the spy hole.

My sister was on the other side, her face tucked into her collar. She was shifting her feet back and forth to stay warm.

I swung the door open. "Have you lost your cold blood?"

She rolled her eyes and pushed past me on a wave of peony-smelling lotion. "I put on a sweater when I played in Phoenix last week." She toed her fluffy boots off. They'd get wrecked in five seconds on the ranch. "It was almost seventy degrees. I was so ashamed."

"You've been away from home too long."

Regret flashed in her eyes, but I pulled her in for a hug. She tossed her arms around me and fiercely returned the embrace.

"I didn't mean anything by that," I explained into her cloud of dirty-blond hair with purple stripes. "I'm happy for you."

She pulled back and flashed me her camera-ready smile. "Aww, thank you."

I kept my hold on her shoulders. I was her sister. She never gave her family that smile. That smile was fake. "What's wrong?"

She sagged in my hold. "I'm not here about me."

"If you're here about me, there's nothing to tell."

Her gaze landed on the half-eaten tub of ice cream. I

had skipped the pints and gone for the half-gallon container of cookies and cream. The last two weeks of setting the stage at work had been exhausting. *Yeah, Gideon went back to work. Silver could only do without him for so long. But, you know, it's fine. I love teaching, and maybe he can work out a remote-work arrangement.*

Each word had widened the crater his absence made in my heart.

"It's treat night."

She stepped far enough into the living room to look at the TV and winced. "It's British-crime-drama bad?"

"I love British crime dramas."

"When you've been through a breakup."

I choked on a sob. "We didn't break up." Tears welled in my eyes. The last two weeks had felt very much like a breakup. "We had a deal. He was always going to leave. I just . . ."

Her mouth dropped open and she blinked. It wasn't often Junie was struck silent. "Oh no. The marriage was fake?"

I nodded. A tear rolled down my cheek.

"And you fell for him anyway."

"So hard."

She hooked my elbow and dragged me to the couch. I took the corner I'd vacated when she'd arrived. My spot was still warm. She disappeared into the kitchen and returned with a spoon and a carton of mint chip.

"I thought you were dairy-free and didn't eat after nine at night?" I'd read the article on her in a magazine. Then I'd laughed with Summer because she used to catch Junie in the closet with crackers and cheese at midnight when she was stressed—like during finals, before prom, and in the months before she'd decided to pursue her singing career.

She plopped on the other end of the couch and tucked her feet under the blanket. As if sensing there were two warm bodies available, Sprinkles strutted back into the room.

"That was for the magazine. And for the record, I said milk made my eczema worse. I never said anything about ice cream or cheese. Besides, ice cream is better than the wine Wynter and I had when she was mopey over Myles."

None of us drank when we were sad. Mama and Daddy had made us associate spirits with good times and family. Thus, the ice cream. "No eating after nine?"

"It's five o'clock somewhere." She took the lid off her carton. "Your heart is broken and the others are worried about you."

"They are?" Scarlett had hovered at school, but I could've rivaled that camera-ready smile of Junie's. I'd worked Wednesday night and both Summer and Wynter had fluttered around me. I'd put on a good show. There was no reason not to. I didn't need to see anyone's pity to know I'd made a mistake when I had thought I could leave the marriage unscathed.

But then, I was still married. Gideon's lawyer hadn't sent the divorce papers yet. I still wore my ring. Had he taken his off? Of course he had. He had no reason to inform anyone about me.

More tears popped into my eyes. I stabbed my spoon in my ice cream.

"Scarlett said you talk like you're reciting lines in a play."

I wrinkled my nose. The only actors Scarlett saw in

plays were the kids during the performances. I did not put on that stilted of a show.

"Wynter said she had to fix five orders behind your back at the bar on Wednesday night."

"She did not." At Junie's direct gaze, I tried to recall the evening. Wynter had been bustling around me and talking to the customers more than usual. I thought it was because I'd told her what the deal between me and Gideon had been and she was avoiding me.

"Summer said you snapped at Tenor."

I couldn't deny that one. Tenor was the most sensitive brother and I still felt bad about biting his head off.

He had actually approached me about a new inventory system that would work for the entire distillery. He'd wanted my input from the bar's standpoint. In my awful mood, I had assumed he'd made his decision already and was placating me.

Then he'd shown me the demo program and the various options he'd researched. I hadn't apologized yet, but I'd gone through the programs and given him my feedback in less than twenty-four hours.

"I haven't been a nice person to be around." Even my students had sensed my dark mood and constantly asked if I was okay. Stuffing my emotions down until the end of the day and pretending everything was all right was *exhausting*. I stuffed my spoon under a big chunk of cookie. I rolled my eyes to clear my tears away. *Don't cry—again*.

"Oh, honey."

I shook my head, but I couldn't meet her gaze. "Tell me about that cutie you're touring with. Is he as single as the tabloids say he is?" *Please tell me everything*. I couldn't spend another night crying over a situation that wouldn't be changing anytime soon.

She smacked her lips, not answering. I was desperate to talk about anything other than how I couldn't look anywhere in the house and not think of Gideon. Of how I'd been almost late for work this morning because I'd had a crying fit in the garage. My car didn't smell like Gideon anymore either. Two whole days was all I'd gotten with his scent before it had been gone.

"Well"—she gestured at me with her spoon—"you, of course, can't tell anyone, but he's seeing the other singer we're on tour with, but they haven't announced it yet."

I exhaled my relief and sank farther into the cushions. I could get lost in other people's drama and forget there was none of my own.

Gideon

A month after I'd returned to Las Vegas, I was a grumpy fuck and everyone in the office kept their distance. My assistant rarely messaged or called, and I canceled more meetings than I kept. That was what a month of shitty sleep did to me.

I'd had the meeting with Taya and Harold the day after I'd returned. He'd asked me a few times if everything was okay and referenced my mysterious family emergency, but I hadn't answered him. Half the time he'd been telling me about his plans, I'd been focused on my left ring finger and how goddamn naked it felt without my ring.

I hadn't given Harold a definitive answer. I had asked to have until the end of the year. Taya was already a yes.

I swiveled around and stared out the window. My office had almost as much square footage as Autumn's house, only it was a completely open floor plan. I had all the light I wanted streaming in, but when the sun went down, the rays turned neon.

I'd done nothing but notice how different this city was. It was like when I'd first arrived for college, only the city didn't seem like the reprieve it had been back then.

Had Dad moved to senior housing? Had he bought new furniture with all the money he'd gotten, or had he hauled the threadbare couch and recliner? Was he making friends instead of watching TV by himself after eating a sandwich?

Worrying about Dad took my mind off Autumn.

How was she doing? Did she miss me? Would she change her mind?

Judging by my quiet phone—no. She was sticking to her decision.

My chest ached. I rubbed the center. I should get some heartburn medicine. This acid would eat my esophagus away if this kept up.

It's not reflux, jackass.

I scrubbed my hands down my face. No one else was talking to me, but I fought with myself all damn day. I needed to focus on work.

The renovations for the parking garage were a go and we were balls deep in logistics. I was overwhelmed and grateful for it. The work kept me rooted to my office. I didn't need to see the sophisticated holiday decorations lining the halls and businesses in Silver.

No fucking thank you.

I loosened my tie—the damn thing was strangling me—and opened my email. A new message sat at the top. The sender: Canyon Legal.

My stomach bottomed out. What the fuck was this?

My mouth went dry as I read the email. Autumn had hired a company to track down a copy of the divorce papers I'd had drawn up. All they needed was a signature from each of us and for the court to sign off. Then I'd be single.

Fire flamed across my skin and burned under my collar. She'd told me to and I hadn't. So she'd done it. She'd made the first move.

She was willing to move on from me. Like everyone else.

Except they didn't, asshole. Dad tried calling and connecting for years.

And he'd done it before he'd sobered up.

Autumn hadn't reached out.

You don't want to be that guy, Gideon.

I'm no closer to knowing the real reason why you don't want kids than when I first asked.

You only gave me a part of you, and that's what I can't stand for.

I hadn't given her a reason to run after me. All she knew of me was that I lived for myself and no one else.

Percival's your legacy, Gideon.

No, it wasn't. I never should've had that pressure on my shoulders. The insidious thought had stolen my life. It'd built up my pride until it was my own worst enemy.

Fuck.

There was a knock on the door. Taya poked her head in. "Can I come in?"

"What do you need?"

She stiffened. I had been keeping my distance because she hadn't been trying to keep hers.

She snuck in and closed the office door behind her. Leaning against it, she crossed her bare legs in a way that might've been meant to entice me.

"This has got to stop, Gideon. You've been an ass since you got back."

I had been. I glanced at the computer screen. The future wasn't looking so hot either.

"Does this . . . does this have anything to do with that redhead?"

"My wife."

"Excuse me?" She blinked her crystal-blue eyes.

"That redhead is my wife. And yes, it all has to do with her."

Taya huffed. Hurt wiped out the astonishment on her face and an angry flush crawled up her skin. "Oh my god, Gideon. What were you thinking?"

"I'd be very careful how you continue."

Tension radiated across her face. She shifted her weight from high heel to high heel. "Okay," she said carefully. "I can read between the lines. You're here and she doesn't seem to be. So, I guess there must be trouble in paradise. Maybe you need to ask yourself what she can give you that you don't already have?"

I didn't have to ask myself. "Everything."

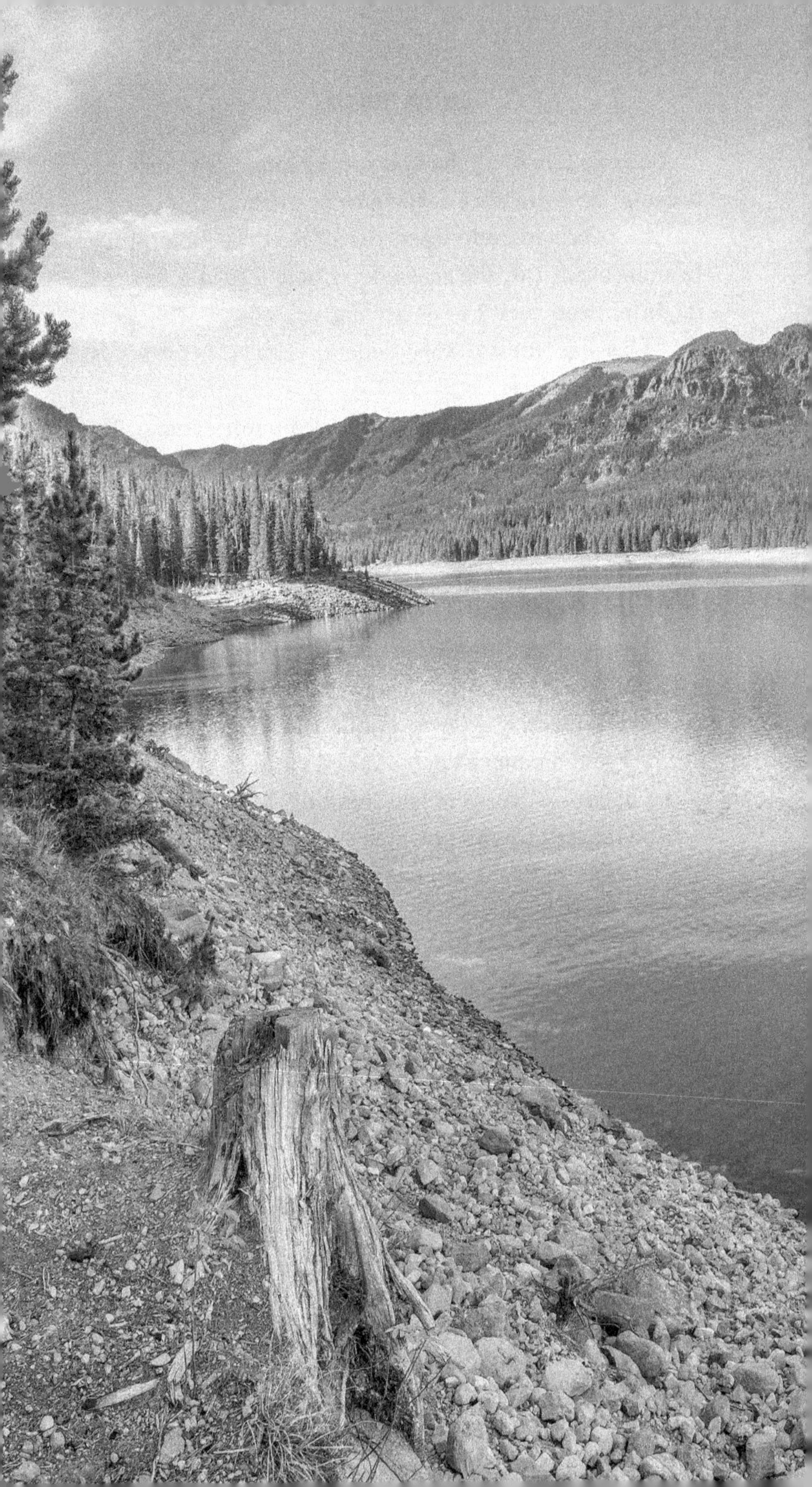

CHAPTER TWENTY-EIGHT

Gideon

Light snow was falling. I got out of my pickup and rolled my shoulders. The drive had been long, the roads had been crap for some of the way, but I'd made the haul in one day.

I faced the modern-looking condo buildings. They were single level and zero entry, hooked together and built in three different sections to make a courtyard that would be nice in the summer. Right now, the gazebo was full of snow. Same with the walking paths.

The sounds of distant engines surrounded me, but this neighborhood was quiet. The light in the unit before me glowed through the closed curtains.

I knocked on the door. The shuffle of footsteps was faint on the other side.

The door swept open without hesitation, not even enough time to have looked through the peephole. Dad's brows lifted. His beard was neatly trimmed, but he wore the same old clothing as before. He was a wealthy man, but he appeared to be living simply still. "Giddy?"

"Hi, Dad."

He didn't move. I didn't move.

He leaned out and looked around. His gaze landed on the brand-new red truck I'd bought the day before last. "You alone?"

So goddamn alone. "Why didn't you sell to me? I need plain words."

He sighed and pushed the door open. "Come on in. We're heating up the neighborhood."

The inside of his unit was completely different than the house I'd grown up in. He'd bought much-needed new furniture. A simple love seat and recliner. Not much more would fit. A small dining room linked the living room and the kitchen.

One thing was the same. The last family photo we'd taken the summer before Mom died hung on the wall across from the recliner. He'd have to look at Mom's smiling face every day. In the picture, I was grinning. Mom had just teased Dad about his crooked mustache and we'd all laughed. The moment was captured for eternity.

I didn't sit. I shoved my hands in my coat pockets. It was the same coat I'd used when I was here last time. "I know you said we all have to be free to live our own life. I think I understand, but I'm afraid I don't. And I have to be sure." My throat threatened to close up. "I have to be certain."

He lowered himself onto the edge of the love seat and pressed his fingertips together. "Did you know your mother wanted to be a teacher?"

Shock hit before a slow burn of dawning horror. The

back of my neck grew hot as a few comments Dad had made when we'd talked last month crept in. "No."

"She wasn't allowed to leave town for college. Her place was the farm. Only child and all."

The dismay seared worse in my gut. "She loved Percival."

"Yeah, she was always good at making lemonade out of lemons." Fondness filled his gaze. "We talked a lot about you, and what would happen when you grew up. She was worried you'd think that this was all there was in life. That her dad would put the same pressure on you that he'd put on her."

I closed my eyes. He had. "I loved Percival."

"I think you felt like you had to love Percival, or you were nothing."

I inhaled sharply. The place had been my home. It'd been the center of all my happy memories. Yet the happiness in those memories came from Mom and Dad. Not the farm.

"Neither of us liked how your grandfather pressured you. He was obsessed with the place, and I think his declining health made him more of a fanatic. He couldn't be around to control everything. Your mom wanted you to be free to live your own life. It was important to her that you had the opportunities she hadn't. She once said that she ought to sell the place to put a stop to her dad's poisonous thinking."

I sank my head into my hands. The sale had been Mom's idea? Blocking me had originated with her? "Why didn't you tell me?"

"I didn't give a shit about the farm or ranch; she wasn't there and I didn't care. I know you hated me for it, but I'd rather have you hate me than her. Your head was filled so full with your grandpa's words, I thought it was all or nothing. Either you're completely free of Percival and you can figure out what you really want in life, or you'd be anchored to that place and you'd die with nothing but your pride while cursing any future kids to my and your mom's fate."

Dad hadn't wanted to be nothing but a farmer or rancher. He'd limited his options for Mom and then he'd gotten stuck out there. If he'd tried to sell when Grandpa Percival was still alive, my grandfather would've made his life hell.

And mine by proximity. "You should've told me. You should've trusted me to put the blame where it belonged." Would it have changed anything?

It didn't matter.

Dad worked his jaw back and forth. "Maybe I was afraid of you resenting her for leaving you with a mess. I didn't want that. For either of us."

We couldn't go back in time and change our actions. And I was so damn tired of being angry. "I'm sorry," I said hoarsely.

"No." Dad shook his head once. "*No.* You do not have anything to apologize for. By the time I sobered up, I was too late to be a good influence. Too late to tell you that you could do anything you wanted."

"I wouldn't have known what I wanted. I would've said Percival."

"It shouldn't have been an all-or-nothing decision," he said sadly.

"Grandpa Percival made it that way."

"You don't know how relieved I am to hear you

acknowledge that. Gives me hope that someday you may not hate me."

I swallowed hard and tipped my head back to look at the off-white ceiling. The walls were plain, but Dad's home was brighter than ours had ever been after Mom died. "I don't hate you."

"You know, I might start to believe that."

"Because I'm here?"

He shook his head. "You didn't bite my head off when I called you Giddy." A smile tipped up the corner of his mouth. "And you called me Dad tonight."

"Shit, Dad." I pushed a hand through my hair. The ball cap I'd worn last was on the passenger seat. "I've been awful to you and I was a selfish ass with Autumn."

"I have to admit I'm glad you're not just in town for me." He pointedly looked at my bare ring finger. My ring was in my pocket. "I've been worried that you two were no more."

"I miss home. I found it again with Autumn and I threw it away." The next part might hurt him, but I had to say it. He'd have the answers. "I'm terrified of losing her. I'm . . ."

"Scared of turning into me?" Sadness filled his gaze. He crossed to me, grabbed both of my shoulders, and hauled me into his arms. I was a few inches taller than him, but I was propelled back in time. He was my old dad, the one from the happy memories I'd never push away again.

When he pulled back, he studied me. "You're scared of turning into me." It wasn't a question.

"I understand, you know. Every time I get upset and want a drink, I think about how much like you I am." I didn't say it to be mean.

Regret passed through his expression. "Hell, Giddy, I'm sorry. If someone had told me before your mom died I'd have an alcohol problem, I'd have never believed 'em. You're aware of the urge. You're already ahead of me. I'm proud of you, you know. Always have been."

His words closed a wound deep inside me that I'd been ignoring. "Autumn wants kids."

"Do you?"

"They petrify me, but . . ." I wanted to be that guy holding all the bags while I took my wife and kids on a trip. "There were several years when my dad was pretty kick-ass. I've had a good role model all along."

His eyes filled with tears and he pulled me into him again. "I needed to hear that, and I didn't even know it."

My arms were pinned to my sides. When was the last time I'd hugged my dad? So many years we'd missed. I embraced him back, awkward as hell, but I did it.

After a minute he pulled away, blinking back his tears. "You left town and then weeks went by. I thought if that girl can't keep you in town, this old man won't bring you back." Hope lit his eyes. I knew what he'd been afraid of.

The urge to tell him everything was strong. *Yeah, Dad. I married Autumn to fool you into selling to me.* But there had been more reasons for walking into that posh chapel with her. She'd captivated me from the very beginning. "The important thing is, now I'm back."

Autumn

. . .

The company Christmas party at Copper Summit was both winding down and livening up. Chance, Brinley, and Darin had gone home with Mama an hour ago. They were sleeping over at her place. Same with Elsa. Myles and Wynter had driven her over, then returned a few minutes ago. They were at a table with Jonah and Summer.

Tenor and Teller were standing around another table, chatting with the distillers and our delivery drivers. Each of my brothers had a glass of bourbon and was gesturing with it like Daddy used to do.

Junie had gone back to Nashville to spend the holiday writing songs with some friends. She rarely stayed in town long, and with her growing popularity, she usually snuck in and out of city limits. She claimed she never wanted coming home to be a story. Summer, Wynter, and I thought she didn't want to run across the high school sweetheart she'd left behind and his adorable daughters.

Tate looked like he was trying to pick up Scarlett, their heads tipped together, both of them smiling and laughing. Tate used to work the crowd when he was the boss, but since he'd taken over the ranch, he'd chat a little, then dote on his wife.

I gulped down my jealousy. Could I use the diarrhea excuse to leave early?

No. No leaving before the party was done. Whenever I heard back from the company I'd hired to do the divorce, I'd be single. I would not wallow in self-pity.

I would not wallow as much.

Maybe one day I would have what Tate, Wynter, and Summer had. Maybe. One day, one year, a long time from now.

I stretched out the fingers of my left hand. *Don't look*.

I was behind the bar. In my safe place. I had on a green Christmas sweater with puffy balls for tree ornaments, a thick brown skirt, and knee-high boots. I looked festive.

I wasn't.

I would eventually have to explain why I wasn't wearing my wedding ring tonight. My sisters had noticed, but they hadn't asked. Too many others around. The ring was at home, tucked into a jewelry box and pushed to the far corner of my dresser. Tonight was the night to debut a bare ring finger.

My "try to announce the end of my marriage without looking pathetic" plan was now in full swing. In the break room at work, my coworkers still asked about Gideon. On Monday, I'd tell them the winter weather and our work were keeping us apart. I'd comment that our lives were just too separate—insert heartbroken pout. His work was important to him. My family was in Montana. I'd field the pitying looks like a champ and then cry to Sprinkles at night.

The worst of my plan would be my brothers. They all "happened" to stop in at the bar and ask how I was doing each night I worked. They never asked about Gideon. They didn't point out that their suspicions might've been right, that Gideon had only married me to manipulate the sale. I didn't mention that yes, he had.

Some things a girl just had to keep to herself.

I'd cry to my cat and my sisters.

But first, I needed the closure of the signed divorce papers. Gideon should've gotten the email a few days ago. The marriage would be officially over any day. The company I'd hired promised me a quick divorce. Vegas was known for quickie weddings. An easy divorce wasn't as heavily advertised, but they offered that too.

Tenor wandered over. His brown eyes were full of concern. He pushed his glasses up. His longish hair hung over the thick frames. "Gideon couldn't make it?"

Of my three brothers, I hadn't thought he'd be the one to broach the subject. Tate and Teller were more direct, but they'd tiptoed around me since Gideon had left town. Tenor had been on the receiving end of my emotions, thanks to the inventory talk, but here he was. Fitting he'd be the first to hear about the end of me and Gideon.

I sipped from the small straw in my Kentucky mule. I hadn't added enough bourbon to make what I had to say any easier and this was my first and only drink of the night. Anxiety swirled in my stomach, but at least it took the focus off the pain around my heart. The only communication between me and Gideon had been the email with the divorce documents, and it hadn't been sent directly from me.

It was time. "We actually decided a divorce would be best."

Tenor cocked his head like he couldn't believe what I'd said. "Divorce?"

"Yep." I popped the p and took another long sip. The lime had enough bite to keep me from getting lost in my own foul mood. Hard to be upset when the taste of summer danced on my tongue. "We tried. So there is that."

"Autumn."

It was the pity. The "I'm so sorry" and "I saw this coming" look I'd been dreading. My pulse kicked up. He was right. I'd known this was coming and I was still devastated.

I was a fool. The worst kind—a fool in love with a broken heart.

"No, no. It's fine. I mean, we tried." My voice caught. Had I tried? Gideon hadn't. But what if I had tried harder?

Teller appeared by Tenor. "What's going on?"

Out of the corner of my eye, I saw Tate making his way around the people at the bar to come our way. Scarlett's gaze was on me, but she'd know having a crowd around me would only make me feel self-conscious. My sisters knew what was up.

I wiggled my ring finger and forced a smile. "The marriage will be officially over soon. Our lives are in different places." I sounded scripted.

Now, I had three brothers with narrowed gazes on me.

"That asshole," Teller growled.

I shook my head. I was disappointed in Gideon, but I couldn't stand hearing them rage about my soon-to-be nonhusband. This had been both of our decisions. "No, it's fine. I mean, everyone saw this coming."

"Maybe that's what we thought at first," Tate said. "But not for long. I really thought he'd find a way to make it work."

He had to want to first.

Teller pushed forward and wrapped me in a bear hug. "We're here for you."

I was crushed against him, and I couldn't move. I also didn't want to. Grief slipped past my wobbly mental barrier and washed over me. No matter how much I'd told myself the marriage wasn't real, it had felt legit. My time with Gideon had been a dream, but I hadn't been imagining it.

I let out a shuddering breath and soaked in the brotherly comfort. Junie's visit had been needed. Now I leaned on my brothers' strength. I needed them to baby me in the way that usually chafed. I was back to being an injured girl scared of her future. The wounds weren't physical and my future wasn't uncertain this time. It was just empty.

I opened my eyes. The other employees would soon hear about the divorce and word would spread. They'd do the work for me. Then it'd be officially over.

My face was still smashed sideways into Teller's chest as Tate stroked a hand down his beard, his brows sewn together. The bell on the door tinkled. He glanced over and did a double take and straightened.

The din in the bar quieted down. Teller's hold eased, and now Tenor frowned at the entrance. I couldn't see around Teller, so I stepped to the side to peek at what kind of guest had made the bar quiet down.

Gideon prowled toward me. His gaze didn't waver to my brothers or any of the other partygoers. He was focused on me.

Now I was dreaming. The divorce was messing with my head.

My brothers didn't part for him. They had all turned to face Gideon and were barriers around me, blocking off the opening to get behind the bar. I tried to nudge Teller and Tenor out of the way, but I might as well have shoved at concrete walls.

"Gideon? What are you doing here?" I had to be hallucinating. But my brothers wouldn't be on guard for some other tall man with broad shoulders, dark hair, and piercing green eyes. Except if Gideon were really here, he'd look like a corporate god instead of dressing in the same clothing he'd moved cattle in and the coat he'd bought for his brief return to a Montana winter.

"I deleted that goddamn email." His voice was smoother and richer than any bourbon we could produce. And it was real. He was here.

"What email?"

His gaze finally jumped to Teller, then Tate, and finally Tenor before swinging back to me. "You know which one."

The only movement behind him were my sisters creeping closer. They were a lot shorter than the guys, but they'd still jump Gideon and hide his body if he hurt me.

Did he have any idea what he had walked into?

Wait—he'd deleted the email. *The* email. "Why? You weren't sending those documents."

Every day I'd cringe when I checked my inbox. Every day, I'd exhale a relieved sigh, then pass through hope to despair, only to fret about checking my email the next day. I couldn't keep doing that. I couldn't keep wondering if he was just too busy to even think about me enough to sever the weak tie between us.

"You're my wife, Autumn. I want to keep it that way."

I laughed. The sound just burst out of me. He wanted to keep me? To keep us? "You won't leave your job."

"I just did."

My vocal cords froze. He'd quit?

"I told them I got married two months ago, and living apart wasn't worth the paycheck." He waved a hand toward the window. "Then I packed my things and bought a pickup to drive here."

He'd bought a pickup. I couldn't read into that. So he had a mode of transportation. Most people did.

The guy rarely left Silver.

But he was here.

"I stopped to talk to Dad first," he said softly. "Or I'd have been here earlier. But I couldn't see you until I cleared a few things up with him."

The ache in my chest lessened. He'd called him Dad instead of Hank. No. I was reading too much into this. His life was in upheaval. "What about the other job offer?"

"I told Harold I'd be interested in investing with him on smaller projects, but first I have some playground equipment to buy for a school in my hometown. I am otherwise unemployed." He shrugged. "Doesn't matter anyway. We're millionaires."

Another laugh burst out of me. Yes, I was financially comfortable. When my family's companies depended on the economy, grain prices, and taxes, we tended to be savers and not spenders. "I'm not rich, Mr. Casino."

"You're my wife. We're rich. My lawyer's going to make the postnup go away—unless you're afraid I'll have some say on your property. It doesn't matter to me because we're never getting divorced." He swung his gaze across my family members. Seemingly undaunted by their presence and the still quiet bar, he continued, "All that money is what I saved to buy Percival. Now it's what I can live on. If you don't mind having a househusband."

I stared at him. Rich. Househusband. None of this was making sense.

He glanced back and forth between Teller and Tenor. They moved aside finally and I was exposed.

"I've missed you." Gideon crossed to me. "I've done nothing but miss you and regret that I couldn't be the guy that you want. Then I saw that damn email. I can't lose you, Autumn. The month I had with you was the best of my life. I want more. I want forever with you. I want kids. I want more cats. A dog. Maybe a bigger house, but our current home will do until our family grows."

Fear tore through me, got smothered by hope, only to turn to disbelief. "Are you sure?"

"I'm so goddamn sure. The talk I had with Dad cleared a lot of things up. I grew up being told everything in my life revolved around Percival and that's not what my mom wanted for me. Dad knew it and that's why he wouldn't sell to me."

"Oh, Gideon." I put my hand on his hard chest. He was so warm. So real.

"It was the best thing he could've done for me. I thought I was losing my legacy, the only place I thought of as home, but you're my home, Autumn. Wherever you are is home." He dug in his coat pocket and dropped to one knee.

Stunned, I could only watch. What was happening?

He opened a small black velvet box. "I know you already have a ring, but this was the one I was going to buy you in the first place."

The five-carat diamond from the wedding chapel. "Gideon."

"I know you won't wear it, but I needed to do this. I have to be the husband I wasn't during our first month. I love you so damn much. So, Autumn Kerrigan. Will you stay married to me?"

My fantasy was on his knee before me, offering me everything I wanted. "Oh god, yes." I flung myself at him. He caught me before my knees hit the floor. I was in his arms again, his mouth pressed against mine, and I no longer felt empty. "I love you too."

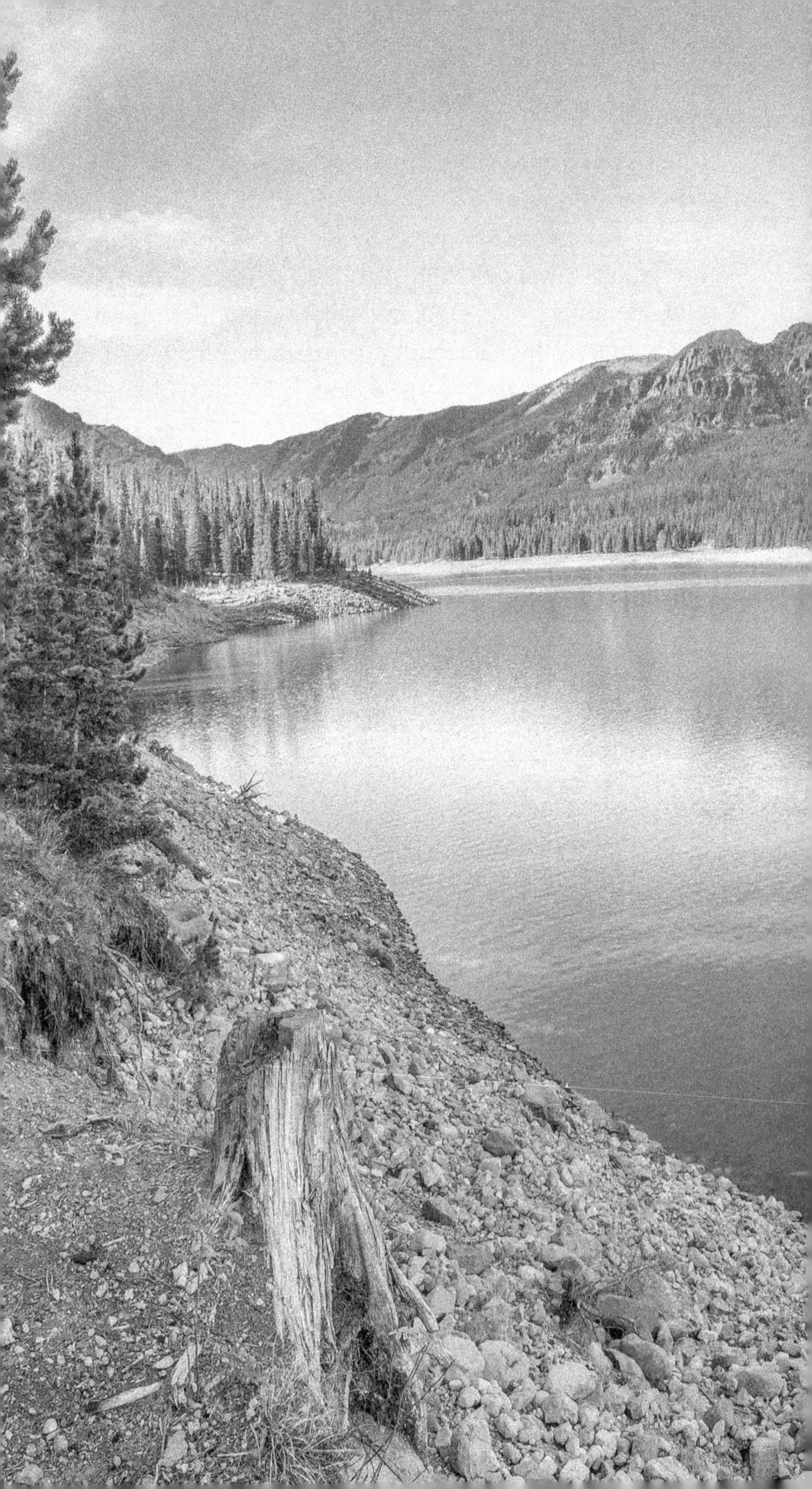

CHAPTER TWENTY-NINE

Gideon

I wanted to take Autumn into the storeroom and shut everyone out. We'd be locked in and I'd have her naked and against the wall in less than a minute. But that'd have to wait. I was behind the bar with her. She was tucked against my side, where she belonged. My ring was on her finger and I'd put mine back on.

Her family had congratulated us, then the various employees of the distillery. Christmas decorations hung in the corners, snowflake lights were around the windows, but the decor didn't annoy me now that I was with my wife.

The claps on the back had been extra hard from her brothers, but I deserved it. They were my brothers now too. My family had grown from me and Dad to a large, thriving crew that had accepted both of us when we'd been less than our best. The Baileys turned their Christmas party into a celebration.

"I can't believe you're here." This was the third time she'd said it.

I lifted her hand, the one with the giant diamond she was almost too paranoid to wear. Her sisters had made her leave it on instead of putting the ring in the box and locking it up for the night.

I brushed my thumb over her warm skin. "Believe it, firecracker. I'm not leaving." I leaned my head down to murmur in her ear. "But I'd like to leave with you."

Her eyes heated. "Let's go. Wynter can close up."

"Your family's here."

She twined her fingers in mine. "They won't want to see what comes next."

I laughed as she grabbed her coat and dragged me out the door. We left on a wave of hoots and hollers.

"Here." I handed her the keys. "We'll come back for your car tomorrow. I want to see your land. You might as well drive."

"It's dark out."

"We'll go again when it's light out."

"The road out there is probably blocked."

She was missing the point. I needed her to know that I was invested in us. I also needed her. We reached the driver's door and I tugged her toward me. Her coat collar puffed around her neck and her hair was a red halo around her face.

She was my very own snow angel. "You know where there's a good place to stop so you can crawl over to my side and get on top of me."

Her eyes widened. "Oh." She snatched the keys out of my hand. "Load up."

The moon was high and there were very few clouds. Still, it was dark on the Baileys' property. I couldn't make out much more than a white landscape with brown grass poking through. We were on a gravel road in the middle of nowhere.

She stopped by a stretch that looked like it could be a turnoff to a long driveway or a narrow road if it was plowed. After she backed in so we were firmly off the road, she killed the lights. "This is the access road. The guys use it for hunting and there's a fishing nook on the edges we sometimes use. I can't wait for you to see it in the spring." She gnawed at her lower lip and gazed into the rearview mirror that showed nothing but darkness. Something was bothering her.

"You can talk to me."

Her expression softened. "I love the simple beauty. It's such an outdoor oasis, I never planned to build a house on it."

"Then we won't."

She peered at me. "As simple as that?"

"As simple as that."

Her lips curved into a smile and she unzipped her coat. "You say all the right things."

"Not enough, but I will. I promise." I shrugged out of my coat and tossed it in the back seat with hers. I had brought very few of my things. I'd get all new stuff. "Now get over here."

My erection was getting uncomfortable. Watching her wiggle out of her winter coat was a personal striptease.

I helped her clamber over the console and I leaned the seat back as far as it'd go. Finally, her weight rested on me. Neither of us moved. Her hands were on my shoulders and her hair hung down.

I drank her in. "You're so fucking beautiful." I cupped her cheek. "I don't deserve you."

"Gideon." She turned her face into my hand. My heartbeat hammered in my cock but I wanted to savor her. She was mine for eternity, but I had to have her now.

"I was a shell before you." I thumbed a puffy ball on her sweater. She was cute in the sexiest way. "Without you, I was an ass no one wanted to be around."

I lifted her sweater enough to expose the creamy mounds of her breasts. The dashboard lights created a halo around her. I palmed each of them. This road probably didn't see much traffic but I wouldn't undress her all the way, just in case. "I can't wait to peel every inch of clothing off you, but right now, I just want to be inside of you."

"Good thing I wore a skirt tonight."

I leaned forward to tongue her nipples through the thin fabric of her bra. Her tight little buds teased me. I'd give them more attention later. "I'm not going to last much longer." I slid my hand up her boots. She could keep those on later too. When I got to her underwear, I slid my fingers underneath. "I don't want to take the time to get these off."

The heat coming off her seared my fingers. I pushed through her wet seam and pushed inside. Her walls clamped around me. She arched her back and rocked into me.

I ripped open my pants with my other hand. There was barely enough room between us. When I finally freed myself, I paused. "I don't have a condom."

She kept rolling her hips, her eyes shut, bliss painting

her expression. "That's okay. We can do other things for now."

"I plan to sink deep into you, but I need to know if you want that too. I need you to know there's been no one but you. And I need to know if you're ready for this."

She stilled and her gaze flew to mine. "You're serious? You'd be okay if I got pregnant?"

"Fuck, yes. And once I got my head out of my ass and realized I was letting fear keep me in the past, I got more than okay. I want kids—with you. I want to raise them—with you. And I want them to have the big fucking support system that's your family and my dad."

She brushed her hand down my cheek and stroked my bottom lip with her thumb. "I want that too. And I want you inside me."

A growl left me. I slipped my finger from her and yanked her underwear to the side. I pushed in as she ground down.

"Fuck," I groaned.

"Gideon," she gasped, her eyelids drifting shut.

When I was fully seated, she met my gaze. My emotions were mirrored in her eyes. This was intense. I could feel everything. Every little ripple.

"You're so fucking wet." All the sensations were amplified and it wasn't just because we were skin to skin. There was nothing between us. She had all of me.

"You make me that way."

I gripped her hips. "I'm never leaving you again."

"Promise?" Her gaze was dreamy as she lazily rode me.

"Never fucking again." I slid my hand around and put my thumb on her clit.

A full-body shudder racked her and she moaned.

"That fucking sound. Do you know how much I dreamed of you?"

"Not as much as I dreamed of you." Her pace picked up.

She was heaven on me and around me. Her needy noises, that cotton-candy smell that left me a starved man while I was in Vegas, and this lush goddamn body. Energy coiled at the base of my spine, cinching everything tight. I concentrated on her; otherwise, I'd be a finished man.

Her breathing hitched. "Gideon. I'm so close."

"You need to come," I said through clenched teeth. "I'm not going to last." It was a damn miracle I'd made it this long.

A cry escaped her lips and her rhythm grew erratic. Finally. I increased pressure on her clit and dragged her head toward me. Thanks to the cramped cab of the pickup, there wasn't much distance to cover before I could capture her mouth and thrust my tongue inside.

She spasmed, the early stages of her climax hitting. With my tongue, I matched the short thrusts I was making in the crowded space. She went taut and threw her head back.

I dropped the gates on my release. Lightning shot through my body, striking every inch of skin as my release poured out of me.

"Fuck. Autumn. *Fuck*."

She convulsed around my cock, gripping and milking. I squeezed my eyes shut and gave myself to her. This was my woman. My wife.

Autumn

We'd recovered after our first round in the pickup, then he'd traded places with me and driven us home. Sprinkles got some quick pets from him before he locked us in the bedroom and ravaged me two more times. Now, I rested my head against Gideon's bare chest and traced my fingers over the planes of his abs.

I was married.

I was *married* married. This wasn't pretend. Not just a deal. It was Gideon and me embarking on a life together.

"What made you change your mind?" I shouldn't question it, but I also knew he'd talk to me. What he'd said in front of everyone at the bar had made him wide open. It was time for us to complete this connection between us. "About kids?"

His chest rose, paused, then fell. "When I talked to Dad, I told him I was afraid of being like him."

I kept swirling my fingers over his skin, sensing he wasn't done speaking yet.

"Being here, with you, it unlocked a lot of memories," he continued. "Good ones. I can't believe I'd forgotten so much. But going back h-home—to Percival—was the key. Images of me, Mom, and Dad rose relentlessly in my head. Same with visiting you at school. The school program. Goddamn trick-or-treating." He shook his head. "Talk about a trip down memory lane."

I caught the way he'd faltered over the word *home*. "Is it going to be hard? Not having Percival in the family? Never mind. Of course it will be."

"Yes and no." He went quiet. I flattened my hand over his beating heart. "It'll always be the home where I grew up. Those memories are mine. I don't have my grandfather's voice in my ear, telling me how I should feel about it. I loved that place. I always will. Do I wish it was still in the family? Yes, but it sort of is. It'll pass down to our kids in a way."

It would as long as Bailey Beef decided not to sell it. But Gideon's name wasn't on any of the papers.

He hugged me closer to him. "When I left home at eighteen, Bourbon Canyon didn't pull at me anywhere close to the way it has for the last month. That was fucking miserable. I tried to ignore it. To continue on my stubborn path. Then you sent those fucking papers. I wasn't willing to give you up," he ended on a growl.

"I was going insane waiting for them to appear in my inbox."

"There was a reason I hadn't told my lawyer to send those papers, firecracker, and that was because I still wanted to be married to you. Being married to you in a different state meant you were still mine. Then you woke me the hell up. I've had blinders on my entire life and you pulled them right off."

I wiggled into him. It shouldn't be possible to get closer to him.

"When I told Dad I was scared of being a father, the fear just drained away."

"Like speaking it out loud took the power away?"

"You remember the party he threw?"

I rolled up to an elbow. He feathered a hand over the tresses of my hair and draped it over his chest. "Yeah?"

"The emotions I felt when I returned were big.

Powerful. And my first urge was to have a stiff drink. It scared me, Autumn. With how I feel about you? Fucking terrifying."

I made the connection without him explaining it. He worried that if something happened to me, he'd be no better than the dad he'd condemned for years.

I pressed a kiss to the hot skin of his pec. "I'm sorry."

"I talked to Dad about that too. I'm not saying the fear isn't still there, but I can handle it. I have you to talk to. Him. That's two more people than I had when I met a sassy redhead on the elevator at Silver."

I laughed. "Just keep talking to me. If you quit, I'll sic my family on you."

He shuddered. "I don't think I'd stand a chance against your mom."

"None of us do." I cuddled against him again. "So . . . househusband?"

"You're worried, aren't you?"

"Maybe a little." Would there be a day when I didn't think this was too good to be true?

He didn't answer right away. I'd asked him at the bar, but I had to hear the specifics. I had to know there'd be nothing to worry about. He had to be as happy as I was.

"I'll hang out with Dad."

I smiled. He said it so simply. There was too much time to make up for between them, but they weren't going to waste more.

"Then, I don't know." He shrugged. "Maybe your brothers need a hired guy."

"You'd work for my brothers?"

"I liked moving cattle with them. I know a thing or

two about farming, and rumor has it they want to start planting in the spring."

Astonished, I blinked at him. "But will you be happy?"

He took my hand. I'd left the giant diamond on. I'd swap it after. Or not. I was becoming a diamond girl. "With you? Always."

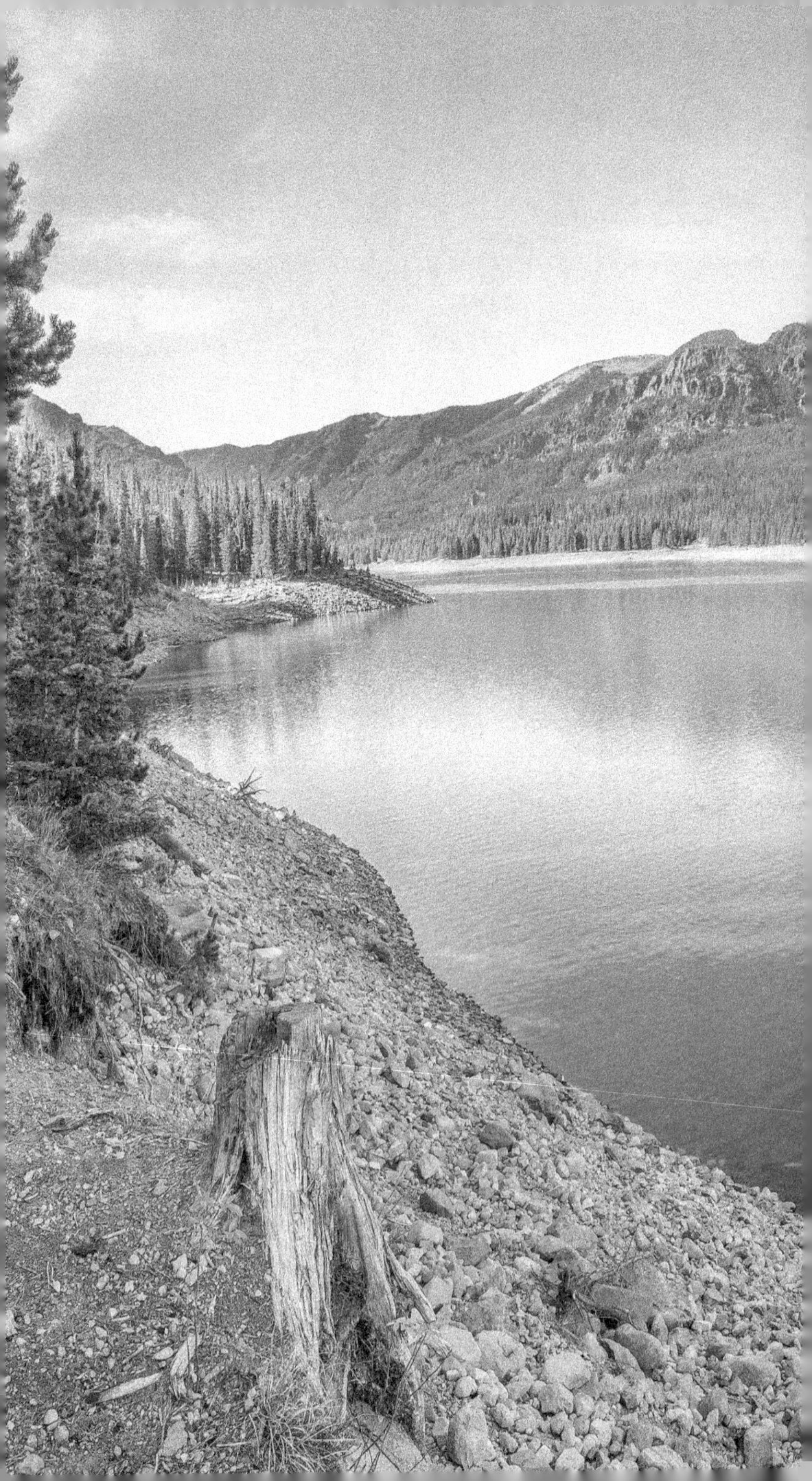

CHAPTER THIRTY

Autumn

Summer tapped her foot against her desk. I'd rushed to Copper Summit after school so I could catch her. The last two months of wedded bliss with Gideon had been perfect. I woke up to him and his egg wraps. I went to bed tucked into his side. And we burned up the sheets so much that Sprinkles avoided our room at bedtime.

"Isn't this what you told Teller you didn't like?" Her eyes were dancing. She liked to turn the tables on our brothers as much as the rest of us did.

"It is precisely what I used to hate." Tenor and Teller had been very diligent about discussing any ideas or changes in the bar with me. I was with them every step of the way for the switch to the new inventory program. But this was different. This was something I had to talk with my sisters about before we broached the request to our brothers.

There was a knock on the door and Wynter entered.

She shut the door behind her. I dug out my phone and dialed Junie.

"This feels so clandestine." Wynter propped a hip on the edge of the desk. "Remember when we used to meet under the stairs to talk about what we were getting all the guys for Christmas?"

Summer rolled her eyes. "They're still awful about finding packages I try to hide. When Jonah made Teller that nightstand in December, Teller walked in on him when he'd just finished it. Jonah tried to act cool and failed, yet he claims I lie like shit."

"You do," I said.

She folded her arms across her chest. "All of us do."

"He-llooo," Junie sang from the phone. "What are we hiding from our brothers?"

I had messaged all of them last night and told them I needed to talk. Junie had been the wild card, but she must've sensed the seriousness of the topic. She'd told us to name a time and she'd make it.

I pressed my hands against my stomach. My nerves were lighting up. There was a reason my sisters were the first ones I was talking to. I trusted my brothers, but if my sisters told me my idea was unreasonable, then I'd have no choice but to drop it. If my brothers said the same thing, my stubbornness would kick in and I'd press ahead out of emotion.

If Summer, Junie, and Wynter said I was out of line, then I'd know their decision was what they felt was the best for the business.

I took a deep breath. "Okay, here's what I'd like to talk to them about."

Gideon

I was stocking the bar while Autumn was in a meeting with her siblings. For the last three months, I'd experienced the kind of wedded bliss I'd thought was a pipe dream. When Autumn was working during the day, Dad and I helped at the food pantry a couple days a week. Some "anonymous" donor had set up a continuous grocery delivery. Dad had just looked at me and shaken his head, a small smile hidden under his trimmed mustache.

All that money I'd socked away for years and invested and grown was finally getting used.

Autumn and I were looking at bigger houses, but we weren't in a rush to move. I'd been helping a little at the ranch, but mostly Tate had tapped Dad's knowledge. The Baileys needed to buy equipment and Tate had asked us to watch auctions and estate sales for good deals.

Dad and I would pore over the ads for farm equipment, and sometimes, we'd take a trip to look a piece over and note our observations. Nothing had been purchased yet, but Dad and I had told them they were running out of time.

I set a crate of Copper Summit's new summer special barrel in the storeroom. I was no longer behind a desk, and my back and shoulders were happy. I didn't need an ergonomic chair if I wasn't sitting for twelve or more hours of the day. When I emerged, Autumn was peeking her head around the wall that bordered the entry.

"You got a minute? The guys want to talk to you."

Curiosity rose, but they probably just wanted to ask

me timeline questions. They might know how to farm, but Dad and I knew that land, how it behaved through the seasons, where it flooded, what parts drained well.

She tangled her fingers through mine. I'd rather walk behind her and admire her ass since she was wearing the same brown skirt she'd worn when I had officially proposed to her. She didn't have the Christmas sweater on, but her loose cream shirt draped over her tits in a way that made my mouth water.

I'd never get enough of her.

The meeting room was on the upper level where the offices were. Inside the rectangular room, family pictures of the Baileys covered the walls. Some images had kids I didn't recognize, but Autumn had said they were the foster kids the Baileys had cared for over the years. Whoever had been under the Bailey roof at the time was in the family picture.

Her siblings were scattered around the table. Teller, Summer, and Tenor on the opposite side. Tate at the head of the table. Wynter was across from Teller. Autumn picked a seat next to her and I took the empty spot beside her.

"Junie's on speaker," Autumn said.

"Hiiii," Junie sang.

"Hi, Junie," I said.

She'd briefly stopped in over the New Year, super enthusiastic and raining gifts on everyone. Autumn was worried about her. According to the tabloids, Junie had broken up with some country music stud and the gossip shows enjoyed showing pictures of him and every other woman who crossed his path.

Her siblings were worried, but Tenor had claimed Junie's troubles weren't man-related. He insisted it was business. I didn't know Junie, but Autumn was worried, so I cared.

Tate tented his fingers together at the end of the table. The two of us were former CEOs dressed down in jeans, a hoodie—his a Bailey Beef sweater and mine an old Silver one. I was finally getting some use out of the merchandise I'd been gifted during my time in charge.

"Autumn approached me a few weeks ago," he said. "Then Summer. And Wynter. Junie."

Summer cocked a brow, looking unrepentant. Wynter smirked. I glanced at Autumn.

Her smile was smug. "I figured it was time for the girls to have a talk before we ran our decision past the guys."

Teller grunted and Tenor nodded.

Tate tapped his fingertips together. "Autumn thinks we need to sell some property."

Myles and Jonah weren't here. Why was I? I didn't have a say about any of their holdings.

Autumn reached for my hand. She beamed. Puzzle pieces were starting to click into place. No. She wouldn't ask Tate to sell—

"She thinks we should sell Percival to you," Tate said, confirming my realization.

They'd just put in all the expense of purchasing the property. I'd love to have a chance to buy my family home, but I didn't want to make financial craters in this family. It wasn't worth it. "What does everyone else think?"

The corner of Tate's mouth lifted. "Seems like the thing to do."

"We all agree," Summer said.

Wynter nodded. Teller folded his arms and leaned back in his chair until it squeaked.

The offer didn't make sense from a business standpoint. They'd be taking a loss. They'd sacrifice the plans they'd made to grow some of their own grains for Copper Summit. They couldn't expand the ranch and use all the new fence Dad and I had repaired. "What's in it for you?"

Tate's smile broadened like he relished my disbelief. This was what having a sibling was like. "Autumn's happiness. Our dad taught us that not every decision needs to benefit the company financially."

" 'Money should never be your first priority all the time,' " Wynter said.

"We wanted to be the buyers to make sure it stayed local." Tate spread his hands. "You're local."

Born and raised and here to stay. I glanced around the table. "What are you charging?"

"What we bought it for."

I had that amount. A few business days, it'd be theirs.

No. There had to be a catch. It was too good to be true. Then it dawned on me. "No."

Autumn squeezed my hand. "Gideon?"

I shook my head. "If you want Autumn's property in exchange—"

"Nope," Teller said. "We don't. Just buy the place back so we don't feel like shit making plans to use it while you work for us and refuse to get paid."

I hadn't refused payment. I'd shamelessly taken Mae's meals as payment.

Tate tapped his fingertips together. "We're not even going to make the sale contingent on contracting with

Copper Summit. But if you want to be a farmer, we'd be happy to do business."

"We can go over my estimates, see what you think," I said. "I've been wanting Dad to have a look." A farmer. From casino and hotel CEO to farming and ranching. "I don't know what I'm doing."

"You've got a helluva resource at your disposal."

Dad.

I huffed out a laugh and considered the top of the table. The wood was glossy and it was filled with epoxy in a way that made it look like a river ran through the middle.

Did I want to farm? To work with the Baileys instead of for them? Teach my kids about the life, take them horseback riding, and show them where we remembered their grandma?

As long as I had Autumn, I didn't give a shit about what I did. But getting Percival? This time, it felt right. These last few months had been an awakening. Farming and ranching were in my blood. Mom had passed on her love for the land, but Grandpa's obsession about who owned what and why had been purged from me. I could just enjoy spending my days outside again. Paying attention to the land and the weather, deciding what equipment to buy, studying the market—it was more rewarding for me than making millions a year for someone else.

More than that was the chance to hang out with Dad again. I couldn't forget the past, but I understood it now. I couldn't wait to pass on my love for the land to my own kids. Only this time, I knew I could do it from anywhere. It didn't have to be Percival. Though if it was . . .

Autumn was chewing her lower lip like she worried she'd overstepped. Home was with her. The rest was just logistics.

"You didn't have to do this," I said to her.

"My god, Gideon. Buy it. We'll figure the rest out."

My wife's eyes were wide, shiny. My world was in that gaze. She wanted me to have it, so I'd buy it. For us. "All right. Get the paperwork ready."

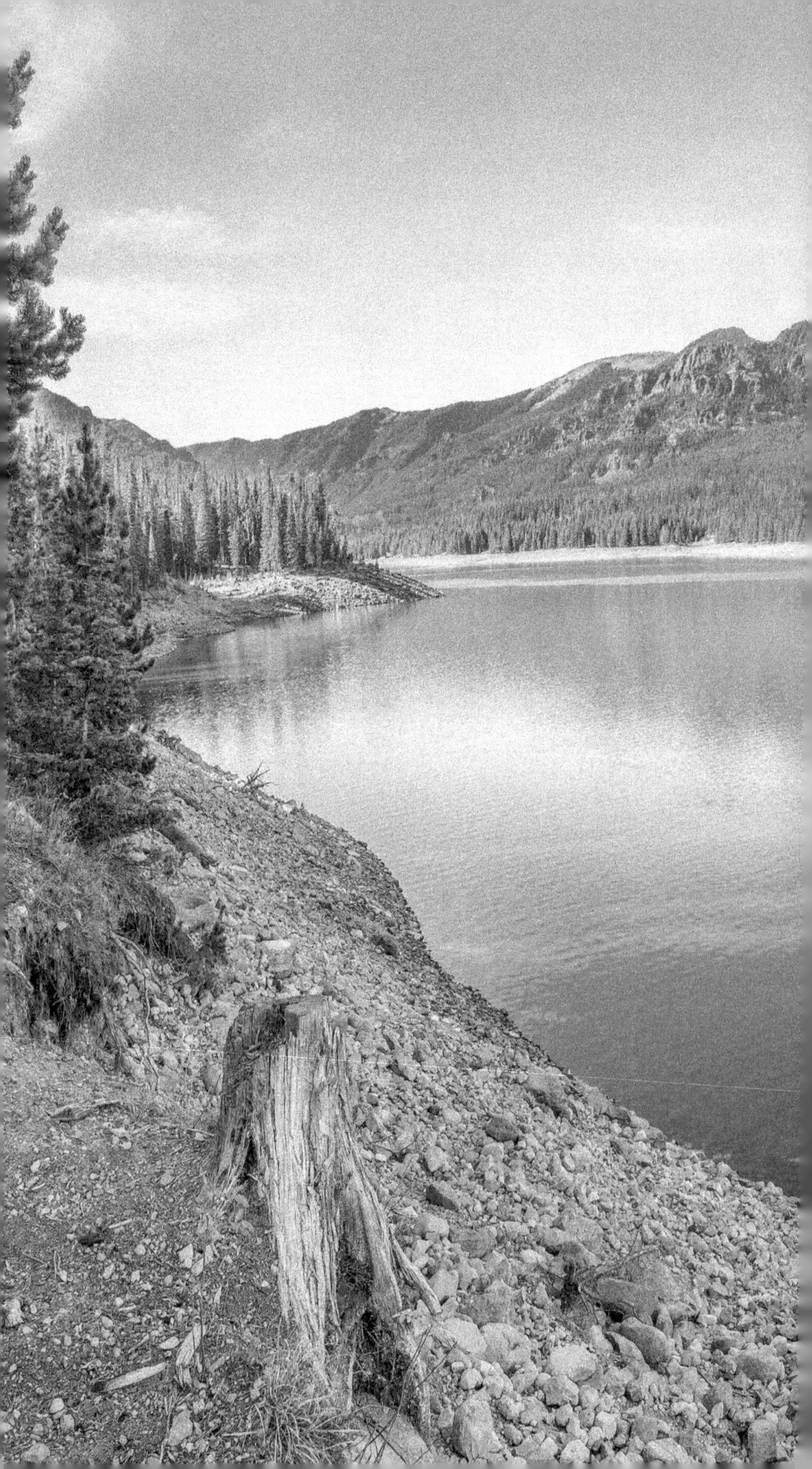

EPILOGUE

Autumn

The doorbell rang at Hank's place. Gideon had the candy bucket and was already opening the door, his dad crowding behind him. They both scooted over so I could see the trick-or-treaters.

Hank was getting a kick out of tonight. This year, I'd told all the kids that they'd have to trick-or-treat at his place since Gideon and I lived at Percival Farms now. We'd remodeled the house over the summer and built an addition. The place was beautiful. Still his childhood home, but also ready for the future.

"What do we have here?" Hank said. He'd been delightedly talking to each kid about their costume. Tonight, he was making up for years of living in the country and missing out on trick-or-treaters.

"Mario!" Deon grinned. He was one of four boys, and he had a cardboard box decorated to look like a car from

Mario Kart. The entire group of boys had coordinated their outfits. There was a Luigi, a Toad, and a Bowser.

Deon held out his blue tote bag. "Trick or treat, Mr. J."

"Evenin', Deon." Gideon doled out the candy.

"No Princess Peach?" I asked the boys.

Deon rolled his eyes. "Caleb didn't want to wear a dress."

"It's cold!" Toad—Caleb—argued.

"Why are you a chef, Mr. J?" Deon asked. The others peered around him, eyeing my costume and Gideon's.

My husband wore a white puffy hat and an apron.

I grinned. At school, I had worn an apron not unlike Gideon's. I'd used an old Amelia Bedelia costume of Scarlett's. But for tonight, I told my students I had a big surprise with my costume. I'd been delighted when Gideon had asked what *we* were dressing up as this year.

I pointed to the image inside the viewing window of the oven costume. "Because I have a bun in the oven!"

I hadn't told my students or coworkers yet that I was expecting. Our family knew and they were ecstatic, no one more so than Hank.

The boys chortled and a few rolled their eyes. I was glad none of them asked why that made Gideon the chef. Teaching them about batter and ovens wasn't my job.

The kids rushed off. No more trick-or-treaters were running up the walk. Hank went to the kitchen, probably to fill his cup of decaf. Gideon closed the door and wrapped his arms around me.

"Happy Halloween, Mrs. J," he murmured in my ear. "Guess what I found this morning when I was unpacking the boxes in the guest room?"

"Hmm . . ." I had all the important stuff unpacked, and we'd bought a lot of new things. The guest room was full of classroom supplies I didn't use often and seasonal decorations. "I can't think of what I should be excited about."

"The red suspenders."

A hum started between my thighs. I was programmed for this man. Completely and irrevocably his. "I seem to recall those."

"I'll make sure you remember."

Hank stood in the dining room, a steaming mug in his hands. "You two leaving for Mae's soon?"

"We've got a few minutes," Gideon said.

Summer and Jonah were at Mama's tonight, showing off their new little boy. Eliott Darin Dunn, an ode to Jonah's late brother, Eli. Tate and Scarlett were taking the kids over, same with Summer and Myles. Hank was staying home and catching up on sleep. He'd been working hard with Gideon to get the harvest in. They hadn't planted all their acreage, but they had a tidy pile to sell to Copper Summit.

I was a farm wife, about to be a mom. I'd come a long way since I'd been refused entrance into a trendy club.

Hank disappeared back into the kitchen.

Gideon pressed a kiss into my hair. "This has been the best year of my life."

"And to think it all started with a bourbon-fueled fake marriage."

"Nothing about us was ever fake." The next kiss was on my mouth. "Our bourbon promises were very real."

. . .

When Junie's tour comes to an end, she needs to go back to her roots. Only the cabin she plans to stay in isn't far from her high school sweetheart's place. And when her car breaks down, he's the first one to stop and help, with his two adorable daughters. Junie's about to get everything she wants in her career, but Rhys Kinkade just might be everything she needs in Bourbon Harmony.

Want to keep reading about Gideon and Autumn? Join them for a very special Las Vegas date in a special bonus epilogue found in my newsletter. Sign up at mariejohnstonwriter.com.

ABOUT THE AUTHOR

I live the dream in my own slice of paradise where I get to enjoy colorful sunsets from my rocking chair while I'm working. I have my very own romance hero with Mr. Rose and there's more than a few little rose buds running around. A couple aren't so little anymore! We keep things interesting with cats and a dog and the critters that roam though the yard (fingers crossed the mountain lions stay away).

walkerrosebooks.com

ALSO BY WALKER ROSE

Bourbon Canyon Series

Bourbon Bachelor

Bourbon Lullaby

Bourbon Runaway

Bourbon Promises